A T...
A TI...
A TIME TO DIE.

201 B.C., Roman province of Campania

Hanno was the son of Hannibal, the great and fearsome general who terrorized Rome. Captured and enslaved by the Roman house of Gallio, Hanno was thrust into the brutal savagery of the arenas. Yet his ferocious fighting skills as a gladiator earned him the name "the Lion of Carthage"—and earned him his freedom.

1859, West Point Academy

Major Anthony Wayne Gallio was the Academy's master swordsman who passed on the military tradition to his three children, Robert, Mark and Maria. The rumors of a devastating war between the states aroused his greatest concern—because members of the Gallio clan would be fighting on both sides, North and South.

1986, Afghanistan

A veteran of Vietnam, Tony Gallio now worked freelance. Smuggled into Soviet-occupied Afghanistan by the CIA, he must assist the freedom fighters in a struggle for arms, power, and justice. But his mercenary mission is deniable. If he is killed, Tony Gallio never existed.

Sons of Glory

The explosive Gallio family saga will continue in upcoming volumes—available from Jove Books!

SONS
OF
GLORY

SIMON HAWKE

J
JOVE BOOKS, NEW YORK

SONS OF GLORY

A Jove Book / published by arrangement with
the author

PRINTING HISTORY
Jove edition / May 1992

ISBN: 0-515-10845-6

Jove Books are published by The Berkley Publishing Group,
200 Madison Avenue, New York, New York 10016.
The name "JOVE" and the "J" logo
are trademarks belonging to Jove Publications, Inc.

PRINTED IN THE UNITED STATES OF AMERICA

10 9 8 7 6 5 4 3 2 1

This book is dedicated to
Jim Morris
with affection and respect,
and gratitude for having faith in this project

Acknowledgments

I would like to express my deepest appreciation and gratitude to all those who assisted in the creation of this novel, either through research, supplying materials, or providing much-needed input and moral support. First and foremost, this novel would not have been possible were it not for the work of those historians and writers whose names appear in the bibliography, and to whom I acknowledge my debt. I would also like to acknowledge the efforts of H. Trask Emery, my primary research assistant, who not only performed yeoman service in searching out specific information I requested, but also took enough interest to pursue avenues of research on his own and make valuable suggestions. I am also indebted to Tracy Ashleigh, who performed miracles in helping organize my notes and whose skill as a neuromuscular therapist kept a painful wrist injury from incapacitating me during the writing of this novel.

Thanks are also due to Ken Detwiler, Frank La Breq, Mike Bakula, Victor Castellani of Denver University, Chris Zinck of Bloomsbury Books in Denver, Brian and Dee Cooper, Rachel Drummond, Kay Cochran, Bill and Lola Molnar of the Gun Room in Denver, Kevin Bishop, Gene Brent, the staff and management of Muddy's Java Café in Denver, John Kennedy, the staff and management of the Tattered Cover bookstore in Denver, Bill Lemieux and Cheryl Green, Ed Bryant, Connie Willis, Cass Marshall, Robert M. Powers, Mark Barsotti, Wil McCarthy, Larry Brown, Marge Sjoden, Ronnie Seagren, Marie Desjardin, Diane Dieter, Bonnie Meadows, Marie Costa, John Stith, David Dvorkin, Emil Marx, Craig Wasinger, Gary Piserchio, David Zindell, Ed McManis, David Mattingly, and Fred "the Bishop" Cleaver. I would also like to thank the people at Presidio Press in San Rafael, California, and the people at Dixie Gun Works in Union City, Tennessee. And my sincere apologies to anyone

I may have forgotten. I plead terminal vagueness and nervous exhaustion.

Special thanks go to my agent, Adele Leone, and to my editor, Gary Goldstein, and to Jim Morris, without whom this project would never have taken off and to whom, with a tip of the Stetson, this book is dedicated.

SONS
OF
GLORY

PROLOGUE

Afghanistan: August, 1986

THE NAME HINDU Kush meant "Hindu Killer." The Pathan tribes who lived in this foreboding mountain wilderness called it *Bam-i-Dunya*, the Roof of the World. To Tony Gallio, the terrain seemed majestically surreal in its savage beauty, a rock-strewn, broken landscape of jagged, twenty-thousand-foot peaks that seemed to stretch into infinity. Rushing torrents of ice-cold snowmelt roared through its steep defiles. Twisted scrub pines and cedar trees grew out of nearly vertical rock walls. The days were mercilessly hot. The nights were biting cold. It was a brutal, unforgiving land that had defied the armies of Darius the Great and Alexander. The hordes of Genghis Khan and Tamerlane had stormed through its precarious mountain passes, but had ultimately failed to conquer it. The British Empire had experienced some of its worst defeats here, humbled by the untamed land and its indomitable people. And now the Soviets were floundering in this fierce and primitive country, throwing everything they had against the freedom fighters of Afghanistan and failing to subdue them. The Hindu Kush killed those who did not belong here.

Tony Gallio was no stranger to harsh, inhospitable country. He had survived the steaming jungles of Vietnam and Cambodia. He had slogged through the dense undergrowth of Nicaragua. He had returned unscathed from covert missions in such places as El Salvador and Lebanon, but he had never before encountered country quite like this. The rocky path they followed was barely a foot wide, with a sheer drop of several thousand feet directly to his left. One false step could prove fatal. Despite being in superb physical condition, Gallio was breathing like a spent marathoner and his clothes were soaked with sweat. It was all he could do

1

to keep up with the seemingly inexhaustible *mujahidin*, the holy warriors of the jihad.

On December 27, 1979, the Soviets had overthrown the communist regime of Mohammed Hafizullah Amin, which had grown too independent for the leaders of the Politburo. The Soviets had other reasons for wanting to invade Afghanistan. Because of their own rapidly growing Muslim population, they were concerned about the rise of Islamic revolutionary movements, and with Afghanistan under their control, all that would separate them from the Bay of Gwadar, which could accommodate the largest aircraft carriers and oil tankers, was the unstable province of Baluchistan. Military bases in Afghanistan would also put them within easy air-strike distance of the vital Straits of Hormuz. A further inducement for their invasion of Afghanistan was its wealth of untapped natural resources. While America was preoccupied with the hostage crisis in Iran, a KGB hit squad had assassinated Amin and installed a puppet government under Babrak Karmal. Then, just as with Hungary and Czechoslovakia, the tanks came rolling in to crush resistance.

The Soviets came with their 103rd, 104th, and 105th Airborne Divisions, along with four motorized divisions that crossed over from the border, spearheading the invasion of Kabul. They came with their Antonov heavy transport planes for carrying troops, their T-54, T-62, and T-64 tanks, and their new, highly maneuverable SU-24 fighter bombers. They brought their armored personnel carriers, their supply trucks, and their fuel tankers. They came with their pipe-laying battalions, capable of laying thirty kilometers of pipe a day to deliver precious diesel fuel to power the invasion. They brought in their MIG-21, MIG-23, and SU-17 jet fighters; their Mi-6 heavy transport and Mi-8 medium transport helicopters for carrying the Air Assault Rangers and Spetsnaz commandos, their tank carriers, their BTR and BMP armored vehicles equipped with 30mm cannon. And they came with one of the most devastating weapons in their entire arsenal, the dreaded Mi-24 Hind helicopter gunships, large, snout-nosed choppers that resembled prehistoric birds of prey, armed with four-barrel turret guns and 128 rockets, four napalm or high-explosive bombs, and laser-sighted cannon capable of firing a thousand rounds per minute. Just one of these awesome juggernauts could raze an entire village in mere seconds.

Pitted against this fearsome military machine was a pitifully small and bedraggled group of freedom fighters armed with hopelessly outdated and just as hopelessly inadequate equipment. The *mujahidin* were armed only with World War II–vintage Soviet Simonov and British Lee-Enfield and Martini Henry rifles. Some of them had nothing better than a flintlock musket. They also used captured Soviet AK-47 Kalashnikov assault rifles and RPG-7 rocket launchers, as well as pistols, shotguns, Czech-made Bren machine guns, American M-1 carbines, and mortars. Anything that they could get their hands on. Sometimes they even threw rocks.

The CIA, in its largest covert military support operation since Vietnam, had been providing the *mujahidin* with arms purchased from Egypt, China, and Israel, but assault rifles, mortars, and antitank rockets weren't much use against heavily armored MIGs and helicopter gunships.

The whole operation, Gallio thought, was like a crazy Chinese fire drill. The Company had provided SAM-7 missiles for the Afghans, despite having learned the hard way in Angola that SAM-7s were virtually useless against the well-armored Soviet jets and choppers. They had also spent $20 million dollars on 12.7mm ammo for the Soviet Dashaka machine guns, the only antiaircraft weapon the freedom fighters had, but most of the ammo they supplied wasn't armor piercing. The United States had spent over $3.2 billion dollars on military aid to Pakistan, which provided an unofficial pipeline to the Afghans, but somewhere in the channel, about 70 percent of the military ordnance simply disappeared, only to resurface in the bazaars of Darra Adem Khiel.

About a half-hour drive from Peshawar, Darra was officially off limits to foreigners, but Gallio had been smuggled in by Pakistani contacts so that he could go through its bazaars. He had never seen anything like it. There were over 250 arms dealers in the bazaars of Darra, most of whom claimed they could copy any weapon the prospective buyer wanted, from rifles to light and heavy machine guns to mortars and rocket launchers. But there was also a profusion of CIA-bought Chinese and Egyptian weaponry, Soviet AK-47 and AKS-74 assault rifles, crates of antitank and antipersonnel mines, SAM-7 missiles, and in one tented shop, Gallio had even seen a howitzer. The streets of Darra sounded like Saigon during the Tet Offensive. There was the constant crackle of automatic weapons fire as buyers tried out the wares. Many of the purchasers were terrorists and drug dealers and even agents of the KHAD, the KGB-trained secret police of the Afghan puppet regime, who had discovered it was cheaper to buy their ordnance in Darra than to get it through their regular channels.

Gallio had been outraged and disgusted. Most of the heroin sold on the streets in the United States came through Peshawar, by way of the "Golden Triangle," and American taxpayers were providing drug lords with cheap weapons through the bazaars of Darra. Monitoring the pipeline was impossible, since both the CIA and Pakistan denied it existed, and what little ordnance got through to the *mujahidin* was nowhere near enough. Gallio, a colonel in the Special Forces, loathed inefficiency, and this was one of the most inefficient operations he had ever seen. The Company sent machine guns to the Afghans, but they neglected to supply spare barrels, so the weapons didn't last long. Spare rounds for the RPG-7 rocket launcher, the world's best light antitank gun, reached the *mujahidin* at the rate of about one a month. A mere six hundred rounds a month was the resupply rate for the Dashaka guns, which was barely enough for a small skirmish. Yet, despite such woefully inadequate support, the Afghans were hanging on relentlessly, fighting the Soviet Goliath with the equivalent of slingshots.

The frustration of the Soviets had pushed them to actions that were barbarous on a scale unlike anything the Viet Cong had ever dreamed of. Their Hind helicopter gunships annihilated whole villages. They dropped butterfly bombs by the thousands, antipersonnel mines that were, ironically, originally developed in the United States. They had a fin that allowed them to flutter to the ground, where their camouflage made them extremely difficult to spot. They were designed to maim, not kill, a terror tactic that was surpassed in savagery only by the hideous toy bombs, brightly colored dolls and plastic birds and toy trucks that were scattered throughout the countryside by low-flying aircraft. Innocent children would pick them up and have their arms or legs blown off.

Gallio had heard dozens of horrifying stories about Soviet atrocities. He had seen the awful evidence in the refugee camps. Among the chemical agents the Soviets were using was a compound known as "liquid fire," a black, tarlike substance that was dropped from aircraft in cluster bomb containers. The containers burst above the ground, releasing a spray that fell down to form globules. If touched, it would immediately adhere to the tires of vehicles or to skin or clothing, bursting into flame that could not be put out. Afghan women were raped and made to watch as their children were subjected to electric shocks and sexual molestation.

Civilians were arbitrarily subjected to nail pulling, sleep deprivation, beatings, torture, being buried alive and crushed beneath tank treads. Pregnant women were bayoneted so they could not give birth to freedom fighters.

Over one-third of the entire population of Afghanistan had fled to refugee camps across the border in Pakistan, a number greater than the entire population of Israel or New Zealand, and still the proud people would not submit to the Soviet aggression. They would not be enslaved. The terror tactics the Soviets had used since Stalin's time were not working in Afghanistan. One of the greatest superpowers in the world could not crush resistance in a tiny, primitive country. Try as they might, they could not intimidate its fiercely independent people.

The *mujahidin* deserved more help than they'd been getting and Tony Gallio had come to give it to them. The administration had finally decided to supply the freedom fighters with the one weapon they so desperately needed, but there were efforts in Congress to block the shipment. However, even as the legislators debated the issue in their subcommittees, Gallio had departed on a covert mission to bring the freedom fighters Stinger missiles and instruct them in their use.

He had been to Peshawar several times before, on fact-finding missions, and he had spoken to resistance leaders and several journalists who had been inside. Both had been extremely wary— the resistance leaders because they'd heard empty promises before and, being Muslim, did not expect much from the West. The journalists were not eager to be debriefed by the CIA, but their sympathies were with the *mujahidin* and several of them were cooperative. Gallio was determined that no part of this shipment of Stingers would wind up in Darra, where terrorists and drug traffickers could get their hands on them. He was going to escort them personally, each and every step of the way.

He had accompanied the shipment to the port of Karachi and personally supervised its unloading. The Stingers had been packed in specially marked crates, which by unofficial arrangement would not be inspected by customs. They were then put aboard Pakistani military trucks and Gallio went with them to the city of Peshawar, close to the Afghan border and thirty miles west of the Khyber Pass. He had brought with him a small, but highly trained mercenary unit recruited through a contact in Geneva, a former British SAS commando who, along with another contact Gallio had in Miami, was capable of putting together a crack assault unit on little more than a moment's notice for covert action anywhere in the world. Some of the mercenaries were former Australian commandos, others were South African, ex-British SAS, or American Special Forces. The purpose of the mercenaries was twofold. One, to provide "plausible deniability" in case anything went wrong. Two, to make sure that no part of the shipment was "diverted."

Peshawar had become the spy capital of the world, crawling with agents of the KGB and KHAD, the Pakistani Special Branch, as well as covert agents from other major powers, arms merchants, smugglers, terrorists, drug dealers, black marketeers, and mercenaries, all of whom would kill to get their hands on Stinger missiles. The key to the success of Gallio's operation was speed. Everything had been set up in advance so that the Stingers would not spend so much as one second languishing anywhere in storage. The mercenaries had accompanied Gallio to Peshawar, where they linked up with representatives of the *mujahidin,* then on to the province of Chitral, where the guerrillas were supplied. The Pakistanis maintained border checkpoints, but although the authorities unofficially looked the other way when it came to delivering supplies to the *mujahidin,* it was still necessary to bribe the border guards.

It seemed to Gallio that everyone in Pakistan had his hand out. Many of the political resistance leaders in Peshawar had Swiss bank accounts. Qhaddafi and Khomeini were both trying to buy them off. The Afghans were Muslim, but they were Afghan first. Afghanistan had never been ruled by a religious leader. The tribal chiefs had more influence among the people than the mullahs. Both Pakistan and Iran were trying to change that. The Arabs gave money to the Pakistanis, who distributed it among the political resistance groups, favoring the fundamentalists with the lion's share.

Gallio had no doubt that much of the personal wealth of the political leaders came from diverted shipments. AK-47s sold in the bazaars of Darra for about $2,800. Some of them wound up in Beirut, where they sold for around $900, others in Tehran, where they were worth about $1,800. Ammunition for Kalashnikovs went for about five hundred Afghanis, or one dollar a bullet. Ironically, the *mujahidin* obtained much of their ammunition by trading with the Soviets themselves, through intermediaries. For a thousand Kalashnikov rounds, a Soviet soldier could receive a kilo of hashish. Before Afghanistan, the Soviets never really had a serious drug problem.

Gallio's shipment of Stingers was marked for the *mujahidin* fighting in the Panjshir Valley under Ahmad Shah Massoud, a young guerrilla leader who had learned his trade from books by Ho Chi Minh and Che Guevara. He was a member of the Jamiat, a fundamentalist resistance group composed primarily of Uzbeks and Tadjiks. Not all *mujahidin* groups were totally united in their resistance. They had constant internecine power struggles and Massoud's chief adversaries were the *Hezb-i-Islami,* a group with strong ties to Khomeini. For obvious reasons, it had been decided that Massoud should be the one to get the Stingers.

The mercenaries had accompanied Gallio only as far as the border, where he had rendezvoused with Massoud's *mujahidin.* Their part of the operation was finished at that point. And that had been the easy part. The Stingers had all made it to the border resupply point with none of them mysteriously disappearing and without any shots being fired. From there, Gallio went on alone across the border with the *mujahidin* and up into the forbidding mountains of the Hindu Kush.

With his dark, Mediterranean coloring, Gallio could easily pass for one of them. He had grown a beard and dressed as they dressed, in loose trousers and a baggy shirt, an olive army anorak beneath his woolen *patou* blanket and a black turban that Sikander, the leader of the group, had wound around his head. They had shown him how to do it several times, but he just couldn't seem to get the hang of it. He wore a pair of Czech-made army boots, as did some of the other Afghans, though most of them climbed the impossibly steep trails wearing only worn-out sneakers or tire-tread sandals.

The supplies and the missiles had been sewn into hemp sacks, then strapped to donkeys, mules, and horses. The greatest danger was in losing any of the animals, with their precious cargo. One mule had slipped and almost gone over the side. Another had been lost when they crossed a rushing stream. They had managed to remove the cargo, but they could not pull the braying, frightened animal out of the water and it was swept away. Its load had been transferred to the backs of several freedom fighters, who bore it uncomplainingly.

They were, thought Gallio, an amazing people. Sikander, the leader, was only in his late twenties, but he looked like a man of forty-five. The life they led was hard and took its toll. One out of every five *mujahidin* was killed. Daoud, the youngest of the group, was a handsome boy of thirteen, with big dark eyes and a flashing smile. He carried an old Lee-Enfield .303 rifle and proudly wore a 9mm Makarov pistol he took off a Russian officer he'd killed. The oldest of the band was Jagran, a white-bearded man of sixty-five, who wore crossed bandoliers of ammo for his AK-47 and had powers of endurance Gallio could not believe.

At the end of the first day, they had stopped at a *chaikhana*, which translated as "teahouse," but was actually little more than a place of refuge on the trail, a sand-colored adobe house with a dirt floor and a pit dug in one corner for a fire. Gallio felt worn out. The altitude was getting to him. He had done some backpacking in the Colorado Rockies and he thought he was in good condition, but just one day on the trail had him panting. He thought he understood now why the standard response to the traditional Afghan greeting, *Ah-salaam aleikum* ("Peace be to you"), was *Astalah mashai* ("May you not be weary").

They built a fire and made *chai* in their blackened teakettles, which they drank with *ghorra*, hard chunks of brown sugar. They gave him *jalghoza*, which were nuts from pine cones, *nan* (bread), and rice with greasy chunks of mutton. They took pains to see he had the choicest pieces of meat and one of the men, Kassim, offered him raisins. In turn, Gallio gave them unfiltered Camel cigarettes, which were a great treat for the *mujahidin*. They smoked the cigarettes with a great show of relish and then reciprocated by offering him *miswah*, a vile chewing tobacco that Gallio bravely stuck between his cheek and gum and proceeded to spit into a corner, just as they did.

"*Allah o Akbar, mordabad Shouravi!*" one of them pronounced, and they all echoed the sentiment. ("God is Great, death to the Soviets!")

A few of them spoke English to varying degrees, but Sikander was most fluent, and as they sat around the fire, smoking and warming their feet, he sat next to Gallio and acted as interpreter.

"You are tired, yes?" Sikander said.

"To be honest, yes, I'm very tired," Gallio replied, with a weary smile. "I thought I was in better shape."

Sikander translated and the others laughed, then one of them, a man named Sadul, spoke in a quick torrent of Pushto, which Sikander translated.

"He says that you are doing very well. We had one of your American journalists with us last month. He said that he had done a lot of running before he came here, to prepare himself, but he grew tired quickly. You are doing much better."

"I should hope to do better than a journalist," said Gallio wryly.

Sikander translated and the others laughed.

"You are an American soldier, yes?"

"Yes," said Gallio.

"You have fought in wars?"

"That's right."

"You have killed Soviets?"

"Not Soviets, no. But I've killed enemy soldiers."

Sikander translated and the others nodded. One of them asked a question.

"Yussuf asks, do you believe in God?"

Gallio hesitated for a moment. He was an agnostic, but to these men, whose faith was strong, it was not an idle question. They each carried a cherished copy of the Koran.

"Well, I was raised a Christian," he explained, "and Christians are taught to believe in God. But I guess I'm not really a Christian anymore."

Sikander frowned. "You have lost your faith?" he asked, with sincere concern.

Gallio considered for a moment before replying. "A man's faith is a personal thing. I believe in myself. I believe in my country. And I guess I believe that if a man wants to pray to whatever power made these mountains and these rivers, then I don't think it matters if he prays to the Christian God or Allah. I think it's really all the same. If his prayers give him strength, then I guess it's good for him to pray."

Sikander translated and the others nodded in approval. One of them asked a question.

"Hassan asks if you wish to pray with us," Sikander said.

"If it's okay for someone who's not a Moslem to pray with you, then I'd be happy to," said Gallio.

The men were pleased with his response. They taught him the words and he joined them outside in their evening prayer, kneeling as they did to face Mecca, with his palms upturned and his forehead touching the ground. Gallio wondered, as he prayed to Allah with them, what Father Antonelli would have said if he could see him now. And he wondered what most Islamic fundamentalists might say if they saw this American infidel kneeling with the *mujahidin* in prayer.

If there was no God, he thought, what harm could it do? And if there was a God, then prayer was prayer, no matter in

what language or what name you used. If Mohammad really
was the messenger of God, then that didn't necessarily mean
Buddha wasn't also, or that Christ wasn't God's son. And if all
people could be as accepting of others as these simple mountain
tribesmen seemed to be, then maybe the world would be a better place.

The days stretched into weeks as they continued on their trek.
The Panjshir Valley, seventy miles long with an elevation of seven
thousand feet, was a three-week journey from the border. Located
forty miles to the north of Kabul, it was a valley of mud and
stone villages, vineyards, wheatfields, and fruit orchards, with one
main entry road to the south flanked by steep escarpments. It was
controlled by the Russians, in as much as they controlled anything
in Afghanistan. They had a base there for the Hind helicopter
gunships. It was a place that Gallio thought should provide some
fine target practice. He was looking forward to shooting one down
himself. It was, of course, strictly against orders. He wasn't even
supposed to be here. He could imagine what would happen if it
ever got out that a colonel in the American Special Forces, working for the CIA, had shot down a Russian helicopter with a Stinger
missile. But there was no way he was going to miss this chance.

Along the way, they frequently saw flights of MIGs passing
overhead. Several times, they observed groups of four or six
helicopter gunships. They remained out of sight, hidden in the
rocks, despite the mounting enthusiasm felt by the *mujahidin*,
who were anxious to try out the Stingers. They had heard about
them, because the forces in Pakistan had been equipped with both
Stingers and Sidewinder air-to-air missiles. There were F-16 jet
fighters in Peshawar, provided as part of the military aid by the
United States, to protect Pakistani airspace and prevent the MIGs
from attacking the refugee camps. The temptation to fire on some
of the helicopters they saw was great, but it was essential not to
give themselves away before they reached their destination. To
ease the tension somewhat, Gallio unpacked one of the Stingers
and gave them dry-run instructions in its use, all without ever
actually firing it. Soon, he told them, the time would come when
they would get the opportunity to use them.

As they continued on their journey they encountered several
groups of *mujahidin* as well as Afghan villagers. The people
were dirt poor, living in simple, thatch-roofed houses with dirt
floors, but always their hospitality was effusive and they shared

what little they had. They lived by their code of *Pakhtunwali*, unwritten laws of social conduct composed of three main dictums. *Melmastia* demanded that anyone who crossed the threshold of their dwelling be treated as an honored guest, even a sworn enemy. *Nanawatai* dictated that asylum must be granted to anyone who sought it, and *Badal,* the strictest commandment of them all, demanded remorseless revenge, payment in blood for any personal affront. *Mordabad Shouravi,* Gallio thought. These were people who believed that it was better to die in battle than in bed. A *shahid*, a martyr who was killed in battle, gained admittance through the gates of paradise. No wonder the Soviets couldn't crush these people. Death held no fear for them and they didn't know the meaning of surrender. They found freedom in death as well as life.

Gallio was unable to keep his group from talking excitedly about the Stinger missiles to those they met on the trail. He tried to caution them, but it was no use. They were like children with new toys. For all he knew, anyone they met could be a spy for the Karmal regime. For that matter, despite all his best efforts, word of what they carried might have leaked out before they had even crossed the border. However, in a very real sense, the operation was no longer his, but theirs. They would get the missiles to Massoud, but if they met the enemy along the way, they'd fight.

They were about five or six days' journey from their destination when they ran into an ambush. A group of Afghans approached them from down the trail, but something in their manner had given them away before they got too close. Whatever it was, Gallio hadn't spotted it, but the others had, and almost before he knew what was happening, he found himself in the middle of a firefight. The "Afghans" were Soviet Spetsnaz commandos in disguise.

The *mujahidin* reacted quickly. Half of them rushed forward and took up position to cover the retreat so the others could escape with their precious cargo of Stingers. But the Russians had prepared for that. The previous night, a flight of helicopters had passed by overhead, an occurrence that had become so common, Gallio hadn't paid much attention to it. The choppers had dropped off several squads of commandos to their rear and they had moved up during the night, setting up a hammer-and-anvil assault to hit them from both sides.

As bullets struck the rocks around them Sikander shouted, *"Boro! Boro!"* ("Let's go! Let's go!") He grabbed Gallio's arm and tried to pull him back out of the way, but Gallio shook him off and took up a position to return the fire with his AK-47, covering the others while they quickly started taking the missiles off the frightened pack animals. They shouldered them and began to scamper up into the rocks like mountain goats. Bullets whined off the rocks around them. Gallio felt a sharp pain as his cheek was lacerated by a stone chipped off by a round from a Kalashnikov. Adrenaline surged through his bloodstream as he returned the fire.

Cries of *"Allah o Akbar!"* and *"Mordabad Shouravi!"* echoed over the sharp, firecracker bursts of the automatic weapons. Then, suddenly, another sound was added to the din as the loud, staccato clatter of helicopter blades filled the air. The Hind helicopter gunships swooped down like screaming pterodactyls, raining a deadly hail of bullets into the mountainside. One of the panicked mules was cut completely in half as the chopper "walked" its fire up the trail and Gallio heard a scream as Sikander's body was reduced to bloody pulp in less than two seconds. He huddled behind the rock outcropping where he had taken shelter, trying to become a part of it as bullets spanged into the mountain all around him, sending dust and stone fragments flying in all directions. Then he heard a loud *whoosh* and a concussive *whump* as the helicopter blossomed into a bright orange fireball.

He glanced up and saw Daoud, the little thirteen-year-old who had paid such close and rapt attention when he had explained the function of the Stingers, lowering the tube from his shoulder, raising his fist, and shouting out triumphantly. He had downed the first Soviet helicopter gunship in the Afghan War.

"Awriight!" Gallio shouted, with elation. *"Yeah, Daoud!"*

The boy waved at him, a wide grin on his face. Then his small body jerked convulsively and fell as it was struck by a burst of machine-gun fire. Gallio screamed hoarsely as he emptied the magazine of his AK-47 into the commando who had killed the boy. He jacked out the clip and slapped a fresh one in. But before he could raise the rifle, he felt a sledgehammerlike blow to his head and everything went black.

He woke up to the jouncing of a truck careening down a rutted road. He was lying on a blood-soaked truckbed, surrounded by the dead bodies of the freedom fighters. The Soviets had discovered it had a demoralizing effect on the *mujahidin* when they took away the bodies of slain freedom fighters, thereby denying them a Muslim burial.

Gallio was surprised to discover he was still alive. His head was throbbing. The bullet must have only grazed him. He no longer had on his turban, but his head was bandaged. The side of his face felt sticky, but he couldn't tell if it was from his own blood or the sticky gore on the floor of the truckbed. He couldn't raise his hand to feel it. They were tied behind his back. His feet were tied as well. He was trussed up like a roped calf, a short cord running behind him from his hands to his feet, arching his back painfully. He was hemmed in by bodies and he couldn't move. The stench was awful.

He had no idea how long he had been out. He had no idea what time it was, whether it was day or night. He heard only the roar of the truck's engine and felt the jarring impact as it bounced over the road. He tried to think. There hadn't been a road close to where they were when the ambush had gone down, so they must have carried him out and loaded him onto a chopper, then transferred him to the truck along with the bodies.

"Well, son," he mumbled to himself, "you finally did it. You really screwed the pooch this time."

The truck braked to a stop. He heard doors slamming and the sound of running footsteps. A moment later, the back gate of the truck was lowered and the tarp was pulled aside. Two men jumped up into the truckbed, walking over the bullet-riddled bodies of the *mujahidin,* and Gallio felt himself lifted painfully and tossed out on the ground. He fell on his side and grunted. His head felt like a thousand hangovers. Someone leaned down and cut the cord running from his wrists to his feet, then cut the cord around his ankles.

"*Vstavai! Vstavai, svolotch!*"

A booted foot connected with his ribs.

Gallio grunted with pain and awkwardly lumbered to his feet. Every muscle in his body felt cramped. It was dusk. The sky was a wild orange purple as the sun set. The wind blew gently on his face. He was in a valley, possibly the Panjshir, though he had no way of knowing for sure. The mountains rose majestically around him. As he quickly glanced around he saw large tents and rows of corrugated iron huts. A hundred or so yards in front of him was a supply depot, with several trucks and armored vehicles parked alongside it. Farther off, he could see a line of rocket launchers positioned near the perimeter of the camp, aimed to fire salvos at the mountain slopes. Nearer, a line of APCs, a couple of fuel tankers, and a row of T-64 tanks. To his right, there were several rows of Hind-24s, huge, ugly-looking choppers with stubby wings and weapons pods. Someone gave him a hard shove and he almost lost his footing.

Four men marched him around the front of the truck and he saw a sight that was right out of *Gunga Din*. It was a huge adobe fort, with thick, thirty-foot walls and gun towers. A gun barrel prodded his back as he was marched through the large, heavy wooden gates. They marched him down a series of dark and narrow corridors, illuminated by lights strung on wire. He heard someone screaming. They brought him to a room and shoved him inside, then tied him to a wooden chair placed behind a folding table. One of the soldiers struck him hard across the face, drawing blood. Gallio spat at him and received a gun butt in his stomach for his trouble. As he fought to get his breath back the door opened and a colonel in the sand-colored uniform of the Spetsnaz commandos entered.

He was tall and muscular, with dark, curly hair and deep-set brown eyes. He was about forty years old, deeply tanned, with sharply chiseled features. Behind him came another man, a swarthy-looking Afghan in the uniform of the Karmal regime. He came up to Gallio and asked him something in Pushto. Gallio didn't understand a word. He simply stared at his interrogator belligerently. The man struck him in the face and repeated his query. Gallio said nothing.

One of the Russian soldiers raised his rifle to strike Gallio in the face with the gun butt, but the colonel quickly said, *"Nyet!"* and the rifle was lowered. *"Ostavteh nas."*

He jerked his head toward the door and the others left, leaving him alone with Gallio.

He took out a silver cigarette case, snapped it open, took one for himself, then held out the case to Gallio and raised his eyebrows. Gallio nodded. The Russian took one out and placed it between Gallio's lips. He lit it, then lit his own and exhaled the smoke through his nostrils.

"My name is Colonel Grigori Andreyvitch Galinov," he said, in excellent, though heavily accented English. "What is your name?"

Gallio gazed at him with an uncomprehending expression and shrugged his shoulders.

"Your pretense at ignorance is pointless," Galinov said matter-of-factly. "I will ask you again, what is your name?"

Gallio did not reply.

"You know that we can make you talk," Galinov said. "You are, no doubt, familiar with our techniques of interrogation. Why put yourself through unnecessary pain?"

Gallio said nothing.

The Russian officer stared at him thoughtfully. "Very well. You do not wish to tell me your name. In that case, I will try another question."

He leaned forward across the table, close to Gallio's face, staring at him intently. He held up a gold signet ring.

"Where did you get this?"

Gallio recognized his own ring, a gold signet inscribed with the symbol of a *gladius,* the Roman short sword, surrounded by the letters PBMMG. He had not realized until that moment that they had removed it from his finger. And as the Russian held it up before him Gallio saw, with a shock, that he was wearing a ring that was absolutely identical.

Galinov saw the expression on his face and his eyes narrowed. He took the cigarette from between Gallio's lips and tossed it aside.

"Where?" he repeated.

"It belonged to my great-grandfather," said Gallio, staring at him with astonishment. "Where did you get yours?"

"It has been in my family for generations," said Galinov. He placed the ring on the table before Gallio and straightened up. *"Pro bono . . . ?"* he said, watching Gallio with an anxious, intense gaze.

Gallio felt a fist start squeezing his insides. He swallowed hard. *"Pro bono maiori, maxima gloria,"* he said, completing the Latin motto that the letters on the ring stood for. He suddenly felt light-headed.

"So you know the words," Galinov said slowly. "But who was the first to say them?"

"Marcus Lucius Gallio. My ancestor." He moistened his lips. "And who did he say them to?"

"To Hanno, son of Hannibal," Galinov replied. He exhaled heavily. *"Chiort vazmi!"* he swore, softly. "Who *are* you?"

"Colonel Anthony Mark Gallio." Suddenly it hit him. He couldn't believe it. He felt as if he had been gut-punched. "Gallio? *Galinov?"*

"We are kinsmen," said the Russian, staring at him with awe. "Jesus Christ! I can't fucking believe it!"

"Your shock is no greater than mine, I assure you," Galinov said. He shook his head. "If this were any other regiment than Spetsnaz, that ring would surely have been stolen."

He took his knife out, went around behind Gallio's chair, and cut his bonds. Then he opened the door and called out, *"Suvorov! Prenehsi butilku vodki."*

A few moments later, a sergeant entered with a bottle of vodka and two shot glasses. Galinov nodded and dismissed him. The man left and shut the door. As Gallio massaged his wrists Galinov opened the bottle and poured them each a shot. "What the devil shall we drink to?" he asked. "You have children?"

"A son."

"I, also. To the children, then."

"To the children," Gallio said softly. They drank.

"Of all the places in the world to meet," Galinov said, offering Gallio another cigarette. He took it and Galinov lit it for him. "You are Special Forces, of course. Yes, you would be." He snorted and shook his head. "You son of a bitch."

Gallio said nothing. He was still in a daze. Galinov refilled their glasses.

"I had thought that my branch of the family was the last," he said.

"So did I," said Gallio.

"A colonel in the United States Army Special Forces, working for the CIA, of course," Galinov said. He shook his head. *"Yob tvayu maht."*

Gallio had some knowledge of Russian. He was familiar with the Russian equivalent of motherfucker.

Colonel Galinov stared at him for a long moment, a strange expression on his face. "What is your son's name?"

"Tony Jr."

"Mine is Alexei," Galinov said. "He will be six years old now. I have not seen him since he was four."

"Mine's eight."

Galinov nodded. "I hate this lousy war."

"I hate the way you're fighting it," said Gallio.

Galinov nodded again, his gaze distant. "Yes. So do I. This is not a war for soldiers, but for butchers. I can no longer sleep without nightmares. What we are doing here fills me with disgust. May God forgive us."

"God?" said Gallio.

Galinov smiled wryly. "You are surprised? Did you think that all of us were atheists? I am Russian Orthodox. And when I return home to Novgorod, if I should return, I shudder at the things I must confess."

"Why?" asked Gallio. "Why kill innocent civilians? Why the atrocities, Galinov?"

"The United States has never committed atrocities, I suppose?" Galinov said sarcastically. "What of your Lieutenant Calley? What of your support of the Nicaraguan Contras?"

"I won't deny the Contras commit atrocities, but we don't control the Contras and Calley was prosecuted. What he did wasn't our policy, as it is yours. You people are committing genocide."

"And your hands are so clean?" Galinov said. "Your country's history is without blemish? What about your American Indians?"

"That was in the past," Gallio said.

"So shall this be, one day," said Galinov. "But whether you believe it or not, I don't like it any more than you do." He refilled their glasses again. "For the first time, there are demonstrations against the war back home. Such a thing has never been before. Our young people do not wish to go. It is like your Vietnam. They injure themselves to get medical exemptions, some even pretend insanity and go to institutions rather than serve in the army." He shook his head. "There is talk we may be pulling out soon. I hope to God it's true."

He shoved his chair back and got up. His manner seemed to change. He drew himself up and looked down at Gallio. Without warning, he punched Gallio in the face, knocking him back over his chair and breaking his nose. As Gallio struggled back up Galinov hit him three more times, powerful, punishing blows that bloodied his mouth and cut the skin over his left eye. Gallio collapsed to the floor.

Galinov opened the door and shouted something to the men outside. They came in, picked Gallio up, and took him to a cell. They shoved him in and he fell sprawling on the dirt floor. There were rats crawling in the corners. The door was slammed and bolted.

The Roman province of Campania, 201 B.C.

"Get up, Carthaginian dog! *Get up,* I said!"

Hanno slowly rose up off the floor and stood, feeling the weight of his chains.

"Outside! Now! *Move!*"

The Roman soldier whacked him on the back with flat of his sword, urging him out of the cell. The blow hurt and Hanno stumbled, but he would not give his enemy the satisfaction of hearing him cry out.

He was herded in line with the other prisoners and taken outside into a walled exercise yard. He noticed training apparatus placed around the yard, wooden poles with sword blades set into them on wheels that turned, dummies for practicing sword strikes, what looked like an obstacle course, and some other apparatus he didn't recognize. They were drawn up into a line by the armed soldiers. A squat, powerfully built, grizzled, and barrel-chested man with a shaved head and numerous scars all over him addressed them. He wore a simple cloth tunic, covered with a chest plate, and sandals.

"My name is Macros," he shouted at them, "and for the duration of your stay here, I shall be your god! You shall grow to fear and hate me, but you shall worship me, because I hold the power of life and death over each and every one of you! You have all been brought here as worthless slaves, but when you leave, assuming you survive, you shall be gladiators! Yours shall be the privilege to fight in the arena for the elite of Rome, and for its people, and if you do well, you shall live and be well cared for. If you do not do well, you shall die, but you shall die with dignity and honor! If you survive, there is a chance that you may win your freedom, as I did myself. But survival is its own reward. Those of you who do not prove suitable, if you survive, shall be taken to labor in the mines. Those of you who become injured, in a manner that renders your usefulness to the republic at an end, shall be put to death. Those of you who disobey, if you are fortunate, I will kill myself, or else you will be crucified. Those are my words. Heed them well, for I shall not repeat myself."

Macros scanned the line and his gaze focused on one man. "You!" he said. "Step forward!"

The man was shoved out of line by one of the soldiers.

"Remove his chains."

The chains were taken off.

"Give him a sword," said Macros.

The soldier handed the man a sword. He looked at it uncertainly.

"Now," said Macros, "kill me."

The man stared at Macros, hesitating.

"I said, *kill me!*"

The man swallowed hard, then lunged clumsily at Macros with the sword. Macros was unarmed, but he easily sidestepped the lunge, grabbed the man's wrist, tripped him, and threw him to the ground, placing one leg over his arm and bending his elbow back against the joint, easily disarming him.

"Get up!" he said.

The man struggled to his feet, moaning and holding his sore arm.

"You see? You know nothing, nothing! Here, you shall learn! Or die in the attempt. Now get back in line!"

As the man returned to stand with the others Macros looked across the line of prisoners again. His gaze settled on Hanno.

"You," he said, narrowing his eyes. He still held the sword he had taken from the first man.

Hanno felt himself shoved forward. His chains were removed. Hanno did not take his eyes off Macros for an instant. The two men stared at each other for a long moment.

"Give him a sword," said Macros.

Hanno took the short sword he was given. It felt good in his hand.

"Now, Carthaginian," said Macros, "here is your chance. The only chance that you will ever get."

Hanno didn't hesitate. He struck at once, a powerful, savage blow aimed at the trainer's head, and Macros barely got his own blade up in time to parry it. He aimed a thrust at Hanno's chest, but Hanno parried it easily and went on the offensive, his blade smashing away at the trainer, driving him backward relentlessly. Hanno grunted with each blow, the fury of his assault pushing the trainer back as he kept advancing, the clang of the blades filling the exercise yard. He kept pounding away at Macros's blade, and moments later, he struck so hard the trainer lost his grip and the sword fell to the ground. Hanno struck him with his left fist, knocking him down, then raised the sword for the killing stroke.

An arrow thudded into the dirt directly at his feet. Hanno hesitated. He looked up to see several archers with drawn bows, standing in the gallery, aiming down at him.

"*Hold!*" cried Macros.

Hanno lowered his sword slowly, then dropped it to the ground. One of the soldiers came up behind him and struck him down with the pommel of his sword. The blow came crashing down on Hanno's skull and he fell headlong into the dirt, fighting to remain conscious as everything started spinning.

"It seems that we have found ourselves a fighter," he heard Macros say above him. "You will do. You will do very well, indeed."

He could not get up. He tasted the dirt in his mouth and then blackness closed in as he lost consciousness.

Panjshir Valley, Afghanistan, August 1986

Gallio awoke hours later to the sound of the bolt being drawn back. The door opened and four soldiers entered. One of them kicked Gallio in the side hard enough to crack his ribs. They tied him up, as before, kicked him again several times, for good measure, then picked him up and dragged him out into the corridor.

They went outside. Dawn was breaking. They dragged him over to one of the Hind helicopter gunships. Its rotors were slowly turning. They picked him up and threw him inside. The chopper rose up into the air. Trussed up as he was, Gallio could barely move. He tried to worm his way backward from the open hatch. All the pilot had to do was bank sharply and he'd simply slide out into space.

"Lay still!" the pilot shouted.

Gallio craned his neck around. It was Galinov. He banked the chopper sharply to the right and Gallio slid back, away from the hatch. They flew for a short while, Galinov keeping the helicopter steady, then descended. They landed and Galinov hurried back. He quickly cut Gallio's bonds with his knife.

"Get out," he said, "quickly, before some of your friends drop one of your damned Stingers in our laps."

Gallio jumped to the ground. Galinov tossed him a pack. "Go home, kinsman!" he shouted, over the churning of the helicopter blades. "Go home and kiss your son!"

He moved back into the pilot's seat, and seconds later the Hind rose rapidly into the air, banked sharply, and disappeared into the distance. Gallio watched it for a long time. He looked into the pack. It contained a Soviet field jacket, some rations, a canteen full of water, a first-aid kit, a compass, a Makarov pistol, and a bottle of Russian vodka.

He looked around. He stood alone on a high plain, in the middle of nowhere, steep mountains all around him scratching at the sky.

Galinov would probably fly back and tell them he'd flown over to one of the Afghan villages and dropped him off—the long way. An example and a payback for the shot-down helicopter. The first, undoubtedly, of many. But at least now the victory of the helicopter gunships was no longer a foregone conclusion.

Gallio tucked the 9mm Makarov pistol into his waistband, took out the compass, and shouldered the pack. He raised his right hand and looked at the gold signet ring Galinov had returned to him.

"Thanks, Great-Grandfather," he said softly.

He had a long, long walk ahead of him, but he was still alive.

BOOK ONE

Come, fill your glasses, fellows and stand up in a row.
To singing sentimentally, we're going for to go.
In the army there's sobriety, promotions very slow.
So we'll sing our reminiscences of Benny Havens, oh!
Oh, Benny Havens, oh! oh, Benny Havens, oh!
So we'll sing our reminiscences of Benny Havens, oh!

CHAPTER ONE

West Point, New York, June 1859

MAJOR ANTHONY WAYNE Gallio stood at the head of the reception line in the entry hall of his modest home, greeting the guests as they arrived. Stocky and barrel-chested, with strong, weathered features and a salt-and-pepper hair and beard, Gallio stood just under six feet tall. On this special occasion, he was dressed in his finest uniform, with his sword and sash and all his medals. To his left stood his two sons, Robert and Mark, both looking handsome in their cadet dress grays, and beside them stood the bride and groom. Gallio's daughter, Maria, the youngest of his three children at sixteen, looked lovely and radiant in her French lace wedding gown. Her new husband, former cadet First Captain Travis Coulter, had just been commissioned as a second lieutenant in the United States Army.

It was a proud and happy day for Major Gallio. After serving in the Mexican War, he had accepted a post as an instructor at the United States Military Academy at West Point. Both his sons were cadets at the Academy. Robert, the oldest, was taller than his father by a head, a trim and muscular, self-assured young man with a quiet and reserved nature. He had graduated with honors at the head of his class and been commissioned as a lieutenant. His best friend, Travis Coulter, had graduated second. He was slightly shorter than Robert, lean and blond, almost towheaded, with fair skin and bright blue eyes. He was soft-spoken, with handsome features and an easy smile, the very image of the Southern cavalier. Gallio's youngest son, Mark, had just successfully completed his second year, much to his family's relief. Mark's rapid accumulation of demerits constantly had him on the very edge of expulsion. He was dark-haired, with deep brown eyes, like his brother and his father, but he had inherited his mother's slight stature. Small and wiry, with a slight droop at the corner of his mouth that gave him the same perpetually wry and insolent expression that his mother had, he looked like a young Lord Byron and he was just about as wild.

His eyes were red-rimmed from the previous night's festivities at Benny Havens's, a nearby pub that was strictly off limits to cadets, though most of them frequently "ran it" to Benny's to enjoy his roast turkey and oysters, and especially his flip, a beverage made of well-beaten and spiced eggs, mixed with ale and heated by a glowing iron poker. If it was left in for just the right amount of time, the hot poker gave the drink a delicious, caramel flavor. If it was left in one second too long, the flip took on the taste of ashes. Benny always knew just how long to leave the poker in and the cadets paid boisterous homage to his skill at every opportunity.

The previous night, following the graduation ceremonies, the faculty had looked the other way while the cadets of the graduating class and a number of underclassmen had repaired to Benny Havens's for a celebration. Robert and Travis, by the look of them, had both been prudent in their partaking of refreshments, but Mark had obviously tied one on. As he stood in the reception line he looked slightly green about the gills.

The only thing Gallio's two sons had in common was a family resemblance. From early childhood, Robert had always been a very serious boy, studious, earnest, and determined. In that, he took after his father. Young Mark, on the other hand, had a streak of Satan in his soul. An irrepressible hell-raiser, Mark had always been difficult and Gallio thought his choice of friends at the Academy left much to be desired. He had, naturally, gravitated to the troublemakers, and his best friend, Cadet George Armstrong Custer, was the worst of the lot. He had finished the year at the very bottom of his class, with Mark barely ahead of him. Gallio had his doubts that either of them would survive the full course at the Academy, but at least Mark had made it through so far. It was touch and go.

Mark made an effort at his studies, if only a halfhearted one, but to Gallio's knowledge, Custer never even cracked a book. Just before the final examinations, someone had broken into Professor Agnel's home and stolen his notes for the French exam. There was no proof, but Agnel was convinced Custer was the culprit and that Mark had probably acted as the lookout. Their intention must have been to copy the exam questions, but Agnel had arrived home early, and in a panic, the thief had torn the notes right out of his book and bolted out the window. In doing so, however, the thief had telegraphed his intentions and Agnel had stayed up late to change all the examination questions, with the result that both George Custer and Mark Gallio had failed spectacularly.

Major Gallio wished there was something he could do to discourage this unfortunate friendship, but he knew Mark well enough to know that anything he said would only make the situation worse. Mark was stubborn and willful. He got it from his mother, who had married Gallio against the wishes of her family. Kathleen always had a sly touch of the leprechaun about her, Gallio remembered fondly. It was one of the things that had made him fall in love with her. She had been the fire to his ice. He wished she could have been with him on this day, that she could have lived to see Robert's graduation and Maria's wedding. She had been dead the past nine years and Gallio still missed her so much that he ached. He had never remarried.

Maria was almost the spitting image of her mother. A ravishing, raven-haired beauty with her mother's bright blue eyes, she was much fairer than either of her brothers, who had inherited their father's dark, Mediterranean complexion. From the first time Cadet Coulter had dinner at their home, Gallio had noticed the attraction between them. After dinner, as the boys were leaving to go back to their rooms at South Barracks, Coulter had lingered and, with as much dignity as he could muster, had politely asked Gallio's permission to call on Maria. Repressing a smile, Gallio had put on a very serious look and asked Cadet Coulter what his intentions were.

The young man had replied, in his soft, South Carolina drawl, "My intentions, sir, are strictly honorable. If, in time, both yourself and your daughter find me acceptable and worthy, I would be proud to ask you for her hand in marriage upon my graduation."

Somewhat taken aback, Gallio had responded, "Well, sir, you are forthright and decisive, I will give you that." Then he smiled. "I appreciate your frankness, Mr. Coulter. And I suppose that time will tell. For the present, if my daughter is amenable, you have my permission to call upon her."

Afterward, Maria had come running up to him, looking anxious. "Did he ask you, Father?"

He had gazed at her, realizing for the first time that his daughter was becoming a woman, and he felt a brief, sharp pang of regret.

"Yes, darling, he did. And I might add that he comported himself in a most direct and gentlemanly manner. I told him he could come and call upon you, if you were agreeable."

Her face had lit up. "Agreeable?" She laughed. "He's the man I'm going to marry!"

Exactly like Kathleen, thought Gallio, who had announced her intention to marry him to her disbelieving family on the first day they met. But unlike his late wife's family, Gallio had not disapproved. Travis Coulter was, indeed, a fine young man. He was from a good, solid, South Carolina family, wealthy and socially prominent citizens of Charleston. He was also one of the best cadets at the Academy, excelling in everything from military drill to academics. He was a brilliant horseman, surpassed in that skill only by Sam Grant, who had graduated some years before him and who held the academy jump record. Coulter had tried repeatedly to best that record, but he was not successful. It was no reflection on him as an equestrian. Grant's ability with horses had been nothing short of supernatural.

For the rest of his stay at the Academy, Coulter had paid polite court to Maria, always acting the perfect Southern gentleman. Maria had once confessed to her father, somewhat disappointedly, that Travis had never even tried to steal a kiss. Often, the two of them simply sat together and held hands, saying nothing, each overwhelmed with emotion. It was chaste and touching, unlike Gallio and Kathleen's courtship. They had been like randy goats, stealing long, passionate kisses at every opportunity. Maria had her mother's hot, romantic blood, but Travis had always remained true to his word about his honorable intentions. The first time he had ever kissed her on the lips was on their wedding day.

It had been a lovely wedding. They were married in the small academy chapel, standing at the altar before the painting of the republic's eagle, flanked by Peace, represented by a pleading woman, and a grim-faced Roman soldier, symbolizing war. Gallio had given his daughter away and Robert had been the best man. The young couple left the chapel and walked arm in arm beneath the drawn sabers of the graduating class, then were driven in a carriage to the reception at Gallio's small stone house on Professors' Row. Gallio was well pleased with his daughter's choice. Coulter was every inch the officer and gentleman. He shuddered at the thought of what might have happened had Maria set her sights on someone like George Custer.

The object of his thoughts suddenly stood before him. "Good afternoon, sir. Allow me to offer my heartfelt congratulations on your daughter's wedding."

Major Gallio took the young man's hand. "Thank you, Mr. Custer. Your sentiments are most appreciated." He cleared his throat. "However, sir, I might add that your hair wants trimming."

As usual, Custer was pushing the regulation about hair length. He was inordinately fond of his flowing blond locks and was constantly receiving demerits for wearing them too long. But his propensity for displaying his insolence was even greater than his vanity, if such a thing was possible. Once, after a particularly severe reprimand, he had shaved his head completely bald. Now his blond mane had grown back, and as usual, it was much too long. Custer merely inclined his head and smiled insolently, then moved on.

Thank God Maria hadn't chosen someone like him, thought Gallio. Like her mother, once Maria made her mind up, it was pointless trying to dissuade her. Fortunately, she was a sensible girl and had disliked Custer at first sight. She referred to him as "the peacock" and had no idea what her brother saw in him. Custer was the worst cadet Gallio had seen at the Academy since Philip Sheridan, who came close to being expelled for constant fighting. As a plebe, young Sheridan had once charged a cadet sergeant with a bayonet. The only thing that saved the upperclassman was some quick footwork and a hasty retreat. Sheridan would have been dismissed if not for the fact that Lee, who was then superintendent, had an inexplicable fondness for the wild young Irishman. Custer had no such guardian angel. He was universally detested by the faculty. If he survived till graduation, Gallio thought, it would be a miracle. He only hoped Custer wouldn't drag Mark down with him.

Gallio's small house wasn't quite up to holding everyone who had been invited to the reception. With the exception of the faculty, the immediate family, and some of Travis and Robert's closest friends among the graduating class, the other guests, mostly cadets, their ladies, and their families, came through the reception line to pay their respects, then went out the back door and around the side of the house to the front lawn, where tables bearing refreshments had been set up. Gallio had been afraid that it might rain, but the weather had cooperated. It was a warm summer day and a gentle breeze was blowing off the Hudson. The cadets and military faculty all looked resplendent in their dress uniforms. The civilian faculty and the parents were attired in their Sunday best and the young ladies were like bright spring flowers in their soft pastels. With their parasols and bonnets and their long, full skirts, they seemed to float gracefully across the lawn on the arms of their cadets.

Gallio was mildly annoyed to see that Custer had chosen to stay inside with Mark rather than go outside with the other underclassmen. However, he decided to say nothing. As he approached the group he realized that they were once more discussing politics. Gallio did not care for talk of politics, but he seemed to be alone in that feeling.

Lately, all anyone at the Academy seemed to talk about was the slavery question. It was impossible to get away from it. People were pushing westward and settling the new territories. American cotton dominated the world market and slave-grown crops had fueled much of the growth. Each year, new immigrants arrived, attracted by America's cheap land and increasing need for labor.

Improvements in transportation had fostered an industrial revolution, particularly in the Northern states, and it had brought about many changes in people's lives. Goods were now being produced primarily for the marketplace rather than for home consumption. Machine production was gradually replacing the work of skilled artisans. Wage labor had increased the gap between the middle and the upper classes, between the workers and the bosses. Society was becoming politically and economically polarized. The birth rate was declining and women were entering the work force in far greater numbers than ever before, especially in the North. Many of them were receiving more formal education and entering the teaching profession. Others were becoming writers for the growing profusion of new "women's magazines." A great many of them were becoming far too independent for Gallio's taste, his daughter among them. Maria had taken it into her head that she wanted to become a writer. She, too, had become interested in politics, but at least now, Gallio thought, that would be her husband's problem and not his.

The changes in society had also widened the gap between the Northern and the Southern states. The economy of the North was centered around industrialization, while the economy of the South was still largely agrarian, dependent on slave labor. Wage labor in the North had brought about tremendous growth, but it had also resulted in the average wage earner feeling much less independent. Their lives were at the mercy of the time clock and many of them had started to equate wage labor with "wage slavery." Such sentiments had given rise to increased opposition to slavery and the growth of the abolitionist movement. The average manual laborer felt degraded by the existence of the "peculiar institution," which seemed to put him on the same footing as a Negro slave. And the South's desire to extend slavery into the new territories was seen as a threat by many Northerners. It was the burning political question of the day.

If slavery was extended into territories such as Kansas, New Mexico, and California, it was almost certain that those territories would enter the Union as slave-holding states, thereby tipping the political balance of power irrevocably toward the South. Free-Soilers and proslavers were battling it out not only in the territories, but in the halls of Congress, where fistfights frequently broke out among the legislators. After giving an incendiary speech against slavery, Charles Sumner, the senator from Massachusetts, had been nearly caned to death by Preston Brooks, a congressman from South Carolina. The only punishment that Brooks received had been a three-hundred-dollar fine levied by a district court, and when the House voted to expel him, Southern opposition had prevented the necessary two-thirds majority. Making the grand gesture, Brooks had resigned anyway and returned home to ask the voters to vindicate him by a reelection, which they promptly did. While Northerners were outraged at this affront, Southerners sent Brooks new canes by the dozens and begged for fragments of the stick with which he'd nearly killed "that damned Yankee abolitionist."

With the entire nation embroiled in the question, it was impossible for the cadets at West Point to remain above it all. Gallio believed soldiers should not concern themselves with politics. It was bad for discipline, a fact borne out by a number of recent events at the Academy stemming directly from the controversy. There had been frequent fistfights between Northern and Southern cadets. On several occasions, swords were even drawn. Some blood had been spilled, but fortunately, no one had been badly hurt. Still, Gallio knew that if this sort of thing kept up, it would only be a matter of time before someone was seriously injured or even killed in some foolish brawl or duel. The sectionalism that was dividing the country was threatening to tear apart the corps of cadets, and the academy staff was at a loss to do anything to stop it.

"If you ask me, the bastard should be caught and hanged," Custer was saying as Gallio approached the group. "They should take a photograph of him dangling and print it in every newspaper in the country as a lesson to other lawbreakers of his ilk."

"Mr. Custer!" Gallio snapped. "I will not have such language in my home, sir! There are ladies present and it is no way for a gentleman to speak, in any case!"

Custer flushed and immediately came to attention. "Forgive me, sir. I meant no disrespect. I beg you to accept my humble apology."

"Your apology is accepted, Mr. Custer," Gallio said stiffly. "See to it that it does not happen again. I remind you that you are a guest in my home, sir, and a West Point cadet. I will insist that you behave accordingly."

"Yes, *sir!*"

"They still ought to hang the murdering scum," Mark said.

"That will be quite enough, Mr. Gallio," his father said firmly. "This is your sister's wedding day and, as such, hardly a suitable occasion for such topics of discussion."

"Hang whom?" Maria asked, coming up behind him with her husband.

Gallio rolled his eyes. "Maria, *honestly . . .*"

"Please, Father," she said, "I am no longer a child, but a married woman. I merely wish to know whom these gentlemen were discussing."

"We were speaking of Osawatomie Brown," said her brother Mark.

"In that case, I must heartily concur with Mr. Custer's sentiments," said Travis. "Hanging's too good for that murdering abolitionist."

They were talking about John Brown again. Lately, a perennial topic of debate. Privately, Gallio agreed with Mark and Custer. Hanging was too good for him. The fanatic, Bible-thumping abolitionist had achieved infamy three years earlier in the massacre of Pottawatomie Creek. In a biblical act of retribution for the near-fatal caning of Senator Charles Sumner, Brown and a band of men, including four of his young sons, had abducted five proslavery settlers from their homes and split their heads open with broadswords. Brown's savagery had so far gone unpunished, and, together with the pillaging of Lawrence, Kansas, by a "posse" of proslavers from Missouri, it had set off a deadly bushwhacking war.

"Bleeding Kansas" had become a battlefield as Free-Soilers and proslavers fought for control of the territory to determine its status. Congress was deadlocked on the issue of whether Kansas should be admitted as a free state or a slave state, and it looked as if the question would not be settled until the next presidential election. Meanwhile, Kansas continued to bleed as the two factions ambushed each other in the night. The newspapers wrote of almost nothing else and John Brown's reign of terror figured prominently in their dispatches.

All the cadets at the Academy knew of the army's efforts to contain the violence in Kansas, but the hit-and-run guerrilla tactics of the combatants rendered their task next to impossible. Many members of the graduating class would undoubtedly soon find themselves in Kansas and they avidly read all the lurid newspaper accounts of the "civil war" in the territory.

"Gentlemen," said Gallio, "I do not wish to repeat myself. This is not a suitable occasion for such inflammatory topics."

"Your pardon, sir," Travis replied, with a courtly bow. "You are quite correct. We shall speak of other things."

"Oh, by all means, let us discuss the weather, or what the other ladies are wearing this afternoon," said Maria, with thinly disguised sarcasm. "Important events may be occurring elsewhere, but we need not concern ourselves with them here. Let us speak of flowers and bluebirds and the breath of spring, the sort of things a woman understands."

"Maria!" Gallio said disapprovingly.

"Come now, Father, why *shouldn't* we discuss the future of the country?" asked Maria. "After all, it is *our* future, too. Why do men think women have no place in such discussions?"

Gallio shook his head in resignation. Cadets would snap to at his slightest word, but his daughter had a will that was entirely her own. He was not about to engage in a debate with her, especially on her wedding day.

"Have it as you wish, then," he said irritably. "But I, for one, do not intend to speak of hangings on my daughter's wedding day." He turned to the others. "There is, in fact, a matter of some import that I would like to discuss in private with my children. With your permission, Mr. Coulter, I would like to take your wife away from you, though only for a few brief moments. Have I your indulgence?"

"Most certainly, sir," said Travis. "We shall await your return so that we may drink our toasts."

"Thank you, Mr. Coulter. Maria, Robert, Mark . . . would you be so kind as to join me in the study? Gentlemen, by your leave . . ."

Gallio's three children followed him to his private sanctum, where he kept his writing desk, his library, and his family mementos. He unlocked the door to admit them, then locked it once more from within after they had entered. Puzzled, they watched their father as he went around behind his desk, then beckoned them to the three chairs he had placed before it. They sat, but he remained standing.

"This is a very special day," he told them. "It is a joyful occasion for our family, but it is also a solemn one. Maria, you have married an excellent young man. A soldier and a gentleman. I couldn't be more pleased. I only wish your mother could have lived to see this day. You would have made her very proud."

"Oh, Father . . ."

"There now, stop that. If you start crying, then next thing, you will have me blubbering like a maudlin drunk and your brothers will be embarrassed for me."

Robert and Mark both grinned.

"Robert . . . or should I say Lieutenant Gallio?" He smiled. "You have made me very proud, as well. You leave behind a record at the Academy that few will be able to surpass. You have exceeded all my expectations. I have no doubt that you have a brilliant career ahead of you and that you will bring honor to the family name."

"Thank you, sir," said Robert, flushing slightly.

"And you, too, Mark, have made me proud," said Gallio, turning to his youngest son. "Although I must admit," he added wryly, "there have been times when you have given me cause for concern."

Mark smiled sheepishly.

"The day will come," Gallio continued, "when you will all have children of your own to carry on the family tradition. One day you will stand before them as I stand before you now, to tell them the meaning of our proud family heritage and how it all began."

He took off the gold signet ring he always wore and placed it on the desk before him so that it faced his children.

"You have often remarked upon that ring and asked me what it signified," said Gallio. "And I have always told you that it symbolized our family tradition, and that when the time came, I would explain its meaning to you fully. That time has now come."

He paused a moment before going on and his children listened eagerly. The ring had long been an intriguing mystery to them. They knew only that their grandfather had worn one exactly like it.

"I have always taught you that family loyalty comes first, above everything else, and that our family tradition of loyalty and service dates back many, many years. The name of Gallio has a long and honorable history. You all know something of that history. You know that your grandfather, rest his soul, fought honorably in the War of 1812 and that his father, your great-grandfather, Colonel Nathan Gallio, fought in the Revolution. You know that our family tradition of military service is, perhaps, the oldest one in all of history, dating back to ancient Rome. But I have never told you of its origin.

"The story of our family tradition dates back to the days of the republic," he continued. "It began with the Second Punic War, when one of the greatest generals in all of history, Hannibal Barca, invaded Spain to make war on Rome's allies and possessions, before attacking Rome itself."

"Hannibal!" said Robert with awe. "Our ancestors fought Hannibal himself?"

"Hannibal *was* our ancestor." Gallio smiled at the thunderstruck expressions on their faces. They were stunned to discover they were descended from the greatest military commander who had ever lived.

"Then . . . we possess *African* blood?" Maria asked with shock.

"Not African, my dear," said Gallio, with a chuckle, "but Carthaginian. Carthage was settled by Phoenicians, a Semitic tribe who once lived in what is now Syria. We are descended from Roman, Spanish, and Phoenician stock. The story of our family began when Hannibal defeated a Spanish tribe known as the Carpetani. Among the prisoners was the wife of the slain Carpetani chieftain, a young woman named Alorca. She is said to have been very beautiful and Hannibal took her for his concubine. She bore him a son named Hanno. Weakened by her arduous journey across the Alps with Hannibal and his forces, Alorca died in childbirth.

"For seventeen long years, Hannibal made war on Rome," Gallio continued, "blazing a trail of destruction throughout Italy.

Hanno grew up a soldier, knowing nothing but war from the moment of his birth. When Hannibal's army was finally defeated by the Roman general Scipio, who thereafter took the name of Africanus to commemorate his victory, young Hanno was among those who were taken prisoner. When his identity was discovered, he was sent in chains to a gladiatorial school in the Roman province of Campania so the citizens of Rome could be treated to the sight of their greatest enemy's son fighting for his life in the arena."

"A gladiator!" Mark exclaimed, with a thrilled glance at his brother. "Think of it, Robert! One of our ancestors was a Roman gladiator!"

"A slave," said Maria softly.

"Yes, a slave," said Gallio somberly. "The life span of a gladiator was often very short. Yet Hanno had been schooled from birth in the arts of warfare. He survived to best all of his opponents and win fame as an indomitable gladiator. The tradition of our family tells us that he became known as the 'Lion of Carthage' and that one day he caught the eye of an influential Roman knight named Marcus Lucius Gallio."

"Then this Roman was our ancestor as well?" asked Robert.

"No, not really, Robert," his father replied. "From Marcus Gallio, we inherited only our name. He was a wealthy and powerful aristocrat who decided to purchase Hanno so that he could boast of having a famous warrior for his slave and so that Hanno could instruct his two young sons in the skills of combat. He wanted them to be prepared to serve as officers in Rome's legions. He gave Hanno a young Thracian slave girl named Cyrene to be his wife, and in time, she bore Hanno a son, who was named Vindix. As the story goes, Gallio treated Hanno well and Hanno served him faithfully, becoming quite attached to Gallio's two sons, who were his pupils. Their names are no longer known to us, but when war broke out between Rome and Sparta, Hanno accompanied Gallio's sons to battle and was seriously wounded saving the life of the eldest. The family tradition makes no mention of the nature of Hanno's injuries, only the fact that he was crippled for life. Gallio rewarded Hanno for this gallant sacrifice and for his years of loyal service by granting him his freedom and adopting Vindix as his grandson, thereby giving him his name and a share of his estate. He also presented Hanno with a gold signet ring that he had made especially for him. It bore the symbol of the *gladius*, the Roman short sword, and the letters PBMMG. They stand for the motto, *Pro bono maiori, maxima gloria.*"

"For the greater good, the greatest glory," Robert said, staring at the ring on his father's desk.

"I see that you have not forgotten your Latin, Robert," Gallio said, feeling pleased. "Yes, 'For the greater good, the greatest glory.' Marcus Gallio presented Hanno with the ring and asked him to wear it always in token of his gratitude, and to pass it on to his son when he was grown so that Vindix would never forget his father's valor or the devotion that had made him a free citizen of Rome. Vindix Gallio grew to manhood as a Roman, but Hanno never allowed him to forget his heritage. He taught him about his grandfather, Hannibal, and the fame he had achieved. And on the day Vindix became a tribune in Rome's legions, Hanno passed the ring on to him, along with an explanation of everything it stood for.

"Ever since that time," Gallio continued, "that proud tradition has been preserved in our family. Regrettably, the stories of many of our ancestors have been lost in time, and doubtless there were many who had fallen away from the tradition. After so many years, there must be many branches of our family throughout the world, more than we could possibly know about, and bearing many different names. To many of them, the tradition and its origins are probably unknown. Yet there has always been a Gallio carrying on the proud legacy of military service. Our branch of the family, which emigrated to the New World with its first settlers, has always maintained the family tradition. We can proudly trace our name all the way back to Vindix Gallio, grandson of Hannibal."

"What a story!" Mark said, grinning broadly. "I can hardly wait to tell the others!"

"No!" said Gallio severely. "That is something you must *never* do, Mark, on pain of being disowned."

The broad smile abruptly faded from Mark's face. "But . . . *why?"* he asked, confused.

"The true story of our heritage, the origin of our family tradition, is something we must always keep only within the immediate family," Gallio replied. "You must *never* repeat it to anyone else, nor tell anyone outside the immediate family the meaning of the letters on the ring. For there may come a day when you encounter someone else who wears the signet. If you ever meet someone who wears such a ring, or a locket, or perhaps a medallion, and who knows what the letters of the motto stand for, as well as the story behind it, then you will know that you have met a kinsman. Our family tradition will form an unbreakable covenant between you. It might even save your life one day, for it supersedes all other allegiances. This motto and this signet, as well as the story of its origin, are how we, the descendants of Hanno and of Vindix Gallio, can recognize each other. It is the key to who and what we are, and as such, it is a secret that must be closely guarded. That is why I have always taught you the importance of our family tradition of loyalty and service."

He turned to his daughter. "Maria, the tradition demands that you do not share this secret with your husband. Now, Travis is a fine young man and I am proud to have him as a member of the family, but the meaning of the signet and its story is only for those who have the blood of the Gallios flowing through their veins. Someday, when you have children of your own and they are grown, you will pass the tradition on to them, as I now pass it on to you. Only in this way can we be certain that those who wear the signet and who know the secret of its meaning are truly of our blood, members of the family."

He turned to his two sons. "Despite the obvious temptation to share this fascinating story with your friends, regardless of how well you trust them, you must *never* do so. Your ancestors before you, dating back to ancient Rome, have kept this sacred covenant and have never broken faith with it. My children must not be the first to do so."

He took the family Bible from the corner of his desk and held it out to them.

"I will now ask the three of you to stand and, with your hands upon our family Bible, swear an oath before Almighty God and on the honor of your family that you will keep this trust and not betray it for as long as you shall live."

The three of them stood and each in turn somberly placed their hands upon the well-worn, leather cover of the Bible.

"Maria?"

"I swear before Almighty God and on the honor of our family that I will keep the trust," she said, with great solemnity.

"Robert, do you so swear? You need not repeat the words."

Robert placed his hand upon the Bible. "I do, Father."

"Mark?"

"I also swear," said Mark.

"Then this is the proudest moment of my life," said Gallio as he reached into his desk drawer and took out a small, velvet-covered

box. He opened it and there, on a bed of purple silk, lay two
gold signet rings, exactly like the one he wore himself, flanking
a golden locket engraved with the signet for Maria. He picked up
his own ring and put it on, then came around the desk and stood
before them.

"Your right hand, Lieutenant Gallio," he said.

As Robert extended his right hand Gallio placed the ring on his
finger, then kissed him once upon each cheek.

"Cadet Gallio, your right hand, please," he said to Mark, and
repeated the ritual.

"And, finally, Maria . . ."

She bowed her head as he fastened the locket around her neck,
then kissed her cheeks. When he stepped back, they saw that his
eyes were moist.

"Today, my children are all grown," he said, in a voice thick
with emotion. "I will now ask you all to join me in a toast."

He went to the sideboard, poured them each a glass of sherry,
then handed them the glasses. He raised his glass.

"Pro bono maiori, maxima gloria!" he said.

"Pro bono maiori, maxima gloria!" they echoed, then drained
their glasses and, following their father's example, shattered them
in the hearth.

"You are now part of a noble and ancient tradition," Gallio said.
"Let it be your source of strength and pride. But remember always
that strength must be tempered with reason, and pride borne with
humility."

"Yes, sir," said Robert solemnly. "We shall remember."

"Father, have you ever met anyone else who wore the signet?"
Mark asked.

"No, son, I never have. When I was young, I heard talk of
relatives we had somewhere in Virginia, but our family had lost
contact with them. I do not know the reason why, but my father
rarely mentioned them. Who knows, perhaps one day you will
meet them. You will know them by the signet. And now that our
private ceremony is concluded, let us rejoin our guests."

As he opened the door the sounds of angry shouting and women
screaming reached them.

"What the devil!" Gallio said, and raced through the house,
with his sons and daughter behind him.

The commotion was taking place outside, on the front lawn.
As they reached the scene they saw the guests crowding around
and Gallio pushed through them. One of the refreshment tables

had been overturned and a young Southern underclassman named Maclean was lying on the grass, his dress gray uniform soaked with punch, his nose bloodied and broken. Another cadet, a brawny Bostonian upperclassman named Debray, was standing a few feet away, being restrained by some of his classmates.

"Let me go, damn you!" he shouted. "I'll teach that young cur a lesson he won't soon forget!"

"Mr. Debray!" snapped Gallio, his loud, commanding voice cutting through the commotion. "What is the meaning of this, sir? How dare you disturb the celebration of my daughter's wedding in this outrageous manner?"

The cadets present all came to attention as the academy staff gathered behind Gallio in a silent show of support. This was his home and it was his place to handle it. He stepped forward.

"Explain yourself, Mr. Debray!"

Peter Debray met his gaze defiantly. "It was a private quarrel, sir. It does not concern you."

Gallio kept his temper in check with difficulty. His face colored and the lines around his mouth deepened. "You have the *temerity* to address me in such a manner, sir? *At my own home?* I asked you a question, mister!"

Debray stared at him sullenly. "He insulted my honor, sir."

"You damned liar!" exclaimed Maclean. "You have no honor to insult!"

"As you *were*, Mr. Maclean!" snapped Gallio, without turning to look at the younger cadet. "I will come to you presently. Now then, Mr. Debray, precisely what was the nature of this insult that it moved you to forget yourself to such an astonishing degree?"

Debray glowered at him. "That miserable little Southern guttersnipe called me a bastard, sir."

"I see," said Gallio curtly. He turned to young Allan Maclean. "Is that true, Mr. Maclean?"

Maclean stood at attention, ignoring the blood flowing down his face. "Yes, sir, it is," he said.

"Stand at ease, Mr. Maclean. You may wipe your face."

"Thank you, sir." He took the handkerchief that Gallio offered him and stanched the blood with it.

"Can you explain what provoked you to address an upperclassman in this manner?" asked Gallio.

"I . . . I would prefer not to, sir."

"I did not ask you what you prefer, Mr. Maclean! Answer my question!"

Maclean hesitated.

"Well?"

"It is not my intention to be insubordinate, sir, but with all due respect, I must decline to repeat Mr. Debray's remark to me," he said. "There are ladies present."

"I see," said Gallio. He turned to the onlookers. "Ladies, I must apologize, but I will ask you to excuse us, please."

Murmuring among themselves, the women withdrew. All except Maria. Gallio glanced at her, but she returned his stare stubbornly and showed no inclination to leave. Gallio drew a deep breath.

"Lieutenant Coulter," he said, "would you be so kind as to escort your wife back into the house?"

"Yes, sir, of course," said Coulter. He offered Maria his arm. "Mrs. Coulter, would you do me the honor?"

Maria hesitated, but not wishing to put her husband on the spot, she relented and reluctantly went back into the house with him. Gallio turned to Cadet Maclean.

"Now then, sir, the ladies have withdrawn and I repeat my question. What provoked you to call Mr. Debray by that name?"

"Several of us were discussing Mr. Lincoln's debates with Senator Douglas, sir," replied Maclean. "In the course of that discussion, I mentioned that a great deal of what the abolitionists say about us Southerners is based on ignorance of how we treat our Negro slaves. Mr. Debray was passing by and overheard. He . . ." Maclean tensed and swallowed hard, then continued. "He commented that Southern gentlemen treat their niggers with a great deal of affection, especially the females, as my dark coloring would readily attest. The remark was insufferable, sir. I called him a lying, no-good bastard and he struck me."

Gallio's lips compressed in a tight grimace. This was what came of political discussions. He turned back to Debray.

"Is this true, Mr. Debray?"

Debray stared at Maclean with loathing.

"Look at me when I address you, mister! I asked you, is it *true*?"

"What if it is?" Debray said. "Everyone knows that so-called Southern gentlemen father children with their female slaves."

Gallio was barely able to restrain his fury. "That will be quite enough, Mr. Debray," he said, struggling to keep his voice even. "You will leave my home this instant. You are confined to quarters, pending my recommendation to the superintendent that a board of court-martial be convened to consider proper disciplinary action. Mr. Sharpton, Mr. Llewellyn, please escort Mr. Debray back to his quarters."

Gallio turned before he lost his temper and started to walk away when there was a sudden shout behind him. He spun around in time to see Debray break away from the two cadets, draw his sword, and lunge at Maclean with murder in his eyes.

Someone yelled, *"Look out!"*

Sunlight flashed off another gleaming blade and there was the clang of steel on steel as Custer leaped forward between Debray and his intended victim. His sword struck down Debray's, then he quickly stepped on the blade and punched the older cadet in the face with the guard of his saber. Debray fell, but immediately scrambled back up, his mouth bloody, his face contorted into a grimace of uncontrolled fury.

Someone called out, "Debray!" and tossed him a sword.

Custer came on guard.

In one smooth motion, Gallio drew his own sword, stepped forward, grabbed Custer by the shoulder and yanked him back out of the way.

"Put down your sword, Mr. Debray, or as God is my witness, I shall run you through!"

Debray paled and swallowed hard. Gallio was the Academy's fencing instructor, and though Debray was an accomplished swordsman, he knew he was no match for him. He looked to his friends for support, but none was forthcoming. There was a deathly silence, then he dropped his sword to the ground. Gallio couldn't even speak. He was trembling. My God, he thought, I was ready to kill him! And on Maria's wedding day!

He felt a hand clasp his shoulder firmly as Superintendent Delafield came up beside him and softly said, "With your permission, Major Gallio, I will take charge of this matter."

Gallio drew a deep breath and put his sword back in its scabbard. "Forgive me, sir," he said. "I—"

"Not now," Delafield said in a low voice so that only Gallio could hear. He turned to Debray and eyed him coldly. "Mr. Debray, you are under arrest. You will be escorted under guard back to your quarters, where you will have precisely one hour to pack your things and be off the post. You are forthwith dishonorably discharged from the Academy. Mr. Sharpton, Mr. Llewellyn, take Mr. Debray in charge. Lieutenant Gallio, call the gentlemen cadets to attention."

"Ah-ten . . . *hut!*" called Robert.

All the cadets present snapped to attention. Delafield glanced at Robert and nodded.

"*Ah*-bout . . . *face!*"

As one, they turned their backs on Debray. The young Bostonian stared at Gallio with hatred before turning smartly and marching back to his quarters with his escort.

"Damn it," said Gallio quietly as he watched Debray move off. "I am so very sorry, Richard. I never should have—"

"It was not your fault," Delafield interrupted, keeping his voice low. "You did exactly the right thing. Another instant and it would have been too late. Mere words would not have stopped them."

Gallio shook his head sadly. "It grows worse and worse every day," he said.

"I know," Delafield replied, with a look of consternation on his face. "I have been dreading something like this. And God help us, I fear it is only the beginning."

CHAPTER TWO

THE STEAMBOAT WAS approaching New York City. Most of the passengers were lined up at the railing on the cabin deck, watching the sights as the boat cruised slowly down the Hudson, past the green banks of New Jersey and toward the busy wharves of Manhattan Island. The verdant countryside gave way to the urban sprawl of New York City, with its tall buildings all crowded together and its citizens bustling about like worker ants. They passed steamboats pulled up at the docks, large wooden ships being unloaded by longshoremen, horses pulling wagons loaded down with freight. Sea gulls circled overhead, emitting their raucous cries.

Maria closed the book she had been reading and leaned back in her deck chair, on the verge of tears. She thought of herself as a strong-minded and practical young woman who did not cry easily, but she had never read a novel that had affected her so deeply. The book had been a parting gift from her best friend, Nancy Snow, and now she wondered at Nancy's purpose in giving it to her. It was the best-selling novel by Mrs. Harriet Beecher Stowe, *Uncle Tom's Cabin*.

Maria cast a worried glance toward Travis, standing at the railing with her brothers and a group of cadets on their way to New York City to enjoy their summer furlough. Maria sighed and bit her lower lip. Much as she loved him, there were some things about being married to Travis Coulter that gave her cause for much concern, things she had never really thought about, had deliberately chosen not to think about, while he had courted her back at West Point.

As she gazed at her husband Maria thought how handsome he looked in his new uniform. In his dark blue trousers with the yellow stripe and his brass-buttoned officer's frock coat with the

44

gold lieutenant's shoulder straps, Travis looked every inch the *beau sabreur*. The high, polished cavalry boots and the sword belt buckled over his red sash made him look dashing and romantic. She especially liked the hat, though both Travis and Robert were less than pleased with their new headgear.

It seemed no one was quite certain what to call the new hats worn by the cavalry regiments. Some called them "Hardee hats," after the man who had designed them, Major William J. Hardee, the author of *Hardee's Rifle and Light Infantry Tactics*. Others referred to them as "Davis hats," after Secretary of War Jefferson Davis, who had overseen the organization of the cavalry regiments and had approved the issue of the headgear. The hats were made of felt, with tall, squared crowns and wide brims pinned up on the right side by a brass eagle insignia. They had crossed sabers pinned to the center of the crowns, gold-braided cords in place of a hatband, and black ostrich feathers worn angled back on the left side of the brim, one feather for enlisted men, two for company grade officers, and three for field officers.

Robert and Travis both preferred the simple Albert cap worn by the dragoons. Mark had decided their new hats made them look like musketeers and had teasingly called them Pathos and Bathos, until they threatened to give him one last hazing, for good measure.

As Maria watched them she wondered how long it would be before they were all together once again. It felt strange to know they were parting. From New York, she and Travis would continue on to South Carolina, where they would stay with the Coulter family in Charleston before Travis had to report to cavalry school in Pennsylvania. Mark would remain briefly in New York City with his classmates and then return to West Point, cutting his furlough short at the insistence of their father, to bone up on his studies. He wasn't very happy about that, yet he had no one but himself to blame, Maria thought. It was what came of his unfortunate friendship with that insufferable peacock Custer. The brash young Ohioan was more stuck on himself than anyone she had ever known. She thought he was a bad influence on Mark. The way they had both accumulated demerits, it was a wonder they hadn't been drummed out of the Academy. She wished Mark would grow up and act more like his older brother. Robert had left behind a superb record at West Point, and from New York he would be going on directly to Carlisle Barracks, where they would later join him. They would be together at cavalry school, but afterward, they would each report to different regiments. The thought of a permanent parting seemed unbearable.

From childhood, they had all been raised in the family's military tradition and there had never been any question about the boys pursuing any other career. As a little girl, Maria had joined them in their military games, despite their teasing that a girl could never be a soldier. How often she had wished that she'd been born a boy so she could grow up to be a soldier, too. She had read books about soldiers, novels and works of history, from the tales of Sir Walter Scott to the writings of Baron von Clausewitz.

Her father had encouraged both her brothers to study Clausewitz as well, and had often bemoaned the fact that military strategy was not taught at West Point. Courses in mathematics and engineering were considered more important. The cadets would not be expected to fight wars, after all, but merely keep the peace on the frontier. Only now there was a great deal of talk concerning war. A civil war.

Neither Travis nor Robert believed it would ever come to that. Robert, who had never talked about such things when Travis was around, insisted that the South was only blustering. There had been threats of secession for years and nothing had ever come of it, he said. It was only politics, grand speech-making by long-winded orators in Congress, and he believed that the political differences between the North and South would eventually be settled at the ballot box. Travis, too, did not believe that it would ever come to war. The so-called fire-eaters of the South were mostly talk, he said, and the South would never leave the Union. The North would give in to their demands.

"Where would the North be without our cotton?" he always said. "All this talk of abolition and the so-called immorality of slavery is merely the chin music of a small minority. Most Yankees could no more see the Negro as their equal than the Southerner could. It's a completely ludicrous notion."

Perhaps it was, Maria thought. Travis would certainly know more about it than she would. She had never known a Negro. She imagined that would change when they reached Charleston, for the Coulter family owned slaves. They had a fine home in the city of Charleston and a large cotton plantation in the country. She had married into wealth. She did not quite realize what that meant yet. Her family certainly wasn't poor, or at least she'd never thought of them that way, but their financial and their social standing could not compare to that of the Coulters. The thought made her feel anxious. What if she would not fit in? What if, through some ignorance on her part, she did something to embarrass Travis? And what if she found herself exposed to the sort of things she had been reading about in Mrs. Stowe's book? The thought filled her with dread. She didn't think she could bear it.

"So, Mrs. Coulter," Travis said, turning toward her with a smile, "how does it feel to be a married woman?" His smile faded when he saw the expression on her face.

"Why, Maria, what *is* it?"

"Oh, nothing really," she replied, with an embarrassed smile. "I've been reading and this story is so very sad and moving!"

Travis glanced down at the book she held in her lap. He frowned. "Where did you get that?"

"It was a present from Nancy Snow. Have you read it?"

"Yes, I'm sorry to say I have," he replied dryly. "And it's nothing but a pack of damned abolitionist lies." He bent down, took the book from her, turned, and flung it overboard.

"*Travis!*" she cried, shocked at his action.

"You should not be reading such trash."

"That was *my* book!"

"I forbid you to read such nonsense."

"You *forbid* me?"

"It has only upset you, Maria, and to no good reason. I thought you had better sense than to waste your time with such drivel."

"Travis Coulter, whatever you may think of my choice of reading matter, you had no right to do that!" she protested angrily.

"I had every right, my dear. I am your husband."

"What's this?" said Mark, turning toward them with a grin. "Are we having our first spat already?"

"He threw my book into the river!" Maria said, in an accusing tone.

"Did he? What book was that?" asked Robert, with surprise.

"That damned abolitionist screed of Mrs. Harriet Beecher Stowe," Travis replied.

"Ah, you mean *Uncle Tom's Cabin*," Robert said. "And you threw it overboard? Rather a severe form of literary criticism, Travis." He smiled.

"Have you read it?" Travis asked.

"No," Robert replied. "I don't waste my time with romantic novels. However, it's hardly possible not to have heard of the so-called Novel of the Age. It's somewhat inflammatory, as I understand."

"It's nothing but an abolitionist polemic," Travis replied. "I'm surprised to see an intelligent woman like Maria wasting her time with such infernal claptrap."

"You'll find, Lieutenant Coulter," said Robert, with a smile, "if you have not discovered it already, that my sister is a woman of an independent and inquiring turn of mind. You may recall I warned you about that."

"Did you, indeed?" Maria asked, with an annoyed glance at her brother. "I'll kindly ask the both of you not to speak of me as if I were not present! And I'll have you know, Travis Coulter, that book was my own personal property! I will expect you to replace it at the first opportunity when we arrive in New York City!"

"I shall do no such thing!" Travis replied, with a frown.

"You shall!" she insisted.

"I shall *not*!" Travis replied firmly. "That detestable novel is a poisonous piece of abolitionist propaganda, written solely to inflame the passions of people who know nothing of the true state of affairs in the South! I doubt that Mrs. Stowe has ever even been south of the Mason-Dixon Line, much less seen anything of the life of slaves on a plantation. She'd have you think that Southerners were all inhuman fiends who took cruel pleasure in torturing their slaves!"

"So then you're saying that such things never happen?" Mark asked.

"I'm not saying that slaves are never beaten," Travis replied frankly. "Slaves are chastised when the occasion merits it, but Mrs. Stowe would have you think that we Southerners treat our slaves worse than a man would treat a dog!" He turned back to Maria. "You will see, my dear, that our slaves are not treated in so cruel a manner. Why, I was practically raised by my Mammy Bess, and I love her almost as much as I love my own dear mother!"

"Why would Mrs. Stowe write such things if they weren't true?" Maria asked.

"Because, my dear, Mrs. Stowe is a fervent abolitionist," Travis replied, "and it suits her purposes to have you believe that Southerners mistreat their slaves. That novel is pure politics, disguised as a romance meant to tug at the heartstrings of impressionable people and influence their opinions against the South. It infuriates me to see the spreading of such lies!"

"Well, if they are lies, then I am glad of it," Maria said. "Yet I cannot help thinking that it must be a sad thing to be a slave."

While she had read the book, she kept thinking of the story their father told them about Hanno, and how they were descended from a slave themselves.

Travis sighed and shook his head. "There speaks the voice of ignorance," he said. "And I mean no disrespect by that remark, my dear, merely that like most Yankees, you really know nothing of our way of life."

"Then families are not torn apart by being sold upon the auction block?" Maria asked.

"Well, I cannot say that never happens," Travis admitted, "but most planters do not break up the families of their slaves. We *care* for our slaves, Maria. It's in our best interest to keep them happy and contented. Slaves who are content are more productive, and their children are an asset to their owners."

"Yes, but assets can be sold," said Mark.

"True," Travis replied, "but what would be the purpose in it? It grieves the slaves to have their children sold. And there is scarcely any profit in it. An adult slave is worth far more than a child and one who has been lashed repeatedly is damaged goods. A domestic slave can cost from four to six hundred dollars. A good field hand easily brings twice that much. If you were to pay such good money for a slave, why would you wish to abuse him?"

"I would not wish to own a slave, myself," replied Mark.

"You say that only because you are a Yankee, Mark, and your livelihood does not depend upon the slave," said Travis. "If you were a planter, you would not survive without them. It isn't work white men would wish to do, while slaves are happy doing it, especially when they are well cared for and well treated. George Washington, the father of our country, was a slave owner. And Thomas Jefferson owned slaves as well. Surely, you would not believe such men were capable of the sort of cruelties that Mrs. Stowe describes?"

"No, I should think not," replied Mark. "And yet it was Jefferson who proposed that neither slavery nor involuntary servitude should be permitted in any state formed from a territory after 1802."

"You've been speaking with some of the abolitionists among the corps, I see," said Travis wryly. "That's one of their favorite arguments. And knowing your standing in your class ranks only above that of Mr. Custer," he added, with a smile, "I can scarcely believe that's a fact you remembered from your studies."

"Perhaps, and yet that doesn't change the truth of it," said Mark defensively.

"The truth of it, Mark," replied Travis rather testily, "is that while Jefferson did, indeed, propose such an ordinance, it was not adopted. And if it had been, it wouldn't have affected him, in any case, as Virginia was already a state."

"Still, the fact remains that he was against the spread of slavery," persisted Mark.

As they spoke, a number of interested parties began to gather around them, to listen to their debate. It was rare to see the issue of slavery discussed in a calm and reasoned manner, without shouts and heated emotion.

"Perhaps this is a subject best left alone," said Robert, who was always careful to avoid any talk of politics. "Friends should not argue about such matters, especially when they are things over which they have no control."

"But we *do* have control over them," Mark countered. "Control that can be exercised at the ballot box."

"Mark . . ."

"No, it's all right," Travis said. "Let him speak. We've always avoided talk of such things at the Academy, while the entire nation speaks of nothing else. There is too little intelligent discourse on such matters these days. If one is to have opinions, then it would be best if those opinions were informed ones."

"Yes, well, we've all seen what such discussions can lead to," Robert replied dryly.

"You mean Debray," said Travis, with a grimace.

"Yes, I mean Debray. If my father hadn't intervened when he had, your wedding day might have been marred by a duel."

"Debray always was a hothead," Travis said scornfully. "However, I am not Peter Debray. Nor is Mark. Debray was a troublemaker and the corps will be better off without him. A man like that has no place in the army."

"I agree," said Robert. "And I also agree that neither you nor Mark is even remotely like Debray. However, friends can disagree on certain matters without striving to change one another's beliefs."

Travis raised his eyebrows. "Are we so far apart in our beliefs, then? It never even occurred to me that you might have abolitionist sympathies, Robert."

"I'm no abolitionist," said Robert. "Nor is Mark. We are neither of us political fanatics. Yet I cannot honestly say that I believe slavery to be a beneficial institution. I make no moral judgments, mind you, but see how it divides the country."

"Yes, I can see that," Travis said, "and malicious writers such as Mrs. Stowe only serve to make things worse."

"I see by your speech, Lieutenant, that you are a Southerner," said one of the bystanders, a tall, lean, sharp-featured man of about forty, with dark hair and a neatly trimmed mustache. He was elegantly dressed in a black suit with a vest of silk brocade, a gold watch chain, and a wide-brimmed hat. "Which state are you from, sir?"

"I'm from South Carolina, sir," Travis replied. "Lieutenant Travis Coulter, at your service. And whom do I have the pleasure of addressing?"

"My name is Van Owen," the stranger said. "Dr. Carl Van Owen, of Boston. And I am one of those 'damned abolitionists' of whom you spoke. Your family owns slaves, I take it?"

"Yes, sir, we do," Travis replied. "And if I have given offense by my remarks, please allow me to tender my apologies."

"Your owning slaves offends me, sir," Van Owen replied flatly. "I take no offense in being called an abolitionist, damned or otherwise, as the case may be. I am of the opinion that slavery is a sin against God and a great evil that will only serve to ruin this country. I'm curious to hear your own defense of the peculiar institution."

"I do not believe it is an institution that requires defense, Dr. Van Owen," Travis said politely.

"Indeed?" Van Owen replied, with an ironic grimace. "And why is that, pray tell?"

"I shall answer your question with another question," Travis replied. "What would you propose as an alternative?"

"Free and honest labor, sir, and not the forced labor of the Negro slave," Van Owen said.

"And without slavery, what would you have the Negro do?" asked Travis. "Employ him as a wage laborer in one of your Northern factories, perhaps, where he would undercut the wages of the white man? I doubt you would find much support for that idea, doctor, even in the North."

"You will find, Lieutenant, that there are many people in the North who believe that it is wrong for one man to own another," said Van Owen tucking his thumbs into his waistcoat, "and that number is growing daily. We Yankees, as you call us, are an enlightened people, who feel a compassion for the injustice suffered by the Negro."

"I remind you that it was the Yankee, sir, who first brought the Negroes to this country," Travis replied evenly, "while it is the Southerner who must bear the burden of maintaining them. While the Yankee now finds it in his interest to cry out against slavery as a social injustice, he nevertheless continues to profit from it. Cotton represents over half of all this country's exports. It makes money not only for the Southern planter, but also for the Yankee who sells, manufactures, and distributes it. Thus, the North receives the wages of slavery while at the same time protesting it is wrong. You abolitionists would have us free our slaves, but only so long as they did not come north, where they would then became a burden to you."

"They need not be a burden to anyone, Lieutenant," said Van Owen, speaking as much for the benefit of their audience as to Travis. "There have been sensible proposals to transport them to Liberia, where they can live undisturbed, among their own kind, laboring for themselves and not for the profit of wealthy Southern planters."

"And if the slaves were all transported to Liberia, then who would pick the cotton?" Travis asked.

"Without the Negro slave working in the fields, the poor white men of the South could do the work," Van Owen said, "for a good and honest wage, without being demeaned by working alongside of slaves."

"Assuming that white men could be found to do such work, which I very much doubt," said Travis, "they would still know that the work was once performed by slaves. It's true that we have poor people in the South, doctor, just as you have in the North, but what makes their life easier to bear is the knowledge that at least their lot is better than that of the Negro slave. Slavery civilizes the Negro, sir, and it promotes equality among free whites. Would you have the poor white man accept a lower station in life by supplanting the Negro?"

Van Owen snorted with derision. "Do not give me the so-called positive good argument of Senator Calhoun, Lieutenant. Slavery is not positive in any manner, except as a positive evil. It serves only the rich Southern planter, who profits by the misery of his slaves. Let them be free, I say, and go back to the land from which they were forcibly abducted!"

Robert cleared his throat uneasily. "Gentlemen, there is little point to this debate. It will not settle the issue."

"But it may serve to clarify it, Robert," Travis replied, intent on continuing the argument. "Dr. Van Owen proposes to transport the Negro to another land, but I wonder if he has thought to ask the Negro if he wished to go? Most slaves in the South were born here in this country. If they were all made free, do you think they would choose to embark upon an uncertain voyage to another land, or to remain in the country of their birth? I can assure you, Dr. Van Owen, that if they were freed, the slaves owned by my family would beg to remain with us, for we treat them kindly, give them a good home, good food to eat, and simple work to occupy their time."

"And a simple lashing now and then to make certain they perform that work like proper beasts of burden?" Van Owen asked sarcastically.

"My husband assures me that they do not whip their slaves," Maria said, coming to Travis's defense.

"If that is indeed the case, Mrs. Coulter," said Van Owen condescendingly, "then your husband's family stand as paragons of virtue in a land that is hopelessly bereft of it."

Travis stiffened, but before he could reply, Robert quickly stepped between them. "There is no cause to be insulting, sir," he said. "As one gentleman to another, I will ask you to retract that statement."

"And if I refuse?" Van Owen said belligerently.

"I do not require you to intercede on my behalf, Robert," Travis said, his face flushed. "I can answer for myself."

"Yes, but you shall not," said Robert firmly, remaining between them. "This has gone far enough. I warned you that such discussions can only lead to trouble."

"Stand aside, Robert," said Travis tensely.

"Stop it, all of you!" Maria said, rising to her feet angrily. A crowd had gathered around them and she knew Travis well enough to know that he would not suffer the insult, especially in front of all these people. "Dr. Van Owen, I am certain it was only the passion of your beliefs that led you to make that remark, and that you intended no insult. My husband has apologized for his remark about abolitionists. I will ask you to kindly return the courtesy and retract that remark you made about the South. As you are a gentleman, sir, surely you would not refuse a lady's request?"

Van Owen was aware of their audience and Maria knew that he had spoken mostly for their benefit. He could look brave in front of them by standing up to a couple of soldiers, but refusing to honor her request would make him look boorish in their eyes, which she was certain he would realize. She only hoped that Travis wouldn't force the issue by doing something foolish.

"As you have made it a request, madam," Van Owen said reluctantly, "then I shall retract the statement and apologize. However, your husband would do well to remember that this country was founded on the principle that all men are created equal, and not upon the supposition that some men are more equal than others. If aristocracy is what you seek, then perhaps you would be better off in England, where they still cling to such outmoded notions."

"By God, sir . . ." Travis began, his face white with fury, but Robert took him firmly by the arm. Maria noticed that Mark and several of the other cadets had quietly moved into position to grab Van Owen from behind, if it became necessary to keep the two of them apart.

"Let it go, Travis," Robert said softly. "Please."

Travis controlled his temper with great difficulty. He took a deep breath. "I do not think of myself as an aristocrat, sir," he said, struggling to keep his voice even, "but merely as a soldier. One who respects your right to your opinions. And as an officer, my personal opinions are of no consequence. My duty is merely to follow the orders of my superiors."

"Very commendable, to be sure," Van Owen said. "A sense of duty can be a painless substitute for conscience."

"That will be quite enough, sir," Robert said, tightening his grip on his friend's arm. "Let us part company in peace, as gentlemen. Good day to you, sir."

"Good day, Lieutenant," said Van Owen, with an ironic tip of his hat and a slight bow to Maria. "Madam . . ."

The boat had pulled up to the dock and the crowd started to disperse, mumbling among themselves.

"What a thoroughly detestable man," Maria said.

"You should not have interfered, Robert," Travis said angrily. "I am quite capable of settling such matters for myself."

"Well, now what would you have done, Travis," Robert asked, "challenged him to a duel? Would you begin your career with a court-martial? The man was clearly seeking to provoke an incident. You would have played right into his hands. Why bother? He's not worth it."

Travis sighed heavily. "Yes, you're right, of course. Thank you, Robert. My temper almost got the best of me."

"It was all my fault," Maria said. "Never mind about that book, Travis. If it provokes such incidents, I do not want it."

"Nevertheless, I apologize," Travis replied. "What I did was wrong and inconsiderate. You can judge the truth of the situation for yourself when we reach Charleston."

They went to gather up their things and disembarked, to see to the hiring of a carriage and the unloading of their trunks. Maria was particularly anxious that their trunks be taken care of, not only for her own clothes and personal possessions, but for the journals they contained.

Before they left West Point, her father had ceremoniously given her some of the bound volumes of their family's history. The original documents had long since been lost. The folios that her father had given her had been carefully preserved and copied many times throughout the years. They were not entirely complete, regrettably, but they were what remained of the writings of their ancestors, soldiers all, many of whom had kept journals of their experiences. The major kept copies of these journals in his library and he had often read his children excerpts from them while they were growing up.

"I've encouraged Robert to keep a journal of his own," her father told her, "but I wanted you to have these. Valerius always was your favorite." He had smiled. "And since you have literary ambitions, these journals will be a help to you. A good writer must understand a great deal about life. In these journals of Valerius, you will find much of benefit in that regard. Take good care of them. Copy those that are showing signs of age. You were always the best Latin scholar in the family and it will be good training for you as a writer."

Maria was very grateful for the gift. She could not have thought of a better one. As a soldier's wife, Maria knew there would be times when her husband was away. The journals of Valerius would help her while away the lonely hours, and she was more concerned about their safety than about any of her other possessions. She did not want to let them out of her sight.

As they disembarked the noise and tumult of New York City assailed them on all sides. From the docks, they would take a coach to the Metropolitan Hotel, have dinner together, and then Mark would join his friends for a brief holiday on the town before heading back to West Point. In the morning, they would continue on to Charleston while Robert would depart for Pennsylvania. Travis had invited him to stay with his family in Charleston so they could all go on together, but Robert had demurred, insisting that this would be a time for Travis to introduce his new wife to the family and he'd only be in the way. Travis had protested, but Robert insisted he was anxious to join his regiment and said he wouldn't really feel comfortable among the high society of Charleston.

"One Yankee in the family will be bad enough," he'd added, with a grin. "Two of us will seem like an invasion."

While Travis saw to engaging a coach and the unloading of their baggage Maria stood on the dock with her two brothers and took in the hustle and the bustle all around them. She had visited New York City before, but each time seemed fresh and new. Each time there seemed to be more people. The city was throbbing with activity. New immigrants were arriving by the thousands every month, and it seemed as if almost every nation of the world was represented among the workers on the docks. She wondered how Charleston would compare with New York City. From what Travis had told her, she imagined a much more pastoral-looking city, marching to a slower and more stately pace, with everyone speaking in a graceful, languid, South Carolina drawl.

I'll be different, she thought. In Charleston, I'm going to be a "Yankee." And she had a good idea of how most Southerners felt about Yankees these days. Travis had told her he'd written to his parents about her many times, and he assured her she'd be made warmly welcome in his family. After all his letters, they were greatly looking forward to meeting her. Yet Maria wondered anxiously how the Coulters really felt about their son marrying a Northern girl. Especially one who did not come from a wealthy and socially prominent family. What if she disappointed them?

Her thoughts were disturbed suddenly by the sounds of shouting. A short distance away, a man came bolting through the crowd, a Negro with a terrified expression on his face. Three white men came on his heels, large and burly-looking men who simply bowled people out of their way as they pursued the running Negro. One of them leaped and brought him down, and as they struggled the other two came rushing up. They grabbed the Negro and pulled him to his feet, but he broke away from them, shoving one man away and punching the other in the face, knocking him down. However, before he could escape from them, the third man clubbed him down with a truncheon and proceeded to belabor him with it. The Negro cried out and threw his arms over his head, trying to protect himself. The man who had been punched got to his feet and started kicking the fallen Negro viciously, shouting, "Lay your hands on me, will you, you nigger bastard?"

"My God, Robert," said Maria, "they're going to kill him!"

"No, they won't," said Robert, stepping forward with a determined expression on his face. He came up behind the man who was kicking the fallen Negro, grabbed him by the shoulder, and threw him down. The other two started toward him, but paused when they saw Mark and the other cadets lining up behind him.

"That's enough," said Robert firmly.

"This is none of your affair, soldier," one of the men said, scowling.

"I'll not stand by and see a man kicked when he's down," said Robert. He looked down at the Negro. "Are you all right?"

"That nigger's a runaway slave, mister," said the man with the truncheon, pointing at the fallen Negro. "You ain't got no right to interfere."

A crowd had gathered. Someone said, "Slave hunters," with derision, and many of the people started booing.

"I'm *not* a slave! I'm a free man!" said the Negro, struggling to his feet. Mark bent down to help him up.

"He's a liar, just like they all are," said the man with the truncheon. "He ran away from his owner in Virginia and we're empowered to bring him back, according to the Fugitive Slave Act."

"I never even *been* to Virginia!" protested the Negro. He looked to Robert for support. "You gotta believe me, Colonel, I'm a free man, I swear to God! I got a job, my boss can tell you! I been here all my life! I got a family! You can't let them take me!"

"Take it easy," Mark said. "Nobody's taking you anywhere."

"You'd best stay out of this," the slave hunter said, pointing at him. "This ain't none of your business. We got the law on our side."

People in the crowd shouted at them angrily. There were cries of "Shame! Shame!" and "Lousy bounty hunters!"

"Can you prove this man's a runaway slave?" asked Robert.

"We don't have to prove nothin' to you, soldier," one of the other slave hunters said, looking around at the crowd uneasily. "We got our rights!"

"And what about this man's rights?" asked Robert.

"He's a nigger," the slave hunter replied, with a sneer. "He ain't got no rights!"

"I beg to disagree," said Robert. "According to the law, you must take him before a magistrate and prove he's a runaway slave before you can take him back and claim your bounty."

"That's just what we was gonna do," the slave hunter replied.

"Indeed?" said Robert. He didn't believe the man for a moment, but he also knew that whether the man was a runaway slave or not, taking him before a magistrate would be merely a formality. He'd have no recourse in a court of law, unless someone who was white spoke up for him. "Well, since you're so concerned about observing the legalities, you'll have no objections if we make some inquiries first concerning this man's claim of being free. We'll go and see his boss together, shall we?"

"We ain't got no time for that!" the slave hunter replied, looking distinctly uncomfortable at the chorus of boos that his remark prompted.

"Then I suggest you go on your way," said Robert. "Apparently, you've made a mistake."

"Yeah, get out of here!" someone in the crowd shouted, setting off a chorus of angry shouts.

"Go home!"

"Go back down south, where you belong!"

"Get out! We don't want your kind around here!"

Realizing they were outnumbered, the slave hunters exchanged nervous glances and decided to give it up. "You lousy abolitionists will get yours one of these days!" one of them said angrily, then cried out as someone in the crowd threw a rock that struck him in the side of the head.

"There'll be no more of that!" Robert shouted, looking around at the crowd. They were getting ugly. He was afraid that in another moment there would be a riot. "You'd best be on your way," he said to slave hunters. "I can't answer for these people."

"Damn Yankees," said the man who'd been struck by the rock. He rubbed his head and scowled at Robert, then turned to his companions. "Come on. Let's get out of here."

"Let them through," said Robert to the crowd. As the slave hunters departed the people in the crowd started to applaud. Several people came up to him and clapped him on the back with words of "Well done, soldier!" and "You showed 'em!"

Robert turned to the man the bounty hunters were pursuing. "Are you injured?" he asked.

"I be okay," the man replied, though he was bleeding from a cut in his head. "I want to thank you for what you done."

"No need," said Robert.

"I be grateful to you just the same," the man said. He turned to Mark. "And you, sir. Might I ask your names?"

"Cadet Mark Gallio," said Mark. "And this is my brother, Lieutenant Robert Gallio."

Robert offered his hand. The man stared at him for a moment, then took it and shook hands with Mark as well. "Isaac Jefferson, at your service," he said. "I won't forget this. If there be anything I can ever do for you, gentlemen, you just say the word."

"Forget it," Robert said. "Just try to stay out of those people's way."

"I do that, sir," said Jefferson. "And I be remembering you gentlemen."

He turned and walked away, a bit unsteadily, as the crowd dispersed. Robert and Mark turned and saw Travis standing with Maria. Maria looked concerned, but Travis stood stiffly, watching them with a tight-lipped expression.

"I've got the carriage," he said as they approached, then turned and walked away without another word.

Maria stared after him anxiously. Robert took a deep breath and let it out slowly.

"He didn't like that, did he?" Mark said.

"We won't speak of it, Mark," said Robert. "I think we've had quite enough politics for one day."

Maria said nothing, but there was a look of great concern on her face.

"Come on, Maria," Robert said, taking her arm gently. "The coach is waiting."

CHAPTER THREE

MARIA WAS GLAD the trip was over at last, but at the same time, their arrival filled her with anxiety. The moment of truth was fast approaching when she would be meeting her husband's family for the first time. She wished she could have had an opportunity to meet them at least once before, on her home ground, with her own family around her for support, but it had not worked out that way. Many of the other cadets had their parents come and visit them while they were at West Point, but the Coulters never came. When other cadets had taken leave to have dinner with their visiting parents, Travis had always been made welcome at the Gallio household.

Maria knew that Samuel Johnson Coulter disapproved of his oldest son entering the army. He had wanted Travis to remain at home and devote himself to the family's business interests, the running of the plantation and their property investments in Charleston. Someday Travis would inherit it all, but for the present he seemed to have little interest in becoming a gentleman planter. What Travis wanted was to command a cavalry regiment.

What concerned Maria was the possibility that Samuel Coulter, already displeased with his son for entering the army against his wishes, would be even more displeased with him for marrying a Northern girl. In the letters Travis had received from home while he was at West Point, letters he had often read to her, his mother had always asked about her and had expressed her eagerness to meet her, but what struck Maria most about those letters was their curiously formal tone. Elizabeth Coulter had always used "My dearest Travis" as a salutation and had signed her letters "All my love," but in between, there had been almost no evidence of personal affection, the sort of heartfelt sentiment one might expect between a mother and her son. And though his mother always wrote "your father sends his best regards," Travis's father had never written to him. Not even once.

Travis had said his father was not the sort to waste his time with letters, as if to dismiss it as being of no consequence, and yet there had been a wistfulness in his expression and his tone that he could not quite conceal. He told her his father had not stood in his way when he expressed his desire to attend West Point and become an officer, but he had disapproved and tried to talk him out of it. However, Travis would not be dissuaded. In that way, apparently, father and son were much alike. Both obstinate and willful. Stubborn. The words Travis had used in describing his father could have applied equally to himself.

Maria imagined Samuel Coulter would have much preferred for his son to wed a Southern girl and remain at home, in Charleston. But he had gone away, against his father's wishes, and now he was bringing home a Yankee wife, and the daughter of a soldier to boot. Maria was afraid he would think Travis had married beneath him. Travis was a gentleman and she expected no less of his father, but there was a great deal of difference between being treated with polite respect and being accepted. She hated the thought that she might unintentionally serve to drive yet a further wedge between Travis and his father.

Back home, everything had seemed so simple. She and Travis were in love and her father had approved. "The major," as his children referred to him among themselves, had been very fond of Travis and had often expressed his wish that Mark would choose someone like Travis for his role model rather than the irrepressible George Custer. In Travis, the major had seen many of the same fine qualities possessed by his good friend Robert E. Lee. To the major's way of thinking, Lee was what every soldier should aspire to be. An officer and a gentleman in every respect, a fine figure of a man, erect in carriage, soft in speech, courteous in manner, and earnest in his endeavors. Mark, regrettably, was none of those things.

Unlike Travis, he was mischievous and boisterous, always breaking regulations and getting into trouble. Mark had been his mother's favorite, much in the same manner that the runt of a litter could command special attention and affection, and as a result, he had been spoiled, most of his youthful transgressions forgiven with a smile. The major had hoped the Academy would give him some discipline, but so far, at least, it hadn't seemed to take.

And Mark, she felt certain, though he did nothing outwardly to show it, harbored some resentment toward Travis, for the obvious affection the major had for him. Maria knew her father did not love Travis more than Mark, for Mark was his own son, after all, but in trying to hold Travis up as an example to him, the major had, perhaps, gone a bit too far. It was always "Travis this" and "Travis that," and "I wish you could be more like Travis." The major might well have said, "I wish you could be more like Robert," for that was how he truly felt, but in trying to avoid showing any favoritism toward his oldest son, he had instead made Mark feel inadequate compared with Travis, which only contributed to Mark's rebellious spirit and resentment.

Now that they were gone, perhaps things would be different. Mark would now have his father's full attention. Without Travis being there, to be constantly held up as an example to him, Mark might settle down and come into his own. Maria hoped so. She hated to think of what would happen if Mark were to be dismissed from the Academy.

About Robert, she had no worries. Her eldest brother was nothing if not capable and she was certain he had a fine career ahead of him. Travis was envious of Robert's being assigned to the Second Cavalry. Only half in jest, he had claimed the assignments must have been reversed by mistake. It was well known that most of the officers of the Second were Southerners. The regiment was commonly referred to as "Jeff Davis's Own," and among its officers were some of the finest graduates of the Point, many of whom she'd known, such as Jeb Stuart, nicknamed "Beauty" at the Academy, an ironic comment upon his supposed lack of comeliness, though he had never been at a loss for female company. Maria remembered how he'd flirted with her, though he had only done it out of playful fondness. She'd been just a child then, and his innocent attention had both flattered and embarrassed her.

Travis thought the Second was the most glamorous of the cavalry regiments, being stationed in the Texas territory, acquired in the war with Mexico. He had been assigned to the First, in Kansas, and the Indians around Fort Leavenworth were mostly peaceful, many of them tribes that had been transplanted from the East during the Jackson administration. The white man's might had already been suitably impressed upon them, and though there were reports of occasional conflict among the tribes, primarily between the new arrivals and those who were already there, such as the Pawnee, the Kansa, and the Oto tribes, Travis did not think there would be much opportunity for action with the First.

The Texas territory, where Robert would be going, was quite another matter, however. Texas was home to the dreaded Comanche, said by some to be the finest light cavalry in all the world, and unlike their Eastern cousins, they were warlike and relentless in their opposition to the white man. Maria had read bloodcurdling stories about their depredations, but Robert had assured her such accounts were much exaggerated. Travis, on the other hand, was not of the same opinion and he felt Robert had received the more desirable assignment, with more opportunities to distinguish himself.

"He'll probably be brevetted to major before I've even made captain," Travis had said ruefully.

There was no real jealousy between them, but Travis was much more ambitious than Robert. More impatient, too. He had barely graduated from the Academy, had not yet even joined his regiment, and already he was thinking of promotions. Maria had discovered he was much the same in bed. Anxious and impatient. But then, perhaps all men were like that. Maria had no basis for comparison. None of her friends back at West Point had been married and it was certainly not a subject she could have broached with any of the older women she had known. She had looked forward, both eagerly and nervously, to their first night together, but it had not been what she'd expected.

During their courtship, Travis had always been the perfect gentleman. Too perfect, she had often thought. Yet, in a sense, that had only contributed to the intensity of their romance. They had been chaste and proper lovers, like two characters out of a novel by Sir Walter Scott, a knight and his fair maiden, and she had thrilled merely to the touching of their hands. She had expected her wedding night would be the culmination of their long and sweet romance, that they would spend hours holding one another, exchanging sweet caresses and tender kisses, but Travis had been terribly impatient. No sooner were they alone in their hotel room than he was fumbling at her clothing and covering her mouth and throat with hot, passionate kisses.

It had been exciting, but Maria wished he hadn't been in such a hurry. In a way, she understood. After all, he'd been waiting a long time for that moment, just as she had been, but while she longed to draw it out and savor it, Travis couldn't seem to wait. He had practically torn her clothes off and carried her to bed, and everything that followed had taken place in a mad rush of passion, so that it was over almost before she knew it had started.

There had been none of the hesitancy Travis had exhibited before they were married. He had put his hand between her legs, pressing her back down onto the bed, all the while passionately kissing her, running his other hand over her breasts roughly and saying things like, "Oh, Maria, oh, my darling," and when she had started to speak, to protest that he was being too quick, too rough, he had shushed her with words of, "Hush, my love, hush now, it'll be all right, don't worry." When he'd pushed her legs apart and entered her, she had cried out with pain, which seemed to please him, and he had put all his weight upon her, thrusting into her roughly and quickly, and in moments she felt the warm gush of his seed spurting into her and it was over. He'd slumped against her, almost suffocating her with his weight, then pulled out of her and rolled over onto his back, breathing heavily. Maria hadn't spoken. It had all happened so quickly, and with such rude abruptness, that she'd been overwhelmed. For a long while she lay silent, almost afraid to speak, and when she finally turned toward him and softly whispered his name, there had been no response. He had already fallen fast asleep.

She had lain awake for a long time, feeling confused and disappointed, wondering if she would become pregnant. Travis had known what he was doing. Obviously, he'd had experience. Maria wondered, briefly, if his experience had been with white women or with slave women. Then she felt ashamed for wondering about that. Perhaps he'd been with prostitutes. She had heard that sometimes fathers took their sons to whores for their first experience, though she could not imagine the major doing that with Mark or Robert. And the thought of Travis with a prostitute, or with any other woman for that matter, black or white, was hurtful.

No reason why it should be, she had told herself. Travis was a man and men are expected to know about such things. It was different for men. And yet, at the same time, she found herself questioning why it had to be that way. It wasn't fair. A man was expected to know everything. Women were expected to know little or nothing. For a man to be experienced in such matters was a mark of sophistication. For a women to be experienced in such things meant she was loose, a wanton hussy. If a woman came to her marriage bed and was found not to be a virgin . . . catastrophe!

Not that she felt cheated in that sense. She had never wanted anyone but Travis. He had been her first love and he would be

her last. She had married him for better or for worse, till death
do you part. There had never been anyone else for her and she
only wished there had never been anyone else for him. She wanted
to say to him, "I waited. Why couldn't you?" She had stared at
him as he slept, then sighed and snuggled up to him, but he had
merely grunted in his sleep and rolled over on his side. Moments
later, he began to snore.

In the morning, he awoke her by climbing on top of her again
for a repeat performance of the previous night. She felt sore
between her legs, but when she tried to tell him that, he said
the same things, "Hush, now, hush, my love," as if she were
not supposed to speak while they were making love. Or, more
to the point, Maria thought, while he was making love to her,
for she did not really feel like a participant. His powerful, eager
thrusts had hurt and she had moaned with pain, yet that seemed to
excite him all the more, and once again it was over fairly quickly.
She felt him climax inside her, and then he collapsed upon her
once again with a heavy sigh, dead weight, and after a moment
he rolled off, got out of bed, and started to perform his morning
toilet. And once again, Maria felt confused and disappointed. She
hadn't expected it to be like this at all. What had happened to the
romantic, gentle, tender suitor she had known?

In other small ways, too, Travis seemed to have changed since
their wedding. His manner toward her had become proprietary,
which was, perhaps, the way it was supposed to be. She was,
after all, his wife and she had promised to obey. But still, she
found it rankled her. Like the way he had taken away her book
and thrown it overboard, and when she had protested that he had
no right to do that, his reply had been an imperious, "I had every
right, my dear, I am your husband." Later, he had apologized and
admitted he was wrong. Yet the fact that he could even *think* of
doing such a thing . . .

To Maria, books were something to be cherished and lovingly
preserved. She loved books with an abiding passion, and it would
never have occurred to her, no matter who had written a book or
why, to treat one in such a callous, disrespectful manner. It made
her feel concerned about the journals. Suppose Travis decided
they were frivolous? The thought chilled her. Surely, he would
not destroy such precious and irreplaceable documents! No, she
thought, he'd never think of doing such a thing. But just the
same, she decided not to let him know about them. She would
keep them with her things, hidden in her trunk among her clothes,

where they would undoubtedly be safe. She would not tell anyone about them.

At first, the thought of traveling by ship to Charleston had been exciting, but the voyage down the coast from New York City had not proved very pleasant. There had been no storms, but Maria had never been aboard a ship before and she had found it was much different from a trip down the Hudson on a steamboat. For much of the voyage, she'd been seasick and that had put a damper on their marital relations. She had expected Travis to be upset with her for that, and she hated being sick in front of him, but he had been very solicitous and understanding. Though he did not suffer from seasickness himself, he said a woman's constitution was more delicate, so he understood completely. For most of the voyage, she had remained in bed, feeling miserable beyond words, and Travis had done everything he could to comfort her. It made her feel ashamed for thinking he was inconsiderate. Now, at last, the awful sickness had abated and they were about to enter Charleston harbor. Maria felt tired and weak. She got dressed and went out on deck with Travis, for her first glimpse of the South. As their ship approached the harbor he pointed out the sights.

Off the coast, there was a string of low and sandy islands, covered with scrub brush and marsh grass, with a few pines and palmetto trees. Narrow strips of swamp land ran along the shore, interspersed with rising savannahs. Travis explained that the flat country along the tidewater was the first part of South Carolina to be settled by the English back in the colonial days.

The state was roughly divided into two regions, he told her, what was called the Low Country and Up Country, each with distinct and separate cultures. Up Country people, Travis said, were mostly Presbyterians, Methodists, and Baptists. The citizens of Charleston were largely Episcopalian, most of the original settlers having belonged to the Anglican faith.

"In Charleston, we often say that no gentleman was ever born above tidewater," he added with a grin.

He told her the areas along the coast had dense forests of cypress and yellow pine, which grew tall and were almost completely free of undergrowth, so it was possible to ride horses at a brisk pace beneath their spreading branches. Maria thought of General Francis Marion, the famous Swamp Fox of the Revolution, riding through these forests with his men, confounding the British with his knowledge of the swampy and heavily wooded terrain that was infested with diamondbacks and copperheads, cottonmouth moccasins, coral snakes, and wildcats known as catamounts. How unlike New York it seemed, Maria thought. Like a tropical jungle, steamy and exotic!

A short way inland, Travis told her, the land began to rise. There, on the coastal plain, was where the original plantations had been established. In the beginning, before the advent of King Cotton, their crops had been primarily indigo and rice. There were many slow-moving rivers and estuaries in this region, which allowed boats, and sometimes even ships, to sail right up to the plantations.

The most desirable locations for plantation homes, Travis explained, were on the bluffs above the streams, safe from high water, where the incoming sea breezes could be caught by the bluffs and disperse the ubiquitous mosquitoes. Most planters came to Charleston in the summer, Travis said, to escape the pestiferous insects and the heat.

In some areas of the Low Country, where the sea drained away, ridges and depressions had been created over time, leaving an infertile, sandy country known as the Sand Hills. Beyond this area was a fertile region known as the Piedmont, which covered roughly one-third of the state, with an abundance of conifer and oak, hickory and chestnut, elm and poplar, pine, cane, and wild pea vines. There were black walnuts and small, shrublike trees called cinquapins, which bore small nuts that had a chestnutlike flavor. There were also wild plum and persimmon trees, which bore the persimmon fruit Travis said was best picked after a frost, for the fruit became naturally candied in the winter, with a tasty, datelike flavor. There were also wild strawberries and blackberries in profusion, and the area was rich in game, providing excellent hunting for deer and partridge.

As Maria listened to him expound enthusiastically upon his native state and watched him gazing at the shore as he spoke, occasionally glancing at her as if to reassure himself that she was taking it all in, she was struck by how much he loved this country and how he wanted her to love it, too. It seemed incongruous, somehow. He had such an abiding affection for the land of his birth, and yet he had gone away to West Point and would soon be en route to Pennsylvania, and then a long assignment on the frontier, so far from his beloved, beautiful South Carolina. If he loved it so much, why then had he not listened to the wishes of his father and stayed?

Yet, so often, she had heard other Southern cadets at the Academy speak the same way of the states from which they came. Whether it was South Carolina or Virginia, Tennessee or Georgia, that same deep and affectionate tie to the land had been there. She couldn't really understand it. She certainly did not feel that way about New York. She would, of course, always think of the green country of the Hudson River Valley as her home, and yet she did not feel the same passion for it that Southerners seemed to feel about their country.

Their *country,* she thought. In a sense, the South really *was* another country, not only geographically different, but culturally different from the North. The North was growing rapidly, and changing with each passing day. The large influx of immigrants, contributing elements of their diverse cultures to their new home, the rapid growth of industry and commerce, the different climate and topography, all contributed to a way of life that was very different from that found in the South. Growth, industry, and progress were the watchwords of the North. Free labor capitalism was the new religion. Meanwhile, the people of the South cleaved to tradition, to their established, genteel, and agrarian institutions. To a much slower, more relaxed and refined way of life.

We Yankees are the workers, she thought, laboring like bees to build a new, progressive future. They are the landed gentry, seeking to preserve their heritage and traditions, not wishing to be swept away in the North's mad rush to an industrial tomorrow. As she listened to Travis she thought she was finally beginning to understand. It wasn't merely about slavery, as so many Northerners insisted. It wasn't merely about Southerners protecting their wealth or their political power. It was something much deeper and more basic than that. They wanted to protect their way of life, their *land,* a land to which they had a much more intimate connection than most Northerners. Slavery was, perhaps, essential to their economy, but in the growing divisiveness between the North and South, it was only the most obvious manifestation of the difference between them. They had grown apart. Changes had swept the North in recent years. The South did not want to change. It wanted to continue going its own way.

She felt almost completely overwhelmed by this epiphany. *Going its own way.* That was the crux of it, the key to what all this talk of secession was really all about. Travis was wrong, she realized. The North would never give in to the South's demands. It couldn't. Regardless of any moral considerations, slavery and free wage labor could not coexist. Already, there was strong resentment among many workers in the North against the bankers and the factory owners, the bosses who seemed to constitute a wealthy upper class, growing wealthier every day at the expense of those who punched the time clocks for them. These workers only needed to look south and they would see another upper class—an aristocracy, as that unpleasant man, Van Owen, had put it—not unlike their bosses, who prospered by the labor of their slaves. And if slaves were property, then were they not much like property themselves, their livelihoods at the mercy of their bosses?

"Maria?" Travis said. "Maria, did you hear what I said?"

"What? Oh, forgive me, Travis, I was lost in thought."

"Well, that's a fine thing," he said with a smile. "Here we are, still newlyweds, and already you're ignoring me."

"I didn't mean to," she replied.

"You had such a faraway look in your eyes," he said. "Feeling a bit homesick?"

She smiled. "Perhaps a little." She was grateful he had misinterpreted her inattention.

"That's only to be expected," he replied. "I felt the same way, the first time I left home. It's a melancholy feeling, but you'll get over it, I promise." He grinned. "You'll have little time for it once we reach home. Everyone is mad to meet you. I expect a ball will be held in your honor."

"A ball?" she said, astonished. "For me?"

"You'll be the envy of every girl in Charleston," he said. "They'll all pale in comparison to you."

"What's that structure over there?" Maria asked, pointing to what looked like an unfinished fortification on a small island in the center of the harbor. She was anxious to change the subject. A ball! *God!* The only balls she'd ever been to were the ones held at West Point, where she was in her element, Major Gallio's daughter, on the arm of Cadet Captain Travis Coulter. She had known the drill, as the major would have said, and had known èxactly how to act and what to expect. But a ball in Charleston, with all their high society in attendance? Held in *her* honor? She dreaded the thought.

"That's Fort Sumter," Travis said.

"Named for General Thomas Sumter, of the Revolution?" asked Maria, grateful to be off the subject of the ball. Somehow, she would have to find a way to talk him out of it. Or, if worse came to worse, perhaps she could pretend to be ill and be unable to attend.

"The major taught you well," said Travis, with a smile. "The government started work on it back in 1829, but it still isn't finished. Probably never will be, at this rate. And over there, coming up on our right, you can see Fort Moultrie, on the tip of Sullivan's Island. It dates back to the Revolution and still has the palmetto-log walls they put up to repel cannonballs. It's in a rather dilapidated state, though. Ahead of us, on that larger island near the mouth of the Cooper River, that's Castle Pinckney. The present fort was constructed for the War of 1812 and it's showing signs of age. I don't think anyone considers these fortifications important anymore. There's really no need for them."

"And that peninsula just beyond Castle Pinckney must be Charleston," said Maria. "I can already see the city from here. What is that body of water on the left?"

"That's the Ashley," Travis said. He grinned. "Down here, we like to say that Charleston harbor is where the Ashley and the Cooper rivers flow together to form the Atlantic Ocean."

She smiled, a bit weakly. So here it was, at last. As the ship sailed past Fort Sumter and into the harbor, she felt as if her nerves were knotting up. She bit her lower lip and wished Travis could have persuaded Robert to change his plans and come to Charleston with them so she could have his strong presence to cling to for support. However, that matter had already been settled. She was no longer just Robert's little sister, she was Mrs. Travis Coulter, and she would have to depend on her husband for support now. She was all grown up, a married woman, and she would have to accept the responsibilities that came with that.

She swallowed hard and took a deep breath. The familiar ramparts of West Point seemed so far very away.

The Coulter family home stood on a tree-lined avenue near the corner of South Bay and Meeting streets, near the southern tip of the peninsula. It was in the middle of a row of elegant, three-story houses constructed of wood and baked brick, looking out across White Point Garden toward the boulevard that ran along the shore. The house faced south, to catch the sea breezes and, like most of the other homes around it, had columned piazzas on each floor, providing shaded, outdoor sitting rooms for warm Carolina evenings. The lower piazza had graceful, Grecian arches above square support columns; the piazzas on the upper floors had round columns extending straight up to the floors above.

The carriage pulled up in front of the house, which was surrounded by a black wrought-iron fence. Beyond it was a garden, lushly planted with fragrant jessamine and oleander, white gardenias and orange trees, as well as a few small ferns in the shaded areas. The stately home was a far cry from the simple stone house the Gallios had lived in on Professors' Row.

Maria hesitated at the gate.

Travis smiled. "There's no reason to be nervous, darling," he said. "They're your family."

"But . . . what if they don't like me?" she said, looking up at him anxiously.

He chuckled. "Don't be silly, they'll love you just as much as I do. Now, come on, they'll all be thrilled to meet you."

They walked down the flagstoned garden path and up the stone steps to the front door. Travis smiled and swung the heavy brass knocker three times. The door was opened by a distinguished-looking, elderly Negro in an elegantly formal black suit. He was bald on top, with short, tightly curled white hair on the sides and handsome, bushy, white side-whiskers. He wore a small pair of round spectacles. As soon as he saw Travis his eyes lit up and he smiled from ear to ear, revealing even, perfect teeth.

"Master Travis!" he exclaimed, in a deep, resonant voice with a strength that belied his advanced years.

"Hello, Jubelo," said Travis, holding out his hand. The butler took it in both of his.

"Oh, come in, sir, do come in! Let me have a look at you!"

They stepped inside.

"Great day in the mornin', don't you look *fine*!" said Jubelo, stepping back and gazing at Travis with warm affection. "You sure are a sight for these sore eyes! And this must be Miz Maria," he added, looking at her. He shook his head. "My, *my*! Welcome, ma'am, welcome, indeed!"

"Thank you, Jubelo," Maria said.

"Jubelo?" a woman's voice called out. "Is someone at the door?"

The woman who came out into the spacious entry hall had strikingly sharp, proud, and attractive features framed by golden hair that was parted in the middle and drawn down at the back and sides. She wore a dark green cotton day dress, full-skirted, with a V-shaped bodice and pagoda sleeves, with black, gathered ribbon trim at the cap and cuff. She was a youthful-looking woman, in her early forties, and the resemblance between her and Travis was unmistakable.

"Travis!"

"Hello, Mother."

She came to him with arms extended and he took her hands in his, stepping in close to kiss her cheek.

"Oh, darling, let me look at you!" Elizabeth Coulter said, stepping back while still holding on to his hands. She smiled and shook her head. "What a fine, proud figure of a man you've grown to be!" She released his hands. "And you must be Maria. Why, my dear, you're even more beautiful than Travis described in all his letters!"

"Thank you, ma'am," Maria said, blushing. "How do you do, Mrs. Coulter?" She curtsied.

"Oh, there now, there's no need to be so formal! Come here, child, and embrace me!"

Somewhat awkwardly, she stepped up and embraced Elizabeth.

"I declare," said Elizabeth, "my Travis, all grown up and married! And to such a charming and attractive girl!"

"Thank you, ma'am," Maria said again, feeling flustered and embarrassed by such effusive praise.

"Ma'am, indeed! You call me Mother, child. You're part of the family now!"

There was a sudden, high-pitched shriek as a flaxen-haired girl came flying down the stairs, practically leaping into Travis's arms. He laughed and swept her up, lifting her off her feet and whirling her around.

"Honestly, Rebecca!" said Elizabeth, frowning. "Now is that any way for a young lady to come entering a room?"

"Young lady, indeed!" said Travis, chuckling. "Why, look at you, Becky! You're all grown up! Maria, meet my little sister, Becky."

Becky was only a few years younger than Maria and she bore the same striking resemblance to her mother that Travis did. Anyone could see at a glance they were brother and sister. She was slightly shorter than Maria, with a lithe, blossoming figure, sparkling blue eyes, fair skin, and sharp, foxlike features. Her blond hair was parted in the middle and worn in corkscrew curls. She turned to Maria, her eyes shining.

"Maria!" she said, throwing her arms around her and kissing her on the cheek. "I've been so looking forward to meeting you!

Travis has told us so much about you in his letters, I feel I already know you!"

"Well, so the prodigal has returned," said a young man, entering from the sitting room. Unlike Travis, his hair was light brown. He was clean-shaven and had sleepy-looking eyes, a somewhat sharper chin, and a wide mouth, like his brother and sister. The family resemblance was there, but it was not as strong. He must take more after his father, thought Maria.

"Maria, this insolent young pup is my brother, Spencer," Travis said. "Spencer, allow me to present my wife."

"Charmed," said Spencer, bowing over her hand and brushing it lightly with his lips. He gazed at her with a glint of amusement in his eyes. "I must say, if all Yankee girls are half as beautiful as you, I can scarcely blame my brother for going north to find one."

"You're very kind," Maria said, unaccustomed to such flattery. She felt herself blushing again.

"And modest, too," said Spencer, with a faintly mocking smile. "See how prettily she blushes."

"You're embarrassing her, Spencer," Travis said, though he was clearly pleased. "Is Father at home?"

"He's in town on business," Spencer replied. "But he said he would be back in time for supper."

"Well, I'm sure Maria must be tired after her long voyage," said Elizabeth. "Jubelo, why don't you show Maria upstairs to her room so she can freshen up? And get Ben and Joshua to help you with their trunks. Meanwhile, I'll have Bess see to some refreshments."

"Come on, Maria," Becky said, taking her by the hand. "I'll show you to your room. Oh, it'll be such *fun* to have a sister! You will stay awhile, won't you? I hope Travis doesn't have to leave soon. You'll make him stay, won't you? The army will allow him the time, won't they? Oh, they simply must, it's been so long since we've all seen each other! And we must have time to get acquainted! There are so many things I want to ask you, I simply don't know where to start!"

Amid an unceasing rush of breathless questions, Rebecca led Maria up the wide, carpeted stairway. The opulence of the house took Maria's breath away. The stair railings were made of lovingly oiled mahogany, and the carpeting must have cost a fortune. The crystal chandelier looked huge, suitable for a hotel ballroom, and the large oil paintings on the walls must have been very expensive, too. They were of members of the Coulter family, each of whom Becky pointed out to her as they passed, speaking with a torrent of warmhearted enthusiasm. This was Grandfather so-and-so, and Great-Uncle this-and-that and grandmothers and great-grandfathers, Maria couldn't keep track of them all. Becky gave her a quick tour of the upstairs of the house, each room seemingly more luxuriously appointed than the last, until finally they came to the room set aside for her and Travis. It was wide and high-ceilinged, painted in muted peach and raspberry, with a beautiful, burgundy and gold-colored carpet and French furniture. The bed was huge and canopied, fit for an Egyptian princess, thought Maria, with a headboard the size of a small dinner table.

"I hope this will be comfortable for you," said Becky.

"Comfortable?" Maria said, with disbelief. "Becky, it's magnificent! It's easily three times the size of my small bedroom back home in West Point!"

"You must tell me all about it," Becky said, plopping down on the bed. "I've never been up north. What's New York City like? Is it really as big as people say? And West Point, Travis wrote that it looks like a medieval fortress. He sent us a tintype of himself and your brother, Robert. He's so handsome! Are all the cadets at West Point so good-looking?"

On and on, the questions came, so that Maria had to laugh, and her nervousness went away completely. Becky was so effusive and openhearted that she immediately felt comfortable with her. She realized all her apprehensions were in vain. These were good, warmhearted people, perhaps not as reserved as those she'd been accustomed to around West Point, though somehow she'd expected the opposite would be true. She had pictured Southern women as being regal and aloof, but judging by Becky and Elizabeth, nothing could be further from the truth.

As they spoke Jubelo arrived, along with two other Negroes carrying her trunks. Jubelo introduced them briefly as Ben and Joshua. They greeted her politely, with respect, though not with the obsequious bowing and scraping that was the popular image of Negroes in the North. They were hardly the eye-rolling minstrels talking with the exaggerated speech that Maria had heard in shows. She noticed they were not referred to as slaves, but as "servants," and each of them assured her that if she required anything during her stay, she had but to ask. Maria also noticed they did not avoid her gaze, staring at the floor, but looked at her

openly, with warmth and friendliness. They certainly did not seem
mistreated or unhappy.

She began to see what Travis meant about Yankees not understanding what things were really like in the South. The Coulters
did seem to match the image of the "wealthy Southerner," but
then they were one of the most socially prominent families in
Charleston, and that was, she realized, only to be expected. On
the other hand, they certainly knew about her background and she
had not encountered the faintest evidence of any condescension.
Southern hospitality was clearly everything Travis said it was.
And Jubelo, Ben, and Joshua seemed a far cry from the benighted
Uncle Tom.

As they brought her trunks in Maria chatted with Becky,
answering her flow of questions and getting to know her better.
She liked her immediately and felt a warm bond with the younger
girl. After all her things were brought up, Becky helped her unpack
her clothing trunk and she changed to go down and join the others
in the parlor, where she met "Mammy Bess," as Travis called her,
who was Jubelo's wife.

Bess was a handsome-looking woman in her sixties, dressed
in a white turban and cotton plaid dress with a white collar
and apron. Her aging face showed character, almost a nobility,
Maria thought, and like her husband, Jubelo, she was well-spoken
and seemed comfortably at ease in her surroundings. There was
nothing servile in her manner, and though she addressed Elizabeth
with polite respect, it was a familiar respect. When she saw Maria,
she took a deep breath and clasped her hands before her.

"Oh, my Lord!" she said, with a maternal smile. "Is this Miz
Maria? Oh, my, Travis, she's such a *lovely* child!"

"Maria, this is Mammy Bess," said Travis. "I've told you all
about her."

"How do you do?" Maria said.

"Why, I'm feelin' older by the minute, child," Bess said, smil-
ing and shaking her head. "It seems like only yesterday I was
washin' this boy behind the ears, and now he done come home
with a wife! Come, sit down, child, I'll fetch you some hot tea
and biscuits. You must be tired, what with the long trip an' all."

They sat and talked, with Elizabeth and Becky asking her all
sorts of questions about herself, her family, the trip down from
New York, her impressions of Charleston, and so forth, with
Spencer occasionally interjecting a question or remark, but for
the most part letting the women do the talking. Maria felt more

and more at ease with them and saw that all her worries were for
nothing. And then Sam Coulter arrived.

Like his sons, he was a tall man, though on the heavy side,
with a ruddy face, a prominent, aquiline nose, a sharp chin, and
light gray eyes. He looked older than Maria had expected, about
sixty-five or so, a man who had obviously started a family late
in life, though there was a quiet strength in his features and his
bearing. His hair was gray and shaggy, worn over the ears to just
above his collar, and he was dressed in a dove-gray frock coat
that draped well over his stout figure. He wore a checked vest
with a gold watch chain and dark trousers that fit snugly about
his waist and narrowed at the ankles. He had a thick, bushy,
drooping gray mustache that covered his upper lip, and it was
clear his son Spencer favored him more than Travis and Rebecca.
He was an imposing-looking man. When he spoke, his voice was
deep and gruff. His children stood when he entered the room, as
did Maria.

"Hello, Father," Travis said, a touch uneasily, it seemed to
Maria.

Sam Coulter looked at him and merely grunted. "So," he said
perfunctorily, "you're home, I see."

"Yes, sir. May I have the honor of presenting my wife, Maria?"

"How do you do, sir?" said Maria, with a curtsy.

Coulter turned toward her, and suddenly all Maria's nervousness returned under the strength of his appraising gaze. For a long
moment he simply looked at her, as if making up his mind, then
he grunted again and said gruffly, "Well, I suppose she'll do."

Maria did not know what to say, but then Sam Coulter's eyes
crinkled with amusement and he chuckled and held out his arms
to her. "Come here, girl."

He hugged her and then he hugged his son, enveloping him in
his strong arms and patting him on the back. "It's good to have
you home, boy," he said. "I hate to admit it, but you look damned
good in that soldier suit. How long has the army given you?"

"Well, sir, I have a furlough of three months, and then I'm to
report to cavalry school in Carlisle, Pennsylvania," said Travis.

"Cavalry school," Coulter said, with a snort. "As if a Southern
gentleman needs lessons in horsemanship!"

"It's not so much to give us lessons in horsemanship as to
accustom us to command and allow us to train new recruits,"
Travis replied. "The tour of duty lasts two years, and then I'm
off to Kansas."

Coulter grunted. "Kansas, eh? Damned Bleeding Kansas. Jubelo, bring us some whiskey and branchwater. I'm going to have a drink with my son."

"Right away, sir," Jubelo said, with a grin.

"So," said Coulter, sitting down, "you've been assigned to the First Cavalry?"

"Yes, sir."

"Why not the Second?"

Travis grimaced. "I'd asked myself the same thing, sir, but the army saw fit to assign me to the First, at Fort Leavenworth."

Sam Coulter grunted. "Well, might not be as good an assignment as Jeff Davis's Own, but I suppose Kansas is a sight better for a married man than Texas. A bit more civilized, at any rate."

"Perhaps," said Travis, "but the chances for promotion would have been much better at Fort Mason. And I would have liked the opportunity to serve with Lee."

Jubelo brought in the whiskey and water, then quietly withdrew.

"Well, we shall leave you gentlemen to your whiskey and your military talk," Elizabeth said, rising to her feet, along with Becky. "Come, Maria."

"I'd like to stay," Maria said.

Elizabeth raised her eyebrows.

"Maria's quite the military scholar, Mother," Travis said with a smile, by way of explanation. "She's not bored by military talk. She's even read the work of Baron von Clausewitz."

The name seemed to mean nothing to Elizabeth, who looked somewhat surprised at this development, but Sam Coulter chuckled.

"Unusual interests for an attractive young woman," he said. "Tell me, do you drink whiskey, too?"

"No, sir," said Maria, thinking she had made a social gaffe. "Perhaps I'd better leave you gentlemen to your talk."

Coulter chuckled again. "No, stay, by all means. I've never spoken with a woman who was a military scholar."

"Come, Rebecca," said Elizabeth, a touch coolly, Maria thought. They left and she glanced at Travis, to see if she had made a mistake, but Travis merely smiled. Becky clearly wanted to stay as well, but she departed with her mother.

"So, Maria," Coulter said, glancing at her wry amusement, "what is *your* opinion concerning your husband's assignment?"

"Well, sir, my brother Robert has been assigned to the Second, at Fort Mason," she said, "and I know Travis wishes it were the other way around. I understand the Second is staffed mostly by Southern officers, some of whom are familiar to me from West Point, and it's probably true that there may be more opportunities for brevets in Texas, what with the Comanche Indians resisting subjugation. The Indians around Fort Leavenworth are largely tribes who have been transplanted from the East, and except for some quarrels among themselves, I understand that they are not really very troublesome. However, I have no doubt that Travis will distinguish himself, wherever he is posted."

Sam Coulter smiled. "I can see you've taken the trouble to learn something of these matters. I find that admirable. A man's wife should take an interest in her husband's business." He grimaced. "Although the business of soldiering is hardly very profitable, especially for a man with a wife and, perhaps before too long, a family to support. However, we've been through all that and I suppose it's just as well my son gets this soldiering bug out of his system while he's still young. Tell me, what do you think of the troubles in Kansas?"

Maria glanced quickly at Travis, but there was no clue in his expression as to how she should proceed. She felt she could be treading on delicate ground. "Well, I'm not entirely certain what you mean, sir," she replied.

"You're aware of recent events there, I take it?" Coulter asked.

"Yes, sir, I read the newspapers."

Coulter grunted. "And what is your opinion of the actions of Osawatomie Brown?"

"I think Osawatomie John Brown is an outlaw, sir," she replied unhesitatingly, "a vicious murderer who must be brought to justice."

Coulter grunted again and nodded. "And as a Yankee, have you no sympathy for his cause?"

"Whatever a man's cause may be," she said, "it cannot justify the murder of innocent people."

"Perhaps," said Coulter, "and yet that was not an answer to my question." He was watching her with interest, awaiting her reply.

"The major . . . that is, my father," said Maria, "has always counseled us to refrain from political involvement. He believes a soldier should not concern himself with politics, but only with his duty, and that his family would do well to pursue the same course."

Travis remained silent, saying nothing of her brothers' interference with the slave hunters in New York, for which Maria was grateful.

"But surely you must have some opinion," Coulter pressed her.

"Maria has read *Uncle Tom's Cabin*," Travis interjected. "She found it very moving," he added wryly. "When I found out she had the book, I became angry and threw it away, but on reflection, I realized that was wrong. I told her that she would soon see for herself how mean-spirited and inaccurate it is."

"I must confess that Mrs. Stowe's novel moved me to tears," Maria admitted. "The thought of a mother and father having their children sold away from them, of slaves being whipped and tracked through swamps with vicious dogs, it all paints a painful and distressing picture. Yet Travis assures me that it's nothing but a pack of lies."

Coulter nodded, staring into his drink. "I've read the book," he said after a moment's pause. "The booksellers here in Charleston couldn't keep it in stock, it sold so quickly. And, of course, it aroused a great many tempers, as you might expect. Mrs. Stowe clearly has an ax to grind. Yet I must admit that the book is not entirely untruthful. And it is that kernel of truth it contains that incenses people so." He paused again, pursing his lips thoughtfully. "Jubelo and Bess had their children sold away from them."

"What?" said Travis, startled. "You've never told me that before! I never even knew they *had* children!"

"It's true," said Coulter, nodding. "We never speak of it, because the memory is painful to them. I had no hand in it, of course. You know I'd never do a thing like that. It happened a long time ago, before you were born, Travis, before we acquired Bess and Jubelo. When I found out about it, I made an effort to track the children down so I could buy them back, but unfortunately I was not successful. Still, Jubelo and Bess have always been grateful for my efforts, even though I failed."

"I never realized," said Travis. "Why, they've never said a thing about it!"

"Nor will they," said his father. "And you must never mention it to them. At the time it happened, they were much younger and their two children were quite small. I doubt they would even remember their parents now. And yet, as you can see, such things do happen." He turned to Maria. "On occasion, slaves are also whipped. Among domestic servants, that is rare, but among field hands on a plantation, it happens with more frequency. As the daughter of a soldier, Maria, and one who is something of a military scholar, perhaps you are aware that whipping is the penalty for desertion in the army. Well, if a slave commits a serious offense that merits such a punishment, then he is whipped, just as a white soldier would be whipped. It's true that some people are freer with the lash than others, but they are the exception rather than the rule."

Maria nodded, saying nothing.

"Despite what Northern newspapers would have you believe," said Coulter, "the Southern plantation is not a Roman galley, where slaves are chained and lashed as a matter of course. You've grown up in the North, Maria, where many people judge us harshly, without knowing us or understanding us. This has brought about a great deal of resentment among the people here. You are my son's wife, and a member of this family, and it is my concern that you are not exposed to such resentment. My friends are all people of good breeding and refinement, and I am certain that you will find them courteous and warmhearted. Yet these are difficult times, and as you yourself have pointed out, slavery is an issue that divides the country."

He paused to take a drink while Travis and Maria sat silently, waiting for him to continue. He wasn't a man to waste any time, Maria thought. He immediately came to the point, putting his cards on the table and confronting the matter of his son marrying a Yankee girl.

"There are those who, like the abolitionists, object to slavery on moral grounds," said Coulter, "and there are those whose opposition to it is largely political. A slave is reckoned in our census as three-fifths of a white man, and Northern politicians believe this gives the South an unfair advantage by virtue of our number of elected representatives. Yet the fact is that if our slaves were not reckoned in the balance, the North, with its greater population, would completely control the legislature. Already, we suffer from tariffs imposed upon imported goods, meant to force us to buy Northern goods rather than European products, which are often cheaper for us. And Northern politicians fear that if slavery were to be extended into Kansas and the other territories, the South would gain a political advantage, while we know that if slavery were excluded from those territories, the North would call the tune in Congress once they were admitted as states. I mention these things because I want you to understand why many Southerners are ill-disposed toward Yankees these days. Our country is suffering from growing pains, and in time, I believe these difficulties will pass of their own accord. However, should you encounter anyone who treats you with discourtesy because you are a Yankee, I want you to bring it to my attention at once and I will see that it does not happen again. You are a Coulter now, and as far as I'm concerned, that means you are to be accorded the respect due not only to a Southern lady, but to a woman of the Coulter family."

"Thank you, sir," Maria said.

"Good," said Coulter, with a nod. "That's settled then. And I would consider it a privilege if you called me Father. You're a member of the family now."

Maria felt gratified and enormously relieved. Travis had been right and she had been wrong to worry. His father had not approved of his choice to become an army officer, and though he hoped Travis would get it out of his system, it seemed he had accepted it. And he had accepted her as well, and had made it clear that if anyone else did not, they would have him to deal with. It would take some time for her to fully get to know these people, her new family, and for them to get to know her, but she felt secure now in knowing they truly welcomed her as one of them. As Travis smiled and took her arm and led her into the dining room for supper, she felt like she belonged. There was no need for her to feel anxious about the new life she had begun.

Everything would be all right.

CHAPTER FOUR

THE CUMBERLAND VALLEY Railroad ran from across the Susquehanna River just the other side of Harrisburg, through Carlisle, roughly twenty-five miles north of Gettysburg, and then continued on in a southwesterly curve to Shippensburg, Chambersburg, and finally to Hagerstown, in Maryland. Lieutenant Robert Gallio got off the train in Carlisle and collected his trunk.

The railroad ran right through the main street of Carlisle, which was dominated by the Mansion House Hotel. Upon entering the Mansion House and asking directions, Robert learned the garrison was about one mile from the town. He arranged for a carriage to take him and his trunk out to the barracks so he could report to Colonel Charles A. May, of the Second Dragoons, who commanded the cavalry school and the garrison. He found Colonel May to be a tall man, about six-foot-four, with a long, dark brown beard and well-trimmed brown hair, penetrating gray eyes, and a courtly demeanor. The garrison commander greeted him in a warm and friendly manner, which seemed to Robert quite informal after the spit and polish of West Point.

"Gallio, eh?" said May, returning his salute. "At ease, Lieutenant. Would you happen to be Major Anthony Gallio's boy?"

"Yes, sir, I have that honor," Robert replied. "Are you acquainted with my father?"

May smiled. "We met during the Mexican campaign. A fine officer." He consulted Robert's orders. "But you've only just graduated from West Point," he said, with a frown. "Surely, you must know you have a three months' leave coming?"

"Yes, sir, I know that," Robert replied. "I requested and received permission to dispense with my leave and report to cavalry school at once so I could get an early start and accustom myself to my new duties."

May smiled. "Eager to get started, are you?"

"Yes, sir."

"Well, we can use you. Have you checked into your quarters yet?"

"No, sir. I reported straightaway to you."

"Well, let's get you settled, then. You can begin your duties tomorrow. We give our newly arriving officers the first day to settle in and receive calls from the other officers on the post, and then they begin their duties on the following day. You'll find the routine simple enough, I am sure, after West Point. We have reveille at five, followed by stable call until seven A.M. Guard mount at eight, mounted drill from nine to eleven-thirty, dismounted drill from one-thirty P.M., to four-thirty, second stable call until five, and then you'll have your evenings off, unless you're on for guard duty. Mess at the usual times, of course. Evenings you'll be free to go into town, and there's often some social occasion or other among some of the local families. Otherwise, we have several local watering holes which provide a congenial atmosphere. Your duties will essentially consist of whipping cavalry recruits into shape, making certain they know one end of a horse from the other, and their right foot from their left. You'll get the hang of it quickly, just look to your noncommissioned officers to show you the drill. Mr. Tremayne!"

"Sir!"

"Show Lieutenant Gallio to his quarters, if you will, and get him settled in."

"My pleasure, sir."

Robert exchanged salutes with May and left with Tremayne, who got a couple of enlisted men to see to Robert's trunk. Robert knew Steven Tremayne from West Point. Tremayne had been a couple of years ahead of him, one of the upperclassmen who, out of sheer perversity, used to make his life miserable. A tall and handsome young Rhode Islander with dark hair, a wide, go-to-hell grin, and mocking brown eyes, Tremayne used to take delight in tormenting Robert. On parade, Tremayne would do everything short of taking a magnifying glass to him, seeking to find some fault with his turnout. And it infuriated him when there was no fault to be found. He never failed to find an opportunity to bedevil him, and Robert grew to loathe him. Now here they were, together, at cavalry school, both second lieutenants. It felt decidedly odd, especially since Tremayne had greeted him like an old friend. Robert had always been under the impression

Tremayne had disliked him intensely.

"You really gave up your summer leave?" Tremayne asked him, with surprise. "What happened? Nothing wrong at home, I hope?"

"No, nothing's wrong at home," said Robert as they walked toward the bachelor officers' quarters. "I simply had no wish to waste the summer lazing around. I've waited five years to become an officer and I was anxious to get started."

Tremayne chuckled. "I see you haven't changed. You were the most somber and serious young plebe I'd ever seen. You drove me to distraction."

"Why?" asked Robert, curious.

"Because you were so goddamned *perfect*." Tremayne laughed. "You know, throughout your entire plebe year, I don't believe I ever even saw you smile."

"You didn't give me much to smile about," Robert replied, wryly.

Tremayne grinned. "No, I suppose I didn't, did I? Do you still resent me for it?"

"I absolutely loathed you," Robert said. "But to be frank, I must admit that you were something of a beneficial influence on me."

"Really?" Tremayne said, with surprise. "How so?"

"You gave me an incentive to excel," said Robert, "because I knew that if I didn't, it would only give you grounds to make my life more miserable. So I suppose I should thank you. Good Lord. I never thought the day would come when I'd say *that* to you!"

Tremayne threw back his head and laughed heartily. In spite of himself, Robert had to smile.

"Lo, the great stone face cracks!" Tremayne said. "So you *can* smile, after all!"

He was seeing a side of Tremayne he'd never seen before, and it was suddenly hard not to find it likable. It was so little like the menace that had hovered over him malevolently all throughout his plebe year.

"Tell me something, Tremayne," Robert said, "why, I mean, for what particular reason, was I singled out above all the other plebes for your tender ministrations? I can scarcely believe it was merely because you thought I was too serious!"

"You want to know the truth?" asked Tremayne.

"Yes, I really do."

"It was because I envied you."

Robert stopped, absolutely startled, and stared at Tremayne with disbelief.

"It's true, you know," Tremayne said. "You were such a *perfect* little bastard, so intent and humorless, you drove me absolutely mad. Do you know what *my* plebe year was like?"

"No."

"I was the worst. I couldn't seem to do anything right. And I tried, oh Lord, how I tried! My drill was sloppy; my uniform always had something wrong with it, some little detail I'd neglected. And I was, at best, merely an average horseman. Oh, I could ride all right, but mounted drill was utterly beyond me until at least halfway through my second year, and I was the worst jumper in my class."

"But you took top honors at the Academy in horsemanship!" said Robert. "And only Sam Grant and Travis Coulter were better jumpers."

"Coulter beat my jumps?"

"Easily," said Robert, taking great pleasure in telling him that. "He tried valiantly to best Grant's record, but no one's ever been able to do that. Grant was like a centaur."

"Coulter, eh?" said Tremayne. "That girlish little Southron?"

Robert smiled. During their plebe year, Travis had suffered at the hands of upperclassmen almost as much as he had because of his remarkable good looks and courtly Southern manners. Yet, unlike Travis, Robert had never tried striking back. There was more than one upperclassman who, unofficially dropping the privileges of senior standing, had agreed to meet Travis clandestinely out behind the stables and been soundly thrashed.

"Well," said Tremayne, "believe me, my skill at horsemanship, at jumping in particular, resulted from hours of arduous practice during most of my free time and rather more than my share of falls. Yet it all seemed to come so easily to you. All of us could tell, right from the start, that you were destined to be the cadet captain of your class."

"Regrettably, I didn't have that honor," Robert said.

"Really? Who made captain in your class?"

"Travis Coulter."

"*Coulter?* You're joking!"

"He improved tremendously in his second year, and after that, there was no catching him," said Robert. "I managed to graduate ahead of him, but only just barely. But look here, Tremayne, you're not seriously telling me that you were jealous of me?"

"I suppose I was, a bit," Tremayne admitted. "I detested your advantages."

Robert frowned. "What advantages?"

"Well, after all, you were Major Gallio's son. You practically grew up at the Academy and you had a head start on us all. So it all came easily to you."

Robert snorted. "Is *that* what you thought? Well, you couldn't have been more wrong. Do you have any idea what it's like being a new cadet with your father on the faculty? All the instructors know you and expect you to be the best, because your father is a decorated veteran of the Mexican campaign. The superintendent and the commandant often came to dinner at our house, and so they knew me and I could hardly escape their critical attention. Add to that the fact that my father was harder on me than on any of the others, for fear of showing any favoritism. You have no idea what a burden that was. I *had* to be best, Tremayne. Anything less would have been unacceptable."

Tremayne pursed his lips thoughtfully. "You know, I hadn't thought of it that way. But you're right, of course. I wouldn't have wanted to be in your shoes. So Coulter made cadet captain, eh? Imagine that. He must have had the ladies swooning when he was on parade."

"Well, one lady, perhaps," said Robert, with a smile. "He married my sister."

"What, little Maria?" said Tremayne.

"She's not so little anymore," said Robert, with a smile. "You'll be seeing them both before too long. Travis has been assigned to the First Cavalry."

"Well, we all knew Maria would grow into a real beauty. But to marry Coulter . . ." Tremayne shook his head.

Robert frowned. "You don't approve? Travis Coulter is a fine gentleman, Tremayne. And he is my closest friend."

"It isn't a question of approval," said Tremayne. "I have no doubt he will treat her well, you understand. It's just that Coulter is a Southron."

"What has that to do with anything?" asked Robert testily. He had found the sectionalism trying at West Point and did not wish to get involved in it here.

"Don't get your back up, Gallio," Tremayne said. "Some of my closest friends at the Academy were from the South. And some of my best friends here as well. But your sister's marriage to Coulter will make things difficult for her when the war comes."

"I don't believe that," Robert said. "All this talk of war is ludicrous. The South's been threatening secession for thirty years or more and nothing's ever come of it. It's all talk and nothing more."

They reached Robert's quarters and went inside. The enlisted men set down the trunk and departed with hasty, and what seemed to Robert, rather sloppy salutes, but he chose to overlook it. After all, he didn't officially start his duties until tomorrow morning. Tremayne didn't seem to mind or even notice their lack of spit and polish. This wasn't the Academy, Robert reminded himself, but the regular army. As Colonel May had said, his duties would simply be to teach them how to tell one end of a horse from the other and not turn them into a crack parade regiment. Still, he thought, that was no reason for poor discipline.

His quarters were small and somewhat Spartan, yet reasonably comfortable. Some former charitable tenant had left behind an inexpensive and somewhat threadbare carpet to cover part of the wood-plank floor. The bed and the other furniture, while little more than utilitarian, were reasonably solid and well made. There was a small iron stove in the center of the sitting room, and the tiny bedroom was through a wood-plank door. Actually, it was more comfortable and spacious than his small room at West Point. Tremayne plopped down into a chair as Robert started to unpack.

"Nothing's ever come of it?" he said, taking out an unevenly colored meerschaum pipe and a well-worn tobacco pouch. "Speak to some of the noncommissioned officers who've been in Kansas. It's considerably more than talk out there."

"A series of minor, albeit bloody skirmishes between Free-Soilers and proslavers is a far cry from civil war, no matter what the newspapers say," said Robert. "Anyway, I understand things in Kansas are already settling down."

"Settling down?" Tremayne said. "With *two* separate territorial legislatures, one for Free-Soilers in Topeka and one for proslavers in Lecompton, each avowing the other is a sham?"

"I thought President Buchanan had recognized the Lecompton constitution," Robert said as he began to put away his things. "As did the Congress."

"The Senate, but not the House," Tremayne said. "Buchanan's been leaning toward Lecompton, to appease the South, but the House wouldn't have any of it. They've sent the constitution back for another referendum. Lord, Gallio, don't you keep up with these things?"

"Not very well, really," Robert replied. "I leave politics to the men in Congress. I found the constant sectional debates at the Academy rather tiresome, not to mention inflammatory. Besides, sooner or later one legislature or the other will be recognized and it will all sort itself out in the end."

"You're wrong, Robert," Tremayne said, shaking his head and lighting up the pipe. "It's only the calm before the storm. What's happening in Kansas is going to ignite a war. You mark my words. It's not a matter of whether it will come or not, it's a matter of when."

"The South hasn't the resources to fight a war," said Robert. "That's why all this talk of secession has been going on for so long and nothing's ever come of it. Besides, even if South Carolina and a handful of other Southern states seceded, Buchanan would never fight a war to stop them."

"Buchanan might not fight, but there's an election coming," Tremayne said.

"So then Douglas will be president," said Robert, with a shrug. "And I doubt the champion of popular sovereignty would make a war over secession, if it came to that."

"No, Douglas has already lost the South," Tremayne said, with a gesture of dismissal. "He opposed the Lecompton constitution as a fraud, which it was of course, the way they stuffed the ballot boxes. Everybody knew it and Douglas had no choice. If he'd supported Lecompton, his victory in the South would have been assured, but he would have gained the South and lost the North, and with it his own constituency in Illinois. He conceived the doctrine of popular sovereignty and he had no choice but to defend it. I understand they're hanging him in effigy all over the South.

"No, if the Democrats run Douglas," Tremayne continued, puffing on his pipe, "the South will bolt and probably run Breckenridge. He's a border stater, but he can't win in the North, not on a proslavery platform, and the Southern Democrats will accept nothing less. The Democratic party will be split. I can't see how it can possibly be avoided. It will split along sectional lines and our next president will be a Republican. You watch. It will be Seward, most likely. Or perhaps Chase. Who knows, maybe even Lincoln. He seems rather a dark horse at the moment, but he gained quite a following and a lot of recognition in his debates with Douglas. Either way, it makes no real difference who the Republicans will run. The Democrats are hopelessly divided, and if a Black Republican is elected president, the Southern states won't stand for it. They will secede and we will have a war."

Robert stared at him for a long moment. He had heard this sort of talk before, but he had never really paid particular attention. Politics had always bored him and he had taken to heart his father's injunction to avoid the subject. However, he had to admit Tremayne's analysis of the situation seemed quite lucid.

"I hope you're wrong," he told Tremayne.

"Come on, Gallio, wake up, for God's sake," said Tremayne impatiently. "Everybody knows it's coming. I don't understand you. How can you affect to be so unconcerned?"

"What possible difference would my concern make?" asked Robert. "Or yours, for that matter? We're soldiers, Tremayne, we do what we are told to do. We don't make policy."

"Doesn't it concern you that you may wind up fighting against your sister's husband and your closest friend?" Tremayne asked softly.

Robert was silent for a moment. "Yes, it concerns me," he finally replied. "It concerns me deeply. But I still think you're wrong, Tremayne. The thought of civil war seems so farfetched . . . and yet, if it ever came to that, I would do my duty as a soldier. As would Travis Coulter. He took an oath to serve his country."

"His country is the South, Robert," Tremayne said, not unsympathetically.

"You're speaking nonsense," Robert said. "You don't know him the way I do."

"He's a Southron, isn't he?" Tremayne replied. "Good Lord, you really don't understand, do you? You think it's all so simple. Duty, honor, country. Has it never occurred to you those words might mean different things to different people? What do you suppose the Southern idea of nullification is all about? Or doesn't it make any difference to you what you'll be fighting for? Southrons don't see the Union in the same way we do. To them, the Constitution is a document pertaining to a confederation of states, with each state remaining sovereign. Any law which threatens that, they see themselves as being free to nullify. Unless Coulter is different from every Southron I've ever met, his first loyalty will be to his native state. And if South Carolina makes good on its threats of secession, he will have to submit his resignation and take up arms to defend the South."

"That would make him a traitor," Robert said. "And Travis Coulter is no traitor."

"He would be either a traitor to the Union or a traitor to his own people," Tremayne replied. "Which do you think he'll choose?"

Before Robert could reply, there was a knock at the door and two young lieutenants entered, carrying bottles of wine. He knew them both from West Point. They were Oliver Sharp and Wendell Phillips, who'd been a year ahead of him at the Academy. Sharp was a Georgian, Phillips was from Maine.

"By God, I told you it was true!" said Phillips, nudging Sharp. "Who else but Gallio would give up his summer leave and report to duty three months early?"

"Keep it up, Gallio," said Sharp. "Given your fine example, soon the army will expect us all to do the same."

"Phillips! Sharp! It's good to see you!" Robert said, feeling genuinely pleased to see familiar faces.

"We have brought libation," Sharp said solemnly, "to toast your excessive and entirely unwarranted devotion to your duty. Here. Damn your zeal and pop the cork."

"I'm afraid I don't have any glasses," Robert said.

"Voilà!" said Phillips, producing a wineglass. He snapped his fingers. "Sergeant Major! Some glasses for the gentlemen!"

A huge, burly, red-bearded noncom entered, carrying a wicker basket, which he placed on the table. From within it, he took glasses, cheese, some bread, and another two bottles of wine.

"Gallio, meet Sergeant Major Mulligan," said Sharp. "Veteran of the Mexican War, the Indian Wars in Texas and New Mexico, and the orneriest sergeant major in the United States Army. Sergeant Mulligan, Lieutenant Gallio, pride of the United States Military Academy at West Point and the sorriest horse's ass you've ever seen."

"Pleasure to be makin' your acquaintance, sir!" said Mulligan, cracking to attention and snapping off a parade-ground perfect salute. Robert returned it, equally properly.

"Thank you, Sergeant Major. At ease. Will you stay and have a drink?"

"Beggin' your pardon, sir, but it ain't proper military etiquette for noncommissioned personnel to fraternize with officers," said Mulligan. "Unless, of course, it was a direct order, sir."

Robert immediately liked the man. "In that case, Sergeant Major, I order you to stay and have a drink."

"Or six or ten," added Sharp.

"Thank you kindly, sir," said Mulligan, accepting a glass from Sharp.

"Mind you, Gallio," said Phillips, "you'll learn a lot from Mulligan if you're smart and pay attention. I've never seen anyone handle men or horses better. And he's fought Comanches, too."

"Did you?" Robert said, fascinated. More than anything, he was looking forward to seeing his first Indians. "I hear they are among the finest light cavalry in all the world."

"Not among the finest, sir," said Mulligan, "they *are* the finest, damn their eyes. Beggin' your pardon, sir. Practically born on horseback, they are, and they can shoot from the back of the horse, no saddles mind you, better than most men can shoot from solid ground."

"I'm anxious to learn more about them," Robert said, but at that moment several other officers arrived and he found himself greeting some more old friends who'd been ahead of him at the Academy. They spoke of the old days at West Point, and then the talk turned to what was happening on the frontier.

Five companies of the First Cavalry had just been sent to the department of Texas, to assist in putting down the Indian uprisings. General Twiggs, who was commanding the department over Colonel Lee, was said to be stripping the Rio Grande frontier of troops. Brownsville, Ringgold Barracks, and Laredo were all to be left ungarrisoned, which meant they would be vulnerable to raids across the border from Mexico. The conversation soon drifted away from Indian fighting toward politics and sectionalism.

Some of the men seemed to feel Twiggs had pulled the troops back from the Rio Grande to deal with the Indian threat, while others were convinced he was purposely weakening the frontier so that in the event of civil war, the garrisons would all be under strength. The South would greatly benefit from having Texas, they argued, especially since it would give them a firm foothold from which to strike out into Mexico. And, like Tremayne, none of them seemed to consider the possibility that there wouldn't be a war. If the Southern states seceded, as the Southern officers maintained they would if a Republican were elected president, the Northern states would fight for the preservation of the Union.

"I cannot believe that war is a foregone conclusion," Robert said. "If the Southern states become truly serious about secession, after having made such empty threats for years, surely Congress would effect some compromise whereby a war could be averted."

"Gallio, my friend," said Sharp, holding a drink in one hand

and clapping him on the back with the other, "it's no use talking. We're going to have a war. I see it coming and all the compromises in the world won't be able to avert it. You'll probably get command of a cavalry regiment and I will go home and ask the governor to give me a cavalry regiment of my own. And who knows but we may move against each other in the war. You'll have the best of it in the beginning, because you Yankees are rich and powerful, while we of the South are poor and weak. Your regiment will have the best of weapons, while mine will have little more than shotguns and scythe blades. Yet for all that, we'll get the best of the fight in the end, because we shall be fighting for a principle, a cause, while you will fight only to perpetuate abuse of power. So here's to you, you blackguard, and here's to glory for us all!"

Toasts were proposed, and as the wine flowed someone nostalgically requested a chorus or two of "Benny Havens." Somberly, they stood and raised their glasses, joining in a song to commemorate the tavern close to West Point, by the Buttermilk Falls, where each and every one of them had often "run it" in defiance of academy regulations and patrolling officers, to bask in the warm glow of good fellowship, the aroma of fine food and warm flip, and the smoldering gazes of Benny's three beautiful daughters.

"Come fill your glasses, fellows, and stand up in a row,
To singing sentimentally, we're going for to go,
In the army there's sobriety, promotions very slow,
So we'll sing our reminiscences of Benny Havens, oh!
Oh, Benny Havens, oh! Oh, Benny Havens, oh!
So we'll sing our reminiscences of Benny Havens, oh!

"Oh, Ryders is a perfect 'fess' and Cozzens all the go,
And officers as thick as hops infest the Falls below,
But we pass them all so slyly by as once a week we go,
To toast the lovely flowers that bloom at Benny Havens, oh!
Oh, Benny Havens, oh! Oh, Benny Havens, oh!
So we'll sing our reminiscences of Benny Havens, oh!

"To our comrades who have fallen, one cup before we go,
They poured their lifeblood freely out *pro bono publico*.
No marble points the stranger to where they rest below,
They lie neglected far away from Benny Havens, oh!

Oh, Benny Havens, oh! Oh, Benny Havens, oh!
So we'll sing our reminiscences of Benny Havens, oh!"

As he sang with them Robert thought of Travis and Maria and
of the friends he'd made at the Academy who were from the
South. If the Southern states actually seceded from the Union,
what would become of them? All his life, there had been threats
of secession from the South. He had come to believe it would
never happen, that Southern politicians were merely acting like
small boys, threatening to pick up their marbles and go home
anytime the game didn't go their way. But Tremayne and the
others all seemed to believe secession was not only inevitable,
but that it would come very soon and that war would inevitably
follow on its heels.

Northern and Southern officers spoke about it without any real
animosity, the Northerners insisting the South was bound to lose
in short order because of their lack of resources, the Southerners
denying it and insisting they would win because their cause
was just. They spoke about the promise of rapid promotions,
of meeting each other on the field of battle as if it were a lark,
some grand adventure to look forward to, and Robert wondered
if they'd all gone quite insane.

In Congress, old men were caning one another senseless and
exchanging feeble fisticuffs. In the Northern city streets, fights
and sometimes even riots broke out over captured fugitive slaves.
He had nearly started one himself. In the Southern cities, Senator
Douglas was being hung in effigy for refusing to come out in
support of slavery in the territories. Free-Soilers and proslavers
in Kansas murdered each other in the night, and here, in his own
quarters, the soldiers who would fight the war, if war would truly
come, bantered good-naturedly with one another and joined in
drinking songs.

What was it Tremayne had said? The calm before the storm?
Was that what this was? Did it really all hinge upon the next
election? Everyone seemed to accept it as a foregone conclusion
that the Democrats would nominate Douglas. During his debates
with Lincoln during the Illinois senatorial campaign, Stephen
Douglas had seemed like a friend to the South, but now all
that had changed. The only way the Democrats could win the
South would be if they adopted a proslavery platform and that
they would not do, for it would lose them the North. And if the
Democratic nominee did not run on a proslavery platform, then

Tremayne was right, and the Southern Democrats would surely bolt and split the party. That would almost certainly guarantee the election of the Republican nominee, whoever he turned out to be. The Southern hatred of the "Black Republicans" was widely known. Would they secede? More to the point, if they did, would the newly elected Republican president allow their peaceful separation?

He really didn't know. His old self-assurance about a peaceful outcome was rapidly beginning to evaporate in the face of the certainty of all the others. They spoke about the coming war as if it were already a reality. If the South were allowed to secede, thought Robert, it would destroy the country. True, the Southern states lacked the resources to fight a war, but what if Britain recognized them and came to their aid? A payback for the Revolution and the War of 1812? Yes, thought Robert, it was possible. Perhaps even likely. Britain needed Southern cotton. And it would surely benefit from a no-longer-United States.

He had always avoided following political developments, concentrating on his studies and trying to become the best soldier he could be. The actual fact of secession seemed so unlikely that he had never seriously considered it a possibility. He wondered if his father had. They had never discussed the subject in their home. He had no idea what the major's opinions were, or even if he had any opinions on the subject. Robert thought about what Tremayne had said.

Doesn't it concern you that you may be fighting against your sister's husband and your best friend?

The thought had never really occurred to him before. He wondered if it had occurred to Maria, who seemed much more interested in politics than he was. Suppose war came and he and Travis met on the field of battle? Or Travis met their father, for the major would surely answer to the call to duty? He was glad Maria wasn't here to listen to such talk, but in only a few short months, she would arrive with Travis and he did not see how she could avoid such conversation, especially with her outspoken nature. And what would they be saying in Charleston now? Would they be telling her she would soon have to choose between her husband and her family?

"Gallio!" said Phillips. "Why so glum? Here, have another drink!"

"He's always glum," Tremayne said, drawing on his pipe.

"He's the most depressingly somber individual I've ever met. But he can smile, apparently. I've seen him do it, hard to believe though it may be."

"He's probably having second thoughts about having given up his leave," said Sharp.

"Who, Gallio?" Tremayne replied. "Nonsense! What would he do on leave? He doesn't even sleep, you know, but stays up all night, polishing his boots."

"Well, we can't have that," said Sharp, "or Colonel May will want us all to polish ours. Here, Gallio, have another drink. We want you sleeping soundly."

Robert had another drink. And then another. He suddenly felt in the mood for getting good and drunk.

CHAPTER FIVE

Carlisle Barracks, Pennsylvania, October 1859

"COME IN," SAID Colonel May.

Robert marched into the office, his hat held in his hand, stopped two feet in front of Colonel May's desk, and came to attention. "You wanted to see me, sir?"

May smiled. "Stand at ease, Mr. Gallio." Robert relaxed his posture only slightly. "How would you like to go to Washington?"

Robert frowned slightly. "Washington, sir?"

"I am in receipt of a communication from the adjutant-general, army headquarters, Washington, D.C., requesting me to use my best discretion in selecting one of the young officers under my command for assignment to the War Department. It seems the general-in-chief is in need of a new aide-de-camp. He prefers a cavalry officer, but he does not wish to detach a man from active duty on the frontier, so as commander of the cavalry school, I have been directed to provide him with one. Would you like the assignment?"

Robert was so stunned, he was speechless. Taking his silence for indecision, Colonel May continued.

"I can understand your hesitation," he said, with a smile. "You are anxious to see duty on the frontier. However, serving as an aide to General Winfield Scott is both a great honor and a privilege. I think you will find it a very valuable experience and it will stand you in good stead in your career. I need not tell you that such an opportunity does not come often. I have not selected you at random. Your record at West Point was nothing short of outstanding, and in the time you've been here, you have impressed me as a diligent and highly capable young officer, one who would reflect well on my judgment."

"What about Lieutenant Coulter, sir?" asked Robert. "His record at West Point was superior to mine."

May smiled. "Perhaps, but not in any significant regard. And it is admirable of you to point that out to me. However, General Scott prefers a man who is unmarried so that he will not be taking time away from that man's wife and family. Also, given the, uh"—he cleared his throat softly—"current climate, if you will, I think it would be best if the postion were filled by a Northern officer. Although that was not specified as a requirement, I was asked to use my 'best discretion,' and I have made my selection accordingly."

"I'm very flattered, sir," said Robert.

"Needless to say, I am not ordering you to undertake this assignment," Colonel May added, "but I would consider it a personal favor if you were to accept. Oh, and did I mention that the posting carries with it the rank of brevet captain?"

"*Captain?*" Robert said, with disbelief. "But . . . but, sir, I have only just been commissioned second lieutenant!"

"Well, the general-in-chief can't have a mere second lieutenant as an aide, can he?" May replied, with a twinkle in his eye. "So . . . do you accept?"

"Sir, I . . ." Robert swallowed hard. Aide-de-camp to the general-in-chief! "I would be very honored, sir."

"Good. Pack your trunk. You leave first thing in the morning. Oh, and by the way, you might care to inform Lieutenant Coulter that this will leave an opening for a lieutenant in the Second Cavalry. Under the circumstances, I think a transfer could easily be arranged."

"Yes, *sir*!" said Robert.

"Dismissed, Mr. Gallio. And my congratulations."

In a daze, Robert left the office. The moment he was outside, he let out a highly uncharacteristic whoop and rushed to give the news to Travis and Maria.

"I can't believe it!" Travis said, when he heard the news. "Breveted to captain already! And serving directly under General Scott! You lucky dog!"

"Oh, Robert, that's wonderful news!" Maria said. "Father will be so proud! You must let me be the first to tell him! I'll write to him at once!"

"When do you leave for Washington?" asked Travis.

"First thing in the morning."

"What, already?" said Maria, with chagrin. "But we've only

just arrived! We've hardly even had a chance to talk!"

Robert smiled. Three months in Charleston and Maria was already beginning to sound a bit like Travis in her speech. Travis had reported for duty at the end of September, bringing Maria with him, and she was full of stories about the time she'd spent in Charleston. The Coulter family had welcomed her with open arms and she had a new best friend in Becky Coulter, who had apparently developed a minor infatuation with him after seeing his photograph. Maria thought Charleston was a marvelous city, so elegant and refined, and she didn't see how Southern women could maintain their figures given their delicious cooking, and the Coulter family had held a ball in her honor, with all the leading citizens of Charleston in attendance, and she had been terrified of not making a good impression, had almost pleaded illness so she could be excused, but everything had come off well and Travis had bought her a beautiful new dress and everyone had been so nice and charming and on and on it went, breathlessly, so he hardly had a chance to get a word in edgewise. She had put on a little weight, which looked becoming on her and added an attractive fullness to her figure, and what was most important, she seemed happy. It was almost a shame to give Travis the good news. The Texas frontier would be a far cry from life in Charleston.

"By the way, Colonel May asked me to deliver a message to you," Robert said to Travis. "He said that my being posted to Washington will leave a vacancy for an officer in the Second Cavalry and he thought that a transfer could be easily arranged. I don't suppose you would be interested?"

"A transfer to 'Jeff Davis's Own'?" said Travis, with a grin. "Need you even ask?"

"Well, see Colonel May about it," Robert said. "He seems to be well aware of your desires. I think he'll be happy to arrange it for you."

"But Robert, can't you wait at least another day or two?" Maria asked.

"I'm afraid not," Robert replied. "One doesn't keep the highest-ranking general in the army waiting, Maria."

"But, it's so unfair!"

"Now, Maria, let's not be selfish," Travis said. "This is a wonderful opportunity for Robert. He'll be rubbing elbows with the most powerful and influential people in the country. Chances are he'll even get to meet the president."

"I know," Maria said, dejected. "It's just that I was counting on our being together for two more years, and now suddenly he's leaving. I'm very happy for you, Robert, but I still can't help feeling disappointed."

He gave her a hug. "I know," he said. "But this is the sort of thing you must grow accustomed to, Maria. As a soldier's wife, there will be times when you'll find circumstances changing without warning. You must learn to adapt to it."

"I suppose I'll have to, won't I?"

"It's already begun," said Robert. "Only a few moments ago, your future plans would have included going to Fort Leavenworth. Now you'll be going not to Kansas, but to Texas. This time, at least, you have plenty of advance warning, but that will not always be the case. A soldier and his family must always be prepared to change their plans on a moment's notice."

"He's right, Maria," Travis said. "Why, only this morning, Robert and I were equals. Now, I'll have to salute my own brother-in-law!" He chuckled. "That will take some getting used to, Captain Gallio."

"I must admit I like the sound of that," said Robert.

"I like the sound of Captain Coulter even better," Travis said. "In fact, Colonel Coulter has rather a nice ring to it, don't you think?"

"Yes, better than General Coulter," Robert added, with a perfectly straight face. "That doesn't sound at all euphonious."

"Well, now, I wouldn't go quite that far." They both laughed. "I suppose a celebration is in order," Travis said. "Have you told any of the others yet?"

"No, you're the very first to know," said Robert. "I came straight from Colonel May's office."

"Well then, we'll have to get word to all the other officers immediately," said Travis. "If you're leaving in the morning, tonight you'll get a proper send-off."

"But Travis, I've made no preparations to entertain!" Maria protested.

"You're a soldier's wife, my dear," said Travis. "You'll have to improvise. I'll go out and find a few enlisted men to pass the word."

"I'll go with you. We'll be right back, Maria."

The moment they stepped outside, Robert took Travis by the arm. "I need a word with you, Travis."

His friend turned toward him with a smile, but when he saw

the sudden, grave expression on his face, the smile faded. "What's wrong?" he asked.

"Walk with me," said Robert. Travis fell in step beside him. "Travis," Robert began, "you are my closest friend in all the world. And you are my sister's husband. We've never had a cross word, you and I, and we've always been able to speak frankly and truthfully with one another."

"I know. And I have always valued your friendship, Robert. What are you getting at?" asked Travis.

Robert took a deep breath. "We've never really spoken of this before," he said, somewhat awkwardly, "but I'm leaving for Washington tomorrow and I don't know when we may see each other again."

"You're worried about the coming war," said Travis.

Robert stopped. "Then you, too, believe that war is coming?"

Travis shook his head. "I don't know," he said, with a sigh. "I never thought it would come to that, and yet, with each passing month, each passing week, each passing day, even, it begins to look more and more likely. I suddenly find myself in the minority, thinking the war won't come. And I still hope it will not. But things have changed, Robert. Maria, of course, was not exposed to any of this in Charleston, and my family took pains to shelter her from it, but the feeling of antipathy among most South Carolinians toward the government in Washington has grown tremendously."

"Yours too?" asked Robert softly.

"I'm a soldier, Robert," he replied. "And I have never wanted to be anything but a soldier in the army of the United States. I regard the breakup of the Union as a great disaster. But as a Southerner, and the son of a planter, I understand how my people feel. Their rights are being trampled on. The North doesn't understand and it seems as if they don't *want* to understand. It isn't only slavery, though slavery might be the central issue. I won't argue with you about morality, but the fact remains that slavery is not a question that may be settled with the stroke of a Northern legislator's pen. Even if our economy did not depend upon it, even if the abolishment of slavery did not utterly ruin the South, it would take years for the question to be settled. I doubt it could be settled in our lifetime.

"It's not only the South, either," Travis continued. "Even in the North, men march in parades with their young daughters, who carry placards reading 'Fathers, save us from nigger husbands!'

Society is not prepared to receive the Negro as an equal. What would they do? How would they live? Even their own spokesmen, among the free Negroes, reject the idea of being transported back to Africa, or to some other country in the tropics. No one can agree on what to do with them. In Charleston, shortly before Maria and I arrived, the Southern business leaders all met in a convention and voted to resolve that all laws pertaining to the prohibition of the African slave trade be repealed. In the North, the talk of abolition grows louder with each passing day. The territories have become the battlefield. If admitted as free states, they tip the balance toward the North. If admitted as slave states, they tip the balance toward the South."

"And you see no other way?" asked Robert.

Travis took a deep breath and let it out slowly. "If this continues, I can see no way of settling the matter short of secession. I am almost certain South Carolina will secede. And if South Carolina secedes, the other Southern states will follow. Whether or not the government will allow a peaceful separation is another matter. That I do not know."

"What if they don't?" asked Robert. "What happens then? What will you do, Travis?"

For a long moment Travis remained silent. "If the people of my state vote to secede, and the government chooses to make war upon them to prevent it, then I cannot in good conscience take up arms against them. I will be forced to resign my commission."

"You'd *really* do that?"

"I'd have no other choice."

"Would you actually take up arms against the government of the United States?"

"In the event of secession, it would no longer *be* my government," Travis replied. "If you're asking me if I would take up arms to defend my country, then the answer would have to be yes."

"And what about Maria?" Robert asked, stunned by his friend's response.

"Maria is my wife," said Travis. "She is a Coulter now, and though she may have grown up in the North, she is now a Southern lady."

"Will she be accepted as such?" asked Robert.

"You have my word on it."

"And you do not think it would break her heart to see her husband go to war against her own family?"

"As much as it would break my heart to think of us upon opposing sides," said Travis. "But I could not be a traitor to my people, Robert."

"So you will force Maria to be a traitor to hers," Robert replied stiffly.

Travis compressed his lips into a tight grimace. "Do not provoke me, Robert, please. Maria is my wife. She joined her fate to mine when we were wed, and she did that of her own free will."

"You have free will as well," said Robert. "You chose to take an oath to serve your country and protect the Constitution and the government of the United States. If you forsake that oath, Travis, then you forsake your honor and brand yourself forever as a traitor to your country."

Travis paled. "If anyone else but you had said that to me, Robert, I would demand satisfaction on the spot. But out of consideration for Maria, I will overlook the insult. However, I do not think we have anything more to talk about."

"As you wish," said Robert. "Under the circumstances, I think it would be best if I were to pack my things and leave tonight. It should only take me a few moments. I will catch the next train from Carlisle. Please convey my apologies to my sister and tell her I will write to her from Washington as soon as time permits."

"I will do so," Travis said, with stiff formality. He snapped to attention and gave Robert a sharp salute. "By your leave, Captain."

"Travis . . ."

"Sir."

"Have it as you wish," said Robert. He returned the salute. Travis stepped back, made a smart about-face, and went back toward his quarters without another word.

Washington, D.C., October 1859

Upon arrival in the capital early on the morning of the seventeenth, Robert paused only long enough to drop his trunk off at the Ebbit House, a popular hostelry for soldiers, before rushing immediately to the offices of the War Department. He was not about to keep General Winfield Scott waiting. He knew how important first impressions were. The general had been his father's commander in the Mexican War and Robert was anxious to prove himself as efficient an officer as his father had been.

The offices of the War Department were in a flurry of activity when he arrived. People were rushing in and out and Robert was impressed with how busy things were, even at such an early hour. He left his name with the adjutant-general and was told curtly to wait in the anteroom. He found another officer already there, a lieutenant like himself, waiting with his long legs stretched out before him. The man was tall, with red hair and a large, full red beard and mustache that gave him the aspect of a Viking warrior. He looked up as Robert entered, frowned slightly, then said, "Aren't you Major Gallio's boy?"

For a moment Robert was nonplussed and couldn't place the man. There seemed to be something familiar about him, but recognition eluded him.

"Jeb Stuart," said the lieutenant, getting to his feet and holding out his hand.

"Good Lord," said Robert. He smiled and took "Beauty" Stuart's hand. "I never would have recognized you! You've grown a beard!"

Stuart smiled. "They tell me it improves my looks by hiding them behind a bush. How is your father?"

"Fine, thank you," Robert said. "What brings you to Washington? I thought you were assigned to the First Cavalry in Kansas."

"That's right," said Stuart. "I was visiting my family when I was called to Washington to present my invention to the War Department."

"What invention?" Robert asked.

"I've devised a new way of attaching a saber to a belt," said Stuart, "more practical than the means currently employed, and I'd been hoping to sell the patent to the government. But it seems they've got their hands full with some sort of crisis at the moment. I've been cooling my heels out here for the past hour or so."

"Do you know what's going on?"

"Something about Harpers Ferry," Stuart replied. "I caught a drift of conversation from some people storming by, but more than that I cannot tell you. What brings you here?"

"I've been assigned as General Scott's new aide," said Robert.

"Have you, now? Good show," said Stuart. "That's what I call a good start, fresh out of the gate. Could be a promotion in it for you before too long."

Robert cleared his throat uneasily. "I've been brevetted to captain," he said, somewhat apologetically. "I haven't had time to procur my new insignia yet."

"What, already?" Stuart said, surprised. Then he came to attention, smiled, and snapped off a sharp salute. "Then allow me to congratulate you, sir."

He held the salute until Robert, somewhat abashedly, returned it.

Stuart grinned. "Damnation," he said. "And you still wet behind the ears!"

"Captain Gallio!" shouted the adjutant-general.

"Sir!"

"The general-in-chief will see you now."

"Hop to, soldier," Stuart said, with a smile.

"I'll let him know you're out here, Jeb."

He was conducted into the presence of General Scott. Winfield Scott was a huge, impressive-looking mountain of a man in his midseventies, weighing nearly three hundred pounds. He looked, thought Robert, less like a general than like Zeus. There was something imperious and almost godlike about the man. His office was filled with memorabilia of the Mexican War and the War of 1812, and in the midst of it all, his commanding presence loomed over the desk he stood behind, along with several officers of his staff.

It was Scott who had instituted the adoption by the army of the rifled musket, which he believed would revolutionize warfare and bring to an end the days of the Napoleonic massed assault. Unlike the smoothbore musket, which fired a patched round ball, it was much more accurate, especially at long range. Robert had used both the smoothbore and the rifled musket and he frankly thought the latter had made the former completely obsolete.

With the smoothbore musket, the lead ball projectile had, of necessity, to be of a smaller diameter than the bore so that it would fit inside the barrel. Consequently, it was necessary, after pouring the powder down the barrel, to cut a cloth patch of an appropriate size—soldiers often simply carried swatches of cloth tucked into their belts which they cut with knives—and place it over the barrel. The ball was then placed on top of the cloth patch and rammed down inside the barrel so that the patch would take up the space around the ball, ensuring a tight fit. The trouble was, on firing, the ball would then rattle around the inside of the barrel before it left the muzzle, which did not make for a great deal of accuracy in its flight. For this reason, infantry tactics had long stressed firing in volleys so that a massed flight of projectiles would be sent hurtling toward the enemy ranks. With the rifled musket, Scott had claimed, the infantry would enjoy a great advantage in superior firepower.

The rifling of the musket, a series of grooves cut into the inside of the barrel, had resulted in a new type of lead projectile called the "Minié ball," named after its designer, Captain Claude Etienne Minié of the French army. It was not properly a ball at all, but a conical-shaped, lead bullet with a hollow cup at the base. Early models had used a wooden plug to fill this cup, but this was soon found to be unnecessary. The Minié ball did not require a patch, which not only greatly simplified the loading procedure, but produced significantly greater accuracy, as well. On firing, the explosion caused by the ignition of the powder would make the hollow base of the bullet expand, and as it traveled down the barrel it would "grip" the rifling of the musket, which would cause it to spin. Its conical shape and its spinning action resulted in a trajectory that was straight and true, accurate out to three or four hundred yards or more. Though Scott was known by the somewhat unflattering sobriquet of "Old Fuss and Feathers," the fact that he had immediately grasped the significance of this new development and urged its adoption by the army as early as 1849 argued well for his military acumen and progressive attitudes.

Robert found himself in awe of the general. Winfield Scott was something of a living legend. Snapping to attention, Robert saluted and said, "Lieutenant, uh, Captain Robert Gallio, reporting for duty, as ordered, sir."

He cursed himself for the slip, but Scott appeared not to notice. "At ease, Captain," he said, with the sort of desultory wave that passed for a salute among generals. "I knew your father. A fine officer. Fine officer, indeed."

"Thank you, sir."

"We have a situation on our hands, Captain, that requires immediate attention, so you'll forgive me if I haven't the time for the proper amenities. You have a mount?"

"No, sir, I've just arrived this morning and have not yet had the time to procure one."

"Well, find one, and find one in a hurry. I've just received word that the arsenal at Harpers Ferry has been captured by a force of raiders. I don't know who they are, I don't know how many they are, in fact, I don't know a goddamned thing about what's going on down there. I need intelligence and I need it quickly. To make matters worse, I've got no troops to send down there right now. All I have is a detachment of ninety marines from the navy, but they've only a lieutenant to command them. The president is going to want some answers, and at the moment I have none to give him."

"I'm on my way, sir," Robert said.

"Wait," said Scott. "Slow down, son. I need to get word to Colonel Lee in Arlington. He's on leave, visiting his family. I want him to report here with all possible speed for a conference with President Buchanan and Secretary Floyd. I want him to take command of those marines."

"Sir," said Robert, "with your permission, Lieutenant Stuart of the First Cavalry is waiting outside in the anteroom. If Lieutenant Stuart were to take word to Colonel Lee, I could proceed at once to Harpers Ferry and have a report ready by the time Colonel Lee arrives with his command."

"Excellent," said Scott. He turned to his secretary. "Write out a message for Colonel Lee at once and have Lieutenant Stuart deliver it. Captain Gallio, you will proceed to Harpers Ferry and report directly to Colonel Lee when he arrives. Dismissed."

"Sir!"

Robert saluted, about-faced, and hastened from the office. Without pausing to speak to Stuart, he rushed to the adjutant-general's desk to inquire where he could get a horse, but there was no one at the desk. He tried to stop a passing officer, but the man brushed past him without pausing. Everyone seemed to be rushing around madly, intent on some urgent errand. One would think the war had started, Robert thought, and then suddenly it came home to him with a shocking realization. My God, he thought, this could be it!

He saw Stuart rushing past him, clutching the message for Lee, and hurried to catch up with him.

"Jeb! I've got to get to Harpers Ferry and find out what's happening! Where can I get a horse?"

"Hell, steal one!" said Stuart as they ran down the corridor together.

People scrambled out of their way to avoid being bowled over as they ran outside and down the steps. Stuart practically flew down the steps and vaulted into the saddle. He spurred his horse into a gallop and disappeared down the street in a cloud of dust, heading toward the bridge.

"Steal one?" said Robert, standing at the bottom of the steps. Looking around, he saw an army colonel dismounting and getting ready to tie his horse up to the railing. "Oh, hell . . ."

He ran up to the colonel and took the reins from him.

"Allow me, sir," he said.

"Why, thank you, Lieutenant," said the colonel. "I appreciate—"

Robert swung up into the saddle, yelled, *"Hah!"* and whipped up the horse with the reins.

"Hey! That's my horse!" the colonel yelled, but Robert was already galloping full speed down the street in Stuart's wake.

Harpers Ferry was in a state of chaos. It began on Sunday morning when a man calling himself Isaac Smith, who had recently rented a farmhouse across the Potomac in Maryland, attacked the federal armory with a band of armed men. They had taken the lone watchman prisoner and, before anyone in the town knew what was happening, had sent out a patrol to take some hostages. The raiders had seized about thirty people returning home from a Methodist service, and they had also captured Colonel Lewis Washington, George Washington's great-grandnephew, who was taken from his home. The raiders had "freed" his slaves after bringing them into the armory, given them pikes, and ordered them to guard their master. They had also captured a local farmer named John Allstadt, along with his eighteen-year-old son.

After taking weapons from the armory, among which were a pistol that had been a gift to George Washington from Lafayette and a sword the nation's first president had received from Frederick the Great, Smith, the leader of the raiders, had decided to move his men from the armory into the engine house. He kept nine of the most prominent citizens hostage and released the others, telling them he had come from Kansas to free all the Negroes in the state and that if he was met with any resistance, he would burn the town.

Almost an entire day had passed before the citizens of Harpers Ferry became aware of what was happening in their midst. By the time Robert arrived, it was all he could do to sort out fact from rumor. At least a dozen men were dead, among them the mayor of Harpers Ferry, Fontaine Beckham, an employee of the Baltimore and Ohio Railroad who had been shot while looking out from behind a water tank. A Negro baggage master had been killed, apparently shot down in the dark by one of the raiders, and a local farmer named George Turner had been shot in the street when he was seen carrying a gun.

Several of the raiders had been killed as well, by locals who had armed themselves after Beckham's murder. One of the captured raiders had been dragged to the Potomac bridge and executed with pistols. His body had been dropped into the water and riddled with balls. Another captured raider was likewise executed and his body used for target practice. Yet another of the raiders, a Negro, had been shot down in the engine-house yard and his body cut to pieces.

When two of the raiders came out of the brick engine house under a flag of truce, the enraged townspeople had shot them down as well. One of them managed to crawl back into the engine house, the other lay bleeding in the yard. Later in the afternoon, two of the raiders had been shot in an attempt to escape across the river. A number of the raiders had apparently managed to escape successfully, but Robert could not determine their exact number. The rest of them had retreated behind the thick walls and heavy doors of the engine house to make a stand. Townspeople and members of several local militia companies divided their time between sniping at the engine house and getting liquored up in the saloons at the hotels. Robert finally found the officer in command of the militia, Colonel Robert Baylor, identified himself, and demanded a report. And it was only then he learned the true identity of the raider leader, "Isaac Smith."

"It's Osawatomie Brown, of Kansas," Baylor said. "At least, that's who he says he is. And I don't know what in hell the mad fool thinks he's doing. Some nonsense about liberating all the slaves. It seems he believed that if he took the arsenal, the slaves would all rise up and come flocking to him so that he could arm them all for a rebellion. If you ask me, he's crazy as a bedbug!"

"Do you know how many men are in there?" Robert asked.

"Not counting the hostages, I'd reckon about five or six," Baylor replied.

"What, that's *all*?" asked Robert, stunned.

"He had about twenty men when he started," Baylor said, "but some have been killed and a few of others have escaped. I sent a man up there under a flag of truce to tell them to surrender. Brown wanted terms. He wants to take his people across the bridge to Maryland, along with the hostages, to ensure their safety. Then he'll release the hostages when he's far enough away. I refused, of course. They asked for a doctor. Seems one of Brown's sons who's with him had been shot, but the doc says he's a goner. He said that aside from the hostages, there's only five of them left in there alive and unwounded, including Brown, who's storming around and waving Washington's pistol and his sword, shouting about hellfire, blood, and damnation. Crazy, like I said. Some of the locals wanted to storm the place, but I wouldn't let 'em, for fear of harming any of the hostages. Right now, it looks as if we've got a standoff."

"You did the right thing, Colonel," Robert said. "Troops are on the way. Keep your men from firing on that engine house. Too many of them have been drinking and we don't want any accidents. I'm going to go up there and try to have a word with Mr. Brown."

"It'll be a waste of time, if you ask me," said Baylor.

"Maybe," Robert said. "But maybe when he hears that troops are coming, he'll see it's hopeless and give himself up."

"What for?" asked Baylor. "He'll only hang. He's got nothing to lose anymore."

"Just the same, I have to try," said Robert. "There's no point to any further bloodshed."

He didn't tell Baylor his real reason for wanting to go up there for a parlay. He didn't want to insult the man. Baylor wasn't a professional soldier, and though his estimation of the situation seemed reasonably accurate, he didn't sound as if he was sure about how many men were in that engine house. In speaking to some of the people on the scene, Robert had heard estimates as to the original number of the raiders ranging from fifteen to eighteen to twenty to more than fifty. No one seemed really sure how many had been killed or how many had managed to escape. Colonel Lee would want a detailed report. He'd want to know their exact number and he'd want to know exactly how many hostages were in there and what sort of condition they were in, as well as what sort of weapons the barricaded raiders had. That was his job. It was why General Scott had sent him down here and Robert knew he'd have to find those things out for himself.

He drew his sword and tied his handkerchief to its blade. Then he handed his pistol to Baylor, held the sword up high over his head, and started to walk steadily and purposefully toward the engine house. It occurred to him there was every chance his flag of truce would not be respected, but Baylor had already sent one man up there for a parlay and he'd returned unscathed, as had the doctor, so the risk seemed justified. Just the same, he felt his stomach knotting up as he approached the heavy doors of the brick engine house.

"That's far enough!" a voice called out to him.

He stopped. "My name is Captain Robert Gallio," he called out, "of the army headquarters staff in Washington. I am unarmed. I would like a word with the gentleman who calls himself Osawatomie John Brown."

"Step up to the door."

Robert moved up to the door, which opened a crack, then opened a bit further to admit him. As he stepped inside someone behind the door reached out and grabbed him. He felt a pistol pressed up against his back. He was quickly searched.

"He's unarmed," a man said.

Someone took his sword from him. Robert quickly looked around. The hostages were all clustered together at the back of the engine house, under guard by two of the raiders. There were nine white men and several Negroes. All of them looked frightened. He quickly counted five raiders. One, a boy, was lying stretched out on the floor, motionless. He appeared to be dead.

"Mr. Brown?"

"I am John Brown, of Kansas," said a tall, gaunt-looking man standing several feet away. He turned from the window to approach him. He was dressed in a dark suit and a black hat. His long and heavy beard gave him the aspect of a biblical prophet. His eyes were deep set and intense. They seemed to glitter with a manic light. "Have you come to offer terms?" asked Brown.

"I have not that authority, Mr. Brown," said Robert. "I have been sent to ascertain precisely what the situation is here and to report to my commanding officer, Colonel Robert E. Lee, who should be arriving shortly along with a detachment of troops. It is Colonel Lee who will decide what terms to offer you, if any."

"Then why have you come to waste my time?" retorted Brown angrily.

"I have told you, Mr. Brown, that my duty is to give a full report of this situation to Colonel Lee when he arrives. In that light, might I ask why you have seized these people, and these premises, and what your intentions are?"

"I have already stated my intentions to those people out there," Brown replied. "I have come to liberate the slaves of this state and take them out of sinful bondage!"

"And did you seriously hope to accomplish this task with such a small force as you have?" asked Robert.

"I had expected help," said Brown glumly, and his face suddenly took on a woebegone expression that, in other circumstances, Robert might have found pathetic.

"I see," said Robert. "Might I ask from whom?"

"From God-fearing and right-thinking men who cry out against injustice!" Brown replied, brandishing Washington's sword. He turned away, looking toward the window. "But it appears that we have been abandoned, both by our fellowman and by Providence. Well, so be it." His mood suddenly shifted once again and he turned back to face Robert with fury in his eyes. "I had this town under my complete control and I could easily have murdered everybody in it! I have killed no unarmed men and yet those Philistines out there shot down two of my people under a flag of truce! Under the circumstances, I think we are entitled to some terms!"

Robert saw no point in pointing out that Brown had never had the town completely under his control. It was not his duty to argue with this man or to convince him of anything, merely to ascertain the facts for his report to Colonel Lee. However, he could not allow Brown's remark that he had killed no unarmed men to pass, since the deaths of the slain townspeople would surely have a bearing on whatever terms, if any, Lee chose to offer him.

"I beg to differ, Mr. Brown," he said, "but several unarmed men were, in fact, shot down by your raiders, among them the mayor of Harpers Ferry. It is unfortunate that your flag of truce was not respected, but I remind you that these townspeople are not military men and were enraged by the murder of their fellow citizens. And by your actions, you have committed treason against the state of Virginia and the United States."

"Is what we're doin' treason?" one of the raiders asked.

"Certainly," John Brown replied impatiently.

"Hell, I thought we just came here to free the slaves!" the man said. "I didn't know it was treason!"

"Be silent!" Brown commanded him. "Captain, if any unarmed men were killed, then it was done without my knowledge, I assure you, and I can only express my deep regret that it was done. My mission here has failed, and the fault is entirely my own, but I remind you that I hold hostages. You tell your superior officer that if he wishes the lives of these people to be spared, my men and I must have safe conduct, with our arms, and with our hostages, across the bridge and into Maryland. When I have satisfied myself that I am not being pursued, I shall release the hostages unharmed. Those are my terms, sir. And now we have nothing further to discuss."

Robert retrieved his sword and left the engine house, walking purposefully, but not quickly, wondering if he would get a bullet in the back. While he had been conferring with Brown, Lee arrived along with Stuart and a detachment of marines under Lieutenant Israel Green. He hurried to report to Lee.

"Robert," Lee greeted him with a curt nod, remembering him from his days as superintendent of West Point. "I am sorry that we must meet again under such conditions. What can you tell me about this situation?"

As quickly as possible Robert gave him his report. Lee listened silently, then nodded.

"The terms that this man asks are impossible to grant," he said. "We must bring this situation to a conclusion with all possible speed. Stuart, I want you to go up there under a flag of truce and tell Mr. Brown that his terms are unacceptable and that he must surrender immediately. If he refuses, then we shall storm the engine house at once with all possible speed. We will employ a party of a dozen picked men, with an equal number held in reserve. There is to be no firing, to avoid endangering the hostages. The men will employ their bayonets."

Lee then turned to Colonel Shriver, the commander of the militia company from nearby Frederick. "Colonel Shriver, do you wish to have the opportunity to make the assault?"

Shriver moistened his lips and looked uncomfortable. "My men have wives and children at home," he said. "I will not expose them to such risks. You and your men are paid for doing this kind of work."

Lee simply stared at him for a moment, then nodded, without comment. He then made the same offer to Colonel Baylor, and Robert realized that Lee, ever the gentleman, was merely doing so out of courtesy and with no real expectation Baylor would take him up on it. Nor did he. Lee then turned to Lieutenant Green, of the marines.

"Lieutenant, do you want the honor of taking your men out?"

Green snapped to attention. "I should be proud to, sir. Thank you very much."

Lee held out his hand and Green shook it earnestly.

"Select a dozen of your best men, Lieutenant," Lee said.

"Colonel," Robert said, "with your permission, I would like to accompany Lieutenant Green. Merely as one of the men under your command, Lieutenant," he added, aware of the difference in their rank.

"If the lieutenant has no objection," Lee said, politely deferring to Green.

"Be happy to have you along, sir," Green said to Robert. "May I offer you a musket?"

"No, thank you, Lieutenant, I'll use my sword," said Robert.

Green nodded. "Lieutenant Stuart, if Brown refuses to surrender, as I frankly expect he will, then speed will be of the utmost essence. The moment you clear the engine-house doors, get out of their line of fire, remove your hat, and wave it. That will be our signal for a charge."

"Right," said Stuart. Green proceeded to pick out his men and instruct them.

Lee finished writing something on a piece of paper, then handed it to Stuart. "Deliver this message to Mr. Brown," he said.

Stuart tied a white handkerchief to his sword and proceeded to walk quickly up to the engine house. In the meantime, with great stealth, Green and his men started to move in. Stuart watched them get into position as he approached the doors, then called out to the men inside.

From within the engine house a voice shouted, "Say your piece!"

Stuart took Lee's message and read it in a loud, clear voice. "Colonel Lee, United States Army, commanding the troops sent by the president of the United States to suppress the insurrection at this place, demands the surrender of the persons in the armory buildings. If they will peaceably surrender themselves and restore the pillaged property, they shall be kept in safety to await the orders of the president. Colonel Lee represents to them, in all frankness, that it is impossible for them to escape, that the armory is surrounded on all sides by troops, and that if he is compelled to take them by force, he cannot answer for their safety."

There was a long moment of silence, then the engine-house door opened slightly, and through the crack, Stuart saw the grim-visaged John Brown, holding a cocked carbine in his hands, aimed straight at him.

Standing at a distance, Lee tensed. The moment of truth had arrived. With Brown knowing that no terms were to be offered except immediate surrender, there was nothing to prevent him from shooting that brave officer.

"I want parole for my men to leave this building undisturbed and cross the bridge," said Brown, reiterating his demands. "The hostages shall be released unharmed only when I have been fully satisfied that there is no pursuit. Those are my terms, sir!"

"And you have heard the terms offered by Colonel Lee," said Stuart. "I am not authorized to offer any others."

From behind Brown, several of the hostages began to shout at once, fearful for their safety, insisting that Lee amend his terms. And then another loud voice overpowered the others and cut clearly through the din.

"Never mind us! Fire!"

From where he stood, Lee heard the shout and recognized the voice of his old friend Colonel Lewis Washington. He smiled and murmured, "The old revolutionary blood does tell."

Brown shouted for silence and the din from the hostages ceased. "Tell your commander that he shall have to offer better terms than that," he said to Stuart.

"You have heard the only terms he is prepared to offer," Stuart replied. "Be sensible, man. Resistance is futile. Give it up."

"Well, I see we can't agree, Lieutenant," Brown said. "You have the numbers on me, but I'm not afraid of death. I'd as soon die by a bullet as on the gallows."

"Is that your final answer?" Stuart asked.

"It is."

Stuart immediately stepped away from the door, flattened himself against the brick wall, and waved his hat. Robert, standing beside Green and his dozen marines, saw Green glance back toward Lee. Lee casually raised his hand. Green barked out a command and three of the marines immediately attacked the door with sledgehammers.

They had moved forward so quickly, the men inside had no vantage point from which to fire at them. The doors shivered under the impact of the hammers, but they held. Robert looked around quickly and spotted a long, heavy wooden ladder. He grabbed Green's arm and pointed to it. Green comprehended instantly. He directed his men to take the ladder and use it as a battering ram. From inside, someone fired a shot as the marines rushed forward with the ladder. The heavy wooden doors gave slightly with the impact, but did not break. On the second try, the wood splintered and caved in.

Keeping low, Robert rushed in with his sword drawn and ducked down behind the fire engine to his left. He was closely

followed by Lieutenant Green. As the marines rushed in behind
them the raiders inside opened fire. One of the marines cried out,
clutched at his stomach, and went down. Using the fire engine for
cover, Robert quickly ran toward the rear of the engine house,
where the hostages were being kept. Someone fired from beneath
the fire engine and Robert felt the ball whistle past him, then one
of the marines spotted the man who'd shot and stabbed beneath
the engine with his bayonet. Robert heard the man cry out, but
he paid no heed as he rushed toward the hostages.

The engine house quickly became filled with gunsmoke and the
sulfurous smell of burned powder, so it was almost impossible to
see. One of the raiders screamed as he was pinned to the wall by
a bayonet. Robert came around the rear of the fire engine and
saw Colonel Washington, standing with the other hostages. Beside
him, kneeling and raising his carbine, was John Brown. Without
pausing, Robert rushed forward, raising his sword, and slashed at
the fanatic abolitionist before he could fire. Brown recoiled from
the flashing sword and caught the cut on his neck. Robert lunged
with his sword and ran him through. The blade went into the left
side of Brown's chest and bent sharply as it struck a rib. Brown
fell without a sound, unconscious.

A shot cracked out behind him and Robert felt something pluck
at the lieutenant's insignia on his right shoulder. He spun around
in time to see Stuart run the shooter through with his sword. He
pulled the bloody blade free as the man went down, then smiled
and tossed off a fencer's salute to Robert. With a grin, Robert
returned it. He felt exhilarated. It seemed as if he could actually
feel the blood pounding through his veins! So this is what it's like
to be in combat, he thought. God, it was marvelous!

It was all over in a matter of minutes. The powder smoke hung
in the air like a thick fog. Robert turned to Colonel Washington.
"Are you all right, sir? How do you feel?"

"Hungry as a hound and dry as a powder horn," Washington
replied calmly. "I believe I could do with a drink."

Outside, a large crowd had gathered. As the marines kept
back the curious onlookers, John Brown was carried out of the
engine house and laid on the ground, where Stuart relieved him
of his bowie knife to keep for a souvenir. As soon as Brown
regained consciousness Lee had him taken to an office in a nearby
building, where Congressman Boteler, Senator Mason, Governor
Wise, Congressman Vallendigham of Ohio, Colonel Washington,
and Congressman Faulkner of Virginia all gathered to interrogate

him. Standing slightly behind Lee and Stuart, Robert thought, how quickly the vultures gather.

"Captain Brown," said Boteler, inexplicably addressing him as if he were a military man, "what brought you here?"

"I came to free your slaves," said Brown sullenly.

"How did you expect to do it, with the small force that you brought?"

"I expected help."

"From whites as well as blacks?"

"I did."

The congressman then asked Brown if he was disappointed not to get that help, and it was all Robert could do to keep from snorting with derision at the stupidity of the question. Lee then interrupted the interrogation softly and told the wounded prisoner that if he was uncomfortable, he could bar all visitors, but Brown replied he was glad for the opportunity to make his motives understood. The men all peppered him with questions. Brown answered freely, but refused to implicate anyone else in what he'd done, insisting no one had financed his effort save himself, out of his own pocket, and claiming once again that had he wanted to, he could easily have burned the town and slain all its inhabitants, but had refrained from doing so.

"How do you justify your acts?" Senator Mason asked him.

Brown turned his piercing gaze upon the legislator. "I think, my friend, that you are guilty of a great wrong against God and humanity. I say it without wishing to be offensive. And it would be perfectly right in anyone to interfere with you so far as to free those you willfully and wickedly hold in bondage. I do not say this insultingly."

"I understand that," Mason replied.

"I think I did right," continued Brown, "and that others will do right to interfere with you at any time and all times. I hold that the Golden Rule, 'Do unto others as you would have them do unto you,' applies to all who help others gain their liberty."

"But you don't believe in the Bible," Stuart said.

"Certainly, I do," said Brown.

"The wages of sin is death," said Stuart, fixing the abolitionist with a level gaze.

Brown calmly met his gaze. "I would not have made such a remark to you if you had been a prisoner and wounded in my hands."

Robert had enough. He left the office and went outside. Most of the crowd had dispersed, most likely to the saloons, to regale each other with tales, both factual and fanciful, of their part in the adventure. He stared up at the night sky. It seemed as if he could still smell the smoke of gunpowder in the air. He'd had his first taste of combat. It had been thrilling and exhilarating, filling him with an exuberance unlike anything he'd ever felt before.

Why now, he thought, do I feel so strangely empty?

BOOK TWO

If you want to have fun,
If you want to see Hell,
If you want to catch the Devil,
Join the Cavalry. . . .

CHAPTER ONE

West Point, New York, February 1861

CADET MARK GALLIO, crisply attired in his dress gray uniform and white cross belts, his polished breastplate gleaming in the sun, halted, about-faced, and smartly transferred his musket from his right to his left shoulder. At the other end of the path, near the academic building, Cadet George Armstrong Custer did the same. Then they started marching toward each other at a slow and steady pace. They would meet in the middle and pass each other, Gallio heading toward the academic building, Custer toward the chapel, then halt, about-face, and march back again.

For both cadets, it was an old and all too familiar routine. The practice was known in cadet parlance as "walking an extra," or serving extra sentinel duty on a Saturday, as punishment, when the other cadets had free time to themselves. As they walked their post they were not supposed to speak to anyone, or to each other, and keep their eyes looking straight ahead. For obvious reasons, they had been ordered not to march side by side, but from opposite ends of their post. However, had the two cadets been strict observers of academy regulations, they would not have been there in the first place, and so, as they approached each other—after a quick glance out of the corners of their eyes to make sure they were unobserved—they would slow down slightly and exchange a few words as they passed each other on the path.

It was a rather time-consuming way to conduct a conversation, but they were both old hands at this sort of thing, having trod the paths of the Academy enough times to walk all the way to New York City and back. They had once tried to reckon the number of miles they had walked in this manner, but had lost track about halfway through their plebe year and given up.

The subject of their current, abbreviated discussion was a long letter written by Maria, which Mark had just received. Maria wrote regularly, seperate letters to Mark and to their father, and the tone of those letters differed accordingly. By unspoken agreement, neither father nor son showed his correspondence to the other, though they often discussed the contents. Mark knew Maria was much more open with her feelings when she wrote to him than when she wrote to the major, because she did not want to cause him any more distress than he already felt. And that was considerable.

She was heartbroken that Travis and Robert had quarreled on the night Robert left for Washington, D.C., and his new assignment as General Scott's aide. Apparently, the rift was permanent, and though she had tried everything she could think of since the day it happened, there seemed to be nothing she could do to mend it. Travis knew she wrote to Robert and that Robert wrote back, and he did not object to it, but he had told her in no uncertain terms he no longer wished to hear Robert's name mentioned in his presence. Mark could clearly envision Travis making the pronouncement, all stiff and formal with affronted Southern honor. Custer thought Travis Coulter was a pompous ass and Mark was in complete agreement with his friend's assessment of his brother-in-law.

From what Maria had been able to piece together of the incident, from the little Travis said about it before forever closing the subject to discussion, and from Robert's letters, which had been more forthcoming, Robert had gravely offended him by saying he would be traitor to his country if he put the interests of his state above those of the Union, or words to that effect. And it was only for the sake of their past friendship, and for Maria's sake as well, that Travis had refrained from seeking satisfaction.

"Robert only told the truth," Custer said. "Coulter took an oath to serve his country. To forsake that oath is treason."

They marched on steadily, in opposite directions, halted, about-faced, and marched back.

"Apparently, Travis doesn't see it that way," Mark replied, on the next pass.

He knew both Travis and his brother were proud and stubborn men. Neither would ever admit he was wrong. So poor Maria had to suffer. For her sake, at least, if not for that of their long-standing friendship, he would have thought the two of them could come to terms and at least agree to disagree without completely severing their relationship, but Travis had his chivalric Southern notions about honor and would not even consider mending fences without a formal apology and a retraction. Robert, of course, would not do either, firmly believing he was in the right. And now that the Southern states had formally seceded from the Union, the situation seemed completely irretrievable.

South Carolina had, not surprisingly, been the first to go. The state convention had voted to secede in December, shortly after Lincoln was elected, and Mississippi, Florida, and Alabama had followed in the second week of January. Then Georgia had voted to secede, followed by Louisiana and Texas. Cadets at the Academy were saying that Tennessee would probably go next. No one could seem to agree about the border slave states, which of them would be the next to go and which would remain loyal or neutral, but of one thing everyone was certain. There would be war. It was now only a question of when the first shots would be fired.

Shots had, in fact, already been fired, though no one was yet willing to call it war. Shortly after voting to secede, South Carolina had sent representatives to President Buchanan, demanding that all federal troops be removed from Charleston. Major Robert Anderson, commander of the forts in Charleston harbor, had anticipated trouble and had moved his troops from the dilapidated Fort Moultrie to the more defensible Fort Sumter, the interior of which had still not been completed.

The lame-duck President Buchanan, who had long been sympathetic to the Southern states and had tried to straddle fences throughout his term of office, found himself unable to vacillate this time. Anderson, it seemed, had acted on his own authority, or at the very least on a very liberal interpretation of his orders from the War Department. He had seen the writing on the wall and had exercised sound military judgment, Mark thought, and most people in the North were of the same opinion. By quietly transferring his command in the dead of the night, under the very noses of the Carolinians, Major Anderson had become a hero to most Northerners and the Southerners were absolutely furious.

Anderson had earlier requested reinforcements and Buchanan had not sent them, seeking to avoid antagonizing the South Carolina representatives. In return, South Carolina promised to make no hostile moves against the forts while the negotiations for their transfer were proceeding. Buchanan had been stalling, hoping to pass the headache on to Lincoln, but Anderson had forced the issue. South Carolina claimed Anderson's moving his garrison to Sumter was a breach of faith and an open act of war. Buchanan was left with no alternative but to make some sort of commitment. The Southerners among his cabinet had resigned in disgust and their places had been filled by strong supporters of the Union, who had argued that if Anderson were ordered back to Moultrie to appease South Carolina, it would be perceived as a disgrace and a surrender and Buchanan would lose all respect and credibility. So, for once making a firm decision, Buchanan had not only refused to order Anderson back, but had agreed to send him reinforcements.

Unfortunately, the matter was not handled with discretion and the newspapers had reported that two hundred soldiers had been dispatched to Charleston on the merchant ship *Star of the West*. The result was South Carolina had been warned of the ship's arrival and their guns had fired on the vessel when it tried to come into the harbor. The ship had taken a hit and her captain came about and headed back out to sea. Had Fort Sumter returned the fire, the war might have started there and then, but Anderson, amazingly, had not been notified that reinforcements were arriving and had received no orders. He was, perhaps, the only one who didn't know what was going on, and so he refrained from acting, not wishing to take it on himself to start a war.

In the meantime, other forts throughout the South were being seized. In Georgia, troops of the state militia took over Fort Pulaski, Fort Jackson, and the arsenal in Augusta. In Alabama, Fort Gaines and Fort Morgan were seized by state militia, and in Florida, troops commandeered Fort Marion and the arsenal at Apalachicola. There had been no resistance offered in any of these actions, except at Fort Barrancas, in Pensacola, where the small body of troops at the garrison had fired on an equally small force that attempted to advance upon them. In Louisiana, Fort St. Philip, Fort Jackson, and the arsenal at Baton Rouge were taken by state troops, along with Fort Pike and the military hospital in New Orleans. Mississippi troops had seized Fort Massachusetts, on Ship Island. And still, incredibly, Mark thought, the government was not willing to concede that this was war.

At the beginning of the month, the peace convention had been organized in Washington, under the leadership of former President Tyler, which seemed rather ludicrous to Mark, since none of the seceded states were represented, and besides, what was the purpose of a peace convention if no one was willing to admit there

was a war? Even as the pointless convention met, representatives
of the seceded states, many of them men who had left Congress
when their states had left the Union, assembled in Montgomery
to elect the officers of their new government. Jefferson Davis, the
former secretary of war, was chosen to be president of the Confederate States of America. Meanwhile, President-elect Lincoln,
en route to his inauguration, was acting like a campaigner on
a whistle-stop tour, making speeches to crowds at every stop
and insisting the crisis was "artificial." It seemed to Mark as if
everyone in the government had lost their senses.

As these events proceeded, Maria's letters had grown more
and more despondent. Travis had resigned his commission when
South Carolina left the Union and had left Carlysle Barracks,
taking Maria with him back to Charleston, where they took up
residence in the Coulter household. Maria was happy to be with
Becky once again, but her delight was dampened by the sad
circumstances of their reunion and by her awkward situation. She
felt like a stranger in a strange land, a Yankee in a hostile country,
and though no one in Charleston had mistreated her in any way,
she nevertheless sensed their discomfort in her presence. Travis
had immediately sought service with the state militia and was
now a captain in the forces guarding Charleston under General
Beauregard.

"At least Coulter and your brother are in the thick of it," said
Custer as he approached, "while we march back and forth like
fools."

Mark was about to make a quick reply, but as they drew even
with each other a sudden loud commotion broke out behind him.
Involuntarily, he stopped and glanced over his shoulder. A group
of about twenty cadets had come out of the mess hall, carrying two
other cadets on their shoulders. They started heading boisterously
in the direction of the steamboat landing.

Custer had stopped as he drew even with Mark and quickly
looked around to make sure no one was watching. "Ball and
Kelley," he said, recognizing the two cadets who were being
borne up by their comrades.

"Leaving for the South?" asked Mark, turning around to face
in the same direction.

Custer nodded. "They're all leaving, damn their eyes," he said.
"But it's hard to fault a man for following his conscience."

They took an oath, thought Mark, just as George had said, and
to forsake that oath, as Travis had forsaken it, was treason. And

yet, according to Maria, Travis did not see it that way. What he had done was not desertion in the face of the enemy. He had formally resigned, just as Ball and Kelley had, and in his view, that resignation had freed him from all obligations of loyalty and service. Mark thought it strange the government had taken no steps whatever to prevent Southern cadets and officers from resigning and going back to their native states. What did they think these men were going to do? There was no question of their remaining neutral in the coming conflict. They would join the forces of the Confederacy, giving the rebels the benefit of the military training they'd acquired at the expense of the government, employing that training to oppose that very government.

Perhaps the men in Washington thought it chivalrous and proper to allow these men to choose according to their conscience, but from a purely military standpoint, it was foolhardy. Suppose the government had refused to accept their resignations? Then these gentlemen of the South would still be bound by their oath of office and would be unable to seek refuge in the fine distinction of their resignation freeing them from their sworn duty.

Mark knew his fellow cadets and he knew the value they placed on their honor. Under such circumstances, he did not believe many of them would have left, much as they might have wished to. For that matter, the government could easily have ordered the arrest and detention of any persons in the military who tendered their resignations. He was not convinced of the legality of such a move, but with war a virtual reality and these men obviously leaving to join the service of the enemy, it seemed a perfectly reasonable course to take. As it was, the Confederacy would desperately need a trained officer corps and the Union was providing them with it.

As they spotted Mark and Custer from their vantage point atop the others' shoulders, Ball and Kelley raised their hats to them in a gesture of farewell.

"Oh, hell," said Custer. *"Ah-ten-hut!"*

Both he and Mark snapped to.

"Pre-sent . . . arms!"

Moving smartly in unison, the two cadets brought their muskets to present, saluting their departing comrades.

Charleston, South Carolina, April 1861

And so it had begun at last. Outside, in the streets, the city of Charleston was celebrating its victory. Fort Sumter had fallen.

Yet, as she sat writing in her journal in the silent shelter of her room, Maria could see no cause for celebration. She felt as if she should weep, and yet her eyes were dry. She could not summon up the tears. She felt as if she should cry out in anger and frustration, and yet she could not find the voice to do so. She felt a void within her, an emptiness such as she had never felt before. Most of all, she felt afraid.

She remembered, not so very long ago, when she first saw Fort Sumter as their ship sailed into Charleston harbor. Even then, she was full of apprehensions about the new life she had embarked upon. She had left behind all that was familiar to her, everything she held near and dear, save for her husband, the man around whom she would build her life, the bulwark of all her hopes and dreams. Even then, she saw those dreams begin to fade, like an early-morning mist burned away by the harsh light of the sun. Oh, what a rude awakening it was!

She often wondered if she was alone in feeling as she did. Did other women feel the same when the expectations of romance were disappointed by the realities of marriage? Did the fault lie with her, in having dreamed too vividly, and in expecting that dream not to dissipate when she awoke? Enough, she thought. The cruel disappointment of her girlish dreams not being fulfilled was a paltry thing compared with the nightmare confronting them all now.

All yesterday, they had watched from the rooftop as Fort Sumter was bombarded. It began just before the first gray light of dawn, when after repeated demands for Major Anderson to surrender, Beauregard had opened fire with his howitzers and mortars. Running low on food, Anderson had sent a message, stating that if Beauregard did not batter him to pieces, he and his command would be starved out in a few days. However, with the ships carrying federal supplies and reinforcements standing just outside the harbor, Beauregard could afford to wait no longer. The first shot of the war was fired at four-thirty in the morning as the harbor batteries began to shell the fort. To the people of Charleston, it was like a grand fireworks display. Maria could not imagine what it must have been like to the men inside the fort.

With the siege under way, the federal reinforcements could only stand off and watch as the guns hammered at the fort relentlessly, all through the day and into the night and the next morning. There had never been any doubt about the outcome. All Anderson could do, at best, was return the fire ineffectually, putting up a token resistance until, finally, with provisions running low, he had no choice but to surrender. Ironically, the only casualty had occurred after the fort had fallen.

Major Anderson had requested, as part of the surrender terms, to fire one last salute to his flag before hauling it down and Beauregard had graciously agreed. While the salute was being fired a burning ember had fallen into some powder and ignited it. Five of Anderson's men were injured in the resulting explosion and one was killed. The first fatality of the war was a private who had died in a senseless accident. A grim omen, indeed, as if fate were commenting ironically on the conflict.

Irony was piled upon irony. Beauregard had been a graduate of West Point, where his gunnery instructor had been none other than Major Robert Anderson. As the weary soldiers from Fort Sumter marched to the wharf to board a vessel from the fleet sent to reinforce them, the soldiers of the Confederacy stood by silently, with their caps removed as a gesture of respect. No one raised a cheer.

Afterward, the city celebrated, and downstairs in the Coulter household, the parlor had been packed with visitors proposing toasts to General Beauregard, to President Davis, to the Confederate States of America, and to victory. Maria felt like a specter at the wedding and she had excused herself and gone upstairs.

For a long time she simply sat in silence, waiting for the tears to come. But the release of tears eluded her. Outside, in the streets, she could hear the sounds of celebration. Inside, she felt hollow, as if she were completely drained of emotion. She thought to write a letter to her father, or to Mark or Robert, but after dipping her pen into the inkwell, she could not think how to begin. She laid her pen aside, went over to her trunk, and dug out the journals her father had given her to keep. The journals of the Roman tribune Valerius Gallio, whose writings she had listened to so often at her father's knee. As she looked through them she wondered how many times, over the centuries, they had been painstakingly copied by her ancestors so the record they had left could be preserved. The originals must have long since crumbled into dust.

She handled them with reverence. They had become her friends, her solace in the quiet moments when she was alone. She often stole out of bed at night and took them out to read by candlelight. Travis didn't know about them. He slept soundly, like a dead man, never moving, often with his arms crossed on his chest in a bizarre, unconscious parody of a corpse laid out in a coffin.

In the first month of their marriage, he had made love to her every night and often in the morning, too. She thought of it just that way, that he made love *to* her, and not *with* her, always with the same rough impatience, like the first time, in a way that never varied. His eager mouth would bruise her lips, his hands would knead her breasts as if they were bread dough, his groping fingers would thrust into her to make her wet, and sometimes he did not even bother with these brief and rough preliminaries, but simply entered her, forcing himself inside, murmuring meaningless endearments as he pounded away at her, faster and faster, harder and harder, till she had to grit her teeth with pain, and then collapsing on her, spent, he would lie still for a few moments, breathing heavily, then roll off and over onto his side, always with his back to her until he fell asleep. Then, in his sleep, he would roll over onto his back and cross his arms on his chest, mouth slightly open, and remain absolutely motionless until he woke up in the morning. Maria no longer tried to speak to him when they were in bed together. She could no longer bear to hear the words, "Hush, now, hush, my darling." They made her want to scream.

In the second month of her marriage, he no longer seemed to want her every night, and only rarely in the morning. In the third month, perhaps once or twice a week. Then less and less and less. Maria did not feel deprived. The thought had crossed her mind that he might have found a mistress, perhaps even more than one, and it was with a bitter melancholy that she realized she did not really care. If there was someone else to spare her from the not-so-tender ministrations of his lust, so much the better. She possessed no more illusions about romantic love. It was the stuff of poems and novels. Knights in shining armor seemed glamorous and noble only from afar. Up close, the odor of their sweaty bodies was oppressive, the bristle of their beards would scratch the skin, and the calluses on their hands made for rough caresses.

She knew Travis would be kept busy with the guests downstairs for hours yet, replying to all their eager questions, regaling them with tales of his exploits at the guns. When he came, she would hear his heavy tread on the stairs and there would be time for her to hide the journal she had selected. This one thing, he would not own. She was his wife, and she now bore his name and lived in the household of his family, but so long as she maintained the secret of the journals, she would have at least one thing that was her own. He had said to her, "You are a Coulter now," but in the quiet, stolen hours she shared with the memories of her Roman ancestor, she could take refuge in who she really was.

She would remain a Gallio.

The Journal of Valerius Marcus Gallio, Cisalpine Gaul, January 49 B.C.

It is the eve of a momentous occasion, an event without precedent in Roman history, and sleep eludes me as I sit alone in my tent and write these words by lamplight. The tension can be felt throughout the entire body of the legion and one perceives the sense of apprehension as well as that of great anticipation.

This evening, as I stood outside my tent in the *praetorium,* I could see the cookfires of my fellow legionnaires all around me, and the flickering flames brought to mind the vision of a flock of fireflies at twilight. Under normal circumstances, on a march or even on the eve of battle, this is a time when soldiers gathered around their fires converse freely in animated tones, taking their ease in the company of comrades or bolstering one another's spirits for the coming strife. One hears shouts and song and laughter. But on this night, all was quiet. There was not a man within the camp who did not know what we would embark upon come sunrise, and what would result from what we were about to do.

As it occurs to me that I am writing for posterity, and for the edification of those who shall come after me, perhaps I should take this opportunity to describe our current situation and the circumstances that attend it. For those who may not be familiar with the manner in which Rome's legions make their camp while on the march, I will briefly describe the procedure that is followed, as it may be of some interest.

Whenever possible, according to the terrain in which we find ourselves, we try to make our camp upon the slope of a hill, in open country and away from wooded areas. The reasoning behind this has to do with military strategy. Making camp near wooded areas would give an enemy the opportunity to make a sudden attack from concealment, and camping in open country denies him this advantage. It is to our advantage, also, to make camp upon a slope so that in the event of an attack, an opposing force must attack uphill, and the disadvantage to the enemy in such a case is obvious. Following this plan, the entrance gates of the camp are always located on the downslope and the rear gates at the crest.

Surrounding the entire camp are earthworks, in the form of a wall built up of soil taken from a ditch that is dug all around the camp, to a depth of nine feet and a width of twelve. The wall itself is always built up to the same dimensions, ten feet high and six feet wide. The reason for the width of six feet is so there will be ample room for defenders to stand atop the wall and hurl their javelins. Timber and brush are used to reinforce the earthworks. The ramparts, if occasion should demand it, may have wooden towers placed upon them, from which archers can shoot down at an advancing enemy. On this occasion, as it was only a temporary camp, we had no need of towers.

The interior of the camp is always laid out in a rectangle, which is divided into three roughly equal parts. These divisions are marked off by two broad streets, the *via principalis* and the *via quintana*, which run the entire length of the camp. The *praetorium* is that section of the camp where the headquarters are located, and where I have my tent, and it is situated in the exact center of the camp. Directly behind the *praetorium* is the *quaestorium*, that section of the camp where hostages, prisoners, booty, forage, and supplies are kept. At the front of the camp is the *praetentura*, which is separated from the *praetorium* by the *via principalis*. One quarter of the cohorts are camped in this section, their tents facing the wall, on either side of the *via praetoria*, the street that leads from the entrance gates to the center of the camp. Here, also, camped between the center and the cohorts, is half the cavalry, the archers and the slingers, situated so that they may quickly move out through the entrance gates to form an advance guard in the event of an attack.

The remainder of the cohorts and the cavalry are disposed on either side of the *praetorium*, as well as in the rear of the camp. Just inside the wall, and running around the entire perimeter of the camp, is a broad street 120 feet wide. This has been found to be the optimum amount of space for the movement of troops defending the walls, as well as to prevent hostile missiles from coming in over the wall and reaching the tents. There are also many smaller streets running the length and width of the camp, separating each cohort from the one beside it.

The plan is such that everything is laid out with logical precision, with a specific allotment of space for the tents, the pack animals, the slaves, and the stacking of weapons. There is no variation from this plan so that our soldiers are well drilled at setting up the camp. Each man works for one hour before he is relieved while other troops form a protective front to cover those doing the work and detachments of cavalry scout the area to provide security. Everything is done with practiced efficiency. If we begin to dig the ditch for the earthworks at midday, the entire task of setting up the camp can be completed before sunset. There is no other army in the world that can match the Roman legions in the field and I am proud to say that I serve as praetor in the finest army ever fielded by Rome, the legions of Gaius Julius Caesar.

Our campaigns in Gaul have covered Rome with glory. As I sit here and reflect upon all we have accomplished I can say with pride that we have subjugated all of Gaul to Roman authority, from the Pyrennees to the Alps, from the Rhine to the Rhone rivers. In our long years of campaigning, we have taken over eight hundred towns, conquered three hundred states, and killed over a million of the enemy, taking as many prisoner. Our glorious general has sent lavish gifts in slaves and booty to the citizens of Rome. He has accomplished all that was asked of him and more. And what is his reward for all these years of faithful, gallant service? Has the Senate seen fit to grant our general a triumph so he may enter Rome in the honored glory he deserves? Glory that we, his loyal and faithful troops, may share with him? No. They have not seen fit to do so. Instead, we have been ordered to disband. We are told the wars are over and Rome has no further need of us. And yet, if this were so, what reason to deny our general the triumph he so well deserves?

The answer to that question is as simple as it is contemptible. Pompey is afraid of Caesar. He considers him a threat to the power that he wields. Once a loyal friend of Caesar's and the greatest general of Rome, Pompey as a statesman has become a Crassus with his power, hoarding it like gold, and he has fallen prey to the evil whisperings of Caesar's enemies. The men around him are corrupt, and Pompey has become corrupt as well. No sooner had Caesar left the city to take his post as provincial governor of Gaul than his former quaestor was brought up on charges of malfeasance in his duties, as part of Pompey's plot to discredit Caesar in the eyes of the citizens of Rome and lay the groundwork for the false charges he planned to bring against him.

And what sort of man is this Caesar, whom they fear so much? Let a soldier who has served with him describe him so that those who read these words will see him clearly, as his troops have seen him. As a man, he is rather plain to look upon, though his appearance is not at all displeasing. He is tall and fair, with the face of a scholar and a somewhat melancholy gaze. His eyes are brown and his forehead is high. Given his many admirable qualities, he may be excused the vanity he exercises in combing what little hair he has over his forehead, and his fastidiousness in keeping his hair carefully trimmed and his face and body depilated is more a matter of cleanliness than vanity. It is this practice, perhaps, that had led his enemies to refer to him as a woman, though never to his face, as they are a venal and a cowardly lot.

I will tell more about this "woman" whom Pompey and the Senate fear so. Caesar has the falling sickness, which has incapacitated many lesser men, and yet it has not prevented him from achieving greatness that not only rivals, but surpasses that of Pompey. He strives to keep the fits at bay with exercise and moderate diet. As a speaker, he possesses considerable gifts, having studied rhetoric in the school of Apollonius of Rhodes, and on the many occasions when he has addressed his troops, as he has always done on the eve of any battle, he spoke to them as man to men, warmly, as a comrade in arms, and with heartfelt emotion. The welfare of his men always came first, before he saw to his own, and unlike many generals, he did not surround himself with luxuries, but lived as his men lived and ate the food they ate.

Though he is a skilled horseman, as he is skilled with the sword, he has often led his men on foot, marching with them like an ordinary soldier. He possesses powers of endurance beyond those of many men, and has often covered over a hundred miles in one day, traveling in light carriages, upon the worst of roads, or where there were no roads at all, at twice the ordinary pace. I have often seen him dictate letters and reports to his secretaries, often as many as four or five at the same time, with never a stray thought or hesitation. He composes poems and scholarly works and has kept an accurate and detailed chronicle of our campaigns in Gaul. His energy is boundless.

In battle, he is completely without fear. As a commander, he is innovative, unpredictable, and brilliant, with a versatility that allows him to easily adapt his strategy to any given situation, no matter how difficult or unexpected. This man, whom his enemies in Rome describe as vain, arrogant, corrupt, self-seeking, and unmanly, is loved by every soldier under his command as no troops have ever loved their general. We would follow him to the far ends of the earth. And tomorrow, we shall follow him where no Roman troops have ever been led by a Roman general before. To the gates of Rome itself.

There is not a man in camp tonight who does not know what this shall mean. Tomorrow, when we cross the Rubicon and march on Rome, it will mean civil war. We, who have fought so hard and for so long to uphold the glory that is Rome's, will now be forced to fight our fellow Romans, and the thought weighs heavily upon us all.

Tonight, the camp is silent, yet few men are asleep. Caesar himself remains awake. I have left him only a short while ago and he was pacing anxiously inside his tent, the strain of his responsibility clearly written on his features.

For my own part, I wish there was some way this bloody conflict that lies ahead of us could be avoided, but the die is cast, and our fortunes now have been cast as chaff upon the wind. There is no avoiding what lies ahead of us, and we must all be stoic as we face our fate. Long ago, the gods decreed that our footsteps would be set upon this path and we must follow where it leads.

My heart is heavy, but I have no fear. I feel confident that we shall prevail. Rome shall survive this coming conflict, and it shall emerge from it to greater glory, but first it must be purged, and purged with blood. As a Roman, I shall take up arms against my fellow Romans, and do so with great regret and pain, but I will do my duty as my fathers before me have done theirs. Tomorrow, I shall follow Caesar, for the greater good, and for the greatest glory.

CHAPTER TWO

Sudley Ford, Virginia, July 1861

IT WASN'T SO much a movement of troops as it was a disorganized ramble, and as Robert stood outside his tent and smoked his pipe he was filled with apprehension about what would happen in the morning. General McDowell seemed confident, or at least pretended to be, but Robert could make no such pretense. Even if the troops, somehow, miraculously, proved capable come morning, there seemed to be more things that could go wrong than he could think of.

Somehow, the rebels had gotten wind of their plans and reinforcements had arrived. Spies, undoubtedly, thought Robert, it was impossible to keep anything secret in Washington for long, and all the time they had wasted on the march was time for the rebels to prepare. In the morning, he would see his first real battle, but it was a battle that would be fought by men who knew next to nothing about being soldiers. He had asked to come on this campaign, to learn and gain experience, but what he had learned so far was not encouraging and what he had experienced was nothing but frustration.

His duties with General Scott had kept him busy throughout the months of April and May, but somehow the time still seemed to drag on interminably. His new assignment at the War Department was both a lot more and lot less than what he had expected. In the beginning, it was exciting to be stationed in the capital, working for the legendary General Winfield Scott and meeting such famous men as Secretary of State William Seward; the former vice-president, Senator John Breckenridge; Treasury Secretary Salmon Chase, whom many had spoken of as the next president before Lincoln had been nominated; the powerful and

135

influential Francis P. Blair; Secretary of the Navy Gideon Wells and Secretary of War Simon Cameron and the president himself, whom he saw not merely on one or two occasions, as he had thought might happen, but frequently enough that the president always greeted him by name. In fact, President Lincoln had remembered his name from the first time they met, a very brief meeting at a time when the president was seeing a seemingly endless stream of people, and yet he had remembered, which was the first indication Robert had that Abraham Lincoln was more than what he appeared to be.

He was, thought Robert, a peculiar-looking man, tall and gangling, with long arms and legs and a melancholy face, a somewhat squeaky, folksy way of speaking, and a rather shambling manner. His clothes never quite seemed to fit correctly, although they did, it was just something about the way he wore them. The president often took his shoes off and liked to put his feet up, as if he were still a country lawyer relaxing in his Illinois office, and he had a most unpresidential habit of storing papers in his stovepipe hat, which exaggerated his already considerable height.

Robert's initial impression of the president wasn't very favorable. Behind his back, some people referred to him in a derogatory manner as "the gorilla," and there was, indeed, something vaguely simian about him. He did not act like a head of state. He was informality incarnate. During the campaign, he had been "Old Abe" or "Abe, the Rail-splitter" or "Honest Abe," but in the White House no one called him Abe and hardly anyone called him "Mr. President." More often than not, it was simply "Lincoln," just as the cadets at West Point had often called each other by their last names. To Robert, who always made a point of addressing him as "Mr. President" and "sir," it seemed highly disrespectful, but the president seemed either not to notice or not to care.

One of the first things Robert found surprising about the president was his accessibility. Congressmen, senators, and cabinet members would simply walk in unannounced, as if they were entering their own home, and though it was usually necessary to get past one of Mr. Lincoln's two young secretaries, either Mr. Hay or Mr. Nicolay, they would simply breeze into the office as if they were entering a saloon. Every day the president would set aside the time to speak with anyone who came to see him, anyone at all, from office seekers to people off the street who came to tell him how to run the country or seek favors or even, on occasion, to ask him for a loan! Robert's first impression was one of slight dismay. What sort of man was this to run the country at a time when the nation faced its greatest crisis?

Yet, from their second meeting onward, Robert's assessment of the president began to change. For all his folksy manner and country bumpkin ways, there was a lot more to the president than met the eye. General Scott held him in high regard and Robert knew a man like Winfield Scott did not bestow his respect lightly. Robert did not have any significant personal intercourse with the president, but he was often present when Lincoln spoke with Scott, or with some members of his cabinet or other politicians, some of whom addressed him in a manner that Robert found not only disrespectful, but highly condescending. Yet he noticed that Lincoln always listened to what any of them had to say, gave the appearance of accepting it without argument, then quietly but firmly did what he intended all along.

After the fall of Fort Sumter, President Lincoln had issued a proclamation calling for seventy-five thousand militia for a ninety-day period of enlistment. War had still not been officially declared. Only Congress had the power to declare war and Congress was not in session at the time. The president had called a special session for the Fourth of July, but in the meantime he took the initial conduct of the war upon himself. At first, things had looked promising, indeed. The fall of Fort Sumter had galvanized public opinion throughout the North, and it looked as if there would be no shortage of volunteers. Ohio had been asked to supply six regiments and they wanted to send twenty. Massachusetts said that troops were on the way. But the governors of the so-called neutral states had protested the president's call for troops.

Governor Letcher of Virginia had flatly refused to send any troops at all, accusing the president of inaugurating civil war by his proclamation. The attack on Fort Sumter, apparently, had not inaugurated anything, nor had the seizure of federal installations throughout the South. Governor Rector had announced that the people of the state of Arkansas would defend themselves "to the last extremity" from Northern aggression. Governor Ellis pronounced that the people of North Carolina would not be party to this "wicked violation of the laws of the country," and Governor Harris said Tennessee would not furnish a single man "for the purposes of coercion." In a matter of days, after refusing the call for troops, these states seceded and joined the Confederacy, making for a total of eleven states in rebellion.

Delaware and Maryland vacillated, apparently waiting to see which way the wind would blow. Kentucky's Governor Magoffin had also refused to supply troops and Missouri's Governor Jackson claimed Lincoln's proclamation was illegal and unconstitutional, "an unholy crusade," and he refused to comply.

The president was greatly concerned about Kentucky, because he felt if the Union lost Kentucky, they would not be able to hold Missouri or Maryland. If Maryland went, then the capital would be surrounded by rebel states and totally cut off. Secessionist sentiment in Maryland was considerable and Virginia troops had already seized the arsenal at Harpers Ferry and the Gosport Navy Yard at Norfolk.

For Robert, these were trying times. His days were full and long, with hardly any time left to himself. General Scott was a relentless taskmaster, a fair and personable man, but a demanding superior. In many ways, Robert felt as if he were repeating his plebe year at the Academy, when he was at every upperclassman's beck and call, performing endless frustrating and demeaning tasks. There was nothing demeaning in what he had to do for General Scott, but there was endless frustration in the feeling that he had somehow stopped being a soldier and had become a secretary and a clerk, a glorified supernumerary.

He prided himself on his efficiency and Scott came to rely upon it more and more. It soon became Robert's responsibility to know everything that was going on and to have ready answers for the general-in-chief at his fingertips. And everywhere things seemed to be going wrong. The forty-seven regulars who had been stationed at Harpers Ferry had been forced to evacuate and had set fire to the arsenal when the Virginia troops moved in, but the rebels had managed to put out the flames and had saved the machinery for making rifles, which they had promptly shipped to Richmond to turn out guns for the Confederacy. At the navy yard, the sixty-eight-year-old Commodore Charles McCauley, in command of eight hundred sailors and marines, as well as some 1,200 cannon and ten ships, including the forty-gun steam frigate *Merrimac*, had not let the ships escape when they still had a chance to do so. The navy's chief engineer, Benjamin Isherwood, had been sent down to the yard by Secretary Welles to oversee the temporary repair of the *Merrimac*'s engines, and the ship had actually gotten up steam to make way for Philadelphia when McCauley countermanded the secretary's orders and refused to let her sail, apparently in the belief it would constitute some sort of provocation and might push Virginia over the line into secession. Then Virginia seceded anyway and the rebels tried to block the ships from sailing by sinking old hulks in the channel.

They had made a bad job of it, however, and the channel remained open, but either McCauley did not know that or else he had panicked, because he suddenly decided the yard couldn't be defended and ordered all the guns spiked, the ships scuttled, and the buildings burned. The task was already under way when reinforcements arrived from Washington and there was nothing to be done but see it through to its completion, but it was ludicrously bungled. Most of the structures had survived because mines had not gone off; the cannon weren't spiked properly and were able to be salvaged; and the *Merrimac*, one of the most powerful ships afloat, had been improperly scuttled and remained essentially intact, easily capable of being raised and repaired. Reports had reached the War Department that the despondent McCauley had been suicidal and was narrowly prevented from taking his own life.

One setback followed another. In April, General Scott had urged the president to offer Robert E. Lee, a man he regarded as the finest officer in the army, the command of the Union forces, but saying he could not raise his hand against his birthplace, his home, and his children, Lee refused and resigned from the army. Robert had been present when Scott told Lee he was making the greatest mistake of his life, but though the courtly Virginian had been deeply saddened at the turn events had taken, he wouldn't be dissuaded. It was a melancholy parting for them all. Robert recalled Lee's words to him at Harpers Ferry, that it was unfortunate they should meet again under such circumstances, and in Washington, they parted under circumstances that were even more unfortunate. Of all the men Robert had ever known, he had always admired and respected Robert E. Lee above all others. He had no idea when, if ever, he would be seeing him again.

Throughout the Union, officers were resigning and departing for the South, and in the capital, despite the early promise of hordes of volunteers, no troops arrived. The president grew more anxious every day. Then, on April 18, a detachment of five hundred men from Pennsylvania finally arrived, though virtually all of them were unarmed. The following day, when the Sixth Massachusetts came through Baltimore, en route to the capital, they were set upon by an angry mob as they changed trains. There was no railroad line through Baltimore and the troops had to get off at the station on the east end of town and march through the city to board another train for Washington. A large crowd had gathered in their path, and as the volunteers marched through the city the shouting mob hurled bricks and paving stones at them. Shots were fired and twelve citizens of Baltimore were killed and an undetermined number wounded. There were four dead among the troops, who arrived in Washington bearing seventeen wounded men on stretchers. To prevent the movement of more troops across their soil, secessionist Marylanders had cut the telegraph lines, torn up the tracks, and wrecked the bridges, leaving the capital cut off.

The result in Washington was panic. Some citizens banded together to form volunteer companies to protect the city, but many fled with all their possessions, convinced the capital was about to fall. Hotels were empty and the streets were practically deserted. Public buildings were barricaded with sandbags and guns were placed on their porticoes. It was a surreal sight.

General Scott had directed Robert to see to the task of fortifying the Treasury Building as a stand of last resort and he had tried to prevail upon the president to leave the capital for his own safety, but Lincoln wouldn't hear of it. He was quite correct, thought Robert, in believing that his leaving Washington would have a demoralizing effect upon the country and would only serve to bolster morale in the South, but it was nevertheless a courageous stand for him to take and Robert's admiration for him grew.

Meanwhile, many people in the capital were sympathetic to the Southern cause and they enthusiastically prepared to receive the troops of the Confederacy, confident they would soon arrive. Colonel Thomas J. Jackson had eight thousand rebel soldiers at Harpers Ferry, and General Beauregard had fifteen thousand troops near Alexandria. If they joined up, all Lincoln had to throw against them were the demoralized Sixth Massachusetts and the Pennsylvanians, who had been quartered in the House and Senate chambers.

The strain was telling on the president. Where were all the promised volunteers? "Why don't they come?" he kept on saying forlornly, pacing back and forth in his office, anxiously looking out the window. He addressed the troops who did arrive in answer to the call, but his words were not well chosen.

"I don't believe there is any North!" he said, with desperation. "The Seventh Regiment is a myth. Rhode Island is not known in our geography any longer. *You* are the only Northern realities!"

It was not, thought Robert as he listened to the president and watched the faces of the men, an auspicious occasion.

Finally, on April 25, the Seventh New York arrived by train, followed by 1,200 volunteers from Rhode Island and the troops of the Eighth Massachusetts, under General Benjamin F. Butler. When he heard about the riot in Baltimore, Butler had detrained his regiment at Chesapeake Bay, commandeered a steamboat, and landed at Annapolis, where he found the torn-up tracks of the Baltimore and Ohio Railroad and one damaged locomotive. Fortunately, Butler had mechanics in his regiment and many of them were railroad men. They had repaired the engine and the tracks and opened up the line to Washington. The capital was no longer cut off. Robert had sent a messenger to Butler from General Scott, directing him to remain at Annapolis and keep the line open so more troops could get through. There was still plenty of secessionist sentiment in Maryland.

"They are closing their coils around us," Scott told Robert as they went to meet with the president. Expecting more trouble, Scott had urged the president to arrest the Maryland legislators before they could vote for secession, but Lincoln balked at this suggestion. The army was already arresting suspected traitors, and the president's suspension of the writ of habeas corpus had resulted in a storm of controversy. In the arrest of a man named John Merryman, who had helped burn bridges and cut telegraph lines in Maryland, and had been recruiting troops for the Confederacy, Chief Justice Roger Taney, serving a tour on the circuit court, had judged the president's suspension of the writ unconstitutional and had ordered Merryman released, but Lincoln defied the chief justice of the Supreme Court and Merryman remained confined in Fort McHenry. The Baltimore police chief had also been arrested, as well as four police commissioners and a number of other citizens for their roles in the Baltimore riot. The president apparently felt arresting the legislators would be going too far, though he did not hold that opinion for very long.

By May, there were ten thousand troops in the capital, with more on the way. It seemed as if the war effort was finally getting under way. Major Robert Anderson, the hero of Fort Sumter, was promoted to general and sent to take command of the federal forces in Kentucky. General John C. Frémont, the celebrated "Pathfinder," was dispatched to Missouri to keep secessionists in line. Harpers Ferry was recaptured, Arlington and

Alexandria were occupied. The cry of "On to Richmond!" began to echo throughout the North.

Richmond was now the rebel capital, moved there from Montgomery. From a strategic standpoint, Lincoln thought this was more to the Union's benefit. Perhaps the Confederate government had reasoned that Richmond was a better site, because it was a larger city and it contained what little industry the South possessed, such as the Tredegar Iron Works, but it was also closer to the border, which meant it could be taken more easily.

Scott, however, turned a deaf ear to the cry of "On to Richmond!" He was a soldier and a tactician who did not believe in having newspapers tell him how to fight a war. The strategy Scott proposed was elegant in its simplicity of concept and would have been more economical in execution than any other plan of action. In discussing it with him, as a preamble to Scott's proposing it to Lincoln, Robert felt it was not only the right way to pursue the war, but it was the only way.

Everyone seemed to believe it would be a short war, and Robert was no exception. He did not see how the South could resist for any length of time, given all the advantages the North held over them. But while popular sentiment was all for ruthlessly crushing the rebellion and teaching the Southerners a lesson they would not soon forget, Scott was more pragmatic.

"Conquering the insurgent states by virtue of invasion would only result in a devastated countryside and heavy loss of life," he said while outlining the plan to Robert as a rehearsal for presenting it to the president, "and it would be necessary, at great expense, to strongly garrison the Southern states for generations thereafter, much as Rome had garrisoned its hostile, conquered provinces. Therefore, instead of invading the Southern states, I propose to envelop them with a naval blockade of their coast and a fleet of gunboats along the Mississippi River, supported by troops that will take New Orleans by an amphibious expedition from the Gulf. In this manner, the South would be cut off and forced to come to terms with less bloodshed than by any other plan."

Robert had nodded in agreement and replied, "It is eminently logical, sir, but to play the devil's advocate, I anticipate the president might respond to this proposal with the observation that it would prolong the conflict."

"Yes, you are quite right," Scott had replied, "however, it would prolong the conflict at considerably less cost to us than to the South, both in resources and in lives. We will also be relying chiefly on three-year volunteers, rather than ninety-day militia regiments, and this will give us ample time to pursue this strategy. The greatest obstacle we face now, indeed, the greatest danger, is the impatience of our patriotic and loyal Union friends. They will urge instant and vigorous action, regardless, I fear, of consequences."

Scott's words had proved prophetic. He had presented the plan to the president and it made sense to Lincoln, but hardly anybody else approved of it. Somehow, word of the plan leaked out to the newspapers, who dubbed Scott's strategy "The Anaconda Plan" and published ridiculous cartoons of giant serpents with their coils wrapped around the Southern states. Scott's plan, though sensible, was not as glamorous as a dashing charge on Richmond and there was nothing in it to cater to the martial spirit of the public. It had no chivalry, and it didn't promise any glory. Most of all, it would take too long. All anyone could see were the rebel forces massing at Manassas, in Virginia, and threatening the capital. The enemy was there and all it would take to win the war would be to crush Bureaugard and Johnston and storm into Richmond unopposed. Why bother with this elaborate, unnecessary, and, some even suggested, cowardly siege?

Yet, while the newspapers urged the army on to Richmond, the troops were green and undisciplined and one embarrassment followed another. The reports that reached Robert at the War Department were uniformly bad. General Butler had attacked J. B. Magruder at Big Bethel, north of Newport News, and although the rebels were badly outnumbered, the raw Union troops became confused, fired into their own ranks, and were driven back by Magruder's artillery. General Patterson's troops clashed with the Confederate forces under Joseph E. Johnston at Falling Waters, and though the casualties on both sides were light, fifty Union soldiers had been taken prisoner.

"It's infuriating and frustrating beyond belief," Robert wrote his father, at West Point. "According to last year's census, the South has a population of a mere nine million, of which perhaps three or four million are slaves, while the North boasts twenty million, with new immigrants constantly arriving. We have twenty-two thousand miles of railroad lines to their nine thousand miles of track. We have more industry, we have greater resources, and we have superior leadership. General Scott has a very low opinion of Jeff Davis. He says that there is 'contamination in his touch' and is amazed that any man of judgment would make him a leader, and yet such a man has been chosen as the president of the Confederacy. President Lincoln has authorized the enlistment of forty-two thousand volunteers for a period of three years, increased the regular army by twenty thousand men and the navy by eighteen thousand. We now have sixty-four volunteer regiments in and around the capital, in addition to some 1,200 regulars, and the naval blockade of the Southern ports is under way. At least that part of General Scott's plan has been adopted.

"At my post in the War Department, I see all these preparations being made and I cannot conceive of how the South can hope to win, and yet each time Union troops have met those of the Confederacy, in the minor skirmishes that have occurred to date, the rebels have made us look like incompetents and fools! It is my firm opinion that this is what results when men are appointed to command by virtue of political considerations.

"A wealthy businessman or politician raises up a regiment of volunteers and outfits them and, by virtue of this fact, appoints himself a general or a colonel, whether he has any military experience or not. And you should see, Father, some of these regiments of volunteers!

"They arrive in every conceivable type of uniform, costumed as if for some society masquerade ball, decked out in flamboyant colors and more brass and plumes and gold braid trim than in a bevy of British admirals! I don't know if the sight of them is more ludicrous or pathetic! They strut about and preen and march . . . well, if you want to call it marching, because for all their brilliant finery, most of them don't know their right foot from their left. They elect their own officers by vote of the majority, without regard to qualifications, but only by measure of their popularity, and they are very good at occupying saloons and storming the affections of young women. As to fighting, they are probably a greater danger to one another than to the rebel troops."

The only exception to these inauspicious beginnings occurred early in June, in western Virginia, where Major General George B. McClellan, commanding the Ohio Volunteers, sent troops to Grafton on the B&O Railroad, from where they marched south thirty miles and surprised the rebels under Colonel Porterfield at Philippi in a night attack. The skirmish, for it could hardly be called a battle, came to be known as the "Philippi Races" for the way the rebels fled headlong through the rainy night.

Then early in July, McClellan followed up his first success by pursuing the rebel forces under General Garnett and outmaneuvering him with flanking actions at Rich Mountain, dividing his force and sending General William Rosecrans to attack his flank. Part of Garnett's forces had surrendered, the remainder retreated across the Cheat River, and Garnett himself was killed at Carrick's Ford, while his command was forced to fight a rear-guard action.

Though McClellan had attended West Point, Robert knew him only by reputation, as they had not been at the Academy together, and at thirty-four, McClellan was an older man who had not made a career out of the army. He had graduated from the Academy near the top of his class, served in the Mexican War and as an observer in the Crimean War, and he had designed a new type of cavalry saddle that bore his name. He then became a railroad man and served as superintendent of the Illinois Central, and later as the president of the Ohio and Mississippi. He had returned to military service when hostilities broke out and, to date, was the only Union commander in the field who seemed to have any inkling of how to fight a war.

And yet, thought Robert, what was one to make of a commander who brought along with him a portable printing press so his words and actions could be instantly set down and reported to the newspapers? The editors, hungry for a hero ever since Anderson at Sumter, were only too eager to publish his pronouncements, but reading them, Robert felt embarrassed for the man.

"Soldiers!" McClellan had addressed his troops after Phillipi, in remarks that had been widely quoted, "I have heard there was danger here! I have come to place myself at your head and share it with you! I fear now but one thing—that you will not find foemen worthy of your steel!"

The newspaper editors thought the speech "Napoleonic." Robert thought it was horse manure. After the defeat of Garnett's troops, once again, the newspapers enthusiastically reported the Napoleonic words of the federal commander.

"Our success is complete, and secession is killed in this country," came the grand pronouncement from McClellan. "Soldiers of the Army of the West! I am more than satisfied with you!"

Pompous as such speeches might have sounded, Robert nevertheless had to admit McClellan seemed to know his business. He apparently believed in winning victories by maneuvering rather than by fighting, and was reluctant to throw his troops against entrenchments or artillery, which was essentially the same approach as Scott's. Yet the so-called Anaconda Plan was in disfavor. The people wanted battle victories and not strategic victories. They wanted "On to Richmond!" Lincoln was well aware of that and he needed the support of the people in order to conduct the war. His aim was to preserve the Union by whatever means he could. If this meant discarding Scott's Anaconda Plan in favor of McDowell's flank attack on the Confederate forces at Manassas Junction, followed by a move in strength on Richmond, then so be it.

General Irvin McDowell had command of thirty-five thousand troops around the capital. Scott did not believe in "a little war by piecemeal," but McDowell saw only the enemy before him and wanted to move against the rebels at Manassas. He admitted that his troops were raw and wanted more time, but believed there was a good chance of success if they were well led, and if General Patterson could prevent the Confederate forces under Johnston in the Shenandoah Valley from reinforcing Beauregard at Manassas. To Robert, that seemed like a lot of ifs, especially for an officer with no experience in field command. Scott was against McDowell's plan, but Lincoln overruled him. The North desperately needed a significant victory and the president wanted to fight before the enlistment of the three-month volunteers ran out. McDowell would move against Beauregard at Manassas and the Anaconda Plan was shelved.

"Sir," said Robert, after he and Scott had left the president, "I have a personal request to make."

"The answer is no, Captain," Scott replied as they walked together, Robert matching his pace to that of the older man, whose years and whose responsibility weighed heavily upon him.

"But you haven't heard my request, sir," Robert said.

Scott stopped and turned to face him. "I know what you're going to ask me, son," he said. "I was young myself once. You want to go with McDowell and see some action, but I need you here."

"May I ask a question, sir?"

"Ask."

"Is it because of my father that you are reluctant to let me go?"

Scott replied without hesitation. "No. I have a warm regard for your father, that is true, but I can assure you that my motives are entirely selfish. In the brief time we have been together, I have come to rely upon you a great deal. You are an excellent officer, the sort who makes it easy to delegate responsibility. You are efficient, dependable, intelligent, and you have initiative, all qualities which I regard most highly. I have also come to feel a personal affection for you. It is not often that a commander encounters a junior officer in whom he can confide without restraint, whose counsel he can seek out and invariably find to be of value. You have a brilliant career ahead of you, Robert, of that I have no doubt, none whatsoever. The army needs intelligent and qualified officers. If something were to happen to you, you would not be easily replaced."

Robert moistened his lips and softly cleared his throat. "Sir, I . . . I appreciate your trust and confidence in me more than I can say. And I would never question your judgment. But, sir, as you yourself have pointed out, the army needs intelligent and *qualified* officers. I am flattered that you think well of my intelligence, but as to my qualifications, at the moment, they are entirely theoretical. I have never had the opportunity to gain any practical experience in the field."

"You were at Harpers Ferry."

"Yes, sir," replied Robert, "but with all due respect, I should hardly think a brief sortie against a mad old man and a handful of untrained civilians qualifies as practical experience."

Scott nodded. "Your point is well taken." He sighed heavily. "Very well. I will inform General McDowell that you will be accompanying him as a member of his staff, temporarily detached from duty at the War Department."

"Thank you, sir," said Robert, "but if I might be allowed to make a suggestion . . ."

Scott grunted, which was often his manner of answering in the affirmative.

"I would prefer to make a personal request of General McDowell to take me along, in whatever capacity he sees fit to employ me. I would, of course, indicate to him that I requested leave of you to do so and that you granted my request, on the condition that this would be acceptable to him."

Scott smiled. "I see that in addition to your other admirable qualities, you are a diplomat. You are implying that if I told McDowell to assign you to his staff, he would think I was sending you to spy on him, as my personal observer."

"I . . . wouldn't have put it quite that way, sir. I would merely prefer that he consent to take me, rather than be ordered to do so."

Scott grunted again. "Yes, well, chances are he may still interpret it that way. And, speaking frankly, I could use a reliable

observer on this campaign. Very well, ask him yourself. I should
hardly think he would refuse. But see here, son, I don't want you
taking any foolish risks. No riding to the sound of the guns, you
understand? That's a direct order. I have no intention of losing
the best aide I've ever had."

"Yes, sir. And thank you, sir."

McDowell had planned to move on July 8, but what with
various problems involving organization and supplies, they did
not leave until the sixteenth. They set out from Arlington with
fifty regiments of infantry, ten batteries of field artillery, and one
cavalry battalion, which made McDowell's force the largest army
on the continent. Their objective at the end of the first day's march
was Fairfax Courthouse, thirteen miles from Arlington. By the
second day, the plan was to make nine more miles to Centreville,
which was within striking distance of Manassas Junction. Yet by
the end of the second day's march, they had not even reached
Fairfax Courthouse.

Getting the green troops moving proved as difficult as prodding
a reluctant mule. For Robert, who was accustomed to the precision
of West Point and to the less precise, but still reasonable efficiency of the regular recruits at Carlysle Barracks, the movement of
the largely volunteer troops was a dismaying revelation. There
was nothing that even vaguely resembled order on the march. The
ranks alternately spread out and bunched together, moving like a
concertina as men were forced to trot in order to keep up or stand
idly in the dusty road and wait while the sluggish troops ahead
of them got moving. During the frequent halts, men stood around
whining and complaining or broke ranks to wander off the road
in search of berries. Most of them were unaccustomed to their
heavy packs and many of them simply discarded their supplies in
order to lighten up their load. Further complicating matters were
the civilians, who came from Washington on horseback and in
carriages, packing picnic lunches for their outing to see the war
firsthand. The traffic on the roads became a hopeless muddle.

Discipline was nonexistent. At the vanguard, word reached
McDowell's staff that many of the men were not only breaking
ranks and wandering off, but were looting the homes along their
route. Robert could scarcely believe it. Riding back along the
column to investigate this report, he heard gunfire coming from
a nearby farm and, wryly recalling Scott's order about "riding to
the sounds of the guns," decided it didn't apply in this case and
galloped up in time to see a group of about fifteen men engaged

in stealing chickens and taking gleeful target practice with the livestock.

"You men!" he shouted. "Stop what you're doing this instant! Have you lost your senses?"

A few of them glanced in his direction, but otherwise ignored him. One trooper, standing not five feet away, finished ramming down his bullet, then cocked and capped his musket. Robert drew his sword and knocked it down just as he fired, thereby saving the life of a Confederate pig.

"Hey, goddamn it!" the man shouted at him angrily, but before he could utter another word, Robert spurred his mount and knocked him sprawling. He sheathed his sword and drew his pistol.

"I will kill the next man who fires a shot," he said.

They stared at him with disbelief, but no one fired.

"You are soldiers, and not chicken thieves," he said furiously. "And when you fight, by God, you will fight rebel soldiers and not pigs! Now get back in ranks!"

Sullenly, they moved to comply, but Robert could not prevent others on the march from looting, and few, if any, of the other officers showed an inclination to control their men. Disgusted, Robert rode back to take his place with McDowell's staff. McDowell made no comment. He seemed preoccupied with his advance scouting parties and with the endless rumors of concealed batteries, every one of which had to be investigated, because McDowell was concerned about his raw troops being surprised. All this wasted a great deal of time, and more time was wasted clearing away trees that had been felled in their path, with the result they did not reach Centreville till Thursday night, after two and a half days on the march.

It then became apparent that most of the men had eaten all their rations and many of them had discarded their ammunition along with other supplies that seemed too heavy. Friday was lost in bringing up more supplies. Saturday was entirely used up by reconnaissance and studying maps and debating various approaches. Robert's advice was not solicited and once, when he ventured to offer a suggestion, McDowell curtly thanked him and informed him that he had matters well in hand. By that time, the ninety-day enlistments of many of the men were up and most of them promptly marched off toward the rear. Nothing McDowell said would stop them. All in all, thought Robert, disgusted beyond words, it was the lamest excuse for an army he could possibly imagine.

Meanwhile, word had reached McDowell that Johnston had given Patterson the slip in the Shenandoah Valley and had moved his troops by railroad to unite with the forces under Beauregard. So much for one if, Robert thought, recalling McDowell's presentation of his plan. As to the second if, the one about a good chance for success if the green troops were well led, he held out little hope for that. However, McDowell was committed. They would attack at first light in the morning.

CHAPTER THREE

Robert's Journal, Washington, D.C., 21 July, 1861

AS I WRITE these words, a misting rain falls upon the capital and the mood of the city is grim. The first battle of the war has been fought and we have lost it. Outside, the troops continue to straggle into the city, disorganized, exhausted, and utterly demoralized. Men huddle in the doorways, wander aimlessly through the muddy streets, or simply drop down where they stand, to sleep on the steps of buildings or up against walls and fences, heedless of the rain falling down upon them. As I look out my window I can see, across the street, two elderly women, well dressed and genteel ladies, standing in the rain behind a table they have set up on the sidewalk and passing out food to the weary soldiers as they trudge by. As the food runs out they send into the house for more, with no apparent thought to the expense or inconvenience, and with no regard for the inclement weather. It is a gray and gloomy day in Washington, and one that is an accurate reflection of my disposition. I grieve for those who have fallen, I burn with resentment and frustration, and I can only imagine how McDowell must feel today, and the weight of the burden he must bear.

General Irvin McDowell, at forty-three years of age, is an imposing figure of a man. He is broad-shouldered and stands six feet tall, with dark brown hair and alert, thoughtful-looking eyes. He wears his beard in the imperial fashion, with a bushy mustache covering his upper lip and the beard covering only his chin, with the cheeks and jaw clean-shaven. He abstains from alcohol and his manner is becoming, courteous, and modest, though he holds firm opinions from which he cannot easily be swayed. My one attempt at venturing an opinion of my own at the outset of the campaign had been politely, yet firmly dismissed, in a manner

151

that quietly reminded me of my place. And quite correctly so. As an officer junior to General McDowell in both rank and age, I was certainly in no position to offer unsolicited opinions, even as General Scott's ex officio observer.

My intent was merely to participate in the campaign and thereby gain practical experience, but unfortunately, as aide to General Scott, there was no way that it was possible for me to appear as anything *but* his observer, which, in point of fact, I was. If General McDowell resented my presence in this capacity, he did not show it. However, I must admit that if I were in his place, I would not have been favorably disposed to having a young, wet-behind-the-ears brevet captain looking over my shoulder and reporting to the general-in-chief.

Unlike many of his junior officers, General McDowell is very much a military man. Though he had never held a field command prior to this campaign, he received his education in a French military academy, where he studied the classical works on military strategy and tactics, and he is also a graduate of West Point, so there is nothing lacking in his training. Nor was he under any illusions as to the limitations of his troops.

He had previously expressed his opinion that there was a good chance for success on the campaign if the men were well led, and if they were formed into small brigades to better facilitate their movement, and if Johnston could be prevented from reinforcing Beauregard. However, he wished for more time and better organization, and had frankly told the president in my presence that the troops were very green. The president's reply had been that the rebel troops were equally green. "You are all green alike," the president had said, as if that solved the problem, and the issue had been settled.

However, I would be remiss if I did not point out that the president seemed motivated primarily by political, rather than purely military considerations. The enlistment period for the three-months men was running out and he wanted an engagement, a victory to appease the public and gain momentum for the war. What he received instead was not a victory, but a crushing and humiliating defeat. The tragedy of this deplorable affair is that the blame will fall upon McDowell, when no commander, under similar circumstances, could have done better.

The public seemed to think that all it would take to bring about the South's surrender would be a determined show of force. Many of the troops seemed to share that opinion as well. For my own part, while I continue to believe that it is not possible for the South to win this war, or even to hold out for very long, I was convinced from the beginning that it would take much more than a mere show of force to bring about their capitulation.

While it is true that the South does not possess the resources of the North, they have most of nation's finest officers. The president was undoubtedly correct in his assessment that the Southern troops are just as green as ours, but there was more to be considered than the organization and discipline of the troops. Many of the men among our troops are city-bred and have never even held a musket. The Southerners are country boys, who have grown up on horseback and have hunted since their early childhood. Perhaps they were green troops, as the president had said, but at least they knew one end of a musket from the other.

General McDowell seemed well aware of this. He had been cautious, both on the march, in his concern over the threat of concealed batteries, and in his strategy. While much fault could be found with the behavior of the troops on the march, none could be found with their commander. However, in all fairness, it must be said that for men with no experience, most of them acquitted themselves with courage when they came under fire.

Manassas, our objective, was an important site, the junction of the Orange and Alexandria line connecting Washington with Richmond and the Manassas Gap Railroad, leading to the Shenandoah Valley. Whoever controls Manassas Junction controls the railroad system in northern Virginia. The plan had called for General Patterson to engage General Johnston's rebel troops at Winchester and keep him from reinforcing General Beauregard at Manassas. While Patterson kept Johnston occupied, McDowell would take Manassas Junction, clearing the way for the push to Richmond. However, things began to go awry almost from the very moment that we left the banks of the Potomac.

Our departure was delayed, and the disorganized march took much longer than anticipated. Time was lost in resupply at Centreville, and more time was lost in having the engineers reconnoiter the territory to pick out the best approach. I had gone with General McDowell to observe the area to the left of our line, in consideration of a move against the enemy's right flank, but we found that the countryside rendered this impractical.

While we were thus engaged, General Tyler had been ordered up from Centreville with two companies of infantry and a squadron of cavalry, to observe the roads leading to Bull Run and reconnoiter the fords. He was directed to avoid engaging the enemy, but make movements aimed to keep up the impression that we would continue to push forward to Manassas. McDowell's plan was to make Beauregard believe that the assault, when it came, would be on his front, while the main column, consisting of General Hunter's Second Division and General Heintzelman's Third Division, would strike the rebel flank.

The plan was sound, but there was only one thing wrong with it, and that was General Tyler. While we were scouting out the countryside to the left of our line, Tyler reached the heights on the north side of the stream at Blackburn's Ford, and seeing enemy troops on the other shore, he opened fire with his twenty-pounders, which at first drew fire from the enemy battery, then silenced it. When called upon to give account for his subsequent actions, Tyler reported that he merely desired more information about the enemy's strength, especially in the woods around the area. However, I have it on the authority of an engineer assigned to his staff that Tyler's ambition got the better of him. His remarks on the occasion, as reported to me in confidence, were that the great man of the war would be the man who got over to Manassas, and he meant to go through that night.

Lord only knows what the man must have been thinking, for he drew up his brigade in a line parallel to the stream and had them open fire, to no apparent effect. While they were engaged in this pointless display the rebels crossed the stream and flanked them, striking at the Twelfth New York on his left and driving them back in complete disorder, with nineteen killed and 38 wounded. So much for the "determined show of force" theory. It was a bad blow to the morale of our troops, and a boon to that of the rebels.

With this inauspicious beginning, the next two days were spent in continuing our reconnaissance. The engineers had discovered an unprotected ford at Sudley Spring, about two miles above Stone Bridge, where the road from Centreville crossed Bull Run. Above the ford, the river could be crossed in many places without difficulty. General McDowell gave orders to General Miles to remain in reserve at Centreville with his Fifth Division, and to detach one of his brigades, along with one of Tyler's, to make a false attack at Blackburn's Ford, the site of Tyler's earlier comeuppance. The main body of the First Division, under Tyler, would then follow the road to Stone Bridge at daybreak, carry it and cross, while the Second and Third Divisions, under Hunter and Heintzelman, would march to the Sudley Spring Ford, make the crossing, and then flank the enemy, taking the defenses of Stone Bridge from the rear while Tyler attacked from the front. Thus united, the forces would then proceed against Manassas Junction.

If there was any flaw in this strategy, I have been unable to discover it. The flaws lay in the execution. We left Centreville at three o'clock on the morning of the twentieth. There was delay in Tyler's division leaving camp, and they were slow in their advance. To what extent this was a result of poor organization, or perhaps to their earlier, sobering confrontation with the rebels, is impossible to determine, but the delay in getting Tyler on the move resulted in the delay of Heintzelman and Hunter, and it took them longer to reach the Sudley Spring ford than was anticipated. The plan called for them to reach the ford by six, and they did not do so until after nine. By six o'clock, Tyler's troops were in position at Stone Bridge and he opened fire with his artillery.

Robert put aside his pen and stared at what he'd written. It was an accurate statement of the events that had occurred up to the point they reached Stone Bridge, but he did not know how to proceed from there. He knew he was writing for posterity, for the generations of his family that would follow, and he felt painfully inadequate to the task. Maria was the writer in the family, and for the first time, he found himself envying her ability with colorful, descriptive prose. Many times she had shown her work to him for his reaction, and he had always commented upon it favorably, but he had never really taken her writing very seriously. That sort of colorful, descriptive writing, meant to evoke emotion and bring fictional characters to life, was not really to his taste. It seemed like a waste of time. It was all right for Maria, because women enjoyed such harmless nonsense and it helped them pass the time, but a man, a soldier, had more important things to occupy his concern.

When it came to writing, a soldier needed to concern himself only with facts and details, stated clearly and succinctly, and Robert was well able to do that. However, while he could set down the facts of what occurred, he felt at a loss to convey the true sense of the actual experience, and it was the actual experience he wanted to capture, for the sake of future generations to whom mere facts and details, no matter how clearly or succinctly stated, could never convey what it was really like to fight a war.

He had wanted to write it all down quickly, while it was still fresh in his mind, while he still felt the full strength of all the conflicting emotions that had raged within him, and he was surprised to find himself feeling those emotions even now, with far greater strength than during the battle itself. He felt exhausted, drained, morose and angry, frustrated and resentful, and the strength of those emotions stymied him. How different this experience was from what he'd felt at Harpers Ferry! There, he had felt exhilaration, an incredible sense of power, as if his blood were singing in his veins, but now . . .

Now he had "been to the hill and seen the elephant," as soldiers said, a saying that hearkened back to the days of Rome's war against Hannibal, his ancestor, and now he knew what war was really like. And it was nothing like what he had expected. The fact that they had experienced defeat, undoubtedly, had much to do with what he felt now. Victory would have made him feel very different, he knew that. Yet that was obvious. That was not what puzzled him, disturbed him. Back on the battle-field of Bull Run, there had come a point when thoughts of defeat or victory were furthest from his mind. That confused him. The thought of victory should have been *foremost* in his mind, and yet at some point, it had ceased to matter altogether.

It seemed, looking back on it now, that in the thick of all the action, he had somehow managed to forget himself. At the same time, he had also found himself, his *essential* self, the very core of his being. He had felt a desperate awareness of his own existence, an awareness that was almost an hysteria, though it was under firm control. He had not expected that.

On the night before the battle, as he stood outside his tent, smoking his pipe, a young lieutenant he had met on the march, a New Yorker named Monroe, had approached him under the pretense of borrowing some tobacco. He had really felt a need to talk.

"You thinking about tomorrow?" Robert asked him as Monroe had packed his pipe.

Monroe nodded. He finished tamping down the tobacco with his thumb, but he did not light his pipe. He merely held it, as if he had forgotten it. "Yes. Are you?"

"I think we all are," Robert had replied.

"May I ask you a personal question, Captain?"

"Of course."

"Do you . . ." Monroe moistened his lips and looked uncomfortable. "Do you worry about being afraid?"

"I think only a fool wouldn't worry about it," said Robert.

Monroe sighed with relief. "I'm afraid of being afraid," he said. "I want to do well, to do my duty, but what if I should prove a coward? I'm more afraid of that than anything."

"There's no shame in being afraid, Monroe," said Robert.

"There's shame in being a coward," Monroe replied.

"What *makes* a coward?" Robert asked.

"Why, fear makes a coward."

"No," said Robert, shaking his head as he drew on his pipe. "Fear merely makes you a man. Allowing your fear to dominate you is what makes a coward. Men will die tomorrow, Monroe. Perhaps you and I will be among those who will fall. But every man must die someday. Suppose you run tomorrow. Not that I think you will, you understand, but for the sake of argument, let's suppose you dust out of the battle and survive. You will have to make the journey back to the Potomac. You could catch your death of cold and die in bed. You could be shot down by some concealed sharpshooter. You could be crossing the street in Washington and be struck down by a runaway horse or carriage. You could be knifed in some alleyway as you are leaving a tavern, drunk. Or you could be shot by a jealous husband."

Monroe grinned. "I begin to see your point. A man could die at any time."

"Not only that," said Robert. "A poet once wrote that a coward dies a thousand times, and a hero dies but once. If you're afraid of cowardice, that's a good thing, a useful thing, because to be a coward is to be constantly afraid. You'll be afraid to go out in the rain, for fear you might catch cold. You'll be afraid to cross the street, for fear you might be run down. You'll live with fear during every waking moment of your life. But tomorrow, you'll have the opportunity to look death in the face. If you die, you die, as we all must die someday. But if you live, you will have seen the face of death, and you'll know that someday he will call for you, but having seen him, you will no longer be afraid."

Monroe stared at him with wonder. "However did you learn to think like that?"

Robert smiled. "I've studied the writings of soldiers all my life. It was all I ever wanted to be. I wanted to prepare myself, and I wanted to learn how soldiers think so that I could be a good one.

Even the greatest of them felt fear at one time or another. Only a fool is not afraid."

Monroe had smiled. "I feel a little better now," he said. "Amid all the bluster of the others, I thought perhaps I was the only one who felt the way I did."

Robert chuckled. "I suspect those who swagger most and talk the loudest are those who are the most afraid."

"You really think so?"

Robert nodded. "They'll be afraid across the river, too. But I learned one thing at Harpers Ferry. When the time comes for action, there's little time to be afraid. And afterward . . ." He smiled. "Afterward, you will feel more alive than you have ever felt before."

The name aptly described the bridge. Stone Bridge was a simple span of stone crossing the stream, with low stone walls and a few trees and shrubs by its approaches on either bank. The road across it was not very wide, but a determined charge would easily have carried it. The sensible course would have been to storm the bridge, deploy skirmishers on the opposite side, and secure it so the rest of the troops could cross. Tyler, however, chose to take up position just before the bridge and open fire on the rebels on the other side.

His batteries threw shot across the bridge, and his troops fired their muskets freely at the rebels on the other side, filling the air with smoke and the crackling of musket fire, all to no discernible effect. And there Tyler remained, implanted, hesitant to commit his troops until the flanking column under Heintzelman and Hunter could arrive. In vain, Robert tried to convince him to move forward.

"I have my orders, Captain Gallio," Tyler replied curtly, "and I will interpret them as I see fit. I've already lost a number of my gallant men and I will not throw away their lives in a foolish rush against the fire of the enemy. We'll wait till they are trapped between us, and then, sir, we will have them!"

That seemed to settle it, and Robert could speak no further. To press his point would have been bordering on insubordination, and there was nothing to be done. He could only sit and stew for the next two and a half hours as they traded fire pointlessly with the rebels, while the whereabouts of Heintzelman and Hunter continued to remain a mystery. Tyler was either a coward or a fool, thought Robert. Had he carried the bridge and moved his troops across, the Southern commander on the opposing shore

would have been convinced their main assault was coming at
his front. Instead, after the meaningless cannonade was kept up
for almost three hours, the rebel commander at Stone Bridge,
General Evans, came to the obvious conclusion that the action
was no more than a feint and he correctly deduced their strategy.
Leaving four companies of infantry behind to keep Tyler occupied, he advanced with his main body on Sudley Springs.

Robert learned later that Hunter had not made his crossing
until ten o'clock, greatly behind schedule. His column came
out of the woods and was confronted by Evans, drawn up in
a line before him, at right angles to his previous position. At that
point, the Southern commander was outnumbered, but instead of
taking advantage of the odds in his favor and properly deploy-
ing his troops for battle, Hunter opened fire on the rebels from
the head of his column as soon as he caught sight of them.
Colonel Burnside's Rhode Islanders were at the head of the
Union column, and they were ordered to advance before the
rest of the troops could be properly deployed. They were cut
to pieces and Hunter himself was seriously wounded and sent
back to the rear. Then Colonels Sykes and Porter came up to
reinforce the beleaguered Burnside on his left and right, which
was what should have been done in the first place, and the
rebels started to give ground, but they were quickly reinforced
by two bridgades coming from the bridge, where Tyler was
still wasting precious time, and they made a stand at Young's
Branch.

Robert spurred his horse and rode away from Tyler's side,
fearful that his self-control would slip and he would tell him what
he thought of him. He rode down the line, toward another officer
whose opinion of Tyler's hesitancy matched his own. Colonel
William Tecumseh Sherman was a red-bearded, regular-army
officer who had left the service prior to the war to practice
law in Leavenworth, but had rejoined when war broke out. He
had impressed Robert as a forthright and aggressive man. He
proceeded to demonstrate these qualities.

"I can stomach this tomfoolery no longer," he said to Robert as
he sat astride his skittish horse. He spoke through clenched teeth.
"We're wasting time, goddamn it! We have to get across! What
in heaven's name is Tyler doing?"

"Interpreting his orders as he sees fit," Robert replied dryly,
which was safe enough, considering it was what Tyler said to
him, and yet his tone clearly conveyed his meaning.

"Is he, indeed?" snapped Sherman. "Well, then, perhaps we should do likewise." He spat out a brown stream of tobacco juice. "There's bound to be another ford around here somewhere. Are you game for it, Gallio?"

Robert recalled his orders from General Scott, about not riding to the sound of the guns, and considered that in searching for a ford with Sherman, he would, in fact, be riding *away* from the sound of Tyler's guns, and so he immediately agreed to go along.

They soon found an unprotected ford, merely half a mile above the bridge, and were able to cross well in advance of Tyler, who waited until Heintzelman arrived to clear the way for him. The brigade of Colonel Keyes followed behind them at a distance, but they disappeared shortly after they had crossed. Robert learned later that Tyler himself had crossed with Keyes's brigade, having left part of his force behind at Stone Bridge, and they made a halfhearted effort to advance up the slopes toward the plateau, but the woods concealed rebel sharpshooters, and Tyler, together with Keyes's troops, retired to the left, behind the shelter of the bluff, and marched away, taking no further part in the battle.

Sherman, however, was not intimidated by the sharpshooters. He advanced up the slope boldly, exhorting his men with shouts and waving his saber as the sporadic firing of the sharpshooters died away and they retreated. Robert caught no glimpse of the enemy until they arrived in time to join the fighting at Young's Branch. The rebels continued to be forced back as the Union forces drew together, and things seemed to be going all their way as they pressed back toward the bridge, but one Southern officer stood firm with his troops, doggedly holding his ground above the bridge while the others all gave way, and his courage must have shamed the others, for they rallied and bought Beauregard the time to re-form his lines on the plateau above the crest.

To Robert, the fighting so far had seemed less like a battle than like a woodland skirmish. He had no real idea of the enemy strength they were facing, and it was only their steady advance toward the bridge that let him know the rebels were giving ground. He saw puffs of smoke and eruptions of sparks coming from the trees ahead of him, but they did not seem real somehow, until Monroe rode up beside him, grinning ear to ear, exultant in his adrenaline-charged state.

"The day is ours!" he cried. "We've got them on the run!"

And then a musket ball struck him squarely in the right temple, blowing out his brains as the .50-caliber ball plowed through his skull. His horse continued on as his body, with its ruined head, slumped in the saddle and then slid off to the left side of the horse, one foot caught in the stirrup. Robert saw him dragged away through the trees.

As the rebels retreated to regroup on the southern end of the plateau, McDowell reformed his lines on the crest above the bridge. Robert spotted him dismounting in front of the Henry house, which stood upon the crest, and he spurred ahead to join him. The upper floor of the house afforded a good vantage point of the plateau beyond, where the rebels had re-formed, and McDowell was standing at the window when Robert came in, looking out toward Beauregard's lines. He heard Robert's footsteps behind him and turned around.

"Gallio," he said. "Where the devil have you been?"

"With Colonel Sherman, sir. We found a ford a little way above the bridge and crossed. Colonel Keyes and his brigade were right behind us."

"Where are they now?" McDowell asked.

"I don't know, sir."

"What do you mean, you don't know?"

"We lost sight of them after we reached the top, sir."

"Wonderful," McDowell said sarcastically. "I don't know where Keyes is, I don't know where Tyler is, and Beauregard's managed to re-form his troops out there." He nodded toward the plateau. "That's where the fight is going to be. Damn that Jackson, anyway. If he hadn't stood firm at the crest, we could have chased them all the way across."

Robert joined him at the window. The plateau was wide and flat, with small streams running on three sides and emptying into Bull Run, south of the bridge, about one hundred feet below. The slopes of the plateau were not very steep, but they were cut with wooded ravines. To the west of the plateau was a wooded area, and directly to the south, the rebels stood.

"I've determined that our best course is to work around the left flank of the rebels, through the woods," McDowell said, pointing at the thick belt of oaks off to his right. "I've ordered Griffin and Ricketts to the top of the ridge there, with their batteries, where they will receive support from the Zouaves and the Fourteenth New York. The guns that command this plateau will determine the action and I intend to waste no time getting them in place."

He glanced at Robert and raised his eyebrows. "Does that meet with your approval, Captain?"

Robert did not know how to respond. "It . . . seems like the proper tactic for the situation, sir," he said.

McDowell smiled. "Clausewitz approves, eh?"

Robert blushed, but McDowell walked past him and back down the stairs before he could think of a response.

Robert rode out with Captains Griffin and Ricketts as they quickly moved their batteries into position, but there was no sign of their support troops.

"Where the devil are they?" Griffin asked, looking around for the Zouaves and the New York regiment. "We're stuck out here like scarecrows in an open field!"

"General McDowell said he sent them forward," Robert said. "They should be arriving any moment."

As he spoke a column of troops came out from the woods about a thousand yards away from them.

"Damn it!" Griffin swore. "Charge your guns!"

"No, wait!" cried Major Barry, Griffin's chief of artillery, staring at the troops intently as they approached. "That's the Fourteenth New York!"

Griffin exhaled heavily. "About damn time," he said. "What the devil were they doing over there?"

"It's not the Fourteenth!" shouted Robert as the troops came closer and he suddenly recognized the mounted officer leading them. It was the same man who had stood firm, immovable, when all the other rebels were in fast retreat back at the ridge. "Look out, it's the—"

The advancing troops brought up their muskets and let loose a devastating volley that tore into the gunners. With the wide profusion of uniforms on the field, troops on both sides were attired in both blue and gray, with all manner of colorful variations in between, and most of the senior Southern officers still wore army blue. General Thomas Jackson, who would forever after become known as "Stonewall" Jackson for his gallant stand against the advancing Union troops, had brought his Virginians out of the woods and Major Barry had made the tragic error of thinking the rebels were the Fourteenth New York regiment, coming to support them. They allowed them to get too close and the result was disaster.

In their first volley, the sharpshooting Virginians succeeded in killing every one of the gunners and most of the horses. Then they charged, giving voice to their banshee rebel yell. Robert heard something whistle past his ear and realized a musket ball had just barely missed him. At the same time another ball plucked at the sleeve of his right arm and he felt a sharp, lacerating pain.

He wheeled his horse around and set his spurs into its flanks, but the frightened animal needed no encouragement as it bolted away from the rebel charge. Behind him, the bullet-riddled bodies of the gunners lay draped over their batteries or collapsed like sacks upon the ground. Wounded horses screamed and thrashed about, unable to stand, and the drifting cloud of smoke blew forward, obscuring everything from view. Jackson's Virginians came charging out of the cloud like grim specters, screaming wildly as they ran forward to capture the guns, the morning sun gleaming on their bayonets.

As Robert galloped away, furious, he almost ran straight into the New York regiment, belatedly moving up to support the already captured batteries. Scott's admonitions about not taking part in any action fled from his mind completely as he turned his horse again and led the men in a charge back toward the guns. He saw the rebels desperately trying to reload, biting off the ends of their paper cartridges and pouring the powder down their barrels, then inserting the balls and ramming them down. He drew his saber and waved it over his head.

"Come on!" he screamed to the men behind him, outdistancing them on his horse as he galloped straight back into the rebels and scattered them.

One rebel infantryman still had burning powder embers in his barrel as he poured down a fresh charge from the cartridge. The powder ignited. The rebel soldier had been leaning over his weapon in his hurry to reload and the flash erupted right in his face. He screamed and dropped his musket, clutching his face as he fell.

Another rifleman was desperately ramming down his ball when Robert came barreling down upon him. Wide-eyed, the man quickly raised his rifle and fired with the ramrod still inside the barrel. The ramrod, followed by the ball, came flying out of the rifle barrel, missing Robert by scarcely half a foot and transfixing one of the charging men behind him. It struck him in the chest, penetrating his back and killing him instantly.

Robert rode down the man who'd fired and started laying about him with his sword. One rebel stabbed up at him with his bayonet and the blade glanced off Robert's saddle, sliding up along his thigh and tearing through his breeches and his skin. Robert brought the saber down in a hard cut at the man's face and laid it open. The rebel fell, screaming, his face a mask of blood.

Then Robert found himself face-to-face with Jackson. Their sabers clanged against each other as they fought on horseback, their mounts shying, almost impossible to control, and then the New Yorkers plowed into the rebels and they were forced apart.

Jackson ordered his men back to regroup, and as they gave ground the batteries were retaken, but the rebels rallied and came back to try and take them once again. The main body of McDowell's troops pressed forward and the rebels were once more pushed back from the guns, and now the battle for the plateau began in earnest.

With the rifled Parrott guns of the Union batteries trading fire with the smoothbore, brass cannon of the rebels, plowing up the field, the tide of the battle ebbed and flowed, back and forth across the plateau, with the sulfurous smell of gunpowder filling the air and smoke covering the battlefield like a blanket.

To Robert, in the thick of it, it looked like an insane melee, with ranks of men moving forward to within thirty or forty yards of the enemy troops, firing and falling back, while other men moved forward and were just as suddenly forced back. It didn't resemble any sort of concerted action, but looked like a hundred little separate wars all being fought on the same field of battle. The din was incredible. Cannon firing, solid shot and canister whistling through the air, striking men and scattering bloody entrails and clumps of earth and grass in all directions, muskets cracking out sporadic fire and shooting powder sparks through the thick smoke, men shouting, screaming, officers vainly trying to make their hoarse-voiced commands heard over all the noise . . . it was bedlam. And the worst was yet to come.

For some reason, Patterson had failed to engage Johnston's rebel troops at Winchester and Johnston himself had arrived on the battlefield before the action had even begun, taking charge of the Southern troops. Beauregard had hastily sent rail transport to bring Johnston's Army of the Shenandoah to Bull Run, and by midafternoon, Johnston's troops were arriving at Manassas Junction and hastening to the front. Beauregard employed them to make another drive across the plateau, and this time the rebels forced the Union troops back and once more recaptured the batteries. McDowell made one final effort to extend his line to the right, in one last hope of flanking the rebels on their left, but

Jubal Early's brigade of the Army of the Shenandoah came up from Manassas Junction to join the fray, and with their arrival, the day was lost.

The entire Union line collapsed and was thrown back across the ridge, over Young's Branch and Bull Run, retiring in complete confusion. After a long and weary day of fighting in the blistering hot Virginia sun, the Union soldiers simply turned and numbly walked off the field of battle, glazed eyes staring from powder-blackened faces, and nothing their officers could say or do would turn them. Not even the most charitable description could call it a retreat. It was a rout.

As the soldiers crossed Bull Run, heading back toward Centreville, the picnicking civilians who had ridden out from the capital to watch the war, as if it were a lark, realized the battle had been lost. Expecting rebel pursuit hot on their heels, they panicked and began to flee. Their horses and carriages choked the roads leading to Cub Run and became tangled up with the army supply wagons and artillery caissons. Somehow, a wagon overturned on the bridge across Cub Run and a cry went up about "black-horse rebel cavalry" bearing down upon them. Hysteria gripped the mob. Their panic infected the weary soldiers and the troops simply broke and ran, without any semblance of order, the men of all divisions intermingled. The officers did not know where their men were, the men did not care where their officers were to be found, and all too many of them could be found galloping away as fast as their mounts could carry them.

The roads became a hopeless quagmire of stalled wagons, panicked horses, more panicked men, and overturned gun carriages. Wagons and coaches were abandoned when they could not get through, blocking the road, and men leaped up on the horses hitched to the carriages and caissons, cut the traces, and galloped away.

Miles, who had been waiting in reserve with his division, had been directed to hold the ridge at Centreville to Blackburn's Ford, but he withdrew, perhaps carried by the momentum of the others, leaving the Union rear completely unprotected. By some miracle, the rebels had not pursued them, except for several detachments of rebel cavalry who followed the retreating Union troops as far as Cub's Run, capturing a number of prisoners.

Robert stopped to aid a wounded Union soldier who had been shot through the leg and was hobbling awkwardly and slowly, using his musket for a crutch. He rode up to the man and held out his hand, taking his foot out of the stirrup so the soldier could climb up behind him.

The soldier took his hand, swung up behind him, and promptly knocked him off his horse and galloped off. Robert fell to the ground, momentarily stunned. As he started to get back to his feet he heard the thunder of hoofbeats and looked up to see a detachment of rebel cavalry bearing down on him. He threw himself to one side, off the road. As the riders galloped past him the officer in their vanguard spotted him and reined in his black stallion. As Robert stood there, helpless, his pistol empty and with nothing but his saber in his hand, the rebel officer leveled his pistol directly at his chest.

· And then, suddenly, he lowered it, easing the hammer back down with his thumb, and Robert recognized Jeb Stuart. With a slight smile on his face, Stuart raised the pistol and touched the barrel to the brim of his plumed hat, saluting him. Robert came to attention, returned the salute with his saber, and Stuart rode off without a word.

Robert sat staring out the window at the rain-soaked streets of Washington. They were a quagmire of mud and dirty brown puddles as the last of the stragglers came trudging past his rooming house, looking like the walking dead. He thought of Stuart, looking ever the dashing cavalier astride his black steed, and he could still see him vividly in his mind's eye, saluting him with the barrel of his pistol, a faint smile playing about his lips. Was it a mocking smile? No, he decided, not from Stuart. Stuart was too much the gentleman to mock a soldier in defeat. It had been a wry smile, perhaps a touch sardonic, acknowledging the bitter irony of their positions. Once comrades-in-arms, now enemies. And yet, somehow, despite it all, still comrades. How to explain such a phenomenon?

Maria, perhaps, with her colorful way with words, might have found a way, but he felt at a loss to convey the proper sense of it. How could he describe his feelings when he saw Monroe, his head burst open like a melon, trailing brains, dragged off into the woods behind his horse? More to the point, how could he describe his curious *lack* of feelings? He had witnessed the horrific sight and it had registered upon his senses, but no more than that. He had not *felt* horrified, he had not, in fact, felt anything at all. What kind of person did that make him? How could he see a man die that way and not feel anything? And he had seen so many men die. . . .

When he had crossed swords with Jackson, briefly, during the encounter at the guns, he felt no hate for him. He had felt no anger and no fury, merely a grim determination to prevail over his enemy if he could, to at least survive if he could not. Was that what happened to men in a pitched battle, or was it a singular reaction that was his alone? He could find no answers. He could only sit there, recalling the events with a bitter melancholy, and wonder at the meaning of it all. Perhaps, he thought, this was, ultimately, what war could be reduced to. The victor felt elation and a sense of accomplishment, the vanquished merely felt morose and numb. Empty. Drained of all emotion.

With a weary sigh, he picked up his pen once more and continued writing in his journal.

McDowell finally ordered Miles back to cover our unprotected rear and the rebel initiative was lost, without ever having been properly taken. Why, I do not know, unless it was because they were as tired and dispirited as all the rest of us. Yet they had good reason for their spirits to be lifted, for they had won the day.

By nightfall, most of our army was safe past Centreville and on the road back to the Potomac. There was little else they could have done, except to walk all the twenty miles back, for there was no organization and there were no supplies. Most of the troops did not stop at the camps, but continued on across the bridges of the Potomac into Washington, where they made a sorry sight, indeed.

My own return to Washington was something less than auspicious, and somewhat embarrassing to boot. After being spared by the gallant and chivalrous Stuart, I began the slow and painful trudge back to the capital, limping along with the other stragglers and half expecting to be ridden down by rebel cavalry. The wound in my leg, which I had scarcely felt throughout the battle, was beginning to bother me severely, and though it was not serious, it was nevertheless quite painful and impeded my progress. I was not looking forward to the long walk still ahead of me.

A short distance past the bridge over Cub Run, the sound of galloping horses reached us, and once again the cry went up about the rebel cavalry, and alarmed stragglers plunged off the road into the brush and fields. Only the horsemen were not rebels, but a detachment of our own cavalry, Palmer's G Company, and who should rein in before me but George Custer, newly commissioned a lieutenant. With the pressing need for officers, his class had been graduated ahead of time and I had not even been aware of his presence on the field. Yet there he was, all cocky grin and flowing blond locks, offering me a hand up.

I rode behind him into Washington, and it was from Custer that I learned Mark had been placed under arrest back at West Point, over a duel in which the affections of a young woman were apparently involved. There was to be a court-martial. Knowing of my assignment as General Scott's aide, Custer tried to find me back in Washington, in the hope that I could somehow intercede on the behalf of my foolish younger brother.

That it was Mark who should be under arrest and not Custer did not really surprise me. Though both were irresponsible young hellions, Mark was always less adept at wriggling off the hook than Custer, and after satisfying myself that my little brother had not been so great a fool as to kill or seriously injure anyone, I promised that I would see what I could do. He was, after all, my brother, even if he was a source of constant embarrassment to me, and I privately resolved that if I could pull his fat out of the fire, I would use my influence, such as it was, to see him assigned as far away from me as possible.

The news of our defeat had reached the capital well in advance of us, carried by the picnicking civilians who had fled the scene on horseback and in carriages, and the mood of the city was subdued. People watched silently from windows and from door-ways as the beaten soldiers trickled in, dragging their weary feet, many of them having dropped their packs and weapons in their flight. They were powder-blackened and begrimed with road dust, which the rain had caked upon them, and the rain made little tracks, like tears, washing through the dirt upon their faces. I suspect there were many real tears intermingled with the raindrops.

It is a sad day for the Union, and for General McDowell, whom I have not seen since we were parted at Bull Run. Already, the vultures have begun to gather and I've heard talk attributing our defeat to McDowell's being drunk, when the fact is that McDowell's abstemiousness stands as an example to every soldier in the army. No matter. The public will demand a scapegoat and the unfortunate McDowell will be delivered up for slaughter, when the blame for our defeat lies elsewhere. What, I wonder, does Mr. Lincoln think of political expediency now?

West Point, New York, August 1861

Mark Gallio entered his father's study and stopped two paces in front of his desk, standing at attention with his cap held under his arm. "Sir, Cadet Gallio reporting, as ordered," he said stiffly.

Major Gallio stared silently at his son for a long moment, then sighed and said, "At ease, Lieutenant. Please sit down."

Mark frowned and looked puzzled at the address his father used, but sat down without a word.

"Yes, your commission has come through," his father said, "and the verdict of the court-martial has been set aside."

Mark looked enormously relieved. "Thank you, sir," he said.

"Don't bother to thank me," his father replied curtly. "I didn't lift a finger to help you. You can thank your brother. Apparently, your friend Custer managed to convince him to intercede with General Scott on your behalf. I don't need to tell you what an acutely embarrassing position that places me in."

"No, sir," Mark said softly, looking down.

Major Gallio took a deep breath and let it out slowly. "I blame myself as much as I blame you," he said. "Ever since your mother died, God rest her soul, I have been entirely too lenient with you. You have been a great disappointment to me, Mark."

Mark stiffened under the rebuke, but made no response. He was well aware of how his father felt. Since his arrest, and his subsequent court-martial, he had neither seen nor heard from the major. Nor had that surprised him. His father had been well aware of his attraction to Nancy Snow, but though he had neither openly encouraged nor discouraged it, it had been clear he disapproved. Nancy had been a friend of Maria's and he had not looked with favor on that relationship, either, but at least Maria had never taken on her friend's flirtatious ways. Maria's heart belonged to Travis Coulter, there had never been any question about that, but Nancy had always loved being surrounded by a flock of male admirers and she delighted in playing them off against one another. Mark had realized this, and had known Nancy was an incorrigible flirt, but he had seen it as a challenge and had somehow managed to convince himself that Nancy favored him above all her other suitors.

He had finally recovered from her spell, but it had taken a harsh dose of reality. Troy Chalmers had made a disparaging remark about her, which in retrospect, Mark realized, had been completely true, and he had gotten his back up and insisted Chalmers take it back. When Chalmers had refused, he challenged him to a duel with cavalry sabers. They had scarcely exchanged two blows when the cry went up that the officer of the guard was coming.

The spectators had scattered, and Mark had turned to run as well, knowing the penalty for dueling, when he felt a crushing blow to the back of his skull. The cowardly Chalmers had struck him from behind with the pommel of his saber and had knocked him senseless. He was discovered still holding the saber in his hand and placed under arrest. Despite the cowardly blow, he had refused to divulge the name of his antagonist and the court had found him guilty. As for the young woman whose honor he had so ardently defended, he'd heard not a word from her.

"I have your orders here," his father said. "And mine as well. I have requested to be placed back on active duty, as I am a soldier first and a teacher only second, and my country is at war. Besides, after this unfortunate event, I would find it extremely awkward to remain at the Academy, in any case. We are both being assigned to the Western front. I shall be reporting to General Frémont in Missouri. You have been assigned to the volunteer forces under General Grant, in Illinois. I have written to Sam Grant and specifically requested that he show you no favoritism on account of your being my son. I have also advised him that as an officer, you do not come highly recommended."

Mark compressed his lips into a tight grimace, but said nothing.

"It is up to you to prove me wrong," his father said. "War can either make a man or break him. As a cadet at the Academy, you have been a source of constant disappointment to me. That you should be commissioned as an officer in the United States Army has less to do with your own efforts than with the efforts of your brother and General Scott's kindly regard for this family. You have been given a second chance. Frankly, you do not deserve it."

Mark sat silent, his face deeply flushed.

"Have you nothing to say for yourself?"

"No, sir. No excuse, sir," Mark replied.

His father pursed his lips and nodded. "Very well. You are dismissed," he said.

Mark stood and snapped off a sharp salute. His father nodded and returned it, then Mark stepped back, pivoted a sharp about-face, and marched from his father's study.

Major Gallio put his head in his hands. This was not the way he would have wished for them to part. It was painful to have it be like this. He was sending his youngest son off to war, knowing there was a chance he'd never see him again, and he wished he could have brought himself to take him in his arms, give him a fatherly embrace, and send him off with warm words of encouragement. However, much as he had wanted to do that, he knew it would have been a mistake. Mark was young, but he was no longer a boy. He was a man, and he would have to learn to act like one, and to accept the consequences of his actions.

Not for the first time, he wondered if it was a mistake for Mark to follow in the family tradition. From early childhood, he and his brother had been very different. Robert had always been the strong and steady one. Mark was like his mother, willful and headstrong, with a touch of the devil in his soul. And yet he had loved him for it, just as he had loved Mark's mother. With Mark, he had been more forgiving. There had always been a warmth about Mark that his older brother lacked. Mark had always been more playful, more spontaneous, more eager to please. And more stubborn, and totally given over to the emotions of the moment. Gallio had hoped the Academy would temper him, would instill in him a sense of discipline, but he had been disappointed in that hope. Perhaps it was wrong for Mark to be a soldier.

He had all the physical abilities. He was very fit, an expert marksman, a good fencer, and an accomplished horseman. Such things had always come easily to him. But perhaps because they had come easily, he did not pursue them with the same dedication as did Robert, who outdid him in all those things, despite having less natural ability. He had never been able to discover if Mark's academic studies were beyond him or if Mark simply didn't care. Mark's response to questions on that subject were usually a shrug of the shoulders or, more often, a simple, "No excuse, sir." Whoever had come up with the idea that West Point cadets should respond to queries concerning their various shortcomings with the admission that there was no excuse for them had failed to anticipate that the admission could also be employed for purposes of obfuscation, Gallio thought wryly.

Had it been cruel of him to send Mark off like that? Perhaps. But it had also been necessary. It had been all he could do, after Mark had been arrested, to refrain from going to see him. Interceding on his behalf had been out of the question. He could not have placed the superintendent in such a position, and the

fact that Robert had gone to General Scott both angered and
relieved him.

Whether Scott had interceded as a favor to Robert or out of
regard for an old friend and subordinate or perhaps out of a
combination of both was immaterial. The fact was that certain
boundaries had been crossed and such things were simply not
done. He had little doubt that for Robert, it must have been
a painfully awkward and extremely difficult thing to do, and
that it had cost him. Scott may have granted his request, but
it would have certainly affected his respect for Robert. Major
Gallio knew just how highly his eldest son valued such respect.
Ever since Mark had enrolled in the Academy, he and his brother
had been drifting further and further apart. This final episode, he
felt certain, had driven an iron wedge between them. He knew his
oldest boy. Robert would never forgive his younger brother.

Not since his wife's death had Gallio felt so despondent. Though
they were both fighting for the same side, there was now a rift
between his sons, and his daughter was living in enemy country,
her husband fighting for the rebels, against her brothers. And now
against her father as well. He had never really believed it would
come to this, to war, though he had seen all the signs and had
chosen to ignore them. His thoughts turned to his daughter.

What must it be like for her? She was Travis Coulter's Yankee
wife and her family was fighting for the Union. He would have
given anything to have some word of her. He hoped she was being
well treated, that the Southerners were not holding her family
connections against her. If he could judge by Travis, and he felt he
could, then the Coulters were fine, upstanding people who would
not hold such things against Maria and would not mistreat her,
but the Coulters were not the only ones she would be in contact
with. Would they be able to protect her? Had he been wrong in
allowing her to marry Travis? Should he have foreseen this and
tried to do something to prevent it? Or could he have prevented
it? He smiled wanly as his thoughts turned to Maria's mother and
how she had married him in spite of all her family had done. No,
he thought, it was better that Maria had married with his blessing
than without it. For better or for worse, she had made her decision
and she was a Coulter now. His family was not the only one the
war had torn apart. Yet he felt as if his daughter were a prisoner
in a foreign land.

There was no greater honor, he had always believed, no greater
glory than service to one's country as a soldier. The Gallios had

held up that fine tradition for countless generations. It was not an easy path to walk, but nothing worthwhile was ever easy. He stared at the ring he wore on his left hand and wondered what had become of the original, the very first. Had it been lost, or did some distant descendant of Hanno still possess it?

From the very first, the Gallios had been warriors. It was in their blood. He took off the ring and held it in his hands, staring at it thoughtfully. The family tradition had been born in blood and violence, those inescapable companions of the ideals of honor and glory. For countless generations, that was the path the Gallios had followed. And it had all started with a slave.

Rome, 193 B.C., the villa of Marcus Lucius Gallio

In the evening, after she had been bathed and dressed by other slaves and anointed with oils, she was brought into a small room near the slaves' quarters on the first floor. The master of the house himself, Marcus Lucius Gallio, walked ahead of her and the overseer as they came into the room, which had only one occupant, who was stretched out on the bed as they came in. At the sight of Gallio, he immediately got to his feet, moving with a heavy, fluid grace.

"I have brought you something," the portly Gallio said, with a smile. "A wife."

She felt as if a huge fist had started squeezing her stomach.

"Her name is Cyrene," Gallio continued. "She is a Thracian. I paid six thousand denarii for her. There were many bidders, considering her youth and beauty, but I wanted only the best for the Lion of Carthage. She should produce strong sons."

Cyrene felt a tightness in her chest as she stared at the man standing before her. In the dim lamplight, his swarthy face was without expression. He looked frightening. He was tall and muscular, and where his tunic left his arms and one shoulder bare, she could see numerous ugly scars. He had scars on his legs as well. He was dark and hairy, massively built, and his dark eyes had a flat, unemotional gaze. He looked horrible, like a beast that walked upright. And this creature was to be her husband.

She had heard all about him from the other female slaves. This was the son of Hannibal, the Carthaginian general who had made war on Rome. His name was Hanno, and after he was captured, he had achieved fame in the arena as an indomitable gladiator before Gallio had bought him for a princely sum. This was the first time she had laid eyes on him, and the other female slaves of the household had told her that being chosen for him was a great honor. Cyrene did not feel honored. She felt terrified. She was fourteen years old.

"I will leave you to get better acquainted," Gallio said, with a smile, and beckoned the overseer after him as he left the room, leaving her alone with the brute that was to be her mate.

She could barely breathe. She did not know what to say or what to do. She had never been with a man before. And she had never seen a man who looked as frightening as this one. His hair was black and cropped short, close to his skull, and his face was wide and square-shaped. There was a long white scar on his cheek that stood out starkly against his dark complexion. His eyebrows were thick and dark, his eyes deeply set, and his mouth had a look of cruelty about it. His arms, shoulders, and chest were heavily muscled. He did not approach her, but simply stared at her. She looked down at the floor and trembled.

She felt as if she should say something, make some sort of effort to communicate with him, but she could not think of anything to say. Nor did he say anything. She could read nothing in those swarthy features. Nothing whatever. There was no trace of tenderness, or lust, or even curiosity. He merely looked at her, then turned and got back into bed.

She simply stood there, uncertain what to do. She was absolutely frozen with terror. She swallowed hard, fighting down her fear. If she displeased him, what would he do? Beat her? She did not think she could survive so much as one blow from those powerful arms. He had killed so many men. . . .

She inhaled deeply, raggedly, trying to summon up her courage. Her hands moving as if of their own accord, she loosened her *stola* and let it fall to the floor. She stood naked before him, feeling more vulnerable than she had ever felt in her life. She could not look at him. She kept staring at the floor. Her knees felt weak. After a long moment she risked a glance at him.

He was simply watching her, his face devoid of all expression. She felt herself shaking. He simply grunted and moved over to make room for her in the small bed.

She closed her eyes and took a deep breath, bit her lower lip, and lay down in the bed beside him, on her back, stiff and rigid. Her mouth felt dry. She tried to swallow and found she couldn't. She shut her eyes again, waiting for him to get on top of her. She hoped it wouldn't hurt too much, afraid that it might anger him if she cried out. She kept her eyes shut, waiting, but nothing happened.

She was afraid to move. Afraid to make the slightest sound. He exhaled heavily, with a groaning sort of sound, and rolled over onto his side, his back to her. Moments later, his labored breathing turned to snores.

She lay there, trembling, and breathed a ragged sigh of relief. She felt the tears start to come and fought to keep from making the slightest sound, for fear she would wake him. She had never felt so lost, so alone, so miserable, and so afraid. She wept and wished that she could die.

There was not much room in the small bed. Her flesh touched his as she gently pulled the bedclothes over her and a tremor of fear and revulsion ran through her. She could smell his maleness. He hadn't touched her. He hadn't even spoken to her. It suddenly occurred to her that perhaps he didn't want her, any more than she wanted him.

Ever since she had been taken into slavery, she had experienced what it was like to be regarded as nothing more than chattel, goods to be sold upon the block, at auction, like so much livestock. She had never thought it could be possible to sink to such a state of degradation. Her life was over. All her dreams had fled. Reality was harsh and cruel, and unforgiving.

She had once dreamed of love. It hadn't been so very long ago, and yet it seemed like an eternity away. She had dreamed about a man who would be kind and gentle, who would treat her with affection and tenderness, who would protect her and take care of her. And she, in turn, would take care of him, and nurture him, and bear his children, and sleep soundly in the warm security of his embrace. Instead, the fates had given her over into slavery, into the hands of this barbarian, a savage Carthaginian who, it was said, had killed over sixty men in the arena. The very thought of it staggered her imagination. And yet he hadn't touched her.

They called him the Lion of Carthage, she was told by the other slaves, and he had been sent to the arena so the citizens of Rome could have the pleasure of seeing the son of their most dreaded enemy fighting for his life to entertain them. His father had terrified them, and they had sought to win back some of their courage at his son's expense. They came, at first, to watch him die, but no opponent could be found to defeat him, to match the ferocity of his indomitable will to win, to survive at any cost. At first, they came to watch him die, and then they came to cheer him.

Now he was freed from the arena, and though still a slave, he no longer had to fight for his existence. That, in itself, Cyrene thought, should have been cause for relief, if not happiness. Yet she had perceived no emotion in him whatever. It was as if some essential part of him was missing. As if something within him had died.

As she lay there, utterly motionless for fear of disturbing the sleeping brute beside her, sleep refused to come and her despondency gradually gave way to a deep-rooted instinct for survival. There was nothing she could do to change her situation. To attempt escape was pointless. She knew she would never succeed. Besides, where could she go? There was nothing left of her home or of her family. She could attempt escape through death, but having confronted that alternative, she chose life instead. Her spirit clung to it tenaciously. Life, no matter how humiliating or degrading, was all she had left and it was precious. She would survive this. Somehow, she would find a way.

Richmond, Virginia, September 1861

It was with mixed feelings that Maria parted from the Coulters. They had tried their best to convince her to remain with them in Charleston, or at the very least, to stay at Tall Pines, the family plantation outside Summerville, where Becky could have gone along to keep her company, but she remained firm in declining all their entreaties as politely as she could.

The Coulters had, of course, supposed that her desire to go to Richmond was motivated by her concern for Travis, that she wanted to be near him, or as near to him as possible. Following the battle at Manassas, many wives and loved ones of those who served on the front lines had gone to Richmond, because news of who had survived and who had fallen was slow in coming. The wounded were brought into Richmond, and if Travis were among them, then that was where he'd be.

Sam Coulter had understood that Maria felt her place was with her husband, or as close to him as she could manage to be, so when he realized she would not be dissuaded, he had provided her with a letter of introduction to one of his old business partners who now had a position in the War Department of the Confederacy. When they said their tearful farewells, Sam Coulter had embraced her warmly and told her he was proud of her.

Maria had felt regret at their parting, for she had come to feel a great deal of affection for them, but she also felt relieved and guilty, for she had other motives in wanting to leave Charleston and the Coulter household. Motives that had nothing at all to do with Travis. Charleston had never felt like home to her, no matter how hard she'd tried to make herself fit in, and Tall Pines might have made a pleasant retreat under other circumstances, but the war had changed everything and there was no retreating from the events that were taking place around her.

The Coulters had never been anything but kind to her and they had accepted her into their family with open hearts. Yet, despite all her efforts, Maria could not make herself feel as if she belonged with them. Through no fault of their own, through no action or lack of action on their part, she nevertheless felt as if she were an interloper. Perhaps the fault was hers, she thought, or perhaps it was merely the circumstances of the war. No matter; she felt alone, cut off, and utterly adrift.

Throughout Charleston, and indeed, throughout all the states of the Confederacy, the women of the South were doing their part to help in the war effort. At the Coulter household, as elsewhere, they would gather in small cooperative societies, to roll bandages from sheets and tablecloths, to sacrifice their linen undergarments to the cause, to knit socks and homespun for the gallant boys at the front, and to talk of the war and the hardships it was visiting upon the South.

The Union naval blockade was having its effect and there were always shortages. The goods the blockade runners were able to bring in could not keep up with the demand and prices rose rapidly as the supplies diminished. The once common calico cloth had quickly doubled in price, from fifty cents to one dollar per yard, and many merchants were demanding even more. Shoes were becoming prohibitively expensive; silk quickly became unobtainable; tea and coffee became impossible to find. The women would exchange recipes for brewing tea from sassafras and other local herbs, and for making coffee from a grind of wheat and rye, or chestnuts. Eggs and butter became scarce, and the impounding of supplies to feed the troops had resulted in many of the farmers refusing to bring their produce in to market for fear it would be seized.

The women of the South, it seemed, had become organized into a vast tribe of seamstresses, making woolen shirts and jackets, cloth caps and overcoats, gloves and quilted blankets, shirts and socks and trousers, all to clothe "our brave boys in the field," as well as to provide what they could no longer buy themselves.

Maria had flinched, inwardly, whenever she heard the phrase "our boys." Yes, her husband was among them, but the words "our boys" could not pass the lips of many Charleston women without a quick, uneasy glance in her direction, for it was widely known that *her* boys, her father and her brothers, were fighting for the Union. Who was to say if one of their husbands or their sons would not fall from a shot fired by her father or, perhaps, one of her brothers?

Maria heard no rude or unkind words from any of the Charleston women with whom she came in contact, yet there was an awkwardness about them whenever she was present that she could not ignore.

She could not escape the feeling that her presence made them feel ill at ease, and often she would excuse herself, pleading a headache or some other ailment, knowing the moment she left, they would all sigh with relief and go on with their conversation, unfettered by her presence. With some of them, she sensed resentment. With others, pity, which seemed even worse. She felt caught between two worlds, unable to belong to either one.

Not that she thought Richmond would be significantly different, but at least in Richmond she would not be trapped in the Coulter household, stuck in the awkward situation of having to watch everyone tiptoe around her sensibilities. While she had been there, guests at the Coulter home could not propose a toast to "the glorious South and the defeat of the damn Yankees" without someone clearing his throat softly and then the speaker glancing at her anxiously and hastily adding, "No offense intended, Mrs. Coulter, to be sure." It had made her feel even worse than if they had said nothing.

In Richmond, where there were many Southern sympathizers from border states like Maryland, chances were her Northern accent would not stand out quite so obviously, and she would not feel pressured by family obligations to take part in the various little get-togethers and sewing circles, where she always felt completely out of place.

Aside from that, there had been the added embarrassment of the fact that she had little talent for such handiwork. Her skills at sewing had been largely limited to things like replacing buttons on her father's uniforms. Her clothes had always been store-bought, and when other girls had spent their idle hours learning to do needlepoint, Maria had preferred to go riding or shooting with her brothers. She could ride as well as any man and shoot better than most, but when it came to things like knitting and sewing, she felt worse than useless. She knew how to cook, but the Coulters had Mammy Bess for that and Bess seemed to feel uncomfortable whenever she tried to help her in the kitchen. She had a need to do something to contribute and she felt superfluous. So when she read about the need for doctors and nurses in the hospitals of Richmond, she announced her decision to go to Virginia and volunteer her services.

Richmond resembled a vast military camp. Regiments mustered in the city and there were constant maneuvers, parades, drills, and parties for the officers and politicians. Newly enlisted troops arrived by the hundreds every day and there was a constant bustle of activity in the city streets. The president, Jefferson Davis, resided in a graceful three-story mansion on a slope overlooking the James River. Commonly known as the Confederate White House, the mansion's light gray stucco walls had caused some people to refer to it as the "Gray House," in keeping with the gray uniforms of the Confederate troops. Although located in the city, it had the look of a plantation house, with its white steeple and eight tall columns lined up in pairs across the veranda, which extended around the side of the house and provided a panoramic view of the James River and the Virginia valley.

Situated on the north side of a bend in the James River, Richmond was surrounded by high ground, so there was often an early-morning mist over the city. A bronze statue of George Washington, a Virginian and a slave owner, stood in the capital square, between St. Paul's Church and the Virginia capitol building. He sat astride his charger, sword at his side, with his raised arm pointing to the south. And in the North, the Union leaders were also looking south, toward Richmond, with its tobacco warehouses and its flour mills, its railroad terminals and the sprawling factory plant of the Tredegar Iron Works, five acres of buildings that housed over 1,200 muscular slaves, working around the clock at the raging furnaces and boilers, turning out guns and ammunition for the Southern armies. If Richmond could be captured, the back of the Confederacy would be broken.

The character of the city had changed with the advent of the war. The black population in the city was growing rapidly, and most of it was male, which made many of the white residents of Richmond ill at ease. The young male slaves were needed to work in Richmond's overburdened factories and in digging trenches and embankments to provide for the city's defense, but with Lincoln promising that slaves used by the South against the North would be freed, the fear of a Northern-encouraged slave insurrection had become greater in Richmond than in any other city in the South. With the population of black males so greatly outnumbering black females, brothels and gambling establishments catering to blacks had sprung up in Penitentiary Bottom and Screamersville, and many white families were sending their women out of the city.

There was also a profusion of new saloons and gambling halls to relieve the white troops of what little money they had. Inflation was taking its toll. The Confederate paper money was losing value by the day. A hotel room in Richmond could be obtained for twenty dollars in Confederate bills. That same hotel room could be had for one dollar in gold coin. A suit of clothes that went for three hundred dollars in Confederate bills could be purchased for thirty dollars in gold. A gallon of whiskey could be had for one dollar and twenty-five cents in gold, but a soldier who was paid in paper money was forced to pay twenty-five dollars for the same amount of whiskey. The eleven dollars per month that a Confederate private was paid was actually worth only fifty-five cents in coin. The price of gold in the North was double what it was in Richmond, so speculation was rampant and there were fortunes to be made by those who were clever and unscrupulous.

It was to this teeming and tense city, so different from the relaxed and refined sensibilities of Charleston, that Maria came in late September, accompanied by Spencer Coulter, who had enlisted in the army and had come along to make sure she arrived safely. Elizabeth had been against Spencer's joining up, not wanting to see both her sons at risk, but Spencer had insisted it would be cowardly for him to remain at home while all the sons of the Confederacy were answering the call to duty, and his father had supported him in his decision. He would join his brother in Stuart's cavalry, reporting in as soon as Maria became settled.

They took a carriage from the station to the Spotswood Hotel, where Spencer took rooms for each of them, paying in gold coin. On the way to the hotel, they passed a gathering of people in the square, and as the carriage slowed to make its way past the crowd Maria asked Spencer what was happening.

"They're holding a slave auction," Spencer said. And turning to the coachman, he added, "Drive on."

"No, wait," Maria said. "I want to see."

The coachman glanced back at Spencer questioningly.

"There's nothing much for you to see," said Spencer. "I doubt you will find it very interesting."

"I've never seen a slave auction," said Maria.

"Ah, well then, by all means, you should stay and watch," said a well-dressed man standing nearby on the outskirts of the crowd. He spoke with a British accent. "You ought to have the opportunity to see what it is your people are fighting for."

Maria turned to stare at him. There seemed to be a hint of derision in his voice, yet he spoke pleasantly enough, in a casual, offhand manner. He stood just under six feet tall, elegantly slim, with curly, light brown hair and light green eyes that seemed alert and clever. He was, Maria guessed, in his early thirties, boyishly handsome, with the same sort of insolent, mischievous expression that Mark's friend Custer had, though Custer had a weak chin, Maria thought, and this man's features were strong and well defined. He wore a well-tailored, dove-gray suit and vest with an immaculate white silk shirt and a neatly tied black cravat. He had a matching gray bowler tilted at a rakish angle, slightly forward on his head. He looked, Maria thought, like an indolent English dandy.

"And who might you be, sir?" asked Spencer stiffly.

"The name is Cord," the Englishman replied. "Geoffrey Cord, of the *London Morning Post,* at your service."

"A newspaperman," said Spencer, with a grimace of distaste.

"A journalist, sir," said Cord, with an engaging smile, "here to observe your gallant struggle and report to my fellow Englishmen back home. Now, I fear you have the advantage of me. Might I know whom I have the pleasure of addressing?"

"My name is Spencer Coulter, sir, of Charleston, and this is my sister-in-law, Maria. And in the interests of not giving your readers the wrong impression, allow me to point out to you that this war is not being fought to preserve slavery, but to preserve self-determination. It is not the South, sir, that is prosecuting this war, but the North. We wish merely to be allowed to go our own way, in peace."

"Yes, and to take your slaves with you, one assumes," Cord replied jauntily. He shrugged. "That strikes me as perfectly reasonable. After all, they are private property, are they not? You paid good money for them, you shouldn't be expected to have to give them up. I understand they're quite handy things to have about, these Negroes. Work hard, don't take up too much space, don't eat much, docile sorts. Reasonably priced, too. A man who's well-off could buy himself an entire family at one of these things. Of course, you don't have to take the whole lot. They'll be glad to break 'em up for you, like that one there is doing.''

Maria looked out toward the platform and saw a Negro woman being parted from her daughter. The woman was perhaps in her late twenties or early thirties. The daughter was perhaps thirteen or fourteen years old. The Negro girl was crying and reaching out for her mother as she was led away. Her mother simply stood there, saying nothing, making no sounds whatever, but Maria could see her shoulders shaking as she sobbed silently.

"They do seem to get attached to one another, don't they?" Cord said, watching the spectacle. "But I understand they get over it. Rather like kittens." He turned toward Maria. "See anything you like? Or are we just window shopping?"

"Now, see here, sir—" Spencer began, but Maria interrupted him.

She turned her face away and quickly said, "Spencer, for God's sake, take me away from here. *Please*."

Spencer glowered at the Englishman, but he acceded to her request and told the coachman to drive on. Maria glanced over her shoulder as they drove away and saw the reporter tip his hat to her cheerfully.

"Lord help us if that's the sort of newspaperman they send here," Spencer said. "You can expect nothing but distortion from his ilk. But they'll come around to recognizing us soon enough when their mills start getting hungry for our cotton."

He glanced at Maria and saw that she was pale and shaken.

"I'm sorry if that man has upset you, Maria," he said solicitously. "I should have gotten down and thrashed him for his impertinence. I have a mind to tell the driver to turn around and—"

"No!" said Maria, shaking her head and looking away. "No, just take me away from here, Spencer. *Please,* just take me away!"

CHAPTER FOUR

Cairo, Illinois, September 1861

OUT OF THE frying pan and into the muck of a drowned fire, Mark thought, when he got off the train in Cairo. Robert may have saved his bacon by using his influence with General Scott, but he had also exacted his revenge. Like an unforgiving Russian Czar, he had effectively exiled him to Siberia. Trust big brother to have me sent as far away as possible, thought Mark, where I won't embarrass him too much.

At first impression, Cairo struck him as an ugly, pestilential town. At second impression, the first impression was confirmed. The place was a soggy breeding ground for fever, dysentery, and mosquitoes. There were swarms of the voracious insects everywhere. In addition to the mosquitoes, there were the rats. Thousands of them. They scurried through the streets and alleyways and darted across the sidewalks. When the Illinois Central trains pulled in along the tracks atop the levee, hundreds of the loathsome, squirming creatures were crushed beneath the wheels. The rats fed on the decomposing carcasses of mules and horses and other refuse that was simply dumped into the river by the waterfront, and the stench was unbelievable. Steam pumps were kept running constantly to keep the water from flooding the sidewalks. The streets were swamps and the mud was everywhere, tracked into the buildings and the soldiers' quarters, clinging obstinately to shoes and trousers. A grown man could easily get stuck just trying to cross the street. The town made Mark think of a giant hog wallow.

Located at the confluence of the Ohio River and the Mississippi, Cairo had strategic significance. At least, General Frémont thought so, and he had sent troops to reinforce Grant's command there, and to ensure that all shipping to the South was blocked. About one hundred miles southeast of St. Louis, with its important railroad junctions, Cairo—pronounced "Kay-ro" by the locals— was a potential base of operations for Union thrusts into Kentucky and Tennessee. However, Mark was convinced anything that happened in Missouri, Tennessee, or farther south along the Mississippi River would only be a sideshow at best. Assuming anything significant happened in the Western Department at all.

Everyone knew the important actions of the war would take place back east, in Virginia. As soon as the Army of the Potomac launched its offensive against Richmond, the war would be over. Virginia was the key. When Richmond fell, the Confederacy would collapse. Custer would be there to share in all the glory, Mark thought with despair, along with Robert, damn his eyes, while he sat in the mud at Cairo, twiddling his thumbs. He would miss out on all of it.

He knew he had no one but himself to blame. He had gotten off easy. Robert could just as well have refused to lift a finger to help him. In fact, Mark had been surprised to learn it was Robert who had interceded for him, and not his father. Time after time, Robert had warned him that one of these days he was going to get himself into trouble unless he straightened up and started taking things more seriously.

"And if you choose to be stubborn and ignore my warning," Robert had told him, "then don't come running to me when you find yourself in over your head."

Well, he hadn't gone running to his big brother. It was Custer who had made the plea on his behalf and Mark knew it must have been an unpleasant and embarrassing experience for his older brother. Robert had a low opinion of Custer and Custer knew it. Robert had always thought Custer was the worst cadet at the Academy, a fact Custer had cheerfully acknowledged.

"But at least," he'd added, with a grin, "I'm not an insufferable stuffed shirt, like your brother."

They'd laughed about it then, because it was true, Robert *was* an insufferable stuffed shirt. He was always so earnest and serious that it was almost comical. The perfect cadet. The model soldier. Custer had always referred to him as "Caesar." Before he'd left for Washington, Custer had stopped in to see him, saying, "Don't worry, old chap, I'll find Caesar and see if I can't get him to pull a few strings, for family's sake. After all, there *is* a war on and they need every able officer they can get. No point in drumming you out for a silly duel that you didn't even get to fight, is there?"

Mark had morosely told him not to bother, because he could not imagine Robert going to General Scott on his behalf. He still couldn't believe Robert had actually done it. Robert was very proud and it must have been a humiliating experience for him. The fact that Scott had granted the request said much about the high regard in which he apparently held Robert, yet Mark knew that in asking the favor, his brother must have fallen a few points in Scott's esteem. He also knew Robert would never forgive him for it. He could hardly blame him for putting as much distance between them as possible. He knew he had been a painful embarrassment to Robert at West Point, as well as to his father, and now he had embarrassed them both in front of the general-in-chief. He wouldn't be surprised if Robert never spoke to him again. As for the major . . .

He had let his father down. He had alienated his brother, and he could not even turn to his little sister for support, because Maria was now in enemy country. For the first time in his life, Mark felt that he was truly on his own. He felt alone, depressed, and overwhelmed with guilt.

He had yet to face the unpleasant task of reporting in to General Grant. He knew it would not be pleasant because of the letter that had preceded him, in which his father had spoken of him in somewhat less than glowing terms.

Originally placed in command of the Twenty-first Illinois regiment in June, Ulysses S. Grant had been promoted to brigadier general in August and ordered to Ironton, to take command of the District of Southeast Missouri. He had shortly thereafter received reinforcements from Frémont, but when they arrived, their commander, Brigadier General Benjamin M. Prentiss, carried orders that had relieved Grant of command. It was apparently a mix-up over seniority. Grant's commission bore the same date as that of Prentiss, but Grant's commission had been backdated, and since Prentiss had actually held the rank longer than Grant, headquarters had assumed he was senior.

However, according to army regulations, if two similarly ranked officers had commissions that bore the same dates, seniority was determined by prior rank in the service. Grant and Prentiss had both been captains in the Mexican War, but while Prentiss had been captain of volunteers, Grant had been a captain of regulars, which meant that Grant, in fact, outranked Prentiss. Before it was all straightened out, Grant had been sent to take command of the

post at Jefferson City. He remained there for only one week before
he received new orders, correcting the situation and putting him
back in command of the District of Southeast Missouri.

General Frémont was concerned about the rebel forces under
General Hardee, south of Cape Girardeau, and he had ordered
Grant to go there and link up with General Prentiss and Colonel Wallace, the commander at Bird's Point, across the river
from Cairo.

The plan had called for Grant to take charge and clear the area
of rebel troops, fortify the defenses at Cape Girardeau, Ironton,
Bird's Point, and Cairo, then move south, making "demonstrations" along the Mississippi, a show of strength to prevent the
rebels from reinforcing General Price and to keep them from
occupying Columbus, with its high bluffs commanding the river,
and Paducah, on the opposite shore.

Unfortunately, when Grant met up with Prentiss at Cape
Girardeau on the first day of September, Prentiss would not
concede that Grant outranked him. He got his back up and and
stubbornly refused to obey Grant's orders. Apparently, he had not
heard from Frémont about Grant's being put back in command
of the district, and when Grant pressed the issue, Prentiss rather
childishly requested a leave. When Grant refused, Prentiss handed
him his resignation. When Grant refused his resignation, Prentiss
placed himself under arrest and departed for St. Louis in a huff,
to take the matter up with General Frémont in person, which left
his troops without a commander and effectively put a halt to the
entire operation.

In the meantime, General Leonidas Polk, the Episcopal bishop
who had gone to West Point and was in command of the rebel
forces in the West, had been alerted by the Union reconnaissance parties that had gone downriver from Cairo to Belmont,
a steamboat landing across from Columbus. Polk had correctly
deduced what the enemy was planning and he wasted no time
in sending General Gideon Pillow in to occupy Columbus ahead
of the federal forces. It was, thought Mark, typical of everything
he had heard about the way things were handled in the Western
Department, under the celebrated General Frémont.

Known as the "Pathfinder of the West," for his years of service
with the Army Topographical Engineers, the flamboyant John C.
Frémont was a very famous, rich, and influential man. He had
mapped the passes of the Rockies with Kit Carson and had helped
bring California into the Union. The Californians had elected him

to the Senate and he had been the Republican party's first candidate for president. With his headquarters at an elegant three-story mansion in St. Louis, Frémont was said to live like some feudal lord, surrounded by a personal bodyguard of three hundred men, all outfitted in resplendent uniforms bedecked with plumes and gold braid, and his personal staff consisted of self-styled European adventurers and soldiers of fortune who had come to America for a taste of the war and had offered their services to the famous Pathfinder.

General Frémont seemed to exist at the center of a storm of controversy. There were scandalous rumors of corruption and patronage involving military contractors in his department, and the only significant battle that had taken place under his command had been the disaster at Wilson's Creek, where General Nathaniel Lyon had fought a combined rebel force under Generals Sterling Price and Ben McCulloch, the former Texas Ranger. Denied reinforcements by Frémont, Lyon found himself outnumbered three to one. His troops were routed after a bloody battle that was the worst Union defeat since Bull Run, and Lyon himself was killed. What was left of his command retreated over a hundred miles, all the way to Rolla, leaving Price free to advance further into Missouri, recruiting guerrillas to his force from the local countryside.

Frémont had caused further controversy by issuing a proclamation declaring martial law. He had announced he was taking over the administrative powers of the state, decreed the death penalty for guerrillas, and freed the slaves of all those who supported the rebellion. This had not endeared him to the president, and Lincoln had ordered him not to execute any guerrillas, for fear the rebels would execute Union prisoners man for man in retaliation. The president also asked Frémont to modify his proclamation in respect to freeing the slaves, in order to conform with acts of Congress. It was, apparently, an effort by the president to avoid ruffling Frémont's feathers by directly countermanding his orders. Nevertheless, the message couldn't have been more clear.

It certainly seemed direct enough to Mark, who would have thought that when the president asked a subordinate to do something, it was generally construed to be an order. However, Frémont had chosen not to see it that way. Not only had he dug in his heels and refused to modify his proclamation in any way without a specific and public order from the president to do so, but he had sent his imperious wife, Jessie, to Washington to see Lincoln in person and explain to him the error of his ways.

When Mark heard about it, he was absolutely astounded. If Lincoln did not immediately remove Frémont from command, he thought, it would be a miracle. Rumor had it that the president was not a firm man and that he was indecisive, out of his depth in running the country, much less the war, but Frémont's behavior was pushing things too far. On such a sensitive issue, the president could not possibly allow himself to be intimidated, because caving in to Frémont would not only make him appear totally emasculated, it would also drive all the Union supporters in Kentucky straight into the arms of Jeff Davis. The entire Western Department seemed to be a circus, Mark thought, a hopeless comedy of errors, and it was into this ludicrous mess that Robert had deposited him.

If any of this caused General Grant undue concern, he didn't seem to show it. After the contretemps with Prentiss, Grant had given up waiting for orders and had gone up the Ohio to Paducah with two regiments, occupying it without firing a shot. The arrival of the rebels had been expected by the townspeople within a matter of hours and they were stunned and not at all pleased to receive Grant's troops instead.

After seizing supplies meant for the Confederates, Grant left a small occupying force at Paducah under General Paine, with strict orders that none of the Union soldiers should harm any civilians, regardless of their sympathies, or engage in any plunder. He then returned to Cairo, only to discover that orders had just arrived from Frémont, allowing him to attempt taking Paducah if he thought it was feasible. Apparently, it was.

Noting the polarization of the Kentuckians, with the residents of Paducah strongly sympathetic to the rebels while the state legislature was still to a large degree pro-Union, Grant sought to soothe potentially offended sensibilities by sending a telegram to the state house of representatives, informing them that "Confederate forces in considerable number have invaded the territory of Kentucky," thereby hoping to provide a justification for his actions.

While well intentioned, this act earned him a slap on the wrist from Frémont, who felt that he himself should be the only one to deal with state officials. As if to underscore this official reprimand, Frémont took Paducah out of Grant's control and assigned its command to General Charles F. Smith. However, if Frémont had intended for Grant to be stung by this transfer of authority, he was doomed to disappointment, for Smith had been Grant's commandant at West Point and there was no soldier in the Army whom Grant respected more. He sent Smith his best troops for reinforcements at Paducah and kept, in his own words, "the raw, unarmed and ragged" for himself at Cairo.

Mark found General Grant seated at his desk in his head-quarters, which were located in a converted bank building. Grant sat slumped over, poring over maps, looking less like a general than a somewhat seedy bank clerk. He glanced up at Mark as he reported in, grunted, and returned his salute with a gesture that was little more than an indifferent wave of his hand.

The commander of the District of Southeast Missouri was not an imposing figure of a man. He stood five feet, eight inches tall and weighed 135 pounds. His sandy brown hair was somewhat unkempt and his beard was long and shaggy. He wore a plain and slightly baggy blue coat with no insignia or decorations save for the shoulder straps bearing the single star of a briga-dier. At a quick glance, it didn't even look like a uniform. A battered, black felt slouch hat rested on a corner of his crowd-ed desk. He was round-shouldered, with a habit of slouching, and as he studied the maps, he smoked a stained meerschaum pipe that was clamped between his teeth. There were tobacco ashes on the desk and he brushed them aside with an absent motion.

"Stand at ease, Lieutenant," he said, looking up at Mark. He nodded. "I remember your father well. In fact, I've recently received a letter from him."

"Yes, sir," Mark said uncomfortably. "I am aware of that."

"As you are aware, I presume, of the letter's contents?" Grant asked, speaking around the pipe clenched between his teeth.

"Yes, sir."

Grant grunted once more. "I understand, Lieutenant, that you narrowly avoided being court-martialed. What was your offense?"

"Dueling, sir."

"Dueling," Grant repeated flatly. "Why?"

"The honor of a young lady was involved, sir."

"I see. And what was the outcome? Of the duel, I mean?"

Mark moistened his lips, nervously. "It . . . never actually came to that, sir. We were interrupted by the arrival of the guard and, uh, when I turned away from my opponent, I was knocked sense-less. And then placed under arrest. Sir."

"And what did you learn from this affair, Lieutenant?" Grant asked.

"To be somewhat more selective of the ladies whose honor I choose to defend. And not to turn my back on an opponent. Sir."

Grant repressed a smile, though not entirely successfully. "Well, Lieutenant Gallio, I would say that those were worthwhile lessons to be learned," he said. "I always make it a point never to turn my back to an opponent. And as for the honor of ladies, I have found that a truly honorable lady generally requires no defense."

"Yes, sir."

"Your father writes to me that your record at West Point left much to be desired," Grant continued.

"Yes, sir, I suppose that's true," said Mark.

Grant nodded. "Well, my own record at the Academy was not especially distinguished. Your father also requests that I afford you no special treatment or consideration on account of any personal feelings I may have for him, and I can assure you that will be the case. He further states that you do not come very highly recommended as an officer." He raised his eyebrows questioningly.

Mark's compressed his lips into a tight grimace. "Yes, sir," he replied stiffly. "He told me that, sir."

Grant grunted. "Well, neither do I," he replied dryly.

Mark stared at him with surprise, not certain he'd heard the man correctly.

"I understand there was considerable debate over my appointment to this command," continued Grant. "They say I drink." He paused and stared down at his desk for a moment. "Well, fact is, I have been known to do that." He looked back up at Mark. "I tell you this, Lieutenant, in all frankness, because I want you to know that while I am not a perfect man, I believe myself to be a fair one. I do not prejudge the men under my command, nor do I expect them to be glittering parade-ground soldiers. I do, however, expect them to be *good* soldiers, and I expect them to have discipline. This is not West Point. This is the army, and these are untrained volunteers, not regulars. I need fighters, Lieutenant, not brass polishers. As far as I am personally concerned, you come to me with a clean slate. What you choose to write upon that slate is entirely up to you. I trust we understand each other."

"Yes, sir," Mark replied, feeling relieved. "And thank you, sir."

Grant nodded curtly. "Good. The men all have their officers, such as they are, but I personally find myself woefully understaffed. There is much to do. We need to build log cabins for our winter quarters, we need supplies, we need artillery, and we need muskets. Those doggone Austrian muskets we were sent are worse than useless. We need tents, we need blankets, we need shoes and shirts—in short, Lieutenant, we need everything and we have no money to get it with. On top of that, the men need to be drilled. I do not expect to put on any grand reviews; I will be satisfied if they know their left foot from their right and if they can hit what they are shooting at. Therefore, since I cannot possibly do everything myself, I will assign you to my staff and work your tail off. That will be all. Report to the adjutant and he will assign you quarters. Dismissed."

"Sir!" said Mark, stiffening to attention and snapping off a sharp salute.

Grant gave him the same indifferent wave and returned his attention to the maps on his desk. Mark stepped back, about-faced, and marched from the office.

He didn't quite know what to make of his new commanding officer. He did not know much about him, except what he'd managed to pick up before leaving West Point. As Grant had admitted himself, his record at the Academy had not been especially distinguished. The only real mark he had left behind was as an expert horseman. There wasn't a single horse he couldn't ride or break and he held the academy jump record. He had not come from a military family. His father was a tanner in Illinois.

He'd been born Hiram Ulysses Grant, but had transposed his initials prior to arriving at West Point, because he had realized they spelled out "hug" and had concluded that this would be an invitation to some levity at his expense. However, as a result of a clerical error in his appointment, his name was entered on the rolls of the Academy not as U. H. Grant, but as U. S. Grant, which led some cadets to speculate mockingly that the initials stood for "United States."

"No," joked an upperclassman by the name of Sherman, "they stand for Uncle Sam," and Sam Grant he became. And with the sole exception of his uncanny ability with horses, he had not left behind any great impression at West Point. He had graduated with the rank of private, twenty-first in a class of thirty-nine.

Mark's father and Grant had served together in the Mexican War, and the major had liked him, had thought he was a good soldier, but afterward, their paths had diverged sharply. The major had come to teach at the Academy, but Grant had left the army in disgrace, forced to resign, it was said, for drunkenness. Word had it that until the war broke out, he had been a deadbeat, wandering around his hometown in a shapeless army greatcoat with all the insignia removed, hauling cordwood, and borrowing money from anyone who'd lend it to him. And now he was a general.

"The final irony," said Captain Kinchloe, puffing his briar pipe alight. "Nobody was willing to trust him enough to give him a commission, much less appoint him to command. He'd failed at being a farmer, he went broke chopping and hauling cordwood, he'd failed at selling real estate, he'd even worked the fields with freed slaves. Only damn job he could get was as a leather-goods clerk, and that was working for his family. Wasn't any great shakes at that, either. He'd failed at everything. The only thing he was any damn good at was being a soldier, but the army didn't want a deadbeat drunk."

Captain John Kinchloe was the officer with whom Mark shared his quarters, a canvas wall tent with upright sides and a sloping roof. It was set up over a wood-plank floor, and as camp accommodations went, it was something of a luxury, with an iron stove and enough room inside for a man to stand up and move about. It was considerably more spacious than the more widely used Sibley and wedge tents, into which the men were often crammed so tightly that if anyone wanted to roll over in the middle of the night, all of them had to do it together. As an officer, Mark was entitled to more comfortable accommodations, and he was assigned to Kinchloe's tent, where a vacancy had recently arisen due to Lieutenant Flemming's death from fever. The adjutant had imparted this information in a rather nonchalant manner that seemed to indicate this was not at all an uncommon occurrence, something Mark did not find especially encouraging.

The officer with whom he would be sharing his quarters was a somewhat phlegmatic, laconic man of forty-six, of average height and with a medium build. He had dark brown hair, worn long, almost to his shoulders, and he was clean-shaven, save for a bushy mustache that covered his upper lip. He was not a West Point graduate, but had served in the regular army. A native of Illinois, he had lied about his age and joined up as an enlisted man when he was just a boy. He'd seen more than his share of army life. He had fought Indians on the frontier, he had seen service in the Mexican War, and he had been in the Fourth Infantry with Captain Grant in 1852, when that hapless regiment had been ordered from New

York to the Pacific coast, by way of Panama. Mark had listened to the story with utter fascination, its telling prompted by his questions about his new commanding officer.

They had arrived during the rainy season in July, at the port built by the financier William Henry Aspinwall as a base for his proposed railroad across the isthmus. A nightmare was awaiting them. When they reached the Chagres River, it was only to discover that the mules meant to transport the men, their families, and supplies had been sold out from under them by an unscrupulous contractor. Trapped in the mud, the endless rain, and the steaming humidity, the men had started to succumb to cholera. As quartermaster, Grant had hired native porters to carry the sick along with the supplies in woven hammocks and he had started the stranded regiment marching to Panama City. One-third of them had died along the way. At Panama City, Grant had turned an old hulk into a floating hospital to nurse those who were sick with fever and himself slept no more than two or three hours a night, doing everything he could to purchase medicines and food for the decimated troops. When they finally shipped north, to Fort Vancouver, over one hundred men had died.

"No one who survived that terrible ordeal will ever forget that man," said Kinchloe, puffing on his pipe as he stared off into the distance. "He was a rock. Even at the worst of times, he kept his head. Nothing rattled him. He had an objective, to reach Panama City and to keep the men alive, as many of them as he could, and nothing would deter him from it."

"Was it then the drinking started?" Mark asked.

Kinchloe gave him a sharp glance, then shook his head. "No. That was later, at Fort Humboldt. A lousy, filthy, little frontier trading post. He was miserable, living in a small log cabin, unable to send for Julia and the boys because he couldn't afford to keep them there on what the army paid him. He thought of resigning from the army, but he knew he wasn't any good at business. All he could see was poverty staring him in the face. Poverty and loneliness. So he started drinking whiskey."

Kinchloe took his pipe out of his mouth and held it absently, looking at it. "Nor was he the only one. Some men can hold their whiskey, though." He shook his head. "Grant never could. Once he got started, he couldn't seem to stop. He showed up drunk for paymaster duty one day and Colonel Buchanan, who had it in for him, made him fill out an unsigned resignation. One more time and he was out. Grant stayed sober for a while, but then at a party, some blamed woman urged him to have a little punch and that was all it took. Next day Buchanan called him in and had him sign that resignation."

Kinchloe paused to light his pipe once more. Mark sat on his cot, listening silently.

"Well, I guess you heard about what happened after that," Kinchloe continued. "The man fell about as low as a man can fall. Even when the war broke out, the army didn't want him, so he drilled volunteers for the state militia as a civilian and cooled his heels in one office after another, trying to get himself an appointment. But it seemed to no avail. The best he could do was get a position as a clerk, copying out orders. That is, until the Twenty-first Illinois came along."

Kinchloe smiled. "Boy, we were the bottom of the barrel, let me tell you. I'd left the army at Fort Humboldt and gone home, having had about enough by then, but I joined up again when the war broke out and they made me a captain, because of my prior service. But in the Twenty-first, that wasn't any great distinction, you can rest assured of that. In the beginning, the Twenty-first was nothing but a bunch of wild, unruly farm boys who didn't know anything about the army and didn't really care to learn. We ran off our first commanding officer. Nobody else wanted us, so they made Grant a colonel and stuck him with the job.

"You should have seen the day he arrived to take command," Kinchloe continued. He smiled at the memory. "He showed up dressed in old civilian clothes, with an overcoat that was worn out at the elbows and a hat that looked as if a mule had stepped on it. The men made fun of him. But not for long. No, sir, not for very long, at all. You see, Sam Grant may not know how to handle business very well, but he can handle men, that's for sure. In a month's time, he'd turned the Twenty-first into soldiers. Still didn't have a uniform. Wore those same shabby civilian clothes with an old saber tied around his waist. The troops took to calling him 'The Quiet Man.' He never raised his voice, never swore, never caused a fuss, and never put on any airs. Just like in Panama. He had a job to do and he steadily went about getting it done."

"And now he's a general," Mark said.

Kinchloe shrugged. "That Congressman Washburne, from his home district, had a hand in that. Just to get a general from his constituency, you understand, so he's not the only congressman around who hasn't got one. Hell, the way they're handing out commissions left and right, there's more generals in this army now than there are men who know how to shoot a musket. They say in Washington, some boy pegged a rock at a stray dog. He missed the dog, you know, but he hit three brigadiers."

Mark grinned. "I hadn't heard that one. But still, for a man with his kind of record . . . He told me there was some debate over his appointment."

Kinchloe raised his eyebrows. "He told you that?"

Mark explained about the letter from his father and the circumstances of his leaving West Point and his posting to Cairo.

"Ah," said Kinchloe, nodding. "I guess that explains it, then. He knows your father and I suppose he must have taken to you. He knows what it's like to be dealt a bad hand, too."

"I should think so," Mark agreed.

"One thing he won't tell you, but I will," said Kinchloe, tapping out his pipe. "He came down with the ague down in the swamps of Panama. Time to time, it takes him again. He starts to sweat and shiver, can't walk, can't stand up . . . Makes people think he's in a drunken fit. Contributes to all the talk about him drinking."

"Why doesn't he tell people, then?" Mark asked, puzzled.

Kinchloe shrugged. "He's not the sort to make excuses, I suppose. He often doesn't say much anyway, unless he's around people he knows and feels comfortable with. He's not a speechmaker, Lord knows. I remember when the troop's term of enlistment was running out and they brought in a couple of congressmen to make speeches, exhorting them to stay." Kinchloe chuckled softly at the memory. "One of them got up and gave the men a rousing, patriotic speech about the flag and country, you know the sort of thing. Then the other one spoke about their girls back home, saying they couldn't go back and face them before they'd even taken part in any battles. Anyway, they got the men all stirred up and then one of them calls on Grant. The men all start shouting, 'Speech! Speech!' And you know what Grant did? He got up and said, 'Men, go back to your quarters.' And that was his whole speech."

Mark grinned.

"Yep," said Kinchloe, "Grant's no orator, like McClellan, nor a dandified popinjay, like Frémont, but you know what? I'd sooner have him as my commander than someone like Ole Fuss and Feathers any day."

"You'd prefer him to General Scott?" Mark said, with surprise.

"Yep," said Kinchloe, putting his pipe away and stretching out on his cot, with his hands behind his head.

"Why?"

"Well," said Kinchloe, "I suspect you'll find that out. Just don't go getting into any more duels, though."

Mark grimaced. "I hadn't planned on it. In fact, the way things are looking, I hadn't even planned on getting into any real fighting."

Kinchloe didn't look at him. "Is that so? Well, you may find you'll have to change your plans," he said.

"Why?" asked Mark. "Do you know something I don't know?"

"Yep," said Kinchloe flatly. "I know Sam Grant."

Mark's Journal, Cairo, Illinois, October 1861

I had not really intended to keep a journal. In all honesty, I must admit that I feel rather foolish about this entire journal business, this long-standing Gallio tradition of preserving our thoughts and experiences for posterity so that future generations of the family may benefit from them. I don't know that I have ever benefited very much from hearing the stories of my ancestors. As a boy, I often found them entertaining when our father would read us various selections by the fire on cold winter nights, or on the porch, during the warmer months.

We each had our favorites, as I recall, among the selections our father chose to read to us. Maria liked that Roman, I cannot recall his name now, Flavius, Vesuvius—no, that's a volcano, isn't it? Well, whatever his name was, the one who served with Julius Caesar. Robert liked him also, but though his tastes were far more varied, he had a favorite as well, and that was Vindix, the son of Hanno, who began the dynasty, as we have always thought of it, and was the first to record his experiences in a journal. My own favorite was our great grandfather, Nathaniel, who fought in the Revolution.

However, to us, as children, these were merely stories, like the stories other parents told their children, and I don't think it made any real difference to us that the stories were true. They were entertaining stories, at least the parts our father read to us, and we enjoyed them as such, without ever giving any thought as to why they were being told to us. The reason was, of course, to ground us early in the family tradition so that when the time came, it would seem only natural for us to take our part. And for Robert and Maria, it seemed natural enough, I suppose. However, for me, it has never seemed so.

It was not that I lost interest. It was merely that I have never truly seen myself as being a part of it all. I am not sure why. Perhaps it was because, as I grew older, I started to discover that I did not have the same talent for being a soldier that Robert has, nor do I seem to possess the ability for scholarship and self-expression that Maria has. Such things have never seemed attainable to me, as my record at West Point will clearly show, and the idea that I have anything of interest or significance to contribute to the family chronicles would seem like the worst sort of self-delusion.

Be that as it may, I have decided to start a journal of my own, for the first time since childhood, when I dutifully recorded all the mischief I got into every day, not because I feel that I have anything of importance to contribute, nor that anyone will find anything of more than passing interest here, but for no other reason than I find myself with some time on my hands and this seems as good a way to pass that time as any. Perhaps, someday, my children will be curious to know exactly what it was their father did in the War of the Rebellion (assuming I survive it and find a wife to bear my children), and in that event, they will be able to consult this poorly written document and read all about how he sat in the mud with Grant at Cairo while their Uncle Robert won the war all by himself back in Virginia.

How I came to be in Cairo is of no great import, and the less said about it, the better. It should suffice to mention that my boyhood talent for getting into mischief has grown into manhood with me and thus I have received this plum of an assignment. At present, we are encamped in this mud hole of a town, frightening the rebels with our close-order drill. We wake up with the morning gun, which is followed by a cacophony of drums and fifes, in the event that anyone has slept through the cannonade. What our bandsmen do to music is usually enough to raise the dead, and so everyone is up and about in time for roll call.

Once we have been reassured that the rebels have not come upon us in the night and slaughtered everyone, the guard assignments are called off and the men are dismissed to perform their morning toilet, which is followed by first mess, which usually consists of something remarkably similar to food. The cuisine generally consists of something very much like meat, potatoes, bread and coffee, and what the men call "desecrated vegetables," which come in pressed sheets that are meant to be broken up and boiled in water. The result is a concoction that resembles the contents of a well-used horse trough, with a liberal sprinkling of dead leaves, and it tastes about the same.

Thus fortified, the troops are then exercised till noon in company and battalion drills, bayonet practice, marksmanship, and whatever else a soldier is supposed to know. As an officer who has graduated from West Point, one of my duties is to pass on my proficiency in such matters to the men under my command, to the best of my ability. However, since my own ability in matters such as these is limited, at best, I do not expect much from my charges and am thus not often disappointed.

I merely try to keep their spirits up and do my best to avoid having them knock into one another. General Grant told me that he would be satisfied if the men knew their left feet from their right, but I had not supposed his remark was anything other than sarcasm until I saw the recruits drilling, with little bundles of hay tied to their left feet and similar bundles of straw tied to their right feet, marching to the commands of "Hay-foot! Straw-foot! Hay-foot! Straw-foot!" On one recent occasion, when there were no senior officers in sight, I followed a command of "About-face!" with "All-e-man left!" and "Do-see-do!" and "Swing your partner!" and for a few minutes, we had ourselves a merry little square dance, which brightened an otherwise dreary and overcast day.

I have promised the men that if they keep their noses clean and refrain from gossiping about our unorthodox close-order drill, I would see what I could do to obtain permission for them to practice marksmanship with live ammunition. They do get a bit depressed, firing blank powder charges at the weeds and failing to mow them down accordingly. On the other hand, it does assure the safety of their officers.

After the second meal of the day, which is only slightly more memorable than the first by reason of the fact that the men have managed to work up an appetite, the troops are given some time to themselves, followed by more drilling, because one cannot get enough of a good thing. Then there is a tent inspection prior to the evening parade, when we have the opportunity to demonstrate to our commander some of what we have managed to learn while the band attempts to do the same with whatever it is they do. Third mess follows, and then the evening social hour, during which we sing and chat and plan the destruction of the rebels, and then tattoo, the signal to retire, and sleep, and dream of another day of equally stimulating activities.

Occasionally, the routine is broken up by one or another incident that merits comment, such as the punishment of miscreants, which is somewhat more creative and considerably less pleasant in the army than the many extras I had walked back at the Point. Desertion in the time of war is punishable by death, but thankfully, to date, I have not seen that particular punishment meted out. Instead, the one episode of desertion we have had since I arrived was punished by whipping.

The regimental surgeon first examined the prisoner to make certain he could stand the punishment, though I do not know what criteria are used in this regard, and then the prisoner was stripped to the waist and tied up to a post by the sergeant of the guard. The orders were then read, and the man given the task of laying on the whip, a soldier who was guilty of a lesser offense, proceeded to go about his grisly task to the count, for thirty-nine lashes.

It was a gruesome sight, and an ordeal for both the deserter and the man laying on the lash, though the deserter had the worst of it, by far. The whip raised ugly purple welts, with drops of blood on the ends of them, and the cries of the prisoner were pitiful to hear. In peacetime, in the regular army, the deserter would then have been drummed out of the service to "The Rogue's March," but this is wartime, and even rogues are useful, so the prisoner was taken down and given to the surgeon's care, to recover and meditate upon his sin before returning to duty.

Other punishments I have witnessed, for lesser offenses, are not nearly as brutal, but are still experiences I could easily do without myself. Bucking and gagging is one such punishment, in which the offender, generally someone who has been either drunk or insubordinate, is made to sit upon the ground and draw his knees up to his chest, then bring his hands out forward, to his shins, where they are tightly bound together. A long stick or board is then inserted beneath his knees and over his arms, and either a gag is fixed in place or else he is made to open his mouth and take a bayonet between his teeth, which is then tied by cords around his head. And so the miserable wretch sits, immobilized, for however long his officer decides to leave him there. It is not only humiliating and degrading, but the discomfort increases by the hour and can apparently become quite painful. The men I have seen released from this peculiar method of confinement were not able to walk and needed to be carried or otherwise assisted back to their quarters.

For more serious offenses, men are sometimes tied up by their thumbs, in such a manner that they have to remain on tiptoe or else experience excruciating pain caused by the weight of their own bodies. Invariably, they weaken and find themselves unable to remain that way, and they begin to do an agonizing sort of dance, wherein their weariness will cause them to get down from their toes and then the resulting pain forces them back up again, and back and forth, and so on, until they are nearly senseless with delirium.

Thankfully, such punishments are not handed out so frequently, and I myself do not possess either the cruelty or the fortitude to make men submit to them. The one time I was faced with a case of insubordination occurred when I had to detail a group of men to perform some work in our makeshift hospital. There was some resistance to this, one fellow in particular insisting he wouldn't do it because it was "woman's work" and he had joined up to fight, not to scrub floors and sweep. Rather than report the man, I took him at his word and struck him down with my fist, then invited him to strike me back if he felt that he was being unfairly treated. He protested that if he did so, he would be accused of striking an officer and punished, but I assured him, on my word of honor, that I would not report him. However, I told him I could not suffer his disobedience and the matter would have to be settled one way or the other, right then and there.

Game fellow that he was, he took me up on it and landed me a blow that knocked me down and nearly broke my jaw, at which point I surmised that perhaps I had bitten off a bit more than I could chew. I got up and came at him again, whereupon once more he knocked me down, and I began to have some serious misgivings about my course of action. Nevertheless, I could not allow myself to be bested by an enlisted man, and so I rose up once more and managed to get in two good blows of my own before he knocked me down again.

Cursing myself for a fool, I struggled to my feet and came at him one more time, only to be knocked sprawling yet again. My mouth and nose were bloody and my eye was blacked, and there was a ringing in my ears like that of a hammer pounding on an anvil, but there was nothing for it and I started to get up again, whereupon the soldier said to me, "Come on, Lieutenant, let's stop now. I don't want to hit you anymore."

As I struggled to my feet I damned his eyes and replied that he would either have to obey my orders or he would have to kill me, because I would not stop. After a glance about at his comrades, who were all watching silently, the fellow replied, "Well, I guess I had best obey your orders, then. Now please, Lieutenant, let me help you."

Whereupon he assisted me back to my tent and ministered to my injuries with all a mother's tenderness, much to the amusement of Kinchloe, who made no comment other than, "Slipped and had a fall, did you?"

I had no more trouble after that with insubordination from any of the men, although I suspect the army would balk at adopting my rather unorthodox approach, no matter how successful it may be. It would probably decimate the officer's corps.

And so I was blooded in the war, and by one of my own men, at that. In the meantime, while I was busy engaging in pointless fisticuffs and drilling, Colonel Mulligan had surrendered his garrison at Lexington to General Price, and General Frémont has set out after Price himself, at the head of his troops, apparently in an attempt to make up for the damage that his wife caused back in Washington. Meanwhile, our commander, General Grant, continues to wait for permission to move against Columbus, but thus far all his requests have come to naught.

Throughout Missouri, we hear of clashes between our troops and the rebels, and while we do encounter them in the occasional reconnaissance, we fight no battles. It seems as if everyone is caught up in the war but us. We continue to occupy the mud at Cairo, holding it secure for the everlasting glory of the Union.

CHAPTER FIVE

Washington, D.C., October 1861

"COME IN, ROBERT," said General Scott. The old man looked tired as he sat behind his desk. "Sit down, please," he said.

Robert took the chair across from him on the other side of the desk.

"I wanted you to hear it from me, first," said Scott. "I have just submitted my resignation as general-in-chief of the army and the president has accepted it. George McClellan is being appointed in my place."

Robert compressed his lips into a tight grimace. "I had been afraid of that, sir."

He had seen it coming. In fact, all of Washington, if not most of the country, had seen it coming, ever since General George Brinton McClellan had been brought in from the Department of the Ohio to replace McDowell, who had taken the fall for Bull Run.

McClellan had arrived in Washington with impeccable credentials. A former railroad man with both the Illinois Central and the Ohio and Mississippi, he had been educated at West Point and possessed a reputation as a strong and capable organizer. As part of the commission sent to observe the Crimean War, he had written a report dealing with the organization of European armies, a critique of the war, and a manual for the U.S. Cavalry, which he had modeled on the Russian cavalry. He had also invented the McClellan saddle, which the army had looked upon with favor, and at the young age of thirty-four was widely considered to be the country's leading expert on the science of war. Aside from all that, he was also widely perceived to be a winner, after his successful campaigns in western Virginia. When he came to Washington to assume command of the Army of the Potomac, he had received a hero's welcome, and almost immediately there was talk of making him general-in-chief.

Robert, however, with his insider's knowledge gained from serving in the War Department, saw McClellan rather differently. He felt himself unqualified to hold any opinions as to McClellan's success in the railroading business, but as a cavalry officer, he had reservations about a cavalry manual written by a man who had never served one day in the cavalry himself. As for the famous McClellan saddle, supposedly derived from a number of different designs McClellan had seen in Europe, Robert had tried it and found it both uncomfortable and impractical. If the army ever saw fit to issue him a McClellan saddle, he'd decided, he would go out and buy his own.

Insofar as McClellan's brilliant successes in western Virginia were concerned, Robert also had opinions that differed somewhat from those held by the newspapers and the general public. He had, after all, access to all the orders and communications and reports. Early on, McClellan had struck him as a prima donna and nothing the general had done in the Department of the Ohio had disabused him of that notion. McClellan had gone over the heads of his superiors in the War Department, directly to the president, to get his father-in-law assigned to his staff and he had been petulant and impatient in his demands for ordnance and supplies, as if his needs were the only ones that mattered. Only four days after being appointed to his command, he had submitted to General Scott his own personal plan to win the war, with himself as the key commander, of course.

Quite aside from the arrogance of presuming to tell the general-in-chief how to conduct the war, McClellan's plan had a number of rather glaring flaws, which General Scott had pointed out to him, such as the fact that it involved very long marches without proper consideration given to supply. For a man who was reputed to be a master "military scientist," George McClellan had submitted a considerably less than masterly plan.

The famous "Philippi Races," of which the newspapers had made so much, had apparently been nothing more than two columns of Union troops led by General Thomas A. Morris coming upon a small body of rebels encamped fifteen miles south of Grafton and catching them completely unprepared. Six rebels had been killed and one Union soldier had been wounded, but the newspapers—and McClellan's own reports—had played it up as a major Union victory. Later, at Rich Mountain, McClellan had, in Robert's view, left Rosecrans to hang, failing to provide support when he heard him engaging Colonel Pegram's forces because the engagement, it seemed, was not going according to McClellan's plan. Fortunately, Rosecrans overran the enemy position, but it was with no help from George McClellan, who sought to pin the blame on Rosecrans for failing to communicate his situation and carry out his orders.

Yet it was Rosecrans who had forced the rebels to retreat from Rich Mountain, leaving behind their guns and their supplies so that Pegram was left with little choice but to surrender, which enabled Morris to drive the rebels under General Garnett from Laurel Mountain, with Garnett himself being killed fighting a rear-guard action. The main part of Garnett's column, however, had escaped, and McClellan had once more pinned the blame on other officers while at the same time congratulating his troops for "annihilating" two armies.

He had, in Robert's opinion, largely taken the credit for the efforts of his subordinates, displayed a marked penchant for self-aggrandizing speeches and pronouncements, and a tendency to involve himself in politics that were outside the scope of his authority. From the moment he arrived in Washington, he had displayed an arrogance and a conceit that, to Robert's way of thinking, was nothing short of egomania. He acted as if he had single-handedly saved Washington from a rebel invasion by the mere fact of his arrival.

He also made no secret of the fact that he considered General Scott a dotard who had long since outlived his usefulness and he didn't even bother to provide Scott with reports. His attitude toward Scott, whom Robert considered one of the nation's finest soldiers, was nothing short of criminal, and his political intrigues had apparently achieved his aims at last. He had brought down Winfield Scott.

"I had heard you might be leaving, sir," said Robert, feeling greatly disheartened, "but I hoped it wasn't true."

Scott nodded. "Yes, I know there's been a great deal of talk about it. But I am an old man, Robert. I am no longer in good health. I can no longer even mount a horse, and I am tired. I am going to retire to West Point."

"You've been pressured into doing this," said Robert, as if it were an accusation.

Scott waved his hand. "It doesn't matter, son. It's time for me to step down. The country needs a younger and more energetic man to conduct the war. The public likes McClellan. The troops like him. He is young, and to date, he is the only general we have who has demonstrated an ability to win." He grimaced wryly. "Granted, we have not quite seen eye to eye, but the president believes that he is the right man for the job and I have given McClellan my support."

"McClellan is a pompous ass," said Robert, with disgust.

"Captain," replied Scott firmly, "I remind you that you are speaking about a senior officer, and the new general-in-chief."

"Forgive me, sir, but I cannot help feeling—"

Scott silenced him with a wave of his hand. "Oh, I know how you feel, son. And I appreciate your loyalty." He sighed heavily. "When George McClellan came to Washington, he had my friendship and my confidence. Well, at any rate, he still has my confidence. But the decision has already been made. I merely wanted to tell you about it myself and to express personally my heartfelt appreciation for your service."

"It's been an honor and a privilege, sir," said Robert, meaning every word of it. "I'll be extremely sorry to see you go."

Scott smiled. "You will be in the minority, I fear. George McClellan is the man of the hour and the public and the press will hail the president's decision."

Robert grimaced. "Have you heard what they're calling him?"

"You mean 'The Young Napoleon'?" said Scott, with a smile. "Yes. He's even had his photograph taken for one of Brady's *cartes de visites*, posing with his hand tucked into his blouse, à la Bonaparte. I understand they're selling very well. But that sort of thing is only to be expected, after all. He's young and all this acclaim is bound to affect him, somewhat."

"That sounds rather like a polite way of saying that it's going to his head, sir," Robert replied.

Scott chuckled. "Yes, I suppose it does, doesn't it? But McClellan knows what he's about. He's a good soldier, even if he is a bit too flamboyant for your taste. And too political for mine. However, that is not what I wanted to speak with you about. As I've already told you, I have found your service to be exemplary, but I know that your heart was never truly in it. I rather doubt McClellan will want my former aide-de-camp on his own personal staff. So before I leave, as a small way of showing my appreciation, I wanted to give you the opportunity to choose your next assignment. I take it you'd like the cavalry?"

"Yes, sir, I would."

Scott smiled. "I thought so. I'm sure General Stoneman will be glad to have you. Oh, and there is one other thing." He opened his desk drawer and took out a small box. "You'd better put these on."

He opened the box and handed it to Robert with a smile. It contained major's shoulder straps. Robert took the box and stared at them, taken completely by surprise.

"Sir, I . . . I don't know what to say."

"You've earned them, son," Scott said. "And Lord knows, you're more entitled to them than a lot of other men I could mention. Some of whom are even wearing general's stars," he added dryly. "Though of course we won't mention any names."

"Thank you, sir," said Robert, feeling overwhelmed. "I . . . I only wish that I could wear them in your service."

Scott grunted. "Well . . . you're quite welcome, Major. Quite welcome, indeed. If I may ask, did you happen to have any plans for this evening?"

"No, sir."

"Well, in that case, there will be a small dinner party at my home tonight, at six o'clock. I would be pleased if you could attend."

"I will, sir. Thank you very much."

"It will be a small, intimate affair, a farewell dinner, as it were. I will be leaving for New York on the morning of the first."

"So soon?" said Robert.

"No point in lingering. I would like it if you could be present with the remainder of my staff to see me off."

"Yes, sir, of course."

"Good," said Scott, nodding. "Well . . . I suppose that's all, then. I know you've been working very hard, Robert, so I've arranged a short furlough for you before you report to General Stoneman."

"There really isn't much point to my taking a furlough, sir," Robert said. "I have no family to visit, under the circumstances, and I'd just as soon get on with my new duties."

"No, Robert, I want you to take the furlough, even if it's only to remain in Washington and have some time to yourself for a few days. You deserve some rest. Find yourself a nice girl and take her out to dinner and the theater. Enjoy yourself. I'll make it my last order to you."

"Yes, sir."

Scott smiled. "Good." He got to his feet, laboriously, and held out his hand. "I'll miss you, Robert."

"I'll miss you, too, sir."

"Good luck."

They shook hands. Robert snapped to attention and gave him a sharp salute. Winfield Scott returned it, then Brevet Major Robert Gallio stepped back, about-faced, and marched smartly from the office.

Belmont, Missouri, November 1861

Belmont was little more than a steamboat landing on some low and scrubby farmland, with the nearest town being Charleston, about twelve miles away. It seemed, Mark thought, a rather paltry object for a military expedition, and an ironic one as well, since until recently it had been in Union hands.

That it was now in the hands of the rebels was a state of affairs that could largely be attributed to General Prentiss, whose childish tantrum over the question of Grant's outranking him had resulted in the troops being pulled back when the offensive stalled. Bishop Polk had seized the initiative and now this seemingly unimportant little piece of ground had taken on significance in light of the rebel occupation of Columbus, on the opposite shore. From Columbus, Polk could use Belmont as a base to cross troops into Missouri. General Frémont, for whom things were not going very well at all, was getting nervous.

On the first of the month, as Winfield Scott was leaving Washington on a gloomy, rainy morning, Grant received orders from headquarters in St. Louis, directing him to have his entire command prepared to march at an hour's notice and make sure they were amply supplied with transportation and ammunition. The next day he was ordered to make demonstrations with his troops along both sides of the river toward Charleston, Norfolk, and Blandville, and to keep his columns moving constantly throughout that area, but without actually engaging the enemy.

Word had reached Frémont that Jeff Thompson, the bold and charismatic rebel general, had a force of some three thousand men gathered south of Ironton, threatening the Union positions, and Bishop Polk was busily sending reinforcements to General Sterling Price, who was causing headquarters considerable embarrassment in the western part of Missouri.

Rumors were already flying that the president was about to remove Frémont from command, and the Pathfinder was clearly anxious to do something that would redeem him in the public eye, and therefore make it difficult for Lincoln to dismiss him. The trouble was, trying for some sort of success also entailed the risk of failure, and Frémont was well aware that Grant's troops were inexperienced. Their role in moving back and forth along the river, making demonstrations, was meant to help drive Thompson back into Arkansas and keep Bishop Polk from sending more troops to General Price.

However, while avoiding a direct engagement with the enemy was a good way to avoid defeat, it was also a good way to avoid accomplishing anything. Somehow, Mark thought it would take a great deal more than simply marching back and forth along the river to make Thompson and Polk start quaking in their boots. General Grant was of the same opinion. The day after he received his orders to make a show of force, Grant called a meeting of his staff. He began by reading his orders from headquarters, then looked up at the small group gathered around him.

"So, headquarters has ordered us to make a demonstration," Grant said, speaking around the pipe perpetually clamped between his teeth. "Well, gentlemen, I intend to demonstrate that we can win."

Grant's chief of staff, John Rawlins, cleared his throat.

"Yes, what is it, John?"

"General, do you really think the troops are ready for an engagement with the enemy?"

"I frankly don't see where anything will be gained by spending more time drilling them," replied Grant. "The more time we spend in preparing our troops, the more time the rebels have to do the same. Besides, our men are tired of drilling. Men learn to fight by fighting, not by putting on reviews. Therefore, I intend to take the offensive."

He spread a map out on the desk and bent over it.

"Colonel Oglesby will take the Eighth, the Eighteenth and the Twenty-ninth, together with four companies of the Eleventh, three companies of cavalry, and a section of artillery, and move on Sikeston, find Thompson, and pursue him wherever he goes. The object of the expedition is to destroy Thompson's force. Colonel Plummer's troops will join the expedition, as well as the troops of Colonel Wallace, who will set out from Bird's Point. I will take the remainder of our force and move on Belmont, to

prevent Bishop Polk from crossing troops in an attempt to cut
the expedition off or reinforce General Price. Colonel Oglesby's
command will get under way tomorrow evening. I will depart with
the remainder of our force three days later, on the sixth, by water
transport. We will proceed in convoy with the gunboats *Tyler* and
Lexington, which will provide cover in the event of a retreat. We
will land the troops at night, here, and commence our attack at
daylight while the gunboats proceed to engage the batteries at
Columbus. Are there any questions, gentlemen?"

There were none. The air was pregnant with anticipation. They
were finally going to fight.

"Very well," said Grant. "Thank you, gentlemen. You are dismissed. Oh, Lieutenant Gallio . . ."

"Sir?" said Mark.

"I want you lead the forward skirmishers at Belmont. You will
select your men from among our best sharpshooters."

"Yes, sir!"

"And no square dancing, Lieutenant, if you please," Grant
added, with a perfectly straight face.

The expedition against Belmont departed on the night of Novem-
ber 6, on schedule, and it was Mark's first real experience with
a troop movement in wartime. Five infantry regiments and two
cavalry companies, making a total of over three thousand men
organized into two brigades, boarded the transports for the journey
upriver to Belmont. For Mark, it was an electrifying spectacle.
The troops were eager and excited as they got aboard the transports. Every man was brimming with enthusiasm and a sense of
purpose.

The two gunboats, the *Tyler* and the *Lexington,* were wooden
sidewheelers, each mounting two thirty-two-pounder guns, as
well as a number of eight-inch shell guns, the *Tyler* mounting
six and the *Lexington* four. They stood offshore, smoke rising
from their twin stacks, waiting to escort the convoy of half a
dozen transport steamers on which the troops were being loaded.

Armored gunboats were being prepared, but for the moment all
Grant had access to were the *Tyler* and the *Lexington.* They were
makeshift vessels at best, not designed for war. However, they
were not meant to play any decisive part in the coming action.
Their task, aside from providing escort to the transports, would
be to engage the batteries at Columbus in order to draw their fire

and keep them occupied while the troops attacked the rebel camp at Belmont.

As they filed up the gangplanks the troops were in an excited, festive mood. Camp life had begun to pall and they were anxious for a chance to have some action. Mark had picked out a company of the best sharpshooters for his skirmishers and they had gone aboard the first boat. The previous night the men had packed their gear and cleaned their muskets, and now they stood around on deck, watching the other troops being loaded, joking among themselves, their spirits high. However, Mark did not share their mood.

He kept thinking about what Grant had told him on the first day he arrived in Cairo. He was starting with a clean slate, and what he chose to write upon it would be entirely up to him. Grant had been extremely charitable in overlooking his lackluster performance at West Point and his knack for getting into trouble. Now that he knew more about his commander, Mark could understand why. As Kinchloe had said, Grant knew what it was like to be dealt a bad hand. He could empathize and give a junior officer the benefit of the doubt. But could that junior officer give himself that same benefit?

Mark knew, better than anyone, the extent of his own shortcomings. At West Point, he had never excelled at anything. He had not only been consistently below average, but he had barely squeaked through the Academy, even discounting the affair of the aborted duel. His father and his brother had always felt it was because he chose not to apply himself. They thought he was simply immature and irresponsible, but the truth was Mark never felt he could measure up to his older brother, no matter how hard he tried.

Robert had always been better at everything. He had always been more intelligent, more athletic, more disciplined, more of everything. In short, more of a man. Mark had laughed with Custer at Robert's stuffy, somber nature, but there had been no denying his superior accomplishments. Mark's own frivolous and somewhat rebellious nature had always been, in part, a compensation for his failings. Now he was to lead a company of skirmishers, the first ones to the attack at Belmont, and he had serious misgivings about the task he had been called upon to perform.

Faced with the prospect of combat, he had suddenly recognized the truth of what it meant to be an officer. If he made any mistakes now, it wouldn't be a mere matter of demerits. Some of these men, perhaps even all of them, could die. That sudden realization weighed heavily upon him.

The men seemed to trust him. Perhaps it was because he was less like some of the other officers and more like one of them. He didn't wear his shoulder straps like a mantle of superiority. He joked with them and carried his authority in an easy, friendly sort of manner, firm, yet not at all officious. When faced with insubordination, he had not hidden behind his rank, but had met the problem like a man, like any one of them would have done, and so they liked him, and they had confidence in him. Only Mark felt no confidence in himself. He felt afraid. His fear was not so much for himself, but for them. Because they had him as their leader. Mark Gallio, the one who could never measure up.

So great was his anxiety over being called on to do something that might be beyond the scope of his abilities that fear for his own life had never even entered the equation. The thought that kept going through his mind was not, "Dear God, don't let me die," but "Dear God, don't let me fail!"

No one had ever expected anything of him before, because his performance had never given anyone cause to expect anything of him. Only now it was different. These men expected him to tell them what to do and how to do it. He was an officer, and not just a volunteer, but a regular who had attended West Point, so they simply took it for granted that he knew what he was doing. For the first time in his life, Mark was faced with a situation where failure would not affect only himself, but the lives of the men under his command, men whom he himself had chosen for the task. As he watched them standing around on deck, smoking and joking among themselves, he thought, Did I pick them out to die?

"You're being very quiet," a familiar voice said at his shoulder.

Mark turned and saw Kinchloe standing beside him. "I suppose I am," he said.

"Worried?"

Mark nodded.

"That's a normal thing," said Kinchloe reassuringly. "It's no sin to feel a mite queasy before going into combat. It happens to everyone at one time or another. Don't worry. You'll do all right."

"That's just what worries me," Mark said, staring off upriver in the direction of Belmont. "What if I *don't* do all right? What if I make a mistake? What if I do something wrong?" He spoke in a low voice so that only Kinchloe could hear. He moistened his lips nervously. "God, what if I get these men killed, John?"

"The mark of a good officer is that he cares about his men," Kinchloe replied. "You'll do your best. That's all a man can do."

Mark smiled ruefully. "That's funny. I never thought to hear myself called a good officer."

"Grant would not have given you the job if he didn't think you could do it," said Kinchloe.

"Maybe he just felt sorry for me, because he's had some hard luck himself."

Kinchloe shook his head. "Not very likely."

"What makes you say that?"

"Sam Grant is not a man much given to sympathy. Not for himself, nor anyone else, for that matter," said Kinchloe. "Sympathy doesn't get you anything, and what Grant wants are results. If he didn't think you could do it, he would have assigned someone else to lead the skirmishers, you can rest assured of that."

"I wish I could rest assured of it," said Mark. He gave a small snort. "You know what he said to me? He said, 'No square dancing, Lieutenant, if you please.' Can you believe it? I had no idea he knew about that."

Kinchloe smiled. "He not only knew about it, he was there."

Mark glanced at him with surprise. "He was there? You mean he *saw* it?"

"We both saw it," Kinchloe said. "He came to watch my men drilling and he wanted to have a look at you and see how you were doing. I told him you were up over the rise a bit, and rode up with him to take a look. We were over by a grove of trees, so I guess you didn't see us."

"Good God! Why the hell didn't you say anything?"

"He told me not to," Kinchloe said, with a shrug.

Mark shook his head in dismay. "He must think me a perfect fool."

"Well, if he thought that, he wouldn't have chosen you to lead the skirmishers, now, would he?" Kinchloe replied. "Nor would be have had you pick the men yourself."

Mark frowned. "I don't understand."

Kinchloe grinned. "You really don't, do you? That silly little square-dance drill of yours may have been poor discipline, but it was good for the men's morale. They were getting tired of doing the same damn things over and over again, and it was showing. But didn't you notice that after your tomfoolery, their spirits picked up and their drill was sharper?"

"No, not really," Mark said, puzzled.

"Well, Grant did," Kinchloe replied. "What's more, the units you've been drilling have shown a marked improvement. It takes more than being good yourself to teach others to be good, you know. It takes a certain knack. You've got it, Mark. The men work harder for you because they respect you. And that's what makes a good leader. That's why Grant chose you to go in first."

Mark stared at him with complete astonishment. "You're saying General Grant thinks *I'm* a good leader?"

"The notion seems to surprise you," Kinchloe replied.

"I can scarcely credit it," said Mark, with disbelief. "I've never been good at anything before."

Kinchloe grunted. "Rather like someone else I know," he replied, then he winked and walked away.

The transports got under way at dawn, making about seven knots. Mark's apprehensions kept pace with the building anticipation of his men. He had a hollow feeling in the pit of his stomach and there was a tightness in his chest. He stood on the deck, gazing upriver, listening to the men talking among themselves in low, excited voices, and he wondered if he was the only one who felt himself in the grip of a desperate anxiety. The banks of the Mississippi seemed to slide past silently in the dim gray mist. The water made slapping sounds against the steamboat's hull. The birds were beginning their morning serenade. It seemed like just another lazy, peaceful morning on the Mississippi, but Mark knew all too well that it would not remain that way for long.

At eight o'clock, they disembarked on the Missouri shore, some five miles north of Belmont. The time the troops had spent in drilling was evident now as they quickly filed down the gangplanks and promptly formed up for the march to the commands of their officers.

Mark took his place at the front with his company of skirmishers. As the troops moved out, their gear clanking with each step, Mark found himself thinking about all the extras he had walked back at West Point.

In an odd sort of way, it almost felt the same, only this time he carried no musket on his shoulder, but a sword at his left side and a Colt Navy revolver in a flap holster at his right. Instead of a West Point dress gray blouse and cross belts, he wore the simple four-button field blouse of a Union officer. Instead of an ornate West Point shako, he wore a plain blue forage cap. And instead of marching back and forth all by himself, or with another miscreant or two, he was marching at the head of a company of men, all of whom would soon depend on him to tell them what to do. He was on the verge of panic.

According to reports, the garrison at Columbus and Belmont had a strength of about ten thousand men. There was at least one regiment of infantry encamped at Belmont, with at least one battery of artillery and probably a squadron of cavalry, but these reports could be misleading. At any time, more troops could be ferried over from Columbus, so there was really no way of telling exactly how many troops they would be facing. The element of surprise would be important. If they lost it . . .

Their formation thinned out as they moved into the forest. The plan was to come up behind the rebel camp, where the forest gave way to cleared ground for about eighty to a hundred yards from the rebel position. When this ground around the camp had been cleared by the rebels to provide a clear field of fire for their artillery, the trees had been used as abatis, the heavier lower portion of their trunks secured upon the ground, the other ends sharpened with axes and elevated, to provide lines of defensive obstacles. Mark and his skirmishers would be the first to cross the open ground and encounter them.

As they approached the rebel camp Grant extended his line through the woods as much as the terrain would allow. The moment they cleared the woods, the line would extend all the way and form a wave to drive the rebels toward the riverbank. It was about half past ten. The last gray mists of dawn had faded and the sun was shining as Grant gave the order to attack.

With a lump in his throat, Mark moved forward with his skirmishers. He shouted out the order for double time the moment they reached the edge of the woods and they started running with their muskets held at the port in front of them, fanning out and moving toward the first line of felled trees that formed the rebel barricades as the remainder of the attacking force moved into position behind them.

They made it almost all the way to the first line of barricades before anyone even noticed their approach. The rebels in the camp were taken completely unaware. Someone shouted "Yanks! Yanks!" and the cry was quickly taken up by other voices in the camp.

Mark drew his saber and gave the order to fire at will. The air became filled with the dull crack of musket fire as the sharp-shooters opened up, some firing from the shoulder, others resting their muskets on the barricades for a steadier platform. Sparks from the ignited powder shot forth from the musket barrels, arcing out toward the rebel camp as the balls hurtled toward their targets.

"Advance! Advance!" Mark shouted, leading his men through the line of barricades.

Those who had fired paused briefly to reload, doing so with practiced precision, reaching into their cartridge boxes, biting the ends off the paper cartridges with their teeth, pouring the premeasured power charges down their barrels, then ramming down the balls and capping their muskets. For many of them, it had at first been an awkward and confusing procedure, and there had been not a few cases where men had put the ball in ahead of the powder or rammed the conical Minié balls in upside down, but with the endless drills, they had become accomplished at the task and they were now able to load quickly.

The main body of Grant's force was moving up behind them fast. The rebel camp was in a tumult. The enemy had been taken completely by surprise. The attacking line was fully extended now and moving in. There was some sporadic firing from the rebel camp.

In the distance, the guns of the *Tyler* and the *Lexington* could be heard, engaging the batteries at Columbus. Powder smoke drifted across the battlefield like a fog. Mark suddenly felt that the saber in his hand was inadequate. He sheathed it and reached for his Navy Colt, hesitated in a brief moment of indecision, then drew the saber once again and transferred it to his left hand so he could draw the revolver with his right.

"Forward! Forward!" he kept shouting, waving his saber as he ran ahead. "Advance! We've got them on the run!"

They did, indeed, seem to have the rebels on the run, but the initial confusion of the enemy did not last long. They formed into a line and started to return the fire, but the Union troops had the advantage of position, having made a rapid advance, and after an aborted charge, the rebel line broke as they turned and fled in complete disorganization toward the riverbank.

With triumphant cries, Grant's men surged ahead into the camp. Mark realized, belatedly, that he hadn't even fired his pistol. His first battle was over, and he hadn't fired a single shot. Nor had any of his men been hit. He felt giddy with relief. He felt like laughing.

The other men seemed to share his mood. They started running through the camp, eagerly ransacking the abandoned rebel tents in search of souvenirs. One of the officers had climbed atop an artillery caisson and started addressing his men, congratulating them on their bravery in battle. Here and there, men clustered together in groups as their enthusiastic officers addressed them, extolling the virtues of the Union cause and their own invincibility as the men cheered and waved their caps, while others paid no heed and ran from tent to tent, like bands of pillaging Huns.

Mark simply stood there, feeling stunned and slightly disoriented. He couldn't believe it was over so quickly. He glanced up at the sun and saw it was high overhead. Impossible. That meant several hours had passed. It couldn't have been that long, he thought, could it?

Kinchloe spotted him and came galloping up. Mark grinned at him foolishly, unaware he was still holding his saber and his pistol in his hands. "We did it, John!" he said. "We did it!"

"Like bloody hell, we did it!" Kinchloe replied, frowning. "What about the goddamn rebels? Or did you forget?"

Mark stared up at him in confusion. "What?"

"The rebs, you fool! They all took off for the riverbank. What the hell do you think they're doing, swimming across?"

Mark stared at him, and then comprehension dawned. He glanced toward the riverbank. The slope kept him from seeing any of the rebels who had retreated, but they were surely there. Trapped between the attacking Union force and the river, they could easily have been forced to surrender. Except no one had asked them to.

The men were all too busy running riot through the rebel camp, brandishing captured weapons and flags and other souvenirs of their victory, and most of their officers were caught up in the festive mood as well. The troops were out of control. As he stared toward the shore Mark could see two boats coming across the river from Columbus, loaded down with men.

"Damn!" said Kinchloe, following his gaze. He set spurs to his horse and galloped off toward the rebel tents, shouting an alarm.

"Lieutenant Gallio!"

Mark, still somewhat dazed, glanced around to see Grant come galloping up.

"Where the devil are your men?" demanded Grant furiously.

"Sir, I . . ." Mark glanced around, helplessly. Most of them were busy tearing through the camp, pawing their way through the equipment of the rebels, laughing and shouting in celebration of their first victory.

Grant did not wait for Mark's response. He had seen the approach of the boats bearing the Confederate troops and his only thought was to regain control of his men.

"Fire the tents!" he said to Mark.

Mark stared at him for a moment, without comprehension. "Sir?"

"*Burn* them!" Grant shouted. "Torch the doggone tents! Maybe that will get their attention!"

He galloped off toward a nearby cluster of men, shouting at them, trying to get it through their heads that they were not yet out of danger. The boats bearing the Confederate troops were fast approaching from across the river and most of the men still seemed oblivious of the threat.

Mark snatched a burning branch out of one of the rebel cookfires and started setting fire to the tents, running from one to the other, sometimes shoving men out of his way, shouting orders at them to start burning the tents and pointing at the boats coming from across the river.

The men responded and soon all the tents were blazing. At the sight of the flames, the rebel batteries from the bluffs on the other side of the river opened up. Perhaps they had held off because they were not certain whether or not their own troops were still there, but as soon as they saw the camp burning they realized it was in Union hands and opened fire.

The burning tents and the shot from the rebel batteries falling among them got through to the troops at last and they finally realized the battle was far from over. The boats from the opposite shore had reached the bank and the rebel reinforcements were disembarking. At the same time as the troops suddenly realized they were under fire and that rebel reinforcements had arrived, a number of them noticed that the rebels who had been driven from the camp had worked their way, unseen, up along the riverbank and were now drawn up in a line between them and their transports. It was like a bucket of cold water dashed into their faces. Their mood changed instantly from jubilation to panic.

"Good God, we're surrounded!" someone shouted, and the cry was quickly taken up by others. Alarmed, the men came flocking to Grant.

"General, we're surrounded!" one of the officers cried, in consternation. "We'll have to surrender!"

"No, not likely," Grant responded, sitting calmly atop his skittish horse as the shot fell among them. "We cut our way in, we can cut our way out just as well."

The men glanced at each other, as if the idea had never even occurred to them. In fact, it hadn't. They saw themselves surrounded and simply assumed there was no way out. But there was Grant, sitting calmly astride his horse, telling them simply and plainly that their situation was anything but hopeless. They had driven off the rebels once already, they could do it once again.

"You heard the general!" Mark shouted. "We've routed them once, we can do it again! Form up! Skirmishers, fall in!"

The men responded instantly. As the rebels struck Grant's men on the flank and rear the Union troops reacted purposefully. Mark moved forward with his skirmishers and they returned the rebel fire with a vengeance, the men once more moving with practiced precision now that their initial bout of panic had worn off. They had a job to do now, and they knew just how to do it. The rebels between them and the transports, already driven off once before and now faced with a firm resolve, gave way after a brief and feeble resistance, and the way to the transports was clear. The men surged ahead, and in their rush to reach the transports, orderly formation was forgotten as each unit hurried with all possible speed to get back to the boats.

As Mark raced ahead with his skirmishers the rebels paced them on their flank, under the cover of the woods. Between the woods and the transports was a cornfield and the men plunged through it to get aboard the boats. The rebel sharpshooters hidden in the woods raked the field with their fire as the Union troops raced up the gangplanks. Mark managed to get aboard safely and he turned back to look for Grant as the rest of the troops came up. There was no sign of him. He scanned the shore anxiously, looking for the general. He couldn't see him anywhere.

Mark caught his breath. Could Grant have fallen? No, wait, there he was! He could see him riding through the cornfield, plowing through it, back and forth. What in God's name was he doing? Then, suddenly, Mark realized Grant was risking his life, riding through the cornfield, checking to make sure all his men had gotten aboard the boats, which were already pushing off.

"Wait, goddamn it!" Mark heard Kinchloe shout as the boat started to pull away from the shore. "The general's not aboard yet!"

The captain quickly ran out a gangplank as Grant reached the riverbank, but the banks were high and the dropoff was steep. With a sinking feeling, Mark realized Grant would never be able to make it down. Then, as Mark watched with disbelief, Grant set spurs to his horse's flanks and the animal moved forward, sliding down the steep riverbank with its forelegs planted in front of it and its hind legs drawn up beneath it. It was a superb display of horsemanship on the part of the rider, and bravery on the part of the animal. The general and his horse slid down the riverbank, then Grant calmly trotted up the gangplank to the cheers of his men as if he did that sort of thing every day.

The boats headed slowly back downriver as the sun began to set. The battle had taken all day. It hadn't seemed that long at all to Mark. It was as if time had somehow been compressed. It wasn't much of a victory, Mark thought. What had they accomplished? They had driven off the rebels, but had then in turn been driven off themselves. Belmont was still in rebel hands. And yet they *had* accomplished something.

The troops had received their baptism of fire. They had proven they could fight and fight well. For a while organization had been lost, but thanks to Grant's clearheadedness, it had not turned into the disaster it could have easily become. They had made the demonstration their orders had called on them to make. They had not managed to take Belmont, but if it was not a victory, then it was not a total defeat, either. It was more of a draw. And Mark realized something else as well.

After a brief moment of hesitation and indecision, he had done exactly what he had been supposed to do and he had fulfilled the task required of him. What was more, he had helped to rally the men after their initial panic and his skirmishers had been the first into the fray, twice during the day. After his initial anxiety and nervousness, he had not felt afraid at all. He had followed his orders with a firm purpose and resolve. He had led his men and he had led them ably. It was, perhaps, the most astonishing realization of them all. He had not failed. He had done what was expected of him and he had done it well.

He was, by God, a soldier.

CHAPTER SIX

Richmond, Virginia, January 1862

FOR MARIA, THE difference between life in Charleston and life in Richmond was dramatic. Richmond had, itself, experienced dramatic changes. The graceful "City of the Seven Hills," often likened by its residents to ancient Rome, with its own Old Dominion aristocracy and rich, albeit relatively young, traditions, now had something of the atmosphere of a teeming, noisy, boomtown. The attractive city streets, lined with shade trees and elegant red-brick boardinghouses standing side by side with slant-roofed private homes and business establishments, now resonated with the sounds of constant traffic.

The central fairgrounds had become Camp Lee, and there was a camp established at Howard's Grove, on the Mechanicsville Turnpike. Richmond College was now the home of the artillery school, and defensive batteries had been built at Yorktown and at Gloucester Point on Jamestown Island. Howitzers had been emplaced on Chimborazo Heights and earthworks were being thrown up for the defense of the capital. There was a constant air of last-minute expectancy about the city, as if everything had to be done quickly, because the Union forces could attack at any time.

The Virginia legislature had vacated the capitol in favor of the Confederate Congress. The Treasury and State Departments had been established in the customs house, as were the office of the president and the cabinet room. The other departments of the Confederate government had been hastily crammed into the Mechanics Institute, an old brick building that was still being remodeled to suit its new purposes when the government moved in. Workmen had still been bustling about with saws and hammers

even as clerks and officials moved in to conduct the business of
government amid the dust and din of construction.

The workers at the Richmond Armory were busily convert-
ing all the old flintlock muskets they could lay their hands on,
replacing the outdated flintlocks with percussion locks, rifling the
smoothbore barrels to enable them to fire Minié balls, and adding
new sights, desperately trying to address the drastic shortage of
arms. The South, unlike the North, was short of everything.
There was a shortage of leather for saddles and harnesses. The
ordnance shops established in the warehouses by the Kanawha
Canal were working feverishly, doing what they could to provide
the Confederate troops with ammunition, despite the shortage of
powder and percussion caps. There were not even enough horses
for the cavalry. Each trooper was required to supply his own
mount.

The smokestacks of the Tredegar Iron Works were constantly
belching forth black clouds as the factory's huge work force of
Negroes toiled around the clock. The ordnance department had
even requested Richmond's churches to donate any bells that
could be spared so they could be melted down and made into
fieldpieces.

Troops were constantly drilling in the city streets and parks
while the citizens of Richmond watched and cheered them on
with cries of "Victory or Death!" Soldiers were everywhere one
looked, with regimental colors flying the magnolia of Mississippi,
or the lone star of Texas, or the Louisiana pelican, each regiment adding to the wild profusion of uniforms. There were the
Georgians, in their green-trimmed, butternut coats; the Maryland
Guard, in flamboyant uniforms of blue and orange; the Louisiana
Zouaves, with their baggy, bright red trousers, gold-braided blue
jackets, white gaiters, and bowie knives tucked into blue sashes;
and the most commonly seen uniform of all, Confederate gray
with yellow trim. There were even the vivandières Maria had
heard so much about, women who followed the regiments, serving
as nurses and sutlers, dressed in military-style uniforms consisting
of baggy Turkish trousers, brass-buttoned blouses, and feathered
hats, a style that, like the Zouave uniforms, had been influenced
by the Crimean War.

The women of Richmond, like the ladies of Charleston, were
pitching in, sewing and knitting socks, shirts, jackets, and blankets
for the troops, mostly out of homespun, for muslin had gone up
to six dollars a yard and even calico could not be had for less

than two dollars now. Confederate-gray homespun was rapidly becoming the fashionable fabric for the city's civilian men, too, as fabrics such as broadcloth and linen became scarce and prohibitively expensive.

The martial spirit was pervasive. The Spotswood Hotel displayed handcuffs in its lobby, taken from Union soldiers at Bull Run and supposedly meant for Jeff Davis and his cabinet. The stores sold sheet music of popular war songs such as "The Bonnie Blue Flag," and the children of the city had their own songs, which they chanted as they trooped around in imitation of the soldiers.

> "I want to be a soldier
> And with the soldiers stand,
> A knapsack on my shoulder,
> A musket in my hand;
> And there beside Jeff Davis,
> So glorious and so brave,
> I'll whip the cussed Yankee,
> And drive him to his grave."

The population of Richmond had doubled and it was growing still. Soldiers were constantly arriving from all over the South, but along with the soldiers came criminals and profiteers and office seekers. Pickpockets were rife throughout the city and robbery and murder had increased. The newspapers complained about the proliferation of gambling halls and houses of ill repute. And adding to the consternation of the white citizens of Richmond, the population of Negroes had risen alarmingly.

In an attempt to keep order in the city, Brigadier General John H. Winder, a West Point classmate of President Davis, had been appointed provost marshal. He administrated the Public Guard, who wore the letters "PG" on their hats and were commonly referred to as the "Blind Pigs" (PG was pig without the "i"), as well as a force of detectives and secret police, the latter meant, ostensibly, to deal with the problem of Union spies.

That there were spies in Richmond was accepted without question, but the methods of the "puguglies" Winder employed to staff his police force were accepted far less readily. There was little, if any, restraint on their behavior. They often commandeered private carriages and confiscated personal property at whim, and a protest could easily result in arrest and incarceration at either Castle Thunder or Castle Lightning, the two military prisons that had been established on Cary Street. Many of the residents of Richmond were shocked and deeply disappointed at what was happening to their fair city. Since becoming the capital of the Confederacy, Richmond was experiencing growing pains and some of the growth spurts were apparently malignant.

Christmas had come and gone, and with it, the latest hope that Britain would enter into the conflict on the side of the South. The *Trent* affair, which had filled the newspapers on two continents when the British vessel Trent was boarded and two Confederate representatives on their way to London had been seized, had finally been resolved when Commissioners Mason and Slidell were released by the federal government and put aboard a ship to England. Thus placated, Great Britain now seemed content to follow a policy of strict neutrality.

For Maria, as for much of the South, it had been a gloomy Christmas. No one believed anymore that the war would be a short one, and the grim realities of warfare were only just beginning to impress themselves on people's consciousness.

After seeing her settled in the Spotswood Hotel, Spencer had gone on to join his unit. Shortly afterward, Maria had moved out of the hotel to the home of Sam Coulter's friend and former business partner, Carson Slater, who insisted she stay with him and his wife.

Slater was a robust and portly man in his late fifties, with a courtly and charming manner. He and his wife, Abigail, lived in a handsome, two-story, red-brick house on Church Hill. They had two grown sons, about the same ages as Travis and Spencer, both with the army. Slater's work at the War Department under the new Confederate secretary of war, Judah Benjamin, kept him away from home long hours and Abigail was grateful to have company around.

Maria found Abigail Slater to be a pleasant, chatty, and socially conscious woman, not much given to intellectual pursuits. She was rather plain, but not unattractive, in her early forties, with chestnut-brown hair that she wore in a chignon. With her husband spending so much time at the War Department, Abigail had become something of an organizer, and when she wasn't spending time at home with her sewing circle, making clothing for the troops, exchanging recipes for gooseberry wine and coffee substitutes, she worked with the Ladies' Aid Society of St. Paul's Episcopal Church, collecting food and supplies for the city's hospitals and volunteering her time to help nurse and visit the wounded soldiers.

Abigail immediately took Maria under her wing and introduced her to the ladies of Richmond society. Unlike the women of Elizabeth Coulter's social circle in Charleston, who had gone out of their way to avoid any reference to Maria's "Yankee connections," Abigail's friends confronted the situation head-on.

"And so the men of your family are fighting for the Union while your husband fights for the Confederacy? Why, you poor dear! How awful it must be for you! You must feel so horribly torn!"

"Isn't that always the way? The men go off to fight their wars, leaving us women at home to bear the brunt of worry. Oh, how I hate this terrible war!"

"My Lord, supposing your brothers should meet your husband on the field of battle! Oh, I simply shudder at the thought! Well, we'll simply say our prayers for all of them, and pray that this awful war comes to a speedy end."

Maria, though initially somewhat flustered at such directness, found she much preferred it to the well-meaning, though uncomfortable avoidance of the subject she had encountered in Charleston. Nor was she the only one among them whose family had been torn apart by the war.

Hetty Morrison had come to Richmond from Baltimore, where half her family had sided with the Union and the other half with the Confederacy. Her husband, Vance, was a Virginian, a captain with the troops under Stonewall Jackson, while her father was a staunch Union man and her sister back in Maryland was married to a Union officer. At one point, Hetty took Maria aside and confided to her that there were ways, for a price, that letters could be smuggled into Washington. Of course, it wasn't really spying, she explained, since no military information was revealed, but she was certain Maria's family was anxious to have some word of her, and if it was nothing more than a strictly personal letter, she couldn't see where there was any harm in it.

"It's really done quite often," she explained, "though, of course, it's not the sort of thing one speaks of out loud, if you know what I mean. Anyway, if you'd like to send word to your father or perhaps your brother in Washington and let them know that you are well, then it could be arranged."

Maria thanked her and said she would, indeed, like to send word to her brother and let him know she was all right. She did not know where her father was, or Mark, for that matter, but she knew Robert was with the Army of the Potomac and doubtless he'd know how to send word to them. It made her feel strange that the prospect of writing a letter to her own brother had suddenly become a clandestine act.

Maria had openly confessed her shortcomings to Abigail when it came to such things as sewing and knitting, telling her she had hoped to find work as a nurse in a military hospital, where she thought she might be of some use. Abigail had understood and immediately supported her in the idea. They had taken a carriage and gone to Chimborazo Heights.

Maria had never seen anything like Chimborazo Hospital. Located on the heights above the city, it was a sprawling complex that occupied forty acres and consisted of 150 single-story, whitewashed buildings divided into five divisions, each one staffed by forty to fifty assistant surgeons under the direction of a surgeon. It had opened in October of the previous year and was under the direction of Dr. James McCaw. The hospital had eight thousand beds, its own herd of cattle numbering two hundred head, and over five hundred goats. It was like a small city unto itself.

Each ward, or pavilion, was detached on three sides from the main corridor, following the design of British military hospitals during the Crimean War. Each pavilion was ridge-ventilated, 187 feet long, 24 feet wide and 14 feet high at the eaves, with two rows of beds on either side of a center aisle and a room at each end, one for nurses and one for supplies.

The hospital received no money from the government, Abigail told Maria, largely because there really wasn't any money to give. It was supported by the community. The tobacco factories had donated the boilers for making soup and the factory workers made the beds and other furniture. Soap was made on the premises from kitchen grease and lye that had been run through the blockade. Beer was brewed on the premises, as well, and ten thousand loaves of bread were baked daily in the hospital bakery. The hospital also had its own dairy and five icehouses, as well as a canal boat that made frequent trips to barter with farmers between Richmond and Lynchburg for eggs, fresh fruit, and vegetables. But as large and modern as the hospital was, its resources were already being strained.

Since the Battle of Manassas, the wounded and the sick had been arriving at a steady rate and there were not enough nurses to go around. There were about five male nurses to every female, and this included soldiers who, for one reason or another, were incapable of serving or those who were too young or too old to join the army. There was about one doctor to every seventy patients, and anyone who was capable of rolling a bandage was welcomed to the cause. Women, in particular, were encouraged to become nurses, for there was a need for the feminine touch, not only to wash and cook and give out medicine, but to provide much-needed moral support by their presence, by reading or singing to the patients, or by writing letters for them and praying with them, or even something as simple as wiping the sweat from their brows. It was, Abigail explained, often a boon to the soldiers to have a woman present by them when they died. It helped them go more peacefully. Maria took in this information silently and grimly.

Mrs. Phoebe Yates Pember, the hospital's chief matron, was well acquainted with Abigail Slater and she welcomed Maria's offer of assistance. A severe, plainspoken and pragmatic woman, Mrs. Pember greeted Maria and put her right to work. And for the first time, Maria got her own taste of the war.

Maria's Journal, Richmond, Virginia, January 1862

Today I have completed my third month of service as a volunteer nurse. It seems as if it has been three years and not three months. I find now that I am capable of seeing the most terrible wounds without feeling faint, or sickened, or struck with horror at the sight. I wonder if this is how the soldiers themselves feel, if after seeing so many awful sights in battle, comrades torn apart by cannonballs and canister shot, their limbs shattered by Minié balls so badly that they require amputation, they look upon such things with no more reaction than they would experience upon a sudden change of weather.

Today, I helped a man to die. Not even a man, really. A boy. A mere boy of seventeen. He had received a wound in battle, I no longer remember or even care which one it was, and it had required the amputation of his foot, just above the ankle, for that bone had been completely shattered beyond any possible hope of healing. He had responded to this mutilation bravely and had looked forward to the eventuality of going home. The war, for him, was over. However, infection had set in shortly following the amputation, and it had been necessary to perform another, this time cutting off his leg below the knee. This, too, he had accepted stoically, saying that it would not really make much difference whether it was a foot he lost or a foot and a calf as well, since it would not make him any more crippled. But then infection had set in once more, and yet a *third* amputation was required, this time depriving him of most of his entire leg, and a third such ordeal had made his spirits fall considerably. He was weak, and wan, and seemed so listless that I feared for his recovery. Nor were my fears in vain. Infection set in once again, relentlessly, and he did not survive.

I sat upon his bed, beside him, his hand holding on to mine, and I prayed together with him. He was feverish, and toward the end, he had become delirious. There was little I could do except to wipe his brow and murmur soothing words to him as he cried out and spoke to me, believing that I was his mother. I did not attempt to disabuse him of that belief. I played the part of his absent mother for him, saying the sort of things that I imagined a mother might say to her dying son, and it seemed to give him comfort as he slowly slipped away into the Valley of Shadow. The war was over for him, indeed.

I remained there, holding on to his cold and lifeless hand for I know not how long. I felt a numbing emptiness. I had no tears. I merely sat and watched his face, his sightless eyes, like the glass eyes of a doll, wide open and staring at the ceiling. I reached out and gently closed his eyelids, then stood and pried my hand away from his grip.

In a daze, I walked down to the nurses' room and sat down at the table. Then, with all the suddenness of a torrential summer rain, my emotions came welling up within me and I could not contain them. I put my head down on my arms and wept. I sobbed uncontrollably, and my entire body felt as if it were spasming with grief. I felt a hand touch me lightly on the shoulder. I thought it was one of the other female nurses, so soft and tender was the touch, but when I glanced up, I saw it was a man. I stared at him, not knowing him, for he was not one of the doctors, nor one of the male nurses, and yet he looked somehow familiar, although I could not seem to place him.

Somewhat awkwardly, he took his hand away, as if thinking that the gesture might have been too familiar.

"We've met before, I think," he said, in a soft voice with a British accent, and when I heard it, I immediately recalled where and when it was that we had met. It was on the first day I arrived in Richmond. "Mrs. Coulter, isn't it?" he said. "You may not remember me. My name is Geoffrey Cord."

"Yes, I remember," I said. "The British journalist."

He nodded. "Somehow we keep meeting at the most unfortunate of circumstances," he said. He glanced back toward the bed of the boy who had just died. "Forgive me, I did not mean to intrude."

I shook my head to indicate that I did not feel he was intruding, for I had no words, yet he seemed to get my meaning.

"You look tired," he said. "When was the last time you had a decent meal?"

I stared at him blankly. For a moment I honestly could not remember. I mumbled something about having eaten a small breakfast in the morning and he said, "I thought as much. It's already almost evening. And you've been on your feet all day, haven't you?"

I suppose it must have been the shock of being with that boy when he died, for I felt confused and rather dazed. I seemed drained of all emotions suddenly. I could only nod in agreement.

"I have a carriage outside," he said. "I would be very pleased if you would join me for dinner, Mrs. Coulter. That is, if you would not think it improper."

I suddenly did not care whether it was proper or not, I only realized that I was famished and not at all in the mood for Abigail's cheerful chattiness. I agreed and he offered me his arm.

We took his carriage to the Exchange House and had our meal in the hotel dining room. We did not encounter anyone I knew, so I was spared from scandalizing any of Abigail's friends by my behavior, yet even so, I honestly would not have cared. I wolfed down my food as if I were some starving Indian while Mr. Cord barely touched his and watched me with curiosity, as if he were a small boy and I some sort of new and fascinating beetle. We barely spoke at all until I had finished, when I felt myself restored to some semblance of my former self and, feeling somewhat ill at ease, apologized for my shameful lack of manners.

He merely smiled and dismissed my remarks with a wave. "Think nothing of it," he said. "The strain of strong emotions can often affect people in strange ways. It usually takes a while before you are fully yourself again."

I nodded. "I thought I had grown accustomed to that sort of thing," I said.

"Have you ever seen a man die before?" he asked me bluntly.

I nodded once more. "Yes, but . . . not like that. I have nursed men who later died, but I have never had a man die while I was actually speaking with him, holding on to his hand . . . That was the first time. And he was just a boy . . ." My voice trailed off. I found that I did not have the words to describe how it had felt. I, who have always fancied myself a writer, could not find the words to describe my own emotions. Yet Mr. Cord seemed to understand.

"There are certain things one can never grow entirely accustomed to," he said. "Human suffering is one of them. If you can look on human suffering without being at all affected, then at that point, you have lost your own humanity."

He looked down for a moment, as if preoccupied with his own thoughts, and then glanced back at me. "I feel I owe you an apology, Mrs. Coulter," he said. "As I recall, I was rather rude to you and your husband at our first meeting."

"It was my brother-in-law, Spencer," I corrected him. "My husband, Travis, is with the army. As is Spencer now."

"Ah, yes. I remember now," he said.

Then I added, "Spencer wanted to go back and thrash you for your impertinence."

"Did he?" This seemed to amuse him. His green eyes twinkled. "Thrash me, eh?" And then he added mockingly, "Not challenge me to a duel?"

"One only fights duels with one's equals," I replied, feeling annoyed at his amused response, and at the same time irritated at myself for having invited it.

I was behaving rather badly. Not only had I allowed him, a complete stranger, to take me, a married woman, out to dinner, but here I was displaying my gratitude by being insulting. Perhaps it was because having eaten and feeling somewhat recovered, I now recalled more vividly his arrogance when we first met, and perhaps also I felt resentful of him for having caught me in a moment of weakness at the hospital. However, my words seemed to delight rather than infuriate him. He burst out laughing.

"Oh, well done, Mrs. Coulter!" he said. "I am properly humbled and chastised!"

I felt suddenly embarrassed. "Forgive me," I said, aware that I was blushing. "That remark was uncalled for."

"Oh, no, I asked for it, at our first meeting," he replied. "It was just rather delayed in coming. Very well, I shall accept your apology if you will accept mine."

I inclined my head toward him. "Your apology is accepted, sir."

"And yours, madam," he replied, mimicking my gesture sardonically.

I found myself feeling rather confused and flustered at the way I was reacting to him. One moment he seemed polite and utterly proper and charming, and then the next he seemed to be making fun of me. However, he had been kind enough to invite me to dinner, and so I thanked him. He graciously thanked me, in turn, for accepting his invitation, saying that he disliked dining alone and was grateful for the company.

We shared some wine and conversation. He seemed most interested in learning about the functions of the hospital, and the duties of a nurse, and my own impressions of what I had seen and experienced there. We progressed to discussing my family background, which also seemed to interest him a great deal.

He had not, of course, known that my father and my brothers were fighting for the North. It seemed to bring about a change in his demeanor toward me. He became more serious, and more solicitous, and it was not difficult to see where his sympathies lay. In fact, that had seemed obvious from our first meeting. I found myself thinking that if his reaction was typical of his countrymen, then the Confederacy would hope in vain to gain recognition from Great Britain.

I understood that his interest in me was primarily of a professional, rather than a personal nature. He was a journalist and was anxious to convey his impressions of the war and its effect on people in America to his readers in London. Perhaps my own ambitions as a writer made me feel sympathetic toward him, or perhaps it was because he listened well, asked thoughtful questions, and was possessed of a quite disarming charm when he chose to employ it. Or perhaps it was because I was simply starved for intelligent conversation, the sort of conversation that men have with one another and in which women are not generally invited to participate. Either way, I told him a great deal—quite surprising now, when I think how *much* I told him—and the time simply slipped away until I realized that it had grown quite late.

Whatever would Abigail think of me, I thought, a married woman, having dinner unchaperoned with a strange man and coming home so late? Even if it was entirely innocent—and of course, it was!—what would people think? I was quite certain I could expect a stern lecture if I told Abigail what I had been up to, so I decided there and then that I simply would not tell her the truth.

Rome, 193 B.C., The villa of Marcus Lucius Gallio

During the day, Cyrene worked in the smoky kitchens of the household, helping the cooks and polishing the bronze utensils. She kept the charcoal burning in the heaters, cleaned the earthenware pots, and swept the stone floors. Sometimes she assisted with the weaving, though she was still learning and her fingers felt clumsy at the looms. Her duties included whatever the overseer of the house decided she should do, as Gallio believed his slaves should know how to do everything, from tending the garden to cooking to making clothes and tapestries to cutting hair. He also placed a premium on education for his household slaves, which was unusual in a Roman citizen, and insisted they all learn how to read and write so they could become properly civilized and undertake secretarial duties if he required it of them.

Gallio's wife had died some years ago, giving birth to his youngest son, and he had not remarried, though he was not at a lack for female company. He entertained lavishly and frequently, and he and his guests fully enjoyed the pleasures of the flesh. Cyrene was never present during the revels and was not asked to serve, because Gallio believed it was improper to tempt his guests with his young female slaves. At such times, Cyrene remained in the kitchens and there was no shortage of work. She was well treated, never beaten or molested, and though her days were full and sometimes exhausting, especially on those days when Gallio entertained, they were not terribly unpleasant. She knew many slaves experienced much worse.

Each day some time was set aside for her and some of the other household slaves to learn their lessons with the tutor, a Greek slave who also taught Gallio's sons. Slowly, she started to become proficient in reading and writing the Roman language, and the tutor, the elderly Antonius, seemed pleased with her efforts and her progress. Sometimes, when she was working in the gardens, she would see Hanno instructing Gallio's two young sons in combat.

The two boys, Drusus and Flavius, were fine, strapping young men and clearly had a deep affection and respect for Hanno, though it was clear they also feared him just a little. It was hard for Cyrene to understand how it was possible for anyone to feel affection for the man who had become, to all intents and purposes, her husband, though there had never been any sort of formal marriage ceremony. Yet, in giving instructions to Gallio's two sons, he was clearly in his element. Gallio had given him free rein in that, insisting only that Hanno be careful not to injure them. He wanted his sons to become fighters, to be strong in body as well as in mind, and he had bought the best fighter in all of Rome to teach them.

Often Gallio would come to watch them train. At such times the boys would try especially hard to impress him with their efforts, and on occasion, their awareness of him would work to their disadvantage.

Crack! "Watch *me* and not your father, boy!" Hanno would whack the younger Flavius with the flat of his wooden sword, hard enough to stagger him and bruise him, but not cause any serious injury. "*Never* take your eyes off your opponent! You are slain! Now go stand over there and watch your brother take his turn!"

Gallio would make no response to such rough ministrations and Flavius would pick up his wooden sword and, rubbing himself where he'd been struck, stand to the side while his brother, Drusus, took his turn at being instructed.

Drusus, a more capable fighter than his younger brother, would engage his teacher with a vengeance, and when he did well, Hanno would merely grunt and nod. When he did poorly, Hanno would correct him, usually in such a manner that the lesson would smart considerably and stay with him. He instructed them as if they were young gladiators, and not the children of his master, but he never forgot his place. He never forgot he was a slave.

During the day, Cyrene almost never saw him, and at night, when they were together in their quarters, he never spoke to her at all. Except when he was instructing Drusus and Flavius, or replying directly to something said by Gallio or by the overseer, he never spoke to anyone. He was a brooding, silent giant of a man, and one blow from those powerful, heavily scarred arms could easily have killed her, but he had never struck her or abused her in any way, as she had expected him to. Nor had he ever taken her.

She came to realize that his roughness was simply all he knew, and perhaps he knew nothing of women, or had no interest in them. He acknowledged her presence, yet only just barely, and his surly acceptance of her was hardly a replacement for love. But then, Cyrene had given up on her dreams of love, and certainly she had no thought of loving him. She was his mate, but to all intents and purposes, that only meant she shared his quarters with him. Cyrene wondered if he even knew what love was, if he had ever even experienced it during his hard life.

After that first night, when she awoke in the morning, she had opened her eyes to find him sitting up in bed and staring down at her with what seemed like curiosity, as if he had suddenly woken to find this strange creature in his bed. Yet the expression on his face was blank, unreadable. She had been afraid to say anything, afraid even to move. He continued to stare at her for a while, then got out of bed and started getting dressed. They both left, to have breakfast in the kitchen with the other slaves, then she was taken in hand to be instructed in her duties and she did not see him again until that night, when once again he made room for her in the bed, but grudgingly, as if he resented sharing it. And, once again, he turned his back to her and simply fell asleep, without even saying anything or touching her.

She tried communicating with him, but could hardly get more than a curt nod or a grunt in response, and after a while she simply accepted this and spoke to him without really expecting a reply. It was almost like talking to herself. Sometimes, at night, he would have nightmares. Perhaps dreams in which he refought old battles in the arena, and he would thrash in the bed, sometimes unintentionally bruising her, and she would shake him awake, more afraid of what he might do to her asleep than his anger at being awakened.

"Hanno! Hanno, wake up! Hanno!"

He would come awake instantly, lunging to a sitting position and looking disoriented for a moment, as if he expected to find himself under attack, then he would realize where he was, see her beside him, cowering in fear, stare at her for a moment, then grunt and go back to sleep.

She had no idea what to make of him. She did not know how to reach him. He was morose and sullen, and somewhere deep inside, there seemed to be a steaming caldron of fury that was always threatening to boil over, though he kept the lid on with an iron self-control. It occurred to her that perhaps he was no more pleased to have her thrust upon him than she was to be given to him. He had given her a grudging acceptance, but nothing more. And, indeed, perhaps he knew nothing else. He had been treated like an animal, and so he had become one. The only trace of humanity he manifested was when he gave instruction to the boys.

One morning she awoke to find him gone. Thinking he had
awakened early and gone out, she thought nothing of it, but
she did not see him for the rest of the day, or the next night,
either. He was not there to give lessons to the boys, and she
realized, with a shock, that he had run away. The slaves whispered
among themselves about it, but whenever she came near, they fell
silent. He was brought back two days later, under guard and in
chains.

She never learned what happened or how he had been captured,
but the soldiers who returned him treated him quite roughly,
though with caution, despite his being chained. Gallio took charge
of him and the soldiers went away. The entire household was
summoned.

"Remove his chains," Gallio said to the overseer.

The chains fell heavily to the floor.

Gallio sighed heavily and shook his head. "I am greatly disappointed in you, Hanno," he said. "Why? Why have you done
this? Why have you betrayed my trust?"

Hanno did not reply.

"Have I ever mistreated you?" Gallio continued. "Have I ever
had you beaten or denied you food or shelter? Have I not taken
you into my own household, away from the arena, and improved
your lot? Have I not, at great expense, given you a beautiful young
wife to care for you and see to your needs? Have I not entrusted
my own sons into your care? Have I not been a good and gentle
master? Is this how you repay me?"

Hanno said nothing, merely continued staring at his feet.

Gallio sighed heavily. "I do not wish to punish you," he said,
"but a runaway slave cannot go unpunished. An example must be
made and you have given me no choice. You have brought this
on yourself." He turned to the overseer. "Bind him."

The overseer approached, but Hanno stepped back away from
him abruptly. The overseer hesitated. Hanno stared at Gallio for
a moment, then slowly turned around and removed his tunic,
exposing his back. He lowered himself to his knees and bent
forward.

Gallio nodded to the overseer. "Thirty lashes," he said, then
turned and walked away.

The overseer took his whip and proceeded to administer the
whipping. Cyrene cried out as the lash fell, then bit her lower
lip. She winced with each blow. Hanno never made a sound.
They all watched while the thirty lashes were administered, then

the overseer turned to them and said, "Remember what you have seen here this day. A slave who runs away steals his owner's property and can be put to death. The master has been lenient. The next offender may not be so fortunate. Now go on about your duties."

She hesitated, but one of the other female slaves took her by the arm and pulled her away. Back in the kitchen, she could not stop trembling. She dropped an earthenware pot and it shattered on the stone floor.

"Clumsy girl!" the cook said. Then, seeing the stricken look on Cyrene's face, her own expression softened. "Go to him," she added quietly.

She found him lying on the bed in their quarters, on his stomach, moaning softly. His back was a latticework of bloody welts. She squeezed her eyes shut at the sight, then forced herself to open them. She bit her lower lip and approached the bed.

She dipped a cloth into some hot water she'd brought from the kitchen, along with some salve, wrung it out into the bowl, and sat down on the bed beside him. Very gently, as carefully and softly as she could, she proceeded to clean away the blood. He winced and made a small sound when she touched him.

"Forgive me," she said, "Oh, it must hurt so very much . . ."

She reached out and gently stroked his hair. He turned and looked at her with a strange expression on his face. He saw that she was crying. He sat up and reached out with one finger to gently touch one of her tears.

"I know that you resent my presence," she said, "and that I was forced upon you . . . but you have never hurt me and . . . I could not stand to watch, and yet I had to. I will leave you if you wish, but I . . . only meant to help . . ."

Her lower lip began to tremble. She brought her hands up to cover her face. A moment later she felt his strong arms go around her and gently pull her close to his chest. She sobbed into it as he hesitantly stroked her hair.

"Forgive me," he said. "I have treated you no better than they have treated me."

It was as if she could suddenly feel the anger ebbing from him, to be replaced with resignation. But she knew, somehow, that he had not resigned himself to her, but to what had become of him, to what he was. For a long time he had been locked deep within himself, driven only by his anger and his instinct to survive, yet the Lion of Carthage had been defeated at last. He had finally resigned himself to being a slave.

And with that resignation, finally, came an awareness that she was just as much a victim as he was. She was just as human. He would not weep, and so she wept for both of them.

BOOK THREE

The army is gathering from near and from far;
The trumpet is sounding the call for the war;
McClellan's our leader, he's gallent and strong;
We'll gird on our armor and be marching along.

WILLIAM BATCHELDER BRADBURY

CHAPTER ONE

Robert's Journal, Washington, D.C., February 1862

I CANNOT RECALL any other time in my life when I have felt so frustrated. Some six months have now passed since George McClellan was given command of the army. When he first came to Washington in late July of last year, the army had numbered some fifty thousand soldiers of infantry, about one thousand of cavalry, and some six hundred and fifty of artillery. Now, George "I can do it all" McClellan is not only commander of the Grand Army of the Potomac, as he prefers to call it, but he has succeeded in displacing Winfield Scott as general-in-chief and the army is over one hundred and fifty thousand strong, with some forty miles of garrisoned fortifications around the capital. And in all that time, we have done absolutely nothing. The daily report of "All quiet along the Potomac" resonates like an ironic commentary upon our inactivity.

McClellan has not been idle, however, to give him his proper due. Since arriving in the capital to a hero's welcome, he has instituted a board review of officers, which has at least disposed of a number of unqualified men, and he has restored order to the capital by appointing Colonel Andrew Porter to the post of provost marshal, with the result that the city's saloons have at last been cleared of errant soldiers, the regiments have been reorganized, and a mutiny in the Seventy-ninth New York has been severely dealt with. Soldiers are no longer allowed within the city unless they have been granted passes to leave the camps. Porter's orders have directed him to see to the "preservation of good order and the suppression of anything that would disturb it." This entails the suppression of gambling houses and what are politely referred to as "disorderly resorts," as well as the regulation of hotels, markets, places of amusement—the "orderly" kind, one assumes—and searches, seizures, and arrests. As to the number of arrests and the like, I cannot testify with any reliable authority, but to my certain knowledge, there are still a good number of gambling houses and "disorderly resorts" that have not been entirely suppressed.

Porter's duties are also concerned with the obtaining of information from the enemy and preventing information from reaching the enemy. The latter, in particular, is of great concern to everyone, as rumor has it that Washington is absolutely infested with Confederate spies. That there are rebel spies here in the capital I do not doubt; however, it would seem there is little they can learn that Jeff Davis cannot read for himself in any Union newspaper. Nevertheless, there is great concern over this spying business, and to address this great concern, the newly organized "secret service" has officially been placed under the provost marshal's jurisdiction. In practice, however, this so-called secret service is directly answerable to George McClellan, primarily in the person of a peculiar little man named Allan Pinkerton.

Pinkerton is a man who, in both appearance and demeanor, has much in common with a ferret. McClellan apparently met him when Pinkerton was a private detective employed by the Illinois Central Railroad. He is now the head of McClellan's secret service, about which little is known; otherwise, of course, it would not be very secret.

Pinkerton is said to have a vast force of spies, or "secret agents," as he prefers to call them, spread throughout the South and reporting on the strength and movements of the enemy. All of this is very mysterious and Pinkerton himself seems obsessed with being mysterious. To aid the mystery, apparently, he prefers to be called by the name of "E. J. Allan," despite the fact that everyone of any importance in Washington knows who he is, and somehow he has managed to tack the rank of major onto his nom de guerre, although, so far as I know, "Major Allan" has never attended West Point and has no military training or experience whatsoever. Yet, when it comes to gathering intelligence about the enemy, he is McClellan's right-hand man.

Pinkerton's reports about the enemy's strength are treated as gospel by McClellan, who quotes Pinkerton's estimates verbatim. Exactly how he arrives at these numbers is also something of a mystery, and they make little sense to me. I cannot see how the South could be capable of raising forces that are so numerically superior to ours, especially given their lack of resources, yet that is what Pinkerton claims. And there is no way that I can see to verify his information, for it is all very mysterious and secret. His reported estimates range from the enemy having over one hundred thousand troops just north of Richmond, to one hundred and seventy, one hundred and eighty, and as many as two hundred thousand. At least some of these estimates, apparently, are based on the interrogation of prisoners who have fallen into Union hands, and yet I have to wonder why anyone with an ounce of common sense would trust information gained directly from the enemy.

Nevertheless, convinced that we are facing a foe vastly superior in numbers, and mindful of the fate of General McDowell in the aftermath of Bull Run, McClellan has determined that the army will not move until it is stronger and sufficiently prepared. Now that he has saved the capital by his arrival, McClellan has embarked upon his plan to save the Union from defeat, and his method of doing this demands a huge Napoleonic army of at least three hundred thousand men, supported by a naval force and railroads. To prepare such a leviathan for a campaign, therefore, it is necessary to enlist more troops, or to obtain them from other areas of the country, and to drill them constantly, holding inspections and putting on reviews, the better to prepare them for the ultimate campaign that will end the war in one decisive and masterful stroke. That is the way to do it, by God, and no one can tell McClellan any different.

Each day, the "Young Napoleon" departs from his headquarters at the home of Navy Captain Charles Wilkes on Pennsylvania Avenue, two blocks from the War Department, and takes his breakfast with his staff at Wormley's Restaurant on I Street. After breakfast, there follows a staff conference, ennobled by the presence of such luminaries as the Prince de Joinville, the son of King Louis Philippe, and the Duc de Chartres and the Comte de Paris, sons of the Duc d'Orléans, who have come to observe the war and have been appointed to McClellan's staff as aides. Joinville is not too difficult for most of the troops to pronounce with some degree of accuracy, but the sons of the Duc d'Orléans have become known as "Captain Chatters" and "Captain Parry."

Following his staff meeting, McClellan then returns to headquarters in order to receive visitors and conduct official business. In the afternoons, he rides out with his staff to conduct inspections and reviews at the camps around the city. Each day, McClellan and his entourage are a familiar sight, galloping through the streets of Washington en route to one camp or another. When they approach the camps, one member of his staff always gallops on ahead to prepare the troops for his arrival.

"Here comes the general, boys! The general! Little Mac is coming! Three cheers for McClellan!"

The men always cheer on cue as "Little Mac" comes riding past, acknowledging them by raising his cap high overhead and giving it a twirl. Often, he will pause to speak briefly with the troops.

"Ready for a brush with the Rebels, boys?" he will inquire.

"Yes, sir!" they will reply, with vigor.

"Good! I'll risk it with you! No more retreats like Bull Run, eh? Forward all the way to Richmond!"

And the men will cheer, and "Little Mac" will wave his cap, set spurs, and off he goes, to raise some more morale. In that, at least, I must admit he has succeeded. The morale of the troops is much improved. They love their "Little Mac," but in all frankness, I must confess that I do not share the high regard in which most of our troops hold our commander. McClellan knows how to organize an army and instill morale, but high spirits and parade-ground tactics are no substitute for battlefield experience. McClellan has taught the army how to move, but it remains to be seen if it can fight.

His excursions to inspect the troops and watch parades normally continue until nine or ten o'clock, when the "Young Napoleon" retires from the field and returns to headquarters following another successful day of command.

In many ways, my duties now remind me of my time in West Point and at cavalry school. McClellan has established schools for his officers to attend, under the direction of his brigadiers, where much of the same elementary ground is covered as we learned in our first year at West Point. Field drills are studied, and army regulations are committed to memory. Our general spends much time in building up his artillery, with an aim to having at least four batteries for each division, which is, for the present, our largest command unit. He intends to postpone the organization of the army into corps until he can select his corps commanders based on observation of their conduct in battle. In itself, this is sound reasoning. But when will we fight a battle?

McClellan drives himself hard, so hard that he fell ill with fever shortly after his arrival in the capital. He is now fully recovered and continues to keep to the same pace. He seems to be so set upon deciding everything himself that he is prevented by this obsession from effectively delegating authority, a necessary faculty in a commanding general, and there are some tasks that he would have done well to delegate, such as the organization of the cavalry.

According to the manual this "war expert" had written following his observation of the conflict in the Crimea, the purpose of the cavalry is to provide guard duty and serve to prevent surprise attacks by the enemy. As I recall, he devoted a mere two pages of his manual to the subject of reconnaissance. Now this general, who has never served in the cavalry himself, has not seen fit to organize the cavalry into an independent unit. Instead, he has distributed the cavalry throughout the army. There is only one brigade, to which I am attached, and that functions only as a temporary training unit. General Stoneman, the cavalry commander, is for the most part little more than an administrator.

The result of this type of organization, or lack of organization, is that the cavalry are scattered all throughout the army and are largely employed as messengers and escorts and orderlies. Many are little more than "dog robbers," a term used to describe a soldier whose duty is to provide whatever his immediate superior requires in the way of supplies or creature comforts, no matter what lengths he has to go to in order to obtain it. The verb "to steal" is often redefined these days as "to requisition."

My own duties entail the training of recruits. The average Union cavalry recruit does not know one end of a horse from the other. Most of them, at first, have no idea of how to get up into the saddle, and after they have been shown, many of them will put one foot into the stirrup and then drop the reins, or push against the horse as they attempt to mount, with the result that the horse will move to the side and a comical ballet ensues as the trooper goes around in circles, one foot in the stirrup and hopping on one leg after the horse, which keeps moving away from him.

Many of our recruits fear the horses, which the animals sense, and so their efforts to control them meet with little success. They hang on to their reins for dear life, pulling back as they attempt to induce their mounts to go forward, and the horses shy, or throw them, or take the bits between their teeth and bolt. Often, the troopers fail to tighten their girths properly, or the horse will inhale deeply as the saddle girth is tightened and the trooper will thus be fooled into thinking it is snug. He will then attempt

to mount up, only to find both saddle and blanket come sliding
down or, worse yet, have it all come loose while he is mounted
and learning how to canter.

I saw an Irish trooper from New York City make a game
effort to stay up on his horse when the animal began to buck,
and though he lost control of his mount, he at least managed to
remain in the saddle for a few moments before he was thrown
soundly to the ground. There he remained, sitting with his legs
spread out, a dazed look upon his face. As I rode up to see if
he was injured he looked up at me sheepishly and said, "Lord,
an' I tried, sir, but I just couldn't stay aboard and calm 'er
down!"

"You should not have used your spurs," I said, for I had
observed him digging in his spurs with a vengeance.

"Faith, sir," he replied, "an' if it wasn't for them holders, I
would've been thrown first thing!"

I could only shut my eyes in weary and long-suffering patience
and think, Cavalry! My *God*!

I think of Stuart's troopers and how they came thundering
down upon our disorganized retreat at Bull Run, like cossacks
born and bred to the saddle, and I despair. The best horseman
in the Union Army is Sam Grant and where is he? Commanding
infantry in Missouri. It seems hopeless. Utterly hopeless. Stuart
will run rings around us.

The rebel infantry does not seem to have many worries, either.
After the disaster at Bull Run, they advanced their lines almost
to the very banks of the Potomac and had emplaced batteries
overlooking the river, endangering our supply lines. In October,
there had been the additional disaster of Ball's Bluff, in which a
force sent across the Potomac to make a demonstration against the
enemy was engaged by a superior rebel force and pushed back
against the steep terrain along the river.

Once again, our troops had panicked, swarming down the bluffs
and into the boats in such numbers that the craft were swamped.
Many had drowned, or were picked off as they attempted to swim
across. In all, 49 men were killed, 158 were wounded, and an
astonishing 714 were reported missing and presumed drowned.
Among the casualties had been Colonel Edward Baker, a former
member of the Senate and a close personal friend of the president.
The blame for this debacle fell on poor General Stone, who had
been in command of the operation, while McClellan, who had
ordered it, escaped unscathed.

To make matters still worse, the new general-in-chief and the president do not get along. What President Lincoln thinks of McClellan I can only guess at, but "Little Mac" has made no secret of what he thinks of the president. It is widely known that McClellan considers the president an incompetent buffoon. Once, it is said, when the president came to call on the Young Napoleon at his headquarters, McClellan ignored him and went straight up to bed. This story caused much amusement when it reached the troops, but if true, it is nothing less than outright insubordination and rudeness of the grossest kind. I cannot imagine how the president could allow such a thing to pass.

Still, despite my personal dislike for Little Mac, I can understand and appreciate his position. McDowell was forced into a campaign before the army was ready and the result was a humiliating defeat, for which, unjustly, he received the blame. McClellan clearly has no intention of repeating McDowell's mistake. He does not wish to risk the army. In the meantime, the newspapers and the public are clamoring for action and delay favors the rebels. Lincoln needs a victory to make up for the disaster at Bull Run. There is also Great Britain to consider. Thus far, the British have remained neutral. They seem to be waiting to see which way the wind blows. However, their textile mills need Southern cotton and the Confederate representatives in London are doubtless working hard to gain British support and recognition. Disagreements between the president and the general-in-chief only play into their hands.

It seemed that nothing would be done until the spring, but at the end of January, the president issued Special War Order 1. McClellan had previously submitted a plan whereby the Army of the Potomac would move against Richmond by water, attacking by way of the lower Chesapeake. In his special order, Lincoln disapproved of that plan and instead ordered that after the defense of Washington had been sufficiently provided for, the army should move in an expedition against Manassas Junction, and that it should do so by the twenty-second of February.

McClellan at once went to the president and objected, requesting permission to submit his objections to the plan in writing. The president allowed McClellan to state his case, and while I was not, of course, privy to the exchange, as a student of military tactics, I can well imagine what McClellan's arguments must have been.

The season is not favorable to a campaign by land. The weather has rendered the roads around Washington impassable. They are a sea of mud. Moving the army by water transport to the lower Chesapeake, from which we could strike at Richmond by the shortest possible land route, where the roads would be in much better condition, would certainly be a complex and expensive operation, yet it would leave the rebel forces threatening Washington with no choice but to pull back and defend their own endangered capital.

An operation against Manassas, on the other hand, would entail moving over roads that are in very poor condition at this time of year and a victory would only gain us the field of battle. A victory at Bull Run, where we have been beaten so badly once before, would be a great boost to morale, but of little strategic value. The rebels could easily retreat back down toward Richmond, fighting holding actions all the way and forcing us either to pursue them across washed-out roads and difficult terrain or abandon pursuit altogether.

McClellan's plan, while undoubtedly complicated and expensive, is nevertheless sound in theory. If a retreat should become necessary, the naval fleet can take advantage of the James and York rivers to provide cover along our flanks. The garrison of Fort Monroe, at the tip of the peninsula, is already in Union hands. And with water transport available, we could then strike at other points in the South, perhaps in South Carolina, or in Georgia. If executed properly, this plan can win the war.

McClellan managed to convince the president of that, although there is still concern about making adequate provisions for the capital's defense. Stonewall Jackson is still on the loose somewhere in the Shenandoah Valley and he is demonstrating a devilish talent for being fast and elusive. In spite of that, the president has rescinded his order in favor of McClellan's plan, but he has insisted that the rebel batteries along the Potomac be cleared away before the campaign begins. And that has apparently become another bone of contention.

The administration is concerned about the safety of the capital. McClellan feels that he has made adequate provisions for the capital's defense and that a strike at Richmond would force the rebels around Washington to rush to its defense. An attempt to clear the rebel batteries from the banks of the Potomac would almost certainly bring on a general engagement and McClellan does not want to engage the rebels here. He wants to do it at Richmond. So once again, there is disagreement, nor is that disagreement confined to those empowered to decide the matter.

Only yesterday, I encountered George Custer in the bar at Willard's and he engaged me in conversation while I was attempting to enjoy a brandy smash. Out of politeness, I offered to buy Custer a drink, but he refused, explaining that a bad experience had convinced him to forswear drinking. The idea of a reformed Custer, who had made so many runs to Benny Havens's that one could almost trace a pathway to his door, seemed so novel that I did not attempt to avoid his company, as I usually try to do. Within moments, he was vigorously arguing that McClellan could do no wrong and that the president should stop trying to interfere with him and let him run the war.

"The man doesn't understand the first thing about military strategy!" he insisted, pounding on the bar for emphasis. "I wish to God Lincoln would just stick to politics and stop trying to play soldier!"

"I think the president has a legitimate concern, George," I replied patiently. "Those batteries have closed the Potomac to navigation and they're threatening the capital."

"They're not threatening much more than Harvey's oysters," Custer said sarcastically.

Harvey's Oyster Salon, on C Street, has become one of the busiest establishments in the city. The demand for oysters, which have always been popular in Washington, has increased tremendously since the arrival of the army. The quartermaster's office often orders as many as four or five hundred gallons at a time, sending the barrels out to the camps around the city, and the Harvey brothers have expanded their business so that it is now the largest restaurant in Washington. However, with the rebel batteries firing on any craft that tries to sail north on the Potomac, the supply of oysters is becoming scarce and the vessels operated by the Harvey brothers brave being sunk each time they run the Confederate blockade. Custer knows I am very fond of oysters and go to Harvey's often. His remark was meant to bait me, something he is always trying to do. I had found that I did not like Custer much better as an officer than I had as a cadet.

Ever since he discovered that my intervention in Mark's court-martial had been bought at the price of Mark's being sent out west to serve with a volunteer infantry regiment, he has made no secret of the fact that he resents it. He and Mark are close friends and were frequent partners in crime back at the Academy, and Custer believes that my arranging for my younger brother to be assigned to Grant's command was petty and vindictive. What galls me is the thought that perhaps Custer is right.

I was angry with Mark for putting me in a position where I had to go to General Scott, with hat in hand, to plead his case. I had asked it as a personal favor, stating the case as briefly and as simply as possible, burning with humiliation all the while. General Scott had simply stared at me for a moment, without saying anything, then he nodded curtly and said, "Very well, I shall look into it."

The matter was never mentioned between us again, and Mark's bacon was saved, but I knew General Scott felt I had presumed on our relationship. Mark had finally gone too far and I resolved to make certain that he would never be in a position to embarrass me again. Custer has made it perfectly clear what he thinks of my actions toward my brother. The most irritating thing about it is that Custer's attitude makes me question my own motives.

For the second time now, my inflexible principles have brought about a rift between me and someone close to me. The first time, it was with Travis. Now it was Mark. We have exchanged letters since I received word from Maria. She had somehow arranged for a letter to be smuggled north to me and I felt obligated to write to Mark and let him know that our sister was safe and well. I had written Mark a letter that was polite and formal, telling him what Maria had said and adding that I was sending her letter on to our father. (It feels strange now to think of him as "the major," as we have always called him, for the idea of holding the same rank as my father, when I have done so comparatively little to deserve it, seems very awkward to me.)

Mark had written back, in a tone equally polite and formal, taking his cue from me, no doubt. He thanked me for sending word about Maria and congratulated me on being brevetted to major. He had briefly described his part in the Battle of Belmont and expressed great admiration for General Grant.

"Take no heed of any malicious gossip you may hear about his being a drunkard," he wrote. "The man is a fine soldier, as determined, brave and able as any I have met. He inspires great confidence in his men and does not hesitate to expose himself to danger alongside them. I am proud to serve with him."

I had raised my eyebrows at that. That did not sound very much like Mark, who has never shown any great respect, much less admiration, for his superiors in rank. Perhaps, although it seems hard to believe, Mark has finally learned his lesson and has started taking things more seriously. Yet there was nothing in his letter to indicate contrition. No apologies, or explanations, or expressions of regret. He scarcely alluded to the incident at all, save for one brief comment at the conclusion of his letter.

"I hope this letter finds you well. Thank you for writing with news about Maria, and for your past efforts on my behalf. Sincerely, your brother, Mark."

What was I to make of that? Was it merely Mark's flippant way of dismissing the affair, or was he so painfully embarrassed over what had happened that he wished to dwell on it as little as possible? Either way, it occurs to me that a stranger glancing at our letters to each other would never guess, from their tone, that we are brothers.

Is Custer right? Have I been too harsh with Mark? Have I, indeed, been petty and vindictive? Or was I right in having Mark posted somewhere where he could neither embarrass his older brother nor suffer by comparison with him, and be forced to make his own way, based on his own initiative? I want to believe the latter, but I cannot dismiss the former, even without Custer around to remind me constantly.

"Tell me something, George," I told him, "why do you even bother with the pretense of camaraderie? We are not friends. We don't even like each other."

"Why, we're old academy mates, you and I," Custer replied, as if frankly astonished that I should even suggest such a thing. "Aside from that, we've fought together at Bull Run. You remember, I gave you a ride back on my horse, because you'd somehow managed to lose yours? Damned careless of you, really. Besides, your brother's my best friend. You remember Mark, your brother? The one you banished to Siberia?"

"Missouri is hardly Siberia," I replied, my annoyance with him growing.

"Ah, well, it's all the same," said Custer, with a shrug. "Probably just as well, too. He won't be able to get into much trouble there. He's better off. Out of sight, out of mind, eh?"

"You're trying my patience, Custer." My tone was intended to convey a warning. He ignored it.

"Am I, indeed?" he replied, raising his eyebrows in an expression of mock innocence. "You mean the great Caesar Gallio is actually capable of losing his temper? Well, well, I would never have guessed it. I've always thought you were an utter paragon of perfection."

I set my glass down on the bar and turned toward him, my patience finally at an end. What was between me and Mark was a family matter and no concern of his. I had decided that I was going to suffer no more of his arrogant insolence.

"For quite some time now, Custer, you've been deliberately seeking to provoke me. Well, you've finally succeeded. If a fight is what you want, then you can damn well have it. Let's you and I go outside and settle this, right *now*."

He smiled faintly. "There is an alley a short way down the street that should do admirably."

"Fine," I replied, through clenched teeth.

"After you, Major," Custer said, with a mock bow.

We left Willard's together and went out into the street. It was growing dark.

"This is quite a treat," said Custer, with a smirk I longed to wipe from his features. "I'm about to have the rare privilege of seeing the perfect cadet, and now the model officer, break regulations and take part in a fistfight. I'm almost sorry I'm the one you will be fighting. I would have dearly loved to watch."

"You'll have a front-row seat," I told him tersely.

"You know, it's going to be a pleasure beating the tar out of you," Custer said as we walked down the street together, to all outward appearances merely two comrades out on the town. "I've been itching to do it ever since I was a plebe."

"Well, you'll finally have your opportunity to try," I said. "I hope you won't be too disappointed."

Custer chuckled. "You know, Robert, I do believe this is the first time I've ever seen you act like a man, and not a textbook. I really think I like you better this way."

If there were ever a more infuriating man, I thought, I have never met him. "I would like you infinitely better if you didn't talk so damned much," I replied, feeling the fury mounting within me.

"Done," said Custer, with a mocking smile, and we walked the rest of the way in silence.

We reached the alleyway he spoke of and turned into it. It was a narrow passageway between two buildings, connecting to the next street. It was strewn with refuse and there were a number of large wooden crates piled up against one wall.

"Let's go a bit further down, behind those crates there," said Custer. "I'd hate to cause you the embarrassment of being caught fighting by the Provost Guard."

I started to remove my coat. I had few worries about the Provost
Guard. They would doubtless have their hands full keeping order
down in the fleshpots of Hooker's Division. Contiguous to Murder
Bay, the capital's most crime-ridden slum, the gambling saloons
and whorehouses between Tenth and Fifteenth streets have been
christened with the name of General "Fighting Joe" Hooker,
whose own well-known taste for bawdy houses has apparently
spurred similar interests in his men. Their camp followers, wanton
trollops all, are known as "Hooker's girls," and soldiers coming
into the city on a pass often make straight for the division to find
themselves a "Hooker."

The Provost Guard could well expect to find trouble down in
the division. They would not likely be looking for it in the much
more genteel vicinity of Willard's Hotel. Even so, I felt reasonably
confident that they would think twice before placing two officers
under arrest, and one of them a major, known to have been an
aide to the former general-in-chief.

I did not care to have such thoughts going through my mind,
for it made me feel as though I were lowering myself to Custer's
level, that of the habitual miscreant, and I was, in fact, no more
than that on this occasion. I knew that and, to my discredit, did
not care. Custer had been a constant irritant ever since West Point
and I had finally reached the limit of my patience. My blood
was up.

Custer started to remove his coat.

"Just tell me one thing, Custer," I said. "Is this on your own
account, or because of Mark?"

"Partly on Mark's account," admitted Custer, "but I have a few
of my own to square with you as well."

"Because I made you walk so many extras at the Point?" I
asked. "You richly deserved each and every one of them."

"I'll grant you that," said Custer, with a shrug. "It's your smug
superiority I never cared for. You always were a stuffed shirt,
Robert. Utterly inflexible. Everything done right by the book. You
wonder why Mark was always getting himself into hot water in
his plebe year? Doubtless you think it was my influence. The fact,
however, is that Mark had a need to prove to the rest of our class
that he was not like you. They loathed you, almost as much as
your friend Coulter, who so dearly loved to bully those smaller
than himself."

I frowned at that. I had always believed that the plebes held
me in respect. Or was Custer merely baiting me again? "I never

bullied anyone," I said. "Nor did Travis Coulter."

Custer laughed with derision. "The only thing Coulter loved more than hazing new cadets was mounting any girl that he could get his hands on."

I felt the blood come rushing to my face at the attack on my friend's honor and, in the heat of the moment, forgot that our friendship had been severed. "You're a damn liar!" I retorted, my hands clenching into fists.

"You mean to tell me you didn't know?" said Custer. He gave a snort. "He had all the girls at Benny's, and he forced himself on half the daughters of the faculty as well. Quite the Southern gentleman, your friend Coulter was. And you let him marry your own sister. How you ever—"

He never finished, for at that moment my right fist landed on his jaw and sent him sprawling.

"Get up!" I shouted. I am ashamed to say I felt such fury that it was all I could do to keep from kicking him when he was down.

Custer put his hand up to his mouth and it came away bloody. "So," he said. "The textbook is human, after all."

He came up charging and ran into me, throwing his arms around my waist and bearing me down to the ground. We fell back against the wooden crates and sent them tumbling. He had always been a strapping fellow, even as a plebe, and while I was his equal in size, I had misjudged his strength. I managed to dislodge him, but he wrestled me down to the ground again before I could fully regain my feet.

We tussled for a few moments, then he managed to get me on my back. He got astride me and struck me twice. One blow caught me in the face, the other glanced off my head as I sought to avoid it. Give the devil his due, he could punch with all the force of a butcher's maul. I dislodged him once again and scrambled away from him. As a wrestler, he was my superior, without doubt, but I had done very well in boxing at the Academy, and once I'd gained my feet, I felt sure I would have the advantage.

We squared off, both of us breathing hard, and he came at me again in that same relentless, head-down charge, like a bull at a red flag. I sidestepped his rush and hooked a fist into his stomach as he passed. It winded him, and he gasped for breath, but recovered quickly. This time he brought his fists up, but whereas I expected him to move more cautiously, catching his breath and waiting for an opening, he rushed in at once, very quickly, and surprised me with a jab to my chin, followed by a hook to the body. I danced away, minimizing somewhat the effect of that second blow, but the first had landed solidly and I could taste blood in my mouth. He pursued me like a juggernaut, always attacking, nothing defensive about his tactics at all, and the sheer ferocity of his assault made up for whatever superior skill I may have possessed.

We traded blows several times, but I was getting the worst of it. This was no polite and sportsmanlike academy boxing match, I realized; the bastard really meant to kill me. I saw I would have to change my own tactics if I was going to survive. He scarcely gave me time to breathe. He simply kept on coming at me, attack, attack, attack, giving no quarter, no opportunity to get away from him, always seeking to force me back against the wall, where he could drive his fists into my body like a blacksmith pounding on an anvil.

I put my own head down, and forgetting everything I had been taught about the art of pugilism, I drove it into his stomach and kept going, forcing him back against the opposite wall so hard that he grunted with the impact. I gave him no time to catch his breath, but belabored him about the face and body, driving him back against the wall each time and giving him no space in which to move.

I was astonished at the amount of punishment he could take. Even as I struck him and landed my blows, he struck back, with telling effect. As I look back on it, and feel the pain of all my cuts and bruises still, we must have presented a horrible sight, like two medieval men-at-arms bashing away at each other, only using our fists instead of swords, with no finesse, no technique, no sporting give-and-take, but merely a bloody, knockdown brawl.

I felt myself weakening and, in desperation, sought to end it with one blow in which I gave my all. I smashed him in the face with all my might, putting the full weight of my body into it, and my fist struck home, landing on his jaw with such force that the sweat sprayed off his hair and face. He fell back against the wall, but amazingly, came right back at me again, and before I could recover my balance, he matched my blow with an identical one of his own and I saw stars.

I do not remember falling, but I must have, for the next thing I remember is lying on my back, vainly attempting to get up. My vision was blurred and everything was spinning. I seemed unable to control my limbs. Dimly, I saw Custer standing over me, as if on his last legs, weaving and swaying like a willow in the wind. Then I heard the sound of running footsteps and men shouting.

I realize now that he must have knocked me senseless for at least several moments, for in the time that I lay on the ground, he had managed to recover somewhat and catch his breath. I saw the men of the Provost Guard come rushing up, and several of them went to Custer, to support him, while two or three others came to bend over me.

I heard someone say, "What happened, sir? Are you all right?"

"Which way did they go?" asked someone else.

"Jumped us . . . coming through the alley," I heard Custer say. He pointed toward the opposite end of the alley, leading to the next street. "Never mind us, we'll be all right. Hurry . . . they went that way . . . you can still catch them!"

The Provost Guard ran off in the direction he had pointed out to them and we were once again alone. Or so I thought.

I saw Custer bending over me as my vision slowly began to clear and control began to return to my limbs. He held out his hand.

"Here," he said. "Let me help you."

I slapped his hand away. "Get away from me, damn you," I said, my voice thick as molasses.

"Come on, Robert, you fought well. Let's be off before they suspect they've been had."

"Leave me alone," I said. "Go to the devil."

He stared at me for a moment, then shrugged. "Fine. Have it your way then," he said.

I saw him stumble over to where he'd placed his coat, pick it up and, with his head high, walk off down the alley. As the sound of his bootheels receded I once again attempted to get up. I managed to achieve a sitting position, only just barely, and could move no more. Then I felt someone's hands upon me.

"Easy, now, soldier," a kindly voice said. "Easy. Allow me to help you."

I felt strong hands supporting me, helping me to my feet, and as I stood, unsteadily, I beheld my benefactor. He was not quite as tall as I, of medium build, and dressed in a dark suit, white shirt open at the neck, and a black felt hat. He had a full, dark, graying beard and a shaggy head of hair. He had a rugged, manly face, but there was a softness about his eyes, a gaze that spoke of kindness.

"Please, lean on me," he said, placing my arm around his shoulder. "I think we should take you to the hospital," he said.

"No," I replied, feeling utterly humiliated.

"I'm afraid I must insist, Major," he said. "We shall go to the general hospital, if only for a short while, so I can tend to your injuries properly. I have some skill at nursing."

I was too weak to protest.

"That other fellow gave you quite a beating," he said as we walked slowly.

I must have given him a sharp glance, for he continued with an explanation.

"I was passing the alley on my way back to my boardinghouse and I heard the commotion," he explained. "I arrived only moments before the Provost Guard, though when they came, I thought it wise to withdraw into the shadow of a doorway. They can be overzealous, on occasion, in the pursuit of their duties. And despite what the other fellow told them, there were no puguglies back there in that alley, but two officers of the United States Army, brawling like a couple of dockworkers. Never fear, however, I shall be discreet. I imagine it was some private affair and therefore none of my concern. However, allow me to say that if you two go after the rebels the way you went after each other, then you shall be at Richmond's gates in no time."

My head had cleared somewhat, though I ached in every bone and muscle of my body. "Who are you?" I asked him.

"My name is Whitman, Major. Walt Whitman."

"Robert Gallio," I replied. "And I am very much obliged to you, Mr. Whitman."

"For whatever it may be worth," said Whitman, "the other fellow looked little better."

"Yes, but he walked away under his own steam," I said, in a disheartened tone. To have been bested by the likes of George Custer was a serious blow to my pride.

"Only just barely," Whitman replied. "It was lucky for him the Provost Guard assumed that you had both been jumped."

Lucky, I thought. That was word for it, all right. Dame Fortune had always smiled on Custer, else his exploits would have caught up with him long since. "Custer's luck," they used to call it back at the Academy.

"Yes, he's always had a lot of luck," I said sourly. "One of these days, he's going to run out of it."

We arrived at the hospital and Mr. Whitman saved me the trouble of further dishonoring myself by explaining that I'd been set upon and beaten. It was, in a way, the truth, only he omitted to say that I'd been beaten up by a junior officer. He also neglected to mention that I had been a willing party to the fray. I was given a chair and a cold compress, and Mr. Whitman saw to my cuts and bruises, probing here and there to see if any bones had been broken. Fortunately, none were, though I would not have been at all surprised to find my ribs busted.

A Negro hospital orderly approached with a bowl of water for Mr. Whitman to wash my face. For a moment he stared at me intently, then his eyes grew wide and he exclaimed, "Lord, I know you, sir!"

I gazed at him, but did not seem to remember him.

"Isaac Jefferson, sir," he said. "You remember, back in New York City, on the docks? You and your brother saved me from the slave hunters."

I recalled him then, but I suddenly felt very weary. I merely nodded, then crawled into a bed, closed my eyes, and fell asleep.

CHAPTER TWO

Mark's Journal, Cairo, Illinois, February 1862

I HAVE BEEN desultory about keeping up my journal. As an amateur historian, I seem to be, at best, erratic. There seems little point in making regular entries when nothing much of import has occurred. All too often, it seems easier to spend evenings in a friendly game of cards, or joining the men in a song or two around the campfire, or simply sleeping, a luxury I have truly come to appreciate, as I seem to be finding less time for it every day. Tonight, however, sleep is difficult in anticipation of our troop movement tomorrow. We are, at long last, about to embark on a campaign!

It has scarcely been two months since our last encounter with the rebels, although it seems much longer, somehow. The weeks following the Battle of Belmont seemed to drag on interminably. The euphoria of the engagement was all too soon replaced by the renewed lethargy of camp life. Our return to Cairo signaled a return to the same old deadening grind of drill and preparation for a campaign that never seemed to come. It was as if Belmont had been an anomaly of some sort, a dress rehearsal for a play that was never meant to open.

Following the battle, we had several meetings with rebel officers from the garrison at Columbus, who came up on steamers under flags of truce. General Grant went down to meet with them, taking along several officers from his staff, and on several occasions he returned the courtesy by paying calls on them, as a number of them were men whom he had served with in the war with Mexico. The purpose of these meetings was to make arrangements for the burial of the dead and for the exchange of prisoners, and on several occasions I was privileged to accompany the general to these meetings.

They were conducted in a most civil and gentlemanly manner, and it seemed at once decidedly odd and yet somehow not unnatural that we should meet our enemies under such polite circumstances. We met with Bishop Polk, the clergyman who has become a rebel general, and learned that during our retreat at Belmont, he had seen General Grant on horseback only moments prior to his daring plunge down the riverbank and, not recognizing him, had invited his sharpshooters to practice their marksmanship on "that Yankee officer."

Both men seemed to regard this incident with some amusement. Later, one of our officers, Colonel Buford, served drinks to our rebel guests, and casting about for a toast that would be acceptable to all concerned, he proposed one to George Washington, the father of our country. Bishop Polk then raised his glass and added, with a smile, "And the first rebel." As no one could reasonably dispute that, we drank the toast and scored a victory for the bishop's wit.

Both sides had claimed that battle as a victory, which seems impossible, and yet both our side and the rebels can, with some justification, make that claim. The rebels claim they won because our troops were driven off and Belmont was back in Confederate hands once more. On the other hand, we had never been ordered to do anything more than make a demonstration in order to prevent reinforcements being sent to Price. In that, we had succeeded, even if Belmont was retaken. In either case, it made little difference to me whose claim to victory was more just, for I had gained a victory all my own at Belmont, a personal victory that I shall treasure always.

I feel now as if I have finally emerged from within the shadow of my older brother. And I have come to look on my assignment to General Grant's forces not as a punishment from Robert, but as an opportunity that he has, perhaps unwittingly, bestowed upon me. At Belmont, I had been given a chance to prove myself, and for the first time in my life, I was not found wanting.

My duties with General Grant's staff have been increased. No promotion came with these new duties, nor any added glory, merely a lot more work. Captain John Rawlins, General Grant's adjutant, is a highly capable man, a successful lawyer in civilian life who had turned down an appointment as a major in a volunteer regiment to accept the lower-ranking post with Grant. Yet for all his administrative and organizational talents, Rawlins has had his hands full and my addition to the staff has proved to be most welcome to him.

One administrative headache kept following another, problems piled upon problems. With McClellan's Army of the Potomac receiving first priority for everything—he and Robert are going to win the war, of course, so I suppose that we should not begrudge them their demands—the situation with supply for our troops has become critical. We have no ambulances; there is not enough clothing to go around, and what little is available is of inferior quality. There is also a shortage of arms. Many of our troops are carrying old flintlocks and the imported Tower muskets. We are badly in need of the new Springfields. There are not enough sword belts for the cavalry and carbines are in short supply. General Grant had me dispatch an urgent request for supplies and funds to headquarters, where we now have a new department commander.

The great Pathfinder has finally been removed from command, undoubtedly because the only successful offensive he had ever launched was in sending his wife to make a demonstration against Lincoln. It succeeded in lighting a fire under the Old Rail-Splitter and the great Pathfinder has finally been deposed. Apparently, the president will take any amount of abuse from his subordinates, but he draws the line at being henpecked by their wives. General David Hunter was appointed to take charge of the department while Frémont was sent home to await further orders from the War Department, which I suspect will be a very long time coming. Hunter's command was only temporary, however, until General Henry Wager Halleck could arrive to assume permanent command.

Our new department commander is known as "Old Brains," and is reputed to be a highly intelligent military tactician. Like the rebel general Hardee, General Halleck has translated a number of military texts. The French generals write them and our generals translate them, all save Grant, who ignores them and relies on common sense, which seems to lose nothing in translation.

The demeanor of our general seems much improved since his family has joined him. I recalled how Kinchloe said he pined for them when they were separated and saw how once Mrs. Grant and the children took up residence on the upper floors of the headquarters building, the change in him was clearly evident. He has trimmed his beard, which had been quite long and unkempt. It is short and well groomed now and effects a marked improvement in his appearance. In honor of the arrival of the general's wife, the troops have named one of our big guns "Lady Grant."

Early in January, we received orders to make another demonstration, this time in support of General Don Carlos Buell, commanding the Department of Ohio. Headquartered at Louisville, Buell was threatened by the rebel forces at Bowling Green, under General Buckner. Our demonstration was intended to prevent Buckner from being reinforced by rebel troops from Columbus, or from Fort Henry and Fort Donelson.

I had looked forward to the movement as a welcome relief from camp life and the constant irritation of dealing with corrupt contractors and suppliers who seem bent on extorting as much money from the army as possible, and with the profiteers engaged in illegal trading with the South. Adding to such problems are the difficulties with rebel sympathizers among the local citizenry. We had lost a number of our picket guards to sharpshooters among the local population, so that General Grant ordered an area of six miles to be cleared all around the camp and made it known that anyone caught within that boundary would be shot. A march seemed just the thing to relieve the tension felt by all the troops, yet General Grant was less than pleased at being ordered to make merely another demonstration.

"I wonder if General Halleck would object to another skirmish like Belmont?" he remarked to me and Rawlins, when he read the orders. Then he added, with a grimace, "I suppose, though, it would hardly do to skirmish hard enough to take Columbus."

We had smiled at this, but we both shared his frustration. There seemed to be little purpose to this maneuvering back and forth, like cautious chess players. What General Grant wanted, what we all wanted, was an engagement with a purpose. That was the only sort of "demonstration" that mattered.

However, our orders were explicit. We were to make a demonstration only. To execute this demonstration, our forces were divided. General Smith proceeded with his column up the west bank of the Tennessee to threaten Fort Heiman and Fort Henry, while the gunboats sailed in support. General McClernand proceeded to western Kentucky, threatening the garrison at Columbus. I accompanied General Grant with McClernand's force.

My relief at leaving camp once more turned out to be short-lived. We were forced to march in beastly weather that wreaked havoc with the roads. We spent a week slogging through mud, snow, and freezing rain, suffering intensely from the cold, and in our misery, we were very much relieved at not having to engage the enemy. The rebels did not attempt to send reinforcements past us, and in that, at least, our movement was successful. Perhaps the rebels simply chose to stay in from the cold, in which case it was the weather, and not our fearsome presence, that deserved the credit. When we finally returned to camp, we were all bone weary and frozen stiff.

On his return, General Smith reported that he thought Fort Heiman could be taken and Flag-Officer Foote concurred. Fort Heiman stood on high ground, commanding Fort Henry on the opposite side of river, which was so high that a portion of Fort Henry had been flooded. This meant that the gunboats could be used with great effect. If Fort Heiman could be captured, Fort Henry would easily fall as well.

The implications of this were immediately obvious. With Fort Heiman and Fort Henry in our hands, the way would be clear for us to conduct operations up the Tennessee and Cumberland rivers, striking at the railroad bridges and disrupting the supply lines of the rebels. General Grant at once left for headquarters to propose the plan, but on his return, we learned that General Halleck had disapproved of it.

General Grant is not a man given to the use of profanity, nor is he the sort to give way to emotional displays, yet I could see that he was very upset at General Halleck's response. I was afraid I knew the reason for it, and my suspicions were shared by Captain Rawlins, as I discovered when we left the general and joined Captain Kinchloe in my quarters.

"It makes no damn sense," said Kinchloe, when he learned that Halleck had turned down the proposed campaign. "Anyone can see the plan is sound merely by looking at a map! Why would Old Brains dismiss it out of hand?"

"Because it came from Grant, that's why," said Rawlins angrily. "Halleck has doubtless heard the rumors being passed about him."

Kinchloe shook his head as he tamped down the tobacco in his ever-present pipe. "I should think Old Brains would have more sense than to listen to malicious rumors."

"Grant has made a lot of enemies," Rawlins replied, with a shrug. "The rebels are not the only ones we have to fight. All that trouble with the contractors has cost him dearly. He broke up their ring and put a stop to their shameless profiteering. So out of spite, they've been spreading lies about Grant's drinking and telling everyone that our administration here in Cairo is a hopeless muddle."

"Why would Halleck give any credence to that sort of talk?" asked Kinchloe. "Surely, when one considers the source—"

"That's just the point. Some of these men have influence," Rawlins replied. "That troublesome lawyer, Swett, for instance."

"The one who complained about the forage contract not being approved?" I said.

Rawlins nodded as he held his cup out for more coffee, which I poured. Even the indefatigable Rawlins seemed tired and dispirited. "He used his influence to have headquarters endorse the contract, only his prices were outrageous and Grant would not approve the vouchers. Swett became furious and threatened to complain to Lincoln."

"Bluff and bluster," Kinchloe said, with a grimace.

"Oh, it was no bluff," Rawlins replied. "Swett and Lincoln were both railroad lawyers in Illinois. They're old friends. Only Sam Grant doesn't take very kindly to threats, even from people who have the president's ear, as Mr. Swett discovered. He told Swett to tell the president anything he pleased, but he would only pay what he believed was a fair price, and if necessary, he would seize the Illinois Central and move the supplies himself. And he said this knowing Swett holds a large interest in the railroad," Rawlins added. "Then he ordered Swett out of Cairo and threatened to have him locked up or even shot if he refused to leave."

Kinchloe grinned. "I bet that took the starch out of his collar. And if I know Grant, he would've done it, too. But I do see what you mean. Sam Grant may be one hell of a soldier, but he will never make a politician."

"Speaking of politicians," Rawlins said, "I received a letter from Congressman Washburne. He's heard reports of Grant's supposed dissipation and has written to me as an old friend, to learn the truth of the matter. Needless to say, I hastened to assure him that I've never seen Grant drunk in all the time I have been with him, but if Washburne's heard enough of these rumors to become concerned, you can be sure that Halleck's heard them also."

That a politician should concern himself with rumors I did not find especially surprising, but that a general in command of the department should pay them any heed seemed worrisome. Yet despite Halleck's disapproval of the plan, Grant did not give

up. Instead, he determined upon a flanking manuever. To this
end, he enlisted the aid of Flag-Officer Foote, who believed
the plan was sound and had urged it from the beginning. He
consented to support General Grant with a dispatch of his own
to headquarters.

Flag-Officer Andrew Foote is a much respected gentleman,
well known for his devout beliefs and his sobriety. He holds
regular devotional services for the men of his command and is
strongly opposed to the use of spirits. When a man of his well-
known temperance gave his support to the proposed campaign,
Old Brains was moved to reconsider.

Perhaps he did so upon reconsidering the plan and seeing its
merits for himself, or because Foote's approval gave it added
weight. Perhaps headquarters had heard from Washburne, after
Rawlins had replied to him. But for whatever reason, today we
finally received orders to move on Fort Henry. There was cheering
at headquarters when the orders arrived. Tomorrow, we embark
on our campaign. No more demonstrations. This time, by God,
we are going to engage the rebels with a vengeance!

Fort Henry, Tennessee, February 3, 1862

The campaign began in much the same way as the expedition
against Belmont, only on a much larger scale. Halleck, once he
had approved the plan, became anxious to improve its chances
of success so he would not be eclipsed by Buell, whom both the
president and General McClellan were urging to take the offensive
in the Cumberland Gap. Buell was being slow to move, however,
so Halleck decided to seize the initiative that Grant had given him
and he'd sent all the reinforcements he could spare.

The troops were in good spirits and filled with strong resolve,
but having routed the rebels once before, only to be routed themselves in turn, they knew now how quickly the fortunes of war
could be reversed. Not all the men who would participate in
this campaign had been at Belmont, but each of them knew
what happened there and why. Grant had given strict orders to
all the regimental commanders. There would be no plundering
this time, no breaking ranks to hunt for rebel souvenirs, no
dramatic speeches made by officers caught up in the emotions
of the moment. The troops were all expressly ordered not to fire
their muskets unless the command was given. Discipline would
be observed.

The steamer transports needed to make several trips up and down the river to move the full force of seventeen thousand men. General McClernand was to command the first wave, which consisted of slightly more than half the total force. Mark waited to embark with Grant and the remainder of the force when the boats came back from landing McClernand's command.

Seven gunboats under Flag-Officer Foote provided escort for the flotilla. In addition to the old wooden gunboats, the *Lexington*, the *Tyler*, and the *Conestoga*, there were now four brand-new ironclads, the *Essex*, the *Cincinnati,* the *Carondelet*, and the *St. Louis*. All together, they made a curious riverboat armada steaming up the Tennessee.

The naval force was much stronger now than it had been at Belmont, with the addition of the new armored gunboats from the shipyards at Carondolet and Mound City. No one had ever seen anything quite like them before. They looked, thought Mark, less like riverboats than like some strange species of gigantic turtle. The gunboats were rectangular and squat, 175 feet long and almost 52 feet in the beam, drawing a mere 6 feet of water. There were embrasures in the armor for three guns in the bows, four guns on each broadside, and two guns at the stern. Their ponderous weight from the iron plating made them slow and ungainly, but though they lacked maneuverability and speed, they would stand up far better to the rebel batteries than the wooden gunboats had.

There were not enough navy men to go around, so men were detailed from the army to fill out their crews, men who had no experience with boats of any kind. Yet Foote was determined to make do with them. He was a naval officer, and the navy had made sailors out of worse material before. Foote's own gunners were spread thin and he found himself short one gun-crew chief. He asked Grant if a good gunner could be spared.

As a West Point graduate, Mark knew he had the necessary experience, and so, with somewhat mixed emotions, he had volunteered. On one hand, he wanted to be with Grant for the land assault on Fort Henry, but on the other, it would be an uncommon opportunity for him as an army officer to get a taste of naval service. Grant thought it over for just a moment before he nodded curtly and temporarily detailed Mark to Foote's command.

The fleet got under way on the morning of the second, the boats making slow headway in the powerful current. Grant wanted to get the troops as near to the enemy as possible without coming within range of their guns, so the plan called for a landing on the banks of the Tennessee River, about six miles below Fort Henry. There would be no hope of a surprise attack this time. If the rebels at Fort Henry were not warned of the fleet's approach, they would certainly see the boats coming upriver from the earthwork battlements.

Grant was counting on the weakness of the rebel position, the high waters of the river, and strategy to win the day. McClernand's troops would be put ashore on the east bank of the river, where they would establish camp. From there, they would move toward the road leading to Fort Donelson and secure it, to cut off the rebel retreat toward Dover. General Smith's column, in the meantime, would move up the west bank toward Fort Heiman, attacking it from the rear and securing the position, so they could deploy their guns and shoot into Fort Henry from the higher ground on their side of the river. The gunboats would proceed upriver and fire on Fort Henry, engaging the water batteries there. With retreat cut off, and reinforcements unable to arrive due to McClernand's holding the road to Fort Donelson, and Smith commanding the superior position at Fort Heiman, the rebels would find themselves pinned down.

Grant seemed confident, but Mark noticed he was nervous. He kept pacing back and forth as the boats departed, staring anxiously back toward the wharf boat moored at Cairo. It wasn't until they had passed out of sight of their departure point that Grant seemed to relax. He took a deep breath and slapped Rawlins on the back with a smile, an uncharacteristic act of camaraderie for the reserved Grant, which took Rawlins somewhat by surprise.

"We seem to be safe now," Grant said, with obvious relief. "We are beyond recall. We will succeed, Rawlins," he added grimly. "We *must* succeed."

With so many setbacks, with so many of his requests turned down by headquarters, Grant had half expected new orders to arrive at the last moment, either recalling the expedition or altering his plans once more, perhaps directing him to make yet another demonstration without engaging the enemy. Grant was sick and tired of this sort of pointless maneuvering, making empty threats and gestures to keep the rebels from moving their forces here or sending reinforcements there. He was longing for a fight, and now, at last, he was going to have one.

By the afternoon of the third, the boats had reached the landing point and McClernand's troops began to disembark. Mark, in the meantime, kept busy familiarizing himself and his landlubber gun crew with the gunboat's weaponry. By the next day, most of the troops had been transported to the banks of the Tennessee. It was raining hard and the waters of the river kept on rising. The boats struggled against the current, their anchors down and their engines laboring to keep from being carried downstream. The river was swollen and full of debris that had been washed away as the Tennessee overflowed its banks. Large pieces of driftwood, tree branches, sections of fencing from small farms and homes situated near the water's edge were carried past the boats, along with some strange white objects that bobbed on the surface of the water.

At first sight, in the mist above the river, they looked as if they were some kind of swimming animals, but as the current carried them closer, it became evident that the cylindrical white objects were torpedoes that had been torn loose from their moorings by the fast current. The men who had been complaining about the weather suddenly saw that it was not without definite advantages. The gunboats might have sailed right into the deadly devices.

"I want a look at one of those," said Foote, directing several of the men to fish one of the torpedoes out as they drifted past the boat. Mark helped to bring the cylindrical device on board and they carefully lowered it onto the fantail deck. Grant, Foote, and a number of the other men drew closer, watching curiously as Mark and one of the gunners started to carefully dismantle the device. Suddenly it started hissing loudly.

The sound galvanized everyone on deck. All save Mark, who stared at the torpedo with dread, frantically looking for a way to stop it from exploding.

Several men jumped overboard into the river. Grant and Foote both leaped for a ladder leading to the upper deck and scrambled madly up the rungs. Then, just as suddenly as it had started, the hissing noise stopped. Mark realized, with a relief so enormous he almost laughed out loud, that it had only been trapped air escaping from the interior of the torpedo. He swallowed hard and drew a ragged breath. His chest felt constricted. For a moment he had been certain he was going to die.

Foote glanced up at Grant, who had managed to scramble up the ladder just ahead of him. Both men had stopped when they heard the noise cease. For a moment there was utter silence, then Foote cleared his throat softly and inquired innocently, "What was your hurry, General?"

Grant grunted. "The army does not believe in letting the navy get ahead of it," he replied gruffly.

Foote raised his eyebrows and smiled. "Well, we shall see about that," he said. They both started back down the ladder.

Grant got down and adjusted his coat. He glanced upstream, toward the fort. By now the rebels could see them easily.

"I wonder what the range of their guns is," Grant mused, aloud.

"Shall we find out?" said Foote.

The gunboats steamed toward the fort to test the range of the rebel batteries. As they sailed past the mouth of a small creek below the fort, the rebel batteries opened fire.

Their first shots fell short, and Mark, along with the other gunners, opened up on the fort. They managed to put several shots into the earthworks protecting the batteries, but then the rebels opened up with a rifle gun and the shot whistled past the gunboat and landed well beyond the stream. Another shot struck the deck near the stern, smashing through the cabin and out into river, fortunately without harming anyone. The boats circled around and headed back downstream, having formally announced their intentions.

"Well," said Grant, looking out toward where the big gun's shot fell just past the creek, "I suppose we shall have to land the rest of the troops beyond the creek." He grimaced. He had hoped to land them closer, but the rebel gunners had too long a reach.

"I will go back to Paducah to bring the rest of the troops," he said. "Even if we cannot get the entire force here by the next day, I will give orders to move on the sixth. The conditions now are very favorable for an assault and I do not wish to delay any longer."

The conditions were much better than could have been hoped for, Mark realized, after their initial tentative thrust against the rebel batteries. Fort Henry was situated on a bend in the river, which allowed its guns to fire downstream. In that, the situation favored the rebels. They had also seen that the rebel camp outside the fort was well entrenched, with rifle pits and fortifications placed about two miles back toward the road to Fort Donelson and Dover. The river was very high, however, overflowing its banks, and this gave a marked advantage to the Union forces.

Fort Henry stood on ground that was now several feet underwater. The river had jumped its banks and the water went well back into woods, at least several hundred yards. As a result, a large portion of the fort had been flooded.

On the opposite bank, Fort Heiman stood on high, dry ground, commanding Fort Henry, but the fortifications were incomplete. Smith would have no trouble whatever in securing that position, because the rebel general Tilghman had already decided that Fort Heiman couldn't be defended and had evacuated it. Unable to defend Fort Heiman, and with the river's height working against him, Tilghman had also concluded that Fort Henry would fall, as well. His powder magazines were almost flooded and the water had risen to within a few feet of his guns. Rather than risk his entire garrison in an engagement, he had ordered a retreat.

Leaving behind only enough men to man the guns, Tilghman sent the remainder of his command to Fort Donelson, where they would make a stand. To buy them time, Tilghman remained behind at Fort Henry with his gun crews, to delay the Union forces as long as possible.

As night fell, Mark stood on deck and watched the rain come down in torrents. It worked both for them and against them. With each inch the river rose, the odds improved in their favor, but for the troops that would have to make the assault by land, the rain brought only hardship. Any regrets he might have had about volunteering to help crew Foote's guns had vanished. The heavy downpour would turn the terrain around the fort into a swamp and the troops encamped on the banks were being deluged. Without tents, they had no choice but to suffer through the night as best they could, huddling beneath their spread-out coats or underneath the trees.

Grant stood on board, near Mark, and looked out toward the camp. He was thinking the same thing about the weather. The Lord was giving with one hand and taking away with the other. Foote came out on deck to join them.

He looked out toward the shore and shook his head. Perhaps recalling Grant's earlier words to him about the army not liking the navy to get ahead of it, he said, "General, I shall have the fort in my possession before you get your men into position."

Grant said nothing.

The attack commenced on the morning of the sixth, shortly before eleven o'clock. As the gunboats started to steam off toward the fort the troops on shore began to move. Mark hurried to join his gun crew as the boats passed a small island about two miles below the fort and formed into a line, four abreast, with the

Essex on the right, then the *Cincinnati*, the *Carondelet*, and the *St. Louis*.

There was a stillness in the air, broken only by the sound of the river flowing swiftly. Foote had given Mark's crew the honor of firing the first shot, signaling the other boats to open fire. Mark gave the command and the big gun roared. Immediately, the rebel gunners at the fort returned the fire, eleven heavy guns opening up on the approaching gunboats.

Mark heard the loud whistle of the shells as they came hurtling toward the boats, and as he looked out through the casemate, he could actually *see* one of the shells coming straight toward them.

"Put your heads down!" he shouted, getting as low as he could as his gunners hasten to comply.

The shell struck the boat just to the left of the casemate, smashing into the iron plate. The sound was deafening. A shudder ran through the gunboat as the armor plating buckled under the tremendous impact and partially gave way. Several bolts were sent flying through into the interior, one of them missing Mark's face by inches, another striking one of the gun crew in the shoulder. As the man cried out Mark rushed to see if he was badly hit, but he bravely shook his head.

"Only a scratch, sir," he shouted, above the din. "I can still shoot!"

"Let them have it, then!" Mark shouted, and they rammed another shell into the gun.

The *Cincinnati* shuddered again and again as the rebel shells smashed into her, one of them penetrating the armor and sending a shower of splinters flying from the side timbers. It was as if some force of giant blacksmiths were pounding on the gunboat with monstrous sledgehammers. The gun crews of the *Cincinnati* returned the fire, doggedly sticking to their task despite the cacophony of the shells ringing on the armor plate and smoke roiling about everywhere so thick it was almost impossible to see.

Mark lost count of how many times they had been hit. Like some sort of machine, he worked the gun with his crew, firing, reloading, and firing again, wiping the powder grime away from his eyes, which were stinging from all the smoke. It was almost impossible for shouted commands to be heard, between the noise and its effects on their hearing. They simply fell into a rhythm, bombarding the earthworks of the fort again and again, seeing the dirt spray up into the air as each shell hit.

Through the casemate opening, Mark spotted the *Essex*, apparently drifting out of control. The *Essex* had been badly hit. Clouds of steam were pouring from her portholes and casemates. One of the rebel shells must have pierced the armor and struck a boiler. Poor devils, Mark thought as he imagined the scalding steam rushing through the boat's interior. He could see men leaping out into the water.

Two of the *Cincinnati*'s guns were now disabled. One man lay dead on the deck, several others lay near him, wounded. Mark could barely breathe now. He and his men were coughing from the smoke and tears blurring their vision. He dreaded to think what it would have been like if the boats had not been armored. They would surely have been reduced to splinters by now. But as telling as the enemy fire was, the fire of the gunboats was having an even more devastating effect.

A number of the rebel guns had now been silenced, several of them exploding into shrapnel from direct hits that had penetrated the protective earthworks. Only four of the fort's guns were returning the fire now as Foote's boats kept up their deadly barrage. Then, through the smoke, Mark could see that the guns of the rebel fort had suddenly stopped firing. A moment later the rebel flag above the fort was lowered. The men broke into wild cheers. It was over. Fort Henry had surrendered.

The men all rushed up on deck as a small boat pulled away from the fort, and moments later General Lloyd Tilghman was brought aboard the *Cincinnati*, along with several members of his staff, to formally surrender the fort to Flag-Officer Foote.

Seven of Tilghman's eleven guns had been disabled and he saw no point in further risking the lives of his men. However, they had not captured his entire garrison. Tilghman had fought the battle with barely a hundred men. The rest had eluded McClernand's troops, which had been bogged down in the swampy roads, and retreated to Fort Donelson. Mark watched as Foote gracefully accepted Tilghman's surrender and both men shook hands, like gentlemen.

He was right, thought Mark. Foote had taken possession of the fort with his gunboats before Grant's troops could even get into position. The navy would receive the credit for this victory, but the important thing was that it *was* a victory. Later in the afternoon, Grant came aboard to congratulate Foote and meet with Tilghman, whom he greeted with courtesy.

The general glanced at Mark's powder-blackened face and smiled. "Well, at least the army was ably represented on this day," he said.

"Thank you, sir," Mark replied. "But if it's all the same to you, sir, I would not care to repeat the experience."

Grant nodded. "I have sent a wire to General Halleck," he told Mark. "I have informed him that Fort Henry is ours and that the gunboats silenced the batteries before we could complete our investment. I think the garrison must have commenced their retreat during the night. Our cavalry followed in their wake, but they had too much of a head start. We found two abandoned guns, so they must have moved quickly."

"It's too bad, sir," Mark said. "If it hadn't been for all the rain, General McClernand would have cut them off."

Grant grunted. "No matter," he replied. "We shall now send Captain Phelps up the Tennessee to destroy the bridge of the Memphis and Ohio Railroad. Then we shall take and destroy Fort Donelson."

CHAPTER THREE

Richmond, Virginia, February 1862

WITH THE FORMAL inauguration of President Davis approaching, and the Confederate House debating for the first time the possibility of enlisting free Negroes into the army, the citizens of Richmond were finally coming to the realization that the war was not going to be a short one, as they had all believed.

There were many recriminations, and a lot of people blamed the army for having lost the initiative after the battle at Manassas. Then, with the Union troops in disorganized retreat, the way was open for an invasion of Washington, D.C. Now, the opportunity was lost and General Lee was keeping his troops busy digging entrenchments, preparing Richmond for defense against the coming federal offensive. They were calling him the "King of Spades," in derision, for one rebel was said to be worth five Yankee fighting men and here were the gallant soldiers of the Confederacy digging ditches, white men doing the work of slaves. This was not the call to glory the men of Richmond had anticipated.

Things were not working out the way Maria had anticipated, either. When she first came to Richmond, she had wanted only to contribute something, and to lose herself in her duties as a nurse. In her work at Chimborazo Hospital, she had found she was able to contribute by caring for the wounded, helping ease their pain and suffering. However, she could not lose herself in her devotion to her task, no matter how hard she tried. She could put in long hours at the hospital, working till her feet ached and her hands felt numb from rolling bandages and binding wounds and bathing soldiers, pushing herself to sheer exhaustion until even the doctors, overworked themselves, prevailed upon her to go home and get some rest, but there was no escape from her emotions, from concern, from nagging doubts and guilt.

Each day she wondered what would happen if she found Travis in the hospital, or if she received word that he'd been killed, or succumbed to illness, for disease was rampant among all the troops. And each day, despite all her efforts to prevent it, she found her thoughts turning more and more to Geoffrey Cord.

"What sort of woman am I?" she wrote in her journal late at night, before crawling exhausted into bed. "What kind of wife can be concerned about the welfare of her husband, facing the deadly trials of war, and at the same time think about another man, one who is almost a stranger? What kind of woman can see the ravaged bodies of the wounded and the dying every day, and have her heart go out to them, and at the same time feel an indecent attraction toward a man other than her husband? My God, what sort of immoral creature have I become? What is happening to me?"

Geoffrey Cord came often to the hospital. He brought his notebook, and he spoke with the physicians and the other nurses. He spent time with the wounded men and heard their stories, but Maria was convinced it was nothing but a pretext for him to see her once again. On the days he didn't come, she found herself feeling a guilty disappointment. On the days he did come, he often waited till she was finished for the day and offered her his carriage.

After the first time, when she had joined him for dinner, he had asked her once again and she'd begged off, saying she was tired and that it would not really be proper. He had never pressed the point, but each time he came, he asked her once again and her resolve had gradually weakened. She told herself that it was only dinner, after all. It was perfectly innocent. Cord was a journalist; he asked her questions for his articles. They spoke about the hospital, the book he planned to write after the war, and it would help the Southern cause to have sympathetic articles appear in British newspapers. They were all sound reasons, yet they were all merely rationalizations and she knew it.

The truth was she enjoyed his company, not only taking pleasure in being with him, but somehow drawing strength from his presence as well. She knew he was attracted to her, though he never even hinted at it or said anything flirtatious, and always acted like the perfect gentleman. And she also felt attracted to him.

There was simply no accounting for it. The first time she had met him, she thought him a perfectly horrid man, but then the second time, at the hospital, he had apologized for his behavior at their first meeting, and though they had never spoken of it again, Maria's thoughts kept returning to it. He had seemed like a completely different person then. Then it finally came to her and she was surprised she hadn't understood it before.

Like many of his countrymen, Cord believed slavery was wrong. When they'd first met at the slave auction, he had quite naturally taken her for an aristocratic Southerner, one of the "ruling elite," contemplating a purchase. In a sense, he hadn't been far wrong, for she had married into one of Charleston's oldest and wealthiest families. A slave-owning family. The change in his demeanor toward her, she realized, had come about when he discovered she was a Yankee.

At their first meeting, she hadn't really spoken with him. Spencer had done most of the talking. Perhaps he had not really heard her clearly, so he could not tell by her speech that she was from the North, or perhaps, though she hadn't realized it, all the time she'd spent in Charleston had influenced her speech and she had started sounding Southern. Indeed, no one ever remarked upon her Yankee accent anymore. Either way, the change in him had come about the day they met again at the hospital, when he had discovered that her father and her brothers were fighting for the Union.

Except for their brief first meeting, he had never revealed his sympathies, but it was clear they did not lie with the South. Why then, she wondered, if his sympathies were with the Union, was he in Richmond, writing newspaper articles about the Confederacy? How could he possibly hope to be objective? Or did he even try? She had never actually seen anything he'd written. Perhaps his articles about the South were far from flattering. Her curiosity finally got the better of her and she came right out and asked him over dinner at the Exchange Hotel.

"You do not approve of slavery, do you?" she asked, point-blank.

He paused with his fork halfway to his mouth and raised his eyebrows. "Do you?"

"Do you always reply to a question with another question?" she countered.

He smiled. "It is the business of a journalist to ask questions," he said. "However, to be quite frank with you, no, Mrs. Coulter,

I do not approve of slavery. I believe it is immoral for one man to own another, like a piece of property. When the founders of your country wrote your Constitution, did they not write that all men were created equal? I don't seem to recall anything about exempting the black man from that sentiment."

"Are you an abolitionist, then?" she asked.

He shrugged. "It would seem that one must be American to be an abolitionist. As a foreigner, I cannot participate in your politics, nor can I condone the actions of men such as John Brown. I do have my own personal beliefs, however, and I believe that slavery is immoral."

"Then, given your beliefs, why have you come to Richmond? How can you hope to be unbiased when you write for your newspaper?"

"Ah. I was wondering where this was leading. Well, to answer your questions, my newspaper already has a correspondent in Washington. In order to achieve a balanced viewpoint, my editor wanted someone reporting from the South. I was offered the opportunity and I would have been foolish to pass it up. As to my own beliefs, I can assure you that I make every effort not to have them influence what I write. The duty of a journalist, as I see it, is to report the facts and not color them with his opinions."

"That would make you a rare journalist," she replied.

He grinned. "Touché. We do not, it seems, live in an age of objectivity, and I fear journalists are no exception. However, be that as it may, I believe that if one is to report the news with any accuracy, one must merely report events as they happen and leave his opinions out of it. If you have an ax to grind, as you Americans say, then you would be better off writing for a magazine, or perhaps writing a book, wherein you can properly dispense with objectivity, as in the case of Mrs. Harriet Beecher Stowe, for example."

Maria nodded. "I read her book."

"Really? What did you think of it?"

"I thought it was wonderful. It moved me to tears."

"Yet you are married to a Confederate officer," said Cord. "The son of a planter who owns slaves. I gather your husband does not share your opinion of *Uncle Tom's Cabin*."

She shook her head. "No, he said it was a pack of lies."

"And did you find it so?"

She sighed and shook her head. "I'm not sure what to believe. The slaves in the Coulter household are well treated and they seem content. They are almost a part of the family. And yet their children had been sold. Not by the Coulters, of course. My father-in-law told me he made every effort to find them and buy them back, but he was not successful. He admitted it was true that some people mistreat their slaves, but he said that on the whole, most slaves in the South are well cared for and content."

"Then why do you suppose so many of them run away?" asked Cord softly.

Maria sighed and shook her head sadly. "I cannot argue with you, Mr. Cord. I cannot defend slavery. In my heart, I think it is wrong, too."

"That must make things rather difficult for you," said Cord.

"When I married Travis," she said, "I never really thought about it. About slavery, I mean. We met at West Point. He was my brother's best friend. He was handsome, and I thought him very dashing and romantic. You may laugh, but I used to imagine that he was Sir Ivanhoe and I was the Lady Rowena."

Cord smiled.

"There was talk of secession even then," she continued, "and there was also talk of war, but none of us believed it. Not I, not Travis, not my brothers or my father. The last time I saw Robert, he and Travis fought. I was not there, so I don't know all that passed between them, but Robert said it would be treason for Travis to support the Southern cause and it brought their friendship to an end. Travis will not even allow me to speak his name. And when I think that they might meet in battle, and that one of them may kill the other . . ." Her voice trailed off.

Cord reached across the table and took her hand. "I'm sorry," he said.

His hand lingered a moment before he took it away, a bit self-consciously.

"Nothing has turned out the way I thought it would," she said.

"Few things in life ever do," Cord replied quietly. There was a strange expression on his face, Maria thought, as if, for a moment, his thoughts were somewhere else, far away from her, far from the war, far from everything except something hidden deep inside. It was a look of such incredible sadness that she almost reached out to touch his cheek, and had actually started to raise her hand to do so, but then caught herself.

"I beg your pardon, Mr. Cord," the maître d' said, coming up to their table, "but there is a gentleman asking to speak with you.

A Dr. Van Owen. I informed him that you were dining, but he insisted that it was most urgent."

"Thank you, Edward," Cord replied, "you may tell him that I will be out directly." He turned to Maria. "Forgive me. Will you excuse me for a moment? I shan't be long."

"Certainly," Maria said. As he got up from the table she frowned. Dr. Van Owen. She did not know anyone named Van Owen, and yet the name seemed vaguely familiar, somehow.

She glanced toward the entrance to the hotel dining room, following Cord with her gaze, and just beyond the entrance, she saw him meet a tall, lean, well-dressed man with dark hair and a mustache. He wore an elegant black suit, a dark red vest with a gold watch chain, and a wide-brimmed, black felt hat. In the moment before he took Cord by the arm and led him away into the lobby, speaking to him earnestly, she recognized him.

His mustache had grown longer and thicker since the last time she had seen him, as had his hair, but it was the same man who had argued with Travis on the steamboat to New York when they had left West Point.

What on earth was *he* doing in Richmond? And what was his relationship to Geoffrey Cord? Maria felt a sudden tightness in her stomach. There was only one reason she could think of why a man like Van Owen, an avowed abolitionist who had expressed open contempt and animosity toward all Southerners, would be in Richmond. Van Owen was a Union spy.

Wait, she told herself, now, don't be hasty. Don't be too quick to judge. There could be another explanation. She tried to think of one and couldn't. On the steamboat to New York, Van Owen had expressed himself in no uncertain terms. He was a fervent, self-professed abolitionist and proud of it. She felt certain he had been prepared to fight with Travis, merely because he was a Southerner, and that had been even before South Carolina had seceded from the Union. Now, with the war on, what would a man like that be doing in Virginia, in the capital of the Confederacy? What possible reason could he have to be here?

She bit her lower lip. He was a spy. What other explanation could there be? And if Geoffrey was involved with him somehow, then perhaps he was a spy as well. Unless, of course, he had some other connection with Van Owen and didn't know he was an abolitionist. After all, as a journalist, Cord had contact with people from all walks of life in Richmond. But then, there were his remarks back at the slave auction when they'd first met, and hadn't he just finished telling her he believed slavery to be immoral?

On the other hand, Cord was a foreigner and why would a foreigner spy for the Union? He was a British citizen and Great Britain was neutral. Unless, perhaps, the British were only outwardly professing neutrality, yet were secretly sympathetic to the Union. It was possible. She knew there was a great deal of antipathy to slavery in Britain, but they also needed Southern cotton. If they openly supported the Union, then there would be repercussions if the South were to win the war. If they recognized the Confederacy, and the Union were to win, then they would find themselves in the same awkward situation. By maintaining neutrality, Great Britain could stay well out of it, at least until the conflict was resolved one way or the other, but if the true sympathies of the British government lay with the North, then it was possible that they might secretly support the Union, and what better way to do it than to send a journalist to Richmond as a spy?

Who would suspect him? Anxious to curry favor with public opinion in Great Britain in the hopes of gaining recognition, the officials of the Confederate government would go out of their way to accommodate him. He was free to go anywhere. He dined with Judah Benjamin; he attended parties at the Davis household; he knew most of the officials in the War Department and visited them frequently . . . and it occurred to her that perhaps she had been flattering herself to think she was the reason why he came so frequently to Chimborazo Hospital.

He spoke with the soldiers, always with his notebook present, and he had such an engaging charm, such a disarming way about him, that the men might have told him more than they intended, might have given him valuable military information without even realizing they were doing it, information about their movements, their supplies, the strength of their troops . . .

"Forgive me," he said, returning to the table. She had been so preoccupied with her thoughts that she hadn't even seen him coming and she gave a guilty start, but he seemed not to notice. "I hope you will accept my apologies, Mrs. Coulter, but I fear I must leave you. Something has arisen that I must attend to. Do please stay and finish your dinner, however. I will leave my carriage for you."

"Is something wrong?" she asked.

"No, no, merely a small matter, but I fear it cannot wait." He smiled. "That's the trouble with journalists, you see, we are always rushing off somewhere. I do hope you will forgive me."

"Of course," she said. "I understand."

"Thank you. We will speak again, and soon, I hope. Good night, Mrs. Coulter. It's been a pleasure, as always."

"Good night, Mr. Cord."

She offered her hand and he bent over it, barely brushing it with his lips, then left the dining room.

She hesitated only for a moment, then she followed him. She had no idea what she was doing. I'm being a fool, she thought as she hurried after him. This was insane. She was jumping to conclusions. There was probably a perfectly reasonable explanation for all this. She was merely letting her imagination run away with her. As if it wasn't bad enough that she was a married woman, keeping company with a single gentleman, now she was running after him, as well, following him like some curious and jealous schoolgirl.

Only what if her suspicions were true? What if he really *was* a spy? What then? Where did her duty lie? Should she report him? He would be hanged or shot. Or would they dare to execute a British citizen? She had no idea, but she had to know the truth, one way or the other.

She paused just inside the entrance to the hotel and saw Cord walking down the street with Van Owen. She stood there, uncertain what to do. Cord had left his carriage for her. She bit her lower lip, hesitating, then decided. She forgot about the carriage and followed them on foot.

They walked quickly and purposefully, so she had to hurry to keep up. Fortunately, it had grown dark and her green calico print dress and black hair easily blended with the shadows. She felt like a skulker, running slightly every few steps to keep up with them. They were moving quickly, cutting through back streets and alleyways that she ordinarily would have balked at entering even in broad daylight. Her suspicions kept on growing stronger as she followed them for block after block, through a neighborhood that grew worse and worse as they progressed.

She started to grow frightened. They were entering a bad section of the city. Once, as she paused briefly to catch her breath, she felt something touch her foot and looked down in time to see a huge rat scurry across her shoe. She raised her knuckle to her mouth and bit down on it to stifle a scream.

The streets were full of Negroes here. They stared at her as she hurried past, trying to keep to the shadows. The two men were talking to each other and were unaware of being followed. She had never been in this neighborhood before, but she knew where she was by the black faces all around her and the saloons and gaming houses she passed, raucous noise coming from inside each open doorway. She was in Screamersville.

The Negro population of Richmond had been growing alarmingly ever since the war began, and the males vastly outnumbered the females. Almost everywhere one looked in Richmond, one could see Negroes lounging about, loitering listlessly in groups. Many of them had come to work at the Tredegar Iron Works, or to help dig the entrenchments, or to work as teamsters. Most of them were freed Negroes, but some were undoubtedly runaway slaves, seeking to blend in with the rest of the population and hoping for a chance to steal past the camps around the city and reach the Union lines. To keep them from becoming a problem, the officials of the city government tolerated Screamersville, a run-down section of the city that had been given over to saloons and gambling halls and sporting houses catering to Negroes. A white face here was as conspicuous as a ball of cotton on a blackberry bush.

The two men turned down another alleyway. Why all this skulking through alleyways if they did not have something to hide? Why on earth were they in Screamersville? And why in God's name, she thought, had she followed them here?

They had been walking very quickly for what seemed like hours, though she knew it couldn't possibly have been that long. She was out of breath from trying to keep up. She turned into an alley after them, and it was so pitch dark in there that she could scarcely see two feet in front of her. Taking a deep breath, she moved forward through the refuse-strewn alley, her nostrils assailed by the smells of rotting trash and God only knew what else. There would undoubtedly be rats here, she thought, with revulsion. If she was bitten by a rat . . .

There was the loud click of a pistol being cocked and a voice from the darkness said, "Stop where you are or you will be shot!"

She gasped and froze with terror. She felt, rather than saw, someone grab her by the arm and push her back against the wall, and she heard more footsteps approaching, then a lantern was uncovered and raised before her, to illuminate her face. She found herself staring into the barrel of a Navy Colt.

"Why, it's a woman!" a voice said, with surprise.

The gun was lowered. She squinted against the glare of the light, unable to make out the features of the men around her.

"Who the devil are you?" asked another voice.

Before she could respond, a third voice with a marked Boston accent said, "Well, I'll be damned! Maria Gallio! Or should I say Mrs. Travis Coulter?"

The light was moved away from her eyes and she saw a well-dressed, muscular young man step into the light. He was a white man, clean-shaven, with dark brown hair. He looked familiar, but in her shock, she couldn't immediately place him.

"You *know* this woman?" one of the others said.

"I should say I do," the young man replied, with an unpleasant smirk. "She is married to a Confederate officer. Her father and I almost crossed swords on her wedding day."

"Peter Debray!" she said, her eyes wide with disbelief.

"Well, I'm indeed flattered you remember me, Mrs. Coulter," he replied. "I wish I could say it's a pleasure meeting you again, but unfortunately, your presence here has proved rather inconvenient. Bring her."

She was conducted, albeit more gently than she had been seized at first, to the end of the alley, where a coach waited. She saw no sign of Geoffrey Cord or Van Owen.

"Where are you taking me?" she asked, frightened.

"Patience, Mrs. Coulter," said Debray, handing her into the coach. He got in after her, along with one of the other men. She could feel the coach move as the third man got up outside, beside the driver. "Would you be so kind as to turn your head?"

Puzzled, she did as she was told and a cloth handkerchief was tied around her head as a blindfold.

"Why are you doing this?" she asked, her voice trembling slightly.

"To prevent you from knowing our destination," Debray replied. "I fear I don't know what we are going to do about you, Mrs. Coulter. You have presented us with a somewhat sticky problem."

The coach lurched and started to move. She swallowed hard, saying nothing, unable to see. Trying to maintain her composure, she folded her hands in her lap and clenched them.

I was right, she thought, and the thought gave her no pleasure. Geoffrey Cord and Van Owen were Union spies. She had stumbled into a whole nest of spies. And she knew at least three of them not only by sight, but by name as well. A sticky problem, indeed. What would they do to her?

She was not certain how long they drove in the coach, but after a while it stopped and she heard the door open. It occurred to her that they had probably driven around to mislead her as to the distance they had gone.

"This way, Mrs. Coulter, if you please," said Debray. "Give me your hand."

She was helped down out of the coach and guided into a building. She couldn't see a thing. There was a bare wood floor beneath her feet and she could smell the odor of tobacco.

"We are coming to a flight of stairs," Debray said, guiding her as she ascended uncertainly.

"And now a landing, and then another flight of stairs to your right," Debray said.

She felt Debray's hand on her arm as she was led down a corridor, or at least what she assumed must have been a corridor, and then they stopped. Someone knocked on a door. Two knocks, a brief pause, then two more, another pause, and then one knock. She heard the sound of a door being opened and then she was ushered inside.

"Good evening, gentlemen," she heard Debray say. "It seems we have an uninvited guest."

"Good God! Maria!"

The last voice was clearly Cord's. The blindfold was removed. She blinked. She was in a small room, with a threadbare, stained carpet on the floor and some aging, inexpensive furniture. There was a large round table in the center of the room and some wooden chairs. Seated at the table were several men, some white, some black, among them Van Owen and Cord. Geoffrey had risen to his feet as she walked in and he was staring at her, astonished. On one wall, she noticed a large map of Richmond and the surrounding area. The military camps were all clearly marked out, and there were numerous other marks on the map she couldn't understand.

"You've become careless, gentlemen," said Debray. "We caught Mrs. Coulter following you."

"I've seen you before," Van Owen said, staring at her intently.

"It was on the steamboat from West Point, Dr. Van Owen," she replied, fighting down her fear and drawing herself up. "You tried to pick a fight with my husband."

"Wonderful," said one of the other men sarcastically. "She knows you by name. And she has seen all of our faces."

"Maria," Cord said, approaching her, "what in God's name possessed you to follow us?"

"I had to know the truth," she said.

"Well, she knows it now," Debray said. "All because the two of you were criminally careless. She'll have all our necks in a noose."

"Oh, Maria, *why*?" asked Cord, stricken.

"She will have to be taken care of," said Debray.

"What do you mean, taken care of?" asked Cord.

"What do you think I mean?" Debray countered. "She's a rebel. She knows us. She can hang us all. She will have to be disposed of."

Cord stared at Debray with disbelief. "*Disposed of?* Have you lost your mind?"

"It seems we have no choice," said Debray.

Cord came up to within a couple of inches of him and looked him straight in the eyes. "Over my dead body," he said, with cold intensity.

"I remind you, Cord, that you have very little say here," Debray replied, steadily meeting his gaze. "Remember, it was you who came to us."

"Damn right," said Cord, "and I remind you, Debray, that I brought my money with me. And that gives my word considerable weight, as I am quite certain these other gentlemen will agree."

"If you want to hang for her, then be my guest," said Debray. "But no woman is going to put a noose around *my* neck."

"That will be quite enough," Van Owen said, separating them. "We will solve nothing by squabbling among ourselves. Geoffrey's right. We did not enter into this to commit murder. That is absolutely out of the question."

"In that case, what do you propose as an alternative?" Debray asked wryly.

Maria felt cold all over. Her life was in the hands of these men. She cursed herself for an utter fool. She had found out the truth, but at what cost?

Van Owen sighed. "We shall simply have to think of something," he said unconvincingly.

"I suggest you think quickly," said Debray.

"You shut your mouth, boy!" said Van Owen, turning on him furiously. "That lip of yours is going to get you into serious trouble one of these days. You would do well to remember who's in charge here."

Debray stiffened, but said nothing.

"What was it, Maria?" Cord asked quietly. "What gave us away?"

"It was me, obviously," Van Owen answered for her. He gave her a hard look. "She must have seen me at the hotel and recognized me. In that, at least, Debray was right. We've become careless. Now we must pay the price for it."

"You asked me why," Maria said to Cord, "now I ask you, Geoffrey. Why? You are a British citizen. This is not your war."

"It is every right-thinking man's war," Cord replied. "I told you that I believe slavery to be immoral. A crime against humanity. That is a war every man must fight."

"Is that how your government feels?" asked Maria.

"That is my earnest hope," said Cord.

"I see," she said. "So they have sent you to spy for the Union."

"Sent me to *spy*?" said Cord. He frowned. "Good Lord, is *that* what you think we're doing?"

Maria stared at him with confusion. "Then you deny that you are Union spies?"

Now it was Van Owen's turn to frown. "We most assuredly do deny it, madam. Is that what you really thought, that we were spies?"

They were all watching her intently. She looked around at them. "Then . . . if you are not spies . . . then what?"

"We are humanitarians, madam," said Van Owen, "not spies. That our sympathies lie with the Union, we do not deny, but we leave military matters to the army. What concerns us is that which the army cannot concern itself with. The freedom of the slaves."

Maria shook her head. "I don't understand."

"We are the Underground Railroad, Maria," Cord said. "We help runaway slaves reach the North, where they can be free."

"Then . . . you are not really a journalist?" she asked.

"Not in the strict sense of the term, no," Cord replied. "I do write articles for the *London Morning Post*, but I am not a journalist by profession. I had volunteered my services to them as a roving correspondent, but I have no need of employment. My father is a very wealthy man and I also have a considerable independent income of my own. However, I have little taste for living a life of pampered indolence while other people are suffering. I could not simply sit by and do nothing. So I came here, to do whatever I could to help. I met these gentlemen in Boston and I offered them my services, which they accepted."

"This is all very touching," said Debray, "but it still fails to solve our problem."

"There may not be a problem, Peter," one of the other men said.

He was young, in his early twenties, good-looking, with jet-black hair, gray eyes, striking features, and a dark complexion. He had been silent throughout the previous conversation, watching Maria carefully. Now he approached her.

"I heard Debray call you by another name," he said to her softly.

He stood very close to her. He clasped his hands before him, at the level of his chest, and looked down at them. Then he looked up at Maria meaningfully, and down at his hands once more.

She glanced down and saw he was toying with a ring on his finger. A heavy gold signet, bearing the sign of a Roman *gladius* and inscribed with the letters "PBMMG."

She caught her breath and looked up at him. Standing only inches away from her, he whispered in a voice too soft for anyone else to hear, "Do you know the words?"

Her hand went to her throat. Her gaze was locked with his as she whispered, *"Pro Bono Maiori, Maxima Gloria."*

She unbuttoned the top two buttons of her dress, allowing him to glimpse the locket at her throat, inscribed with a signet to match the ring. Her heart stood still as she stared at him, eyes wide.

He nodded. "Well met, cousin," he said, with a slight smile.

CHAPTER FOUR

Robert's Journal, Washington, D.C., March 1862

IT SEEMS THE joke has been on me. Custer was right, after all—damn the lead-fisted bastard—and it was not so much my concern for Mark as my anger and vindictiveness that were the motives for my having him posted to Missouri. In return, fate has served me up a deep dish of humble pie.

While the general-in-chief and the president remain at loggerheads, and the grand Army of the Potomac remains in camp, Grant has taken the offensive in Missouri in what can only be described as a spectacular coup. No, it can be described in many other ways as well, for the newspapers are battling with one another to find suitable aggrandizing adjectives with which to compose his accolades. "We know now what the 'U.S.' in U.S. Grant stands for," they proclaim, "Unconditional Surrender!"

I have eagerly combed the papers for further details of the campaign, which first struck up the Tennessee at Fort Henry, then on a march to Dover, where with support from gunboats that had sailed up the Cumberland, Fort Donelson was taken. From all that I have been able to learn, the success was due less to Grant's brilliance, as the papers claim, than to impossible conditions for the rebels at Fort Henry and incompetence on the part of the Confederate commanders at Fort Donelson. Nevertheless, the credit belongs deservedly to Grant, who took the bold offensive and used every opportunity afforded him, as well as overcoming many disadvantages.

General John B. Floyd, the former secretary of war, was the rebel commander at Fort Donelson. However, Floyd is a not a military man, but a politician, and a corrupt politician, at that. He is not only inexperienced and possessed of no real qualifica-

tions as a soldier, but he has fled to the Confederacy to escape
prosecution for embezzling government funds and remains under
indictment in Washington. The second-in-command at Donelson
was General Gideon Pillow, whom Grant had served with during
the war in Mexico. Grant seems to have thought little of him
and told his staff and troops that with any force, no matter
how small, he could easily march to within gunshot of Pillow's
entrenchments. This, in fact, proved to be the case.

Situated two miles north of Dover, Fort Donelson was a valuable outpost for the Confederacy. It occupies some one hundred
acres, fronting the Cumberland River on the east, with Hickman's
Creek to the north, and a ravine with a stream running through
it on the south, emptying into the Cumberland. The fort stands
on high ground, one hundred feet above the river, with its well-
protected guns facing the water and emplaced in the bluffs. There
was a line of rifle pits dug to the west, two miles back from river,
as at Fort Henry, only in superior positions, disposed along the
ridges, with a long defensive abatis formed from felled trees. The
terrain around the fort is reported to be rough and broken, cut with
ravines and densely wooded. By all appearances, it would seem a
formidable position for the enemy to occupy.

Little Mac undoubtedly would have planned an extended grand
campaign with siege cannon, heavy mortars, and entrenchments,
but Grant chose not even to wait for the reinforcements promised
him by Halleck. He moved, by God. McClellan would have
thumped his chest over the capture of Fort Henry and spent
months, no doubt, in fortifying it to make certain it could not
fall into rebel hands again. Grant simply chose to move on to
the next target and make certain of the same goal by taking the
rebels into his own hands.

Some reinforcements did arrive in time for the offensive, in
the form of Colonel Thayer and his Nebraska regiments, which
Grant immediately sent in convoy with the gunboats. General
C. F. Smith initially remained behind to guard Fort Henry with
part of his division, and General Lew Wallace moved on the left to
Hickman's Creek while General John McClernand took the right,
covering the road to Charlotte by which the enemy could retreat
from their position. Grant apparently saw no need for entrenching,
choosing instead to use the natural terrain along the crests and
ridges to protect his men and guns. The weather the troops faced,
by all accounts, was abysmal, with guns sinking in the mud, and
snow and freezing rain bringing much hardship to the troops,

many of whom left their blankets and their overcoats behind at camp, for the weather had been mild when they set out.

They faced some twenty thousand well-entrenched rebel troops. After some brief skirmishing over position at the outset, Grant's troops settled in and waited for the gunboats to engage the water batteries. On the night of February 13, Flag-Officer Foote arrived with the ironclads *St. Louis, Louisville*, and *Pittsburgh*, along with the wooden gunboats *Tyler* and *Connestoga*, convoying Thayer's troops. Thayer landed on the morning of the fourteenth. Wallace arrived at about the same time, took charge of Thayer's force, and made up a new division to take the center. Smith was brought up to command upon the left.

On the afternoon of the fourteenth, Foote moved up with his whole fleet against the water batteries. The gunboats attacked from close range and took much damage. Foote's boat was reported to have been hit at least sixty times, with several shots passing near the waterline and one entering the pilothouse, killing the pilot, destroying the wheel, and wounding Foote as well. Disabled, the gunboat drifted out of action.

That night, the gunboats were withdrawn, and the troops on land suffered through intense cold, made all the more miserable for their having no tents within which to take shelter, nor the ability to make fires, due to the weather and the proximity of enemy batteries and sharpshooters. McClernand's troops had made an attempt to capture the batteries opposing them, but were repulsed. While the gunboats engaged the water batteries, the batteries of both the rebels on the heights and Grant's troops facing them continued to trade fire, as did the sharpshooters of both sides, in their independent manner, but there was no general engagement.

The next morning, as I have it in a long letter from Mark, Foote asked to see Grant on board his gunboat, the *St. Louis*, as he was wounded and could not come to Grant's headquarters himself. Mark accompanied Grant to the meeting. Grant left his troops with orders to hold and avoid engagement until he returned. At the meeting, Foote told Grant the condition of the boats and explained the necessity of returning to the shipyards at Mound City for repairs, saying that he could return in ten days' time, which speaks highly for the efficiency of the workers at Mound City, or for Foote's ability to get things done, or both. It seemed, wrote Mark, that for at least ten days, there would be no further action, but the rebels apparently had other ideas, and my little brother, who had tasted an infantry skirmish at Belmont and a naval bombardment at Fort Henry, suddenly found himself in the middle of his first full-scale engagement.

Fort Donelson, Tennessee, February 15, 1862

As Grant and Mark stepped out of the boat that brought them ashore from their conference with Foote, a rider came galloping toward them at breakneck pace, his horse lathered with foam. Mark recognized Captain Hillyer, of Grant's staff, as the officer reined in, his snorting horse's hooves sending up divots of damp earth. His face was chalk white.

"They've struck us, General!" he shouted. "The enemy have come out in force and attacked on the right! McClernand's division is scattered! They are in retreat!"

Without a word, Grant swung up into the saddle and set spurs. Mark had to ride hard to keep up with him. They outpaced Hillyer, whose horse was winded from his ride, and had to gallop hard for about five miles to reach Smith and Wallace. As they arrived Grant got down off his horse and exchanged salutes with his field commanders.

Wallace was surly. "This army wants a head," he grumbled.

"It seems so," Grant replied curtly, and asked what the situation was.

The attack had been made on the right, by Pillow's troops, supported on their flank by Forrest's dismounted cavalry. Smith's command had not been involved in the engagement, but the fighting had reached Wallace's position in the center and he had sent in Thayer's brigade to support McClernand, whose troops had run out of ammunition. The intent of the rebels was immediately clear. They had to drive McClernand's forces back to open up the road to Charlotte and Nashville, enabling a retreat. Why they had not done so earlier was a mystery to Mark. That road was vital to Grant's success. With Smith on the left, Wallace in the center, and McClernand on the right, Fort Donelson was now enclosed in a semicircle on all sides except the river, and when the gunboats returned, the rebels would be trapped. That they had waited so long and allowed themselves to become surrounded by the Union troops displayed extremely poor judgment on the part of their commander.

However, the enemy had finally come out and tried to cut their way through past McClernand. The Union troops ran out of ammunition and part of the division broke and fled, but most only fell back. When Thayer came up to reinforce them, the rebels retired within their entrenchments. Grant took this all in calmly as Wallace reported the events in a crisp and succinct manner.

Grant nodded and replied, "Some of our men are pretty badly demoralized, but the enemy must be more so, for he has attempted to force his way out, but has fallen back. The one who attacks first now will be victorious, and the enemy will have to be in a hurry if he gets ahead of me."

He mounted and motioned to Mark and Colonel Webster, who was also on his staff, to follow. "We need to make a strong attack on the left," he said to General Smith, "before the rebels can reform and redistribute their forces. And we must do so immediately. General Smith, I will require a charge to your front with your entire division. You will find slim opposition, as the main force of the enemy has just made a strong assault upon our right. You must overwhelm their position and take the fort, if you can."

"I will do it," said Smith simply, mounting his own horse with a spryness that belied his advanced years.

As Smith rode off, Grant turned to Mark and Webster. "Ride with me and call out to the men to fill their cartridge boxes quick and get into line; the enemy is trying to escape and must not be permitted to do so."

They kicked up their horses and galloped toward McClernand's forces, on their right.

"Though Floyd is not a soldier, we can expect a fight," said Grant as they rode. "He will be afraid. As secretary of war, he took an oath to maintain the Constitution and he betrayed that trust. Before leaving the cabinet, he removed arms from Northern to Southern arsenals. He was already working for the Confederacy while still in Buchanan's cabinet. If he should fall into our hands, he knows he will be tried for treason, so he will be desperate."

"He'll make mistakes, then," Mark replied.

"Perhaps, if he counts on Pillow to pull his fat out of the fire. Pillow was lucky today, but he should never have withdrawn back to the safety of his entrenchments once he broke McClernand's line. He should have pressed on, but he lacks the mettle for it. The man who worries me is Buckner."

As they rode they shouted to the troops they passed, rallying them, and the men responded instantly on seeing Grant. His calm steadiness inspired them. They did not cheer for him or wave their hats, or give him colorful nicknames, for Sam Grant was not even remotely flamboyant. The one name they had for their unpretentious general was the Quiet Man, but this quiet man had the ability to make his firm resolve contagious. He never panicked. He was a source of strength and calm in the eye of the storm and his presence on the field galvanized the troops.

All night long, they froze without shelter or sleep, many of them double-timed around and around in circles by their officers in an effort to keep warm, and they had just suffered an enemy attack in which 1,500 men had fallen, yet Grant was determined to counterattack with everything he had. He had sent a dispatch to Foote, asking him to show his damaged gunboats, if only to throw a few shells at the enemy from long range. Then he rode along the line, rallying his men and bucking up their spirits with his presence. The troops moved forward on the right to reclaim their former position, encountering only slight resistance from the enemy batteries and sharpshooters. Meanwhile, Smith attacked furiously on the left.

The old man led the troops himself, sitting erect and walking his horse in front of them across tangled and heavily overgrown terrain, his hat held up on the tip of his sword so everyone could see him clearly, the enemy included. As the rebels fired on their advance Smith kept talking to his troops, urging them on, swearing blisteringly at those who lagged behind. Miraculously, though bullets buzzed all around him like angry hornets, he was unhit. He reached the crest and drove the rebels back from their entrenchments into the fort, and as night fell he camped within their lines.

It wasn't over yet, but for a time there was a respite. Mark was kept busy galloping from place to place, carrying out Grant's orders and seeing to it that the troops were resupplied and given rations. The wagons were brought up and everyone was utterly exhausted. The farmhouses in the vicinity were commandeered and turned into field hospitals, where the surgeons worked without rest all through the night. Dead men were laid out in rows, their faces pale and frozen. Everywhere, dead and wounded men were lying on the ground amid a blasted landscape. Branches had been sheared away by gunfire, trees had been cut in two by cannonballs, and craters dotted the torn-up ground everywhere.

Grant kept moving without rest, and Mark, trying to keep up with him, wondered where he got the energy. At one point, they reined in and Mark saw Grant staring toward a spot on the ground where a wounded Union officer lay beside a rebel private. The officer was trying to give the rebel a drink from his canteen, but he could barely move.

Without a word, Grant dismounted and approached them. "Does anyone have a flask?" he asked.

Mark produced one, filled with brandy. Grant took it, knelt, and gave each of the men several sips.

"Thank you, General," the rebel managed.

The Union officer attempted to salute, but he was too weak to manage it.

"Send for stretchers," Grant said to Mark, returning the flask.

He remained with the wounded men until Mark returned with a stretcher party. The stretcher bearers picked up the Union officer, but made no move to help the rebel private. Grant scowled.

"Take this Confederate, too," he ordered them. "Take them both, the war is over between them."

Grant watched them move away impassively, then mounted his horse. All around them, wounded men limped back toward the camps; others, too badly wounded to move, lay moaning and screaming, waiting for the stretchers. There were many more who could no longer moan or scream and would never move again.

" 'Man's inhumanity to man makes countless thousands mourn,' " Grant murmured, quoting Emerson. He took a deep breath and glanced at Mark. "Let's get away from this dreadful place, Lieutenant."

They returned to the farmhouse of Mrs. Crisp, where Grant had set up headquarters, and ate for the first time since breakfast. All night long, the noise of the restive army continued unabated. They heard the creak of wagon wheels, the rumbling clatter of gun carriages being moved, the shouts of stretcher bearers, and the cries of the wounded. Grant removed his coat and blouse and stretched out wearily on a mattress thrown on the kitchen floor. Mark felt exhausted, but he couldn't sleep. He sat in a chair near the fire with his coat off and his blouse unbuttoned, staring into the crackling flames.

John Rawlins was slumped down nearby, looking half-dead, his eyes shut. They did not speak, though both men were awake. The crackling logs in the fireplace made the only sounds within the room. Outside, they heard the hoofbeats of the Four Horsemen, riding back and forth on picket duty.

Where was the glory? Mark thought. There was no glory here, only death and desolation. And for the living, there was only numb, dispirited exhaustion. Throughout the day, there had been no time to think, no time to feel anything, time only to take in that which was perceived by the senses and do what must be done, and now, in the late hours of the frozen night, the weary mind made an attempt to catalog all it had registered throughout the day and there was simply too much, far too much to deal with. There were only pictures, random images that at some point in the future might make sense, only not now. In the morning, only hours away, it would all begin again.

The door opened to a blast of wind and General Smith came in. "Where is the general?" asked the former West Point commandant.

"In the kitchen," Mark said, rising wearily to his feet. "I'll go and get him, sir."

Mark went into the kitchen and roused Grant. When they came back in, Grant buttoning up his blouse, Smith was standing by the fire, warming himself. "There's something for you to read, General," he said, handing Grant a piece of paper. "Anyone have a drink?"

Mark handed him his brandy flask, now almost empty.

As Grant unfolded the paper Smith took a couple of short sips from Mark's flask and handed it back to him with a nod of gratitude. He stared down at his feet.

"I've scorched my boots," the old man said absently. "I slept with my head on the saddle and my feet too near the fire. The soles of my boots are burned."

"This is from Buckner," Grant said. He read aloud. " 'Headquarters, Fort Donelson, February 16, 1862. Sir: In consideration of all the circumstances governing the present situation of affairs at this station, I propose to the commanding officer of the federal forces the appointment of commissioners to agree upon terms of capitulation of the forces and fort under my command, and in that view suggest an armistice until twelve o'clock today. I am, sir, very respectfully, your obedient servant, S. B. Buckner, Brigadier General, C.S.A.' "

Mark stared at him. "They're giving up," he said, with disbelief.

Grant nodded. "What answer shall I send to this, General?" he asked Smith.

The old man looked up sharply, fire in his eyes. "No terms to the damned rebels!" he snapped.

Grant chuckled. He turned to Mark. "Lieutenant, take down my reply, if you will be so kind."

Mark sat down at the table and prepared to write.

"Headquarters, Army in the Field, Camp near Donelson, February sixteenth, 1862," Grant dictated. "General S. B. Buckner, Confederate Army. Sir: Yours of this date, proposing armistice and appointment of commissioners to settle terms of capitulation, is just received."

He paused, waiting for Mark to catch up. When Mark glanced up at him, he continued.

"No terms except an unconditional and immediate surrender can be accepted. I propose to move immediately upon your works. I am, sir, very respectfully, so on and so forth, U. S. Grant, Brigadier General."

He waited until Mark had finished, then he signed it and handed it to Smith. Smith grunted. "It's the same thing, only in smoother words," he groused, then he folded the dispatch and went out the door. Grant smiled at the old man's feistiness.

"What happens now?" asked Mark anxiously.

"We wait, Lieutenant," Grant replied. He sat down at the table and leaned back in the chair. "Now we just wait."

The response to Grant's reply was not long in coming. It read:

> Headquarters, Dover, Tennessee
> February 16, 1862
>
> To Brig.-Gen. U. S. Grant
> U.S. Army
> Sir: The distribution of the forces under my command, incident to an unexpected change of commanders, and the overwhelming force under your command, compel me, notwithstanding the brilliant success of the Confederate arms yesterday, to accept the ungenerous and unchivalrous terms which you propose.
> I am, sir,
> Your very obedient servant,
> S. B. Buckner,
> Brig.-Gen. C.S.A.

Grant merely sighed and shook his head at the phrasing of Buckner's acceptance. "It's ironic," he said, looking off into the distance. "Buckner is an old friend of mine, you know. He loaned me money once when I was in bad straits."

He sighed once more and drew his lips together in a tight

grimace. Outside, the first gray light of dawn was beginning to show. Grant got up.

"Well, gentlemen, let us go and join my old friend General Buckner for breakfast."

Robert's Journal, Washington, D.C., March 1862

News of Grant's victory spread like wildfire. There was cheering on the Senate floor and McClellan was congratulated for his brilliant arrangement of the campaign. McClellan, of course, took as much credit as he could for the first significant Union victory. The rebels were now in full retreat in Kentucky and Tennessee. Sam Grant, previously an unknown brigadier, has become the nation's hero.

The Confederates have been humiliated. General Floyd fled in ignominy, after first turning his command over to Pillow, who declined it and chose to flee as well. As the two senior rebel commanders took to their heels, the command of the fort fell to Simon Buckner, who held out while they escaped by transport to Nashville with about three hundred troops. One rebel officer refused to surrender. Colonel Nathan Bedford Forrest broke out with his cavalry in the middle of the night and made his way clear. Other rebels managed to slip away after the surrender, but this was of little import, for Grant gave paroles to those who asked for them rather than encumber himself with a large amount of prisoners. He had won the forts, which was his chief concern, and he trusted to their honor that they would not again take up arms against the Union. So the first initiative has been taken, not by Little Mac with his grand Army of the Potomac, but by Sam Grant and his as yet unnamed volunteer army, out in the West, where no one, least of all myself, expected it.

I read Mark's letter describing the campaign to Walt Whitman and to Isaac Jefferson, who has become my orderly since the night we met again at the hospital. Unable to join the army, since Negroes are not yet being accepted, but eager to do something to participate, Jefferson came to Washington, leaving his wife and son in New York with friends. He had volunteered to work at the hospital, but was sorely in need of money, so I offered to make him my orderly.

Isaac Jefferson is the first black man I have ever known to any great extent. He is twenty-eight years old, slightly under six feet tall, and powerfully built from years of working on the docks. He is very dark, which suggests that his African blood is pure, and he has never been a slave, having been born a preacher's son in New York City. He is a man of quiet disposition, soft-spoken and well mannered, and he has had some education. In conversation, he has an admirable tendency to consider what he is going to say before he says it. While I have never felt the need for an orderly and did not even use plebes in such capacity when I was at West Point, as many upperclassmen did, my rank and pay entitle me to one, and I am glad I took him on, as I find his company enjoyable. He is industrious and does many things without being asked, because he likes to keep busy and feel that he is "pulling his weight," as he puts it. But what he wants more than anything is to enlist in the army. Being my orderly, he says, has brought him one step closer, which is, regrettably, as close as he may come for the present. I have come to like him a great deal.

Walt Whitman, too, has become a good friend since the night Custer and I nearly beat each other to a pulp. I was not severely injured, though I received the worst of it. I have not seen Custer since that night, but I am told his face is a symphony of cuts and bruises. The belief, among those who are privy to the incident, is that we were both set upon by a gang of robbers or rebel sympathizers. Aside from Custer and myself, only Jefferson and Whitman know the truth. Strange, the ironies of fate. Here am I, the cadet who was often compared with Lee, "the Marble Model," though I had always felt ill at ease with the comparison, and there is Mark, who narrowly avoided being court-martialed, and it is as if we have changed places. Mark has proved himself a soldier and I have proved myself a common brawler. And an unsuccessful one, at that.

However, even though I fared poorly in the fight, it gave me no end of satisfaction to get in my licks with Custer. I had fancied myself something of a pugilist, and how he stood up to my best blows so well astounds me. The man is a bull. He was simply relentless. For that, if nothing else, I must admire him. Yet, even after I had nearly healed from the cuts and bruises I sustained, I still could not understand exactly why I did it. Certainly, it was not the first time I had been provoked, and though it was a fight I could have easily avoided, it seemed to settle something, perhaps not so much between Custer and myself, but between me and my own conscience.

It was Whitman who helped me understand it. We were speaking in his room, after having dined together. I had learned he was a poet and he offered to read some of his verses to me, which offer I could have readily refused, as I have never really had an ear for poetry. Still, I felt obligated to him. I liked him and did not wish to offend him, so I pretended an interest. To my surprise, I found his verses vivid and compelling, not at all what I expected. They were about the war and they evoked strong feelings in me. I read him the letter I received from Mark and we discussed it at great length. Our conversation moved to the rift between Travis and myself, and my feelings about Mark and Custer.

"I don't think it was Custer you wanted to fight so much as you wanted to fight someone, anyone," Whitman told me. "Anyone at all." He smiled. "Well, perhaps not just anyone, but someone against whom you felt some animosity so that you could justify it to yourself. Someone who could give as well as he got."

"What are you saying, Walt?" I asked him. "Are you suggesting that I *wanted* to get beaten up?"

"Well, in a way, I suppose you did," Whitman replied. "Perhaps the thought wasn't foremost in your mind, but I suspect it must have been there, concealed deep inside and festering like an open sore."

I frowned with puzzlement, and he took it for disapproval.

"Forgive me, Robert, I don't mean to presume," he said, "nor do I pretend to know your thoughts, and yet it seems to me you have a great deal of anger stored up within you."

"Anger? At Mark, you mean?" I asked him.

"Perhaps," Whitman replied, "but I think it's more anger at yourself. I don't claim to understand a great deal about life, but I'm a poet and a poet understands emotions. They are his stock in trade. There've been times when I've felt such strong emotions that they threatened to make me burst if I couldn't find some way to express them. I'm sure you've felt that way as well. I'm more fortunate than you, however, for I have my poetry to give vent to my feelings and you, my friend, have nothing to give vent to yours. Or perhaps I should say that you have *had* nothing, until recently. You mentioned that you had begun to keep a journal. Now, though I admit to being curious, I don't ask to read it, because a journal is a very private thing. I don't know what you write in it, but I suspect you've been writing in your journal and expressing thoughts, or feelings, that you had never bothered to confront before. Am I correct, or do I presume too much?"

I shook my head, impressed by his perception, and said, "No, you are quite correct. Go on."

"Well, from what you've given me to understand, your brother and his friend George Custer are very unlike you in that they are largely creatures of emotion. They were the two hell-raisers at West Point, as you say, always getting into trouble, skylarking and breaking regulations. You, on the other hand, have always felt a strong sense of duty to your father and have tried to be the sort of officer and gentleman he would be proud of. And I'm certain he is very proud of you. Yet let us consider your brother for a moment.

"You've exerted all your efforts and applied yourself diligently to the task of becoming all your father wanted you to be," he continued. "And there's nothing wrong in that. It's very admirable. However, have you ever paused to consider how difficult it must have been for Mark to follow in your footsteps? I have never met your brother, but from what you tell me, I imagine it must have been quite difficult for him to live up to the example that you set him. Perhaps he was afraid of failing to live up to it, and so he chose someone like Custer for a friend, someone who was so very different from his older brother. You tell me Custer was the worst cadet at the Academy, and that your brother was not far behind him. You were among the best, with your friend Travis, were you not? And not only did Mark have you and Travis to live up to, but he had to do it in the presence of your father, who was there to see his every shortcoming. Well, perhaps he couldn't be among the best, as you were, so he chose to be among the worst."

"But why?" I asked.

Whitman smiled. "So that less would be expected of him."

"That's foolish," I said.

"Is it, really? Perhaps he wasn't as strong as you are, Robert. And perhaps he feared disappointing you as much or even more as disappointing your father, so he chose a course that would not lead to many expectations on your part."

I frowned. "What makes you think so?"

"Remember that I'm a poet, Robert," he replied, with a smile. "Words are my stock in trade. I weigh them very carefully, and give great consideration to their meaning, to which words I must use, exactly, to produce the desired effect. The words in Mark's letter expressed love for his older brother, perhaps not literally, but the sense of it was clearly there. They expressed a sense of pride and accomplishment that he wants you to share. Perhaps even more so than his father, he wants *you* to be proud of him. It is *your* approval he desires."

Jefferson nodded in agreement as he listened. "I think Mr. Whitman's right, sir," he said. "Sound like he want his big brother to be proud of him."

"He's never told me that," I said.

"No, of course not," Whitman replied. "He has his pride, as you have yours. You say you're ashamed at having lowered yourself to Custer's level, and at the same time you tell me you gained a lot of satisfaction from it. But was it really Custer you were angry at? Was it really Custer you were striking, or was it Mark, or Travis, or even yourself? Or perhaps all three together?"

"I hadn't thought of it that way," I replied. "But strangely, ever since the fight, I haven't really felt angry at Mark. I still feel angry at Travis, though. If the things Custer said about him are true . . ."

Whitman raised his eyebrows, as I had not yet told him of Custer's accusations. However, I had no wish to repeat them and merely explained that Custer had impugned my brother-in-law's moral character. Whitman seemed curious, but did not press me to elaborate.

"Well, not knowing Mr. Custer, I cannot, of course, express any opinions as to the truth or falsity of his allegations," Whitman said, "but let us suppose, for the moment, that they are untrue so that we can disregard them. The bonds of friendship are often stronger than familial ties. Despite whatever quarrel you may have with your brother, he will still remain your brother. That bond shall always exist between you and cannot be severed. Whereas with a friend, once the friendship is severed, the bond is broken unless pains are taken to renew it. The loss of a friendship is often felt more profoundly than a quarrel with a member of the family, because one always feels a certain obligation to one's family, as you felt when you interceded in Mark's arrest. Whatever he may have done, he was part of the family, and would always be. Yet friendship is an obligation one *chooses* to incur, and so it is more fragile and its loss more keenly felt."

I nodded in agreement and admitted that while I had felt disappointed in Mark, I felt betrayed by Travis. It was that feeling of betrayal that made me unable to dismiss Custer's accusations. If they were true, then I had been betrayed, indeed, and Travis Coulter had only pretended to be a gentleman, when in fact he was a scoundrel. If that were true, then I should have moved heaven and earth to prevent his marriage to Maria. The one letter I had received from her had made no allusion to his being anything other than a gentleman and a good husband, and yet its tone was melancholy and even bitter in places. It would be simple to blame that on the war, and perhaps it is no more than that, though Lord knows, it is enough. But Custer's words have left a nagging doubt that lingers like an illness that cannot be shaken.

I pity poor Maria and wish that I could see her, speak with her, and ascertain the truth. But I cannot. As this nation has been torn apart, so has our family. This morning, I received a letter from my father, which I enclose here in this journal, for his words echo my thoughts and feelings, and express the hopes and dreams we all must share.

                                        25 February 1862
                                        Nashville, Tennessee

My dear Son,

Nashville is ours. Yesterday, General Buell marched our troops into the city, which we took without firing a shot. News of our approach preceded us, as Hardee's rebels retreated through the city, setting off a great panic among the citizens. The state legislature fled, taking all their papers with them and leaving the beleaguered mayor to surrender the city. Many of the residents had fled as well, fearing we would shell them, or run rampant on a spree of looting and pillaging like the hordes of Genghis Khan.

Our arrival was delayed by the condition of the roads and the necessity to effect repair on bridges, so that by the time we reached the city, the consternation caused by the news of our approach had already brought Nashville to its knees. Many of the homes and businesses had been abandoned, hotels stood empty with their doors bolted, and the streets were deserted.

There had been talk, apparently, of setting fire to the city to prevent our taking possession of it, but fortunately, Nashville had been spared the flames. Cooler heads prevailed, chief among them that of Nathan Bedford Forrest, who escaped with his cavalry from Fort Donelson and arrived in Nashville just in time to take a firm hand and prevent the city from descending into anarchy.

In an attempt to mollify the fears of the citizenry, it seems the mayor had promised to distribute whatever government stores the Confederate troops would leave behind. The result of this announcement was that large crowds had gathered at

the warehouses in an attempt to prevent the removing of
supplies. I heard that Forrest was forced to quell the riot
by ordering his troops to lay about them with the flats
of their sabers and turn hoses on the crowd. A singularly
noteworthy officer, this Colonel Forrest, who has repeatedly
demonstrated extraordinary competence for a man with no
military training. Before the war, it's said he was a slave
trader by profession. By the time our troops arrived, he had
succeeded in seeing most of the supplies removed by rail
and making his retreat to Murfreesboro, where he joined
with Johnston and Hardee. With Grant's victories at Fort
Henry and Fort Donelson, and our capture of Nashville,
the rebels have now lost Kentucky and most of Tennessee.
Johnston has suffered reverses from which he shall not be
able to recover. Yet, though we have succeeded in crippling
the rebels in this part of the country, I remain filled with a
disquieting apprehension.

You will recall that right up to the moment South Carolina
seceded from the Union, I had not believed a war was possible. Even then, I thought it was no more than some temporary aberration and that the conflict we are now engaged
in could be avoided. However, now I see it was inevitable
and I am deeply saddened at the gulf that exists between the
North and South. How could we have grown so far apart?
And how can we ever mend the rift between us? I have no
doubt of Union victory, but I fear that victory will not solve
all the problems that we face, nor bring an end to the bitter
resentment against us in the South.

I take the field with my troops against men I've known for
years and served with as my brother officers, many of them
men I have regarded as close friends. Whatever differences
we may have had between us in the past had never interfered
with our respect and love for one another, and in a strange
sort of way, they still do not. Though there are those who
look upon the officers who enlisted in the cause of the
Confederacy as traitors, I feel no animosity for men like
Sidney Johnston, a man I much admire, and I cannot believe
he bears any animosity toward me. Yet, if we meet upon the
field of battle, each of us will do our utmost to destroy the
other. Has there ever been a conflict such as this? Caesar,
when he crossed the Rubicon and marched on Rome, took
the field against men he believed, with good cause, to be

his bitter enemies. I take the field against men I still think of as my friends.

Is it because we fight to bring an end to slavery and the South fights to perpetuate it? I do not approve of slavery, but I must confess that I have never felt strongly enough to count myself an abolitionist, nor do I believe that many Union soldiers have any fondness for the Negro or concern about his plight. On the other hand, Lee is but one among many rebels who does not keep slaves. Do we fight because we read the Constitution differently, because we believe that the government in Washington must be the glue that bonds the Union, while the Southerners believe that states' rights must supersede it? I have met many rebel soldiers to whom that question would be meaningless, simple farmers who neither own slaves nor give any serious thought to the meaning of the Constitution. They fight simply to defend their country. Perhaps that is where the answer truly lies.

Somehow, we have become, without ever realizing it, two separate countries, each with a different way of life, a different society, and different points of view. Each of us, the Northern and the Southern man, fights to preserve his way of life and one must win at the other's expense.

We say that slavery is wrong, yet if we fight this war to free the Negro, will our victory truly make the Negro free? Will it make him the equal of the white man? Will it somehow make a place for him in our society? What will he do and how will he be treated? There are many Negroes who clamor for a place among our troops, a role thus far denied them, and there are those who believe, as I do, that they should be armed and enlisted in the cause. Yet there are also many Union soldiers who say they would lay down their arms if asked to accept the Negro as their equal. They fight to preserve the Union, not to free the slave. Yet, if our fight is to preserve the democratic Union and slavery is but a secondary consideration, then does the survival of democracy require that the majority must rule by the minority's forcible suppression? Can this truly be what our founding fathers had in mind?

I have always taught you that a soldier's concern is with his duty, first and foremost, and that he should do his duty without question. Yet, given the tragic struggle into which our nation has been plunged, how can any man of conscience not ask questions?

Do not mistake my meaning and think that I am plagued with doubts about my duty, for I have no doubt whatever on that score. I see my duty clearly. What I do not see clearly is the path that lies before us. Clausewitz has written that the result of war is never final, that through victory, we can compel the enemy to do our will, but there is no way to compel the enemy to think as we do. We can defeat the South and we can preserve the Union, but how *united* will that Union be?

It is not only the prosecution of the war that must concern us, but its aftermath as well. We do not fight to conquer another nation, but to preserve the one our forefathers have created. Yet it seems that we must conquer to preserve, and how can we preserve our country's strength and unity if half the nation is a suppressed and subjugated people? The rebels have chosen to follow their own flag. Will they love the stars and stripes of the United States after the stars and bars of the Confederacy have been trampled in the dust?

I am deeply saddened to learn of your quarrel with Travis. You say the breach between you is irreparable, but if that is really true, then there is no hope for the future of our country, for the conditions that have brought about your quarrel are the very same conditions that have brought about this war. If, God willing, we survive to see the end of this calamity, then we must find a way to overcome those things that have divided us and come together once again, else there will have been no purpose to this war and many brave men will have died in vain.

It is the sworn duty of a soldier to protect his country and defeat his enemy, my son, but there is nothing in your oath that requires you to hate him. You write that you are anxious and frustrated with McClellan's inactivity, but the Army of the Potomac will be on the march soon, and when that day comes, there is one thing I would like you to remember. Be gracious in your victory and charitable to your enemy in his defeat. Treat the rebel soldier with respect and allow him to retain his dignity. When your prisoner lays down his arms, then you must lay down your hostility toward him.

As you have fought with Travis and must one day find a way to make amends, so we are now fighting with the rebels and must one day make a peace, because as with Travis and yourself, so with the North and South. We are all a family. For the present, we seem to have forgotten that. My earnest prayer is that one day, may it come soon, we shall remember.

> With all my love,
> and prayers for your continued safety,
> your father,
> Anthony Wayne Gallio
> Colonel, United States Army

It was not until the second time I read my father's letter, when I read it aloud to Jefferson and Whitman, that I noticed he had been promoted. The major was not the major any longer. Now he was the colonel. Except for the way he signed his letter, which was a matter of pure form, I never would have known. He had not said a thing about it.

CHAPTER FIVE

Richmond, Virginia, March 1862

RICHMOND WAS UNDER martial law. The Confederate Congress
had called for the destruction of the cotton and tobacco crops to
prevent their falling into Union hands if the Yankees advanced
any further into Virginia. In the West, the Union gunboats were
wreaking havoc along the rivers and the South had lost two of
its finest generals when both McCulloch and McIntosh fell in
the Battle of Pea Ridge. General Van Dorn was in retreat. After
its brilliant success against the wooden warships of the Union
Navy, the *Merrimac,* the former Union steam frigate that had
been scuttled at the Gosport Navy Yard, raised and converted to
an ironclad and rechristened the *Virginia,* met the Union ironclad
Monitor in a grueling four-hour duel in the harbor at Hampton
Roads. Though both vessels had been damaged after pounding away at each other relentlessly, neither had been able to
prevail over the other and the initial elation at the *Virginia*'s
superiority over the wooden vessels of the Union Navy dis-
sipated. All that came of the battle between the two ironclads
was the realization that the day of wooden fighting ships was
over and the bitter knowledge that the blockade would not be
broken. The Confederacy had thought to raise the stakes with
the *Virginia,* but the Union had matched them with the *Monitor.*

Conditions in the city were growing worse with each passing
day, as seemed to be the case throughout the entire Confederacy. Burnside was pressing the Confederate troops hard in North
Carolina and word had reached the capital that McClellan would
soon be on his way, moving the entire Army of the Potomac
on a flotilla of water transports to the peninsula. Richmond was

preparing for a siege and there was a great deal of apprehension among the citizens.

Maria was no exception. Whatever control she had retained over her life seemed to have completely slipped away. Perhaps it began on the day she married Travis, or on the day South Carolina seceded from the Union. Perhaps it started when she came to Richmond, or when she first met Geoffrey Cord. But it all came to a head on that night she chose to follow Cord and Van Owen and came face-to-face with the family tradition in the person of Drew Michaeljohn, who was, despite his name, a Gallio.

In the days just prior to the Revolution, when Boston had been seething with rebellion, Drew's grandmother had committed the unpardonable sin of falling in love with a British officer who had been quartered in their home. He had left her with a child, and rather than disgrace her family, she left home and went to New York, where she married a loyalist who believed she was a widow, for she had assumed the name of the absent father of her son. They eventually settled in Virginia, and though she had lost touch with her family, she kept to the tradition, passing it on to her children.

"Grandmother always hoped the family would reunite one day," Michaeljohn had said that night, "but here we are, almost a century later, and one is still a rebel, the other still a loyalist."

Only Maria could not see it that way. With her husband fighting for the Confederacy while the rest of her family fought for the Union, how could she possibly take sides? She felt caught squarely in the middle. Yet to men like Van Owen and Debray, she was a rebel, married into a wealthy, slave-owning South Carolina family, wife to an officer in Jeb Stuart's rebel cavalry. And while Carl Van Owen was apprehensive and seemed uncertain what to do about her, Peter Debray had no such doubts.

Debray had always been a troublemaker back at West Point, she remembered, a violent brawler and a firebrand. Maria recalled only too well the scene he had caused at her wedding reception. If her father had not intervened, Debray might well have killed that Southern underclassman. If it were not for Cord and the others, he might well have killed her, too.

Her distant cousin was far more willing than the others to give her the benefit of the doubt. What had happened to his grandmother was, in a way, not much different from what had happened to Maria. Because of love, both had been separated from their families, finding themselves on opposing sides in a bitter conflict. Drew Michaeljohn also knew the strength of the family tradition and respected it. He had explained to the others that Maria was related to him, but that did not quite satisfy their apprehensions. Especially Debray's.

"You suppose because she is a distant cousin of yours, she can be trusted to keep our secret safe?" Debray asked. He snorted with derision. "Yours would not be the first family divided by this war. Besides, what sort of family ties are there between you, anyway? You admit you've never even met her till tonight. I tell you, she means nothing but trouble for us. She knows me from West Point, where I had made no secret of my sympathies. She knows you as well, Carl. It seems that Cord is acquainted with her also. And now we learn that Michaeljohn is her long-lost cousin? That strikes me as a rather incredible series of coincidences."

"What are you suggesting, Debray?" asked Cord tensely.

"Oh, come on! It's obvious! She's been sent to spy on us!"

"That's absurd," said Cord.

"Is it? What is she doing in Richmond? Travis Coulter is from Charleston."

"She came here to volunteer as a nurse at Chimborazo Hospital," said Cord. "She explained all that. She's staying with Carson Slater and his wife, who are friends of the Coulter family."

"And Carson Slater only happens to work in the Confederate War Department," Debray countered. "Another coincidence, I suppose. Undoubtedly, she followed you and Carl all the way to Screamersville merely because she was out for an evening stroll."

Maria simply stood there, stunned, unable to think of anything to say in her own defense. What Debray was saying sounded infinitely more plausible than the truth and she had no idea how she could convince them otherwise.

"There is only one explanation," Debray continued. "We've been betrayed."

"Then why haven't we been arrested?" Cord asked.

"Because they want to get the rest of us as well," Debray replied, "not merely one small group, but the entire organization."

"Are you implying it was I who betrayed the group?" Michaeljohn asked, in a level tone.

"You were the last to join us," said Debray, pointing at him accusingly. "And you are Virginia born and bred, for all your so-called moral qualms concerning slavery."

Michaeljohn stiffened. "Have a care, Peter," he said softly. "You go too far."

"Do I, indeed? How do we know she is really your cousin? We have only your word and hers. How do we know the two of you are not confederates . . . in more ways than one?"

Michaeljohn's fist lashed out and Debray fell, blood spurting from his nose.

"That's enough!" Van Owen snapped.

"Not *nearly* enough," Debray replied, getting to his feet with a murderous look in his eye.

He pulled a .31-caliber Baby Dragon from his coat pocket, but as his thumb cocked the hammer of the pistol Michaeljohn's hand flashed inside his coat and then out in a blindingly quick motion. With a sound like a cleaver striking meat, the ten-inch bowie plunged into Debray's right shoulder, just below the collarbone. He cried out and the gun went off, but the ball only struck the floor.

It had all happened so quickly none of the others had a chance to react and there was a moment of stunned silence in the room. No one moved. Maria watched with shocked disbelief as Debray dropped the pistol and gasped, clutching at the knife protruding from his shoulder.

"Damn it," swore Van Owen, the first to break the silence. He went over to Debray and motioned Cord to help him. They picked him up and laid him on the table. "Easy now," Van Owen said.

They tore away his clothing and Van Owen looked closely at where the knife had gone in. "Get my bag," he said.

One of the others rushed to fetch it.

"Bastard!" gasped Debray. "I'll kill the bastard!"

"You won't be killing anyone," Van Owen said. "Now, settle down and stop squirming before you open an artery."

He grasped the hilt and carefully pulled out the knife. Debray cried out with pain.

"Hmmpf," snorted Van Owen, examining the wound. "You're a lucky man, Debray. And a very stupid one as well."

Maria stared at Michaeljohn as Cord and Van Owen worked over Debray. Michaeljohn simply stood there, watching them dispassionately. When Van Owen laid the bowie knife down on the table, he walked over and picked it up, wiped it on some of Debray's torn clothing, and returned it to the plain leather sheath on his belt, beneath his coat. Maria started shaking.

"You could have killed him!" she said.

"I meant to," Michaeljohn replied flatly. "I seem to be in need of practice."

"He's lost consciousness," Cord said.

"He'll survive," Van Owen replied dryly. "But as soon as he's well enough to move he's going back to Boston. After this, I want no part of him."

"He could make trouble," Cord replied.

"If he knows what's good for him, he'll keep his mouth shut," Van Owen said. "However, to be safe, we'll have to move our operation and increase our caution. It's not only our lives I'm concerned about, but the lives of the people in our charge. We'll have to move up our timetable."

"This is all my fault," Maria said.

"You were not the one who pulled a pistol," Van Owen replied as he stitched up the wound. "I've never felt very secure about Debray. He's a hothead with an evil temper, though I never dreamed he'd do anything like this. We'll be well rid of him." His compressed his lips into a tight grimace. "You, on the other hand, have presented us with something of a problem."

"I will not betray you," she replied. "I came here to help people, not see them hanged or shot."

"Then why did you follow us tonight?" he asked. "Because you thought we were Union spies?"

She shook her head. "I . . . I didn't think. I just had to know."

"Why?" asked Cord.

She looked him straight in the eye. "I had to know if you were using me."

He nodded. "I see."

"Were you?"

"No, of course not. At least, not in the way you think. I was, in part, using you as a source of information for my newspaper articles. I did tell you the truth about that from the beginning. However, that was only part of it. The truth is, I enjoyed your company. I liked being with you. What's more, I think you enjoyed it, too."

"You forget yourself, Mr. Cord. I'm a married woman."

"I haven't forgotten that," said Cord, gazing at her steadily. "But you followed me just the same."

She looked away.

Van Owen finished dressing the wound and came over to them, wiping his hands. He sighed. "If infection doesn't set in, he should recover fully. If he doesn't, he'll have no one but himself to blame." He glanced at Michaeljohn. "You were very quick with that knife of yours."

Michaeljohn simply shrugged. "My life was at stake."

Van Owen appraised him carefully. "You have some unusual talents, Drew."

"It's no more unusual for a Southern boy to learn to throw a bowie knife than to ride or shoot a gun," Michaeljohn replied. "Or do *you* suspect me, too, now?"

Van Owen shook his head. "I'd be dishonest if I said Debray did not succeed in planting a kernel of doubt. However, we've all been under a great strain of late." He sighed again. "When we embarked on this undertaking, I knew there could be violence, but I had hoped to avoid it. What I had not expected was that there could be violence among ourselves." He glanced back toward Debray, lying unconscious on the table. "I had a bad feeling about him from the very start. I should have listened to my better instincts. However, Debray was right about one thing. Mrs. Coulter does, indeed, represent a risk to us."

He turned to Maria. "Perhaps our coming together like this is, indeed, no more than a remarkable series of coincidences, but the world sometimes turns on coincidences. Perhaps it's fate. Do you believe in fate, Mrs. Coulter?"

Maria shook her head. "I don't know."

Van Owen nodded. "Well, I do. You recall the day we met, on that steamboat to New York? I freely admit I sought to provoke your husband, but his words to you provoked me. I could not help overhearing what he said to you, about how Mrs. Stowe's book was nothing but a pack of lies and how slaves in the South are generally well treated by their owners and satisfied with their lot. Those words incensed me. I know Mrs. Stowe, you see. Her father, Henry Ward Beecher, has been a friend of mine for many years. He is passionate about the cause of abolition and his daughter shares his beliefs. The book she wrote was not some fantasy, derived from whole cloth, but a story based on incidents that really happened. You can ask any of these men here. They know."

She looked around at the others and saw them nodding in agreement. They were all risking their lives here, especially the Negroes among them. She didn't need to wonder what would happen to them if they were caught.

"I was with John Brown in Kansas," said Van Owen. "I see that shocks you. Well, I went to join him because I believed what he was doing was right." He shook his head. "It wasn't. I saw him commit acts that were unspeakable. They say he was mad. But I believe it was his fate to do what he did, and to die as he did, for in dying on the gallows, he became a martyr to the cause and gave it a strength it never had before. Brown used to say that the Lord Jehovah was a vengeful God, and that he was the chosen instrument of His vengeance. I think we were all afraid of him. I think we all thought he was a little mad. Perhaps more than just a little. But the Lord works in mysterious ways, and if slavery is madness, as I believe it to be, then perhaps it took a madman to destroy it, or at least to set our feet on the path to its destruction.

"I resolved to avoid violence if I could," he continued. "I could have chosen to become a soldier. I am in the prime of life, and fit, and I have means. I could have raised a regiment and become its colonel. However, I believed there was more important work for me to do and that was to continue what John Brown had started. Only it is not my wish to foment an insurrection among the Southern slaves, Mrs. Coulter, nor to kill their masters, if it can be avoided. What I want is to help as many of them as I can to freedom. Help them to cross over into Union lines, where they may choose a new life for themselves. Help them through my friends, in places like Boston, and New York, and Washington, help them to form regiments of their own, if they so choose, for who has more reason to fight this war than they? It will come to pass, Mrs. Coulter. There *will* be Negroes in the uniform of Union soldiers, many of them men who were once slaves. And when that day comes, then those who believe the Negroes are an inferior race will see the error of their thinking. The color of their skin is different from ours; perhaps their ways are different, too. If some of them seem simple and childlike, then it is because they've learned the hard way that such behavior is expected of them. If you were to meet a man like Frederick Douglass, Mrs. Coulter, an intelligent, well-spoken, and educated man, a gentleman, then you would see that the only difference between the black man and the white aside from the color of his skin is the opportunity that he is given."

He got to his feet. "Come with me, Mrs. Coulter. There are some people I would like you to meet."

She was blindfolded once again, then taken down the stairs and into the coach. They drove for a short distance and then stopped, and she was carefully handed down out of the coach, conducted into a building and up another flight of stairs. The blindfold was removed.

For a moment she thought she was in a hospital, one of those that had been set up inside a warehouse, for it was a warehouse they had brought her to. The large, open space that stretched out before her was filled with crude cots and improvised bedding placed around the floor. Only instead of wounded soldiers, what she saw were black faces staring at her, men and women and small children, even infants. They were all slaves, or they had once been slaves, for they had made their desperate bid for freedom and were now awaiting their turn to be conducted north, beyond the Union lines.

Van Owen led her around the room, along with Cord and Michaeljohn, and as they moved among them many of the Negroes greeted them with warm affection, touching them and thanking them for all that they were doing. One young woman Van Owen addressed as Eliza held an infant to her breast, clutching it protectively. Van Owen spoke to her solicitously as she clasped his hand and gazed up at him with a look of gratitude no words could have expressed, then they moved on.

"Eliza had three children," Van Owen said to Maria. "The infant boy is all she has left now. The other two were sold, you see, along with their father, all to different masters. She has no idea where they are, or if she will ever see any of them again. In all likelihood, they are lost to her forever. Her life has been sold away from her, piecemeal."

They stopped once more and spoke briefly to a young man about the same age as Michaeljohn. His name was Solomon. Van Owen introduced him to Maria.

"Solomon," Van Owen said, "I have brought this lady here in the hope that she might better understand what we are doing. Could I ask you to remove your shirt, please?"

Solomon stared for a moment at Maria, then took off his shirt and turned around. Maria gasped. His entire back was crisscrossed with cuts and welts, some old, some recent and not yet completely healed.

"Yes, indeed," Van Owen said, looking at the horrified expression on her face. "Slaves are treated well here in the South. Thank you, Solomon."

"Thank *you*, Dr. Van Owen, sir. God bless you."

Around the room they went, stopping here and there and speaking briefly with some of the runaway slaves, hearing something of their stories. By the time they'd made a full circuit of the room, Maria's cheeks were wet with tears.

"No more," she said, her voice barely above a whisper. "Oh, please, no more."

"Perhaps now you understand," Van Owen said softly. "I do not pretend to be a noble man, Mrs. Coulter. I do not even claim to be a good man. But there comes a time when you must make a stand for something, and this is where I've chosen to make mine. What about you, Mrs. Coulter? Your people in the North are making a stand for what they believe is right. Your husband has chosen to oppose them, but you see what he is fighting for."

Maria could not stop the flow of tears. She shook her head. "No . . . I can't believe that he means . . ." her voice trailed off. She felt utterly miserable and helpless.

"I don't mean to suggest that your husband is an evil man, Mrs. Coulter," Van Owen said. "Nor that his family are evil people. I don't know them. But surely you can see this is wrong. That *they* are wrong to support any cause that would perpetuate such human suffering. Now *you* have a choice to make. You will not be able to find this place, nor the place we were before, but you know our faces and you know who we are. You can go to General Winder and tell him about us. His men will conduct a search and they may find this place before we have a chance to move these people, and we shall all be hauled off to Castle Thunder to await our fate. As to the fate of these people here, you can well imagine what it will be. Or you can keep silent about what you have learned tonight, if not for our sake, then certainly for theirs."

He looked back at the people in the room behind them. Then he turned back to face her. "There is still a third choice. You can choose to make your own stand for what you believe is right. We can use a nurse for some of these people, and we need medicines as well. Think about it, Mrs. Coulter. Mr. Michaeljohn will take you home."

The villa of Marcus Lucius Gallio, Rome, 192 B.C.

Hanno never tried to escape again. He was treated no differently following his escape attempt than he was before, and neither Gallio nor anyone else ever made mention of it. He continued to instruct the boys Drusus and Flavius and to perform other tasks for Gallio when called upon, but something in him had changed. He walked a little heavier now, and a little slower, and the surly look of anger that had been his perpetual expression was gone now.

Just as Cyrene had surrendered to her circumstances when she first stood before him, naked, so he had finally surrendered to his fate as well. But in spite of this, he was not broken.

"I no longer hate the Romans," he said to Cyrene one night as they lay in bed together. "For years, I have hated them, wanting to kill them all, but I could not and so, in my anger, I killed all those they sent against me. Men whose only crime had been falling into Roman hands. Men no different from myself."

"You had to survive," Cyrene said.

"Did I?" he replied. "At what cost? I was filled with hate, driven by it, so that nothing else existed for me. And what had I become? How was I different from them? I was no different in the way I treated you, just as my father was no different in the way he took my mother. I was born a slave. The Romans only made me realize it." He reached out and touched her swollen belly. "He will be born a slave as well."

"The child may be a girl," she said.

"The way he kicks? No, he will be a boy."

"I think so, too. But it may still be a girl. Will you be disappointed?"

"It matters not. What matters is that Gallio has promised not to sell the child. That is the most important thing. There are worse masters than Marcus Gallio, but whether the child is a boy or girl, it will be still be born a slave. And that is what I hate now. More than I have ever hated the Romans, I hate that one man can make another his slave. My father's people did it, too. I never truly understood until I became a slave myself."

"The strong have always prevailed over the weak," Cyrene replied. "That is the way of the world."

"Then the world is wrong," said Hanno. "But that is our misfortune, for we cannot change the world."

"Perhaps we can, someday," Cyrene replied. She took his hand and squeezed it as it rested on her belly. "Perhaps, one day, our child can help to change it."

He shook his head. "Not in our lifetime."

"Then in the lifetime of our grandchildren. Or their children. Or their children's children. But someday, it will change."

"You can still have hope?" he said.

"Hope is all we have to live for," she replied. "It is the only thing worth living for."

He gently rubbed her stomach. "No, not the only thing."

"A child *is* hope," she said.

"Then I shall live for hope," he said, and took her in his arms.

Maria's Journal, Richmond, Virginia, March 1862

I have not been able to write of this till now. I have been afraid to set these things to paper. What if somebody should read them? At the Slater house, each time I sat down to write in my journal, I would always wait until it was late and the Slaters were asleep. I have kept this journal like a guilty secret, fearful of what might happen if anyone should find it and have access to my innermost thoughts. I write my journal in Latin now, which takes more time, but seems a great deal safer, and am always trying to think of better ways to hide it.

Abigail was waiting up for me when I returned. It was very late, a most indecent hour to be coming home. There was no excuse that I could make, although I suppose I could have claimed that I'd been needed at the hospital, or that I had lain down to rest and fallen asleep, but I did not have my wits about me to think up any such excuses and my face must have betrayed my guilt, though Abigail did not suspect the actual reason for it. She had reached her own conclusions.

"Maria," she said, when I came in, "I shall not ask where you have been. I do not want to know. This war has imposed . . . certain hardships upon all of us. But you have a husband, and he is fighting for his country, and Sam Coulter is a very close friend of ours." She moistened her lips and clasped her hands before her, clearly suffering discomfort in what she had to say, but resolved that she would say it. "I know that you are young, and that you have been lonely, and that Mr. Cord is a very charming and handsome man."

I started to say something, to protest, but she held me off firmly.

"I do *not* wish to discuss this," she insisted. "I will simply ask you to consider our position . . . and yours. That is all I have to say. We will not speak of this again. Now it is very late and I am going to bed. Good night, Maria."

And she left me there, my face burning with shame, for what, I know not, for I had done nothing wrong. Or had I?

"You're in love with him, aren't you?" Drew had asked me as he took me home.

I stammered some sort of protest, I do not remember exactly what I said, for his bluntness had shocked me. I did not think that I could take any more shocks, after a night like that.

"Well, he is in love with you," he said.

I told him he was talking nonsense, but he shook his head.

"No, anyone can plainly see it," he persisted. "You can see it in the way he looks at you, the way he speaks to you, the way he acts in your presence."

"I have not been unfaithful to my husband," I insisted. That much I can remember clearly, for I said it very forcibly, though I wonder which of us I was trying harder to convince.

"I didn't say you were," he replied, "except, perhaps, in spirit. Do you love your husband?"

"What a thing to say! Of course I love my husband! A gentleman would never think of asking such a thing!"

"I never said I was a gentleman," he replied. "But I have to wonder why a woman who claims to love her husband keeps company with another man and follows him in the middle of the night, because she is afraid he may be using her."

I flushed deeply, condemned by my own words, and could think of no reply.

"Cord is a good man, Maria," he said. "Unlike me, he *is* a gentleman. I cannot believe that he would take advantage of you."

"Why do you say you are not a gentleman?" I asked him.

"Because, Cousin Maria, I'm not," Drew said. "And I will not be hypocritical. It's my nature to speak bluntly and act directly. If I were a gentleman, there's a good chance I wouldn't be alive right now. Had I been a gentleman, I would have been demanding satisfaction of Debray and asking him to name his seconds, and in the meantime, he would have shot me. Being a gentleman has numerous disadvantages, you see. Geoffrey Cord, on the other hand, *is* a gentleman, and being a gentleman, he would never make love to another man's wife, not even the wife of a rebel officer." He grinned. "For my own part, I find such limitations inconvenient."

I was aghast at his remarks. "How can you admit to such a thing?" I asked him.

He laughed. "Because I'm not a gentleman. I am a rake, a cad, a gambler, and altogether a complete scoundrel."

"You're only saying these things to shock me," I replied. "If you were really all you claim to be, you would not be helping Dr. Van Owen."

"Ah, well, Van Owen's not entirely a gentleman himself," Drew replied, "though he is more of one than I am, I suppose. We each have our own reasons for what we do."

"And what are yours?"

"Oh, they are entirely selfish. When I was a small boy, you see, my family kept several domestic slaves. We had no plantation, and we didn't call them slaves. We called them servants. It sounded ever so much more genteel. One of them, our cook, had a daughter about my age named Charlotte. We used to call her Charlie. We were very close. Charlie was my constant playmate and I was extremely fond of her. I was an only child and she was like a sister to me. We were inseparable. But as we both grew older my father came to believe that our fondness for each other was unhealthy and improper. I suppose you can imagine what he must have been afraid of, though that thought never entered my own mind, nor Charlie's, I am sure. We simply did not think of each other in that way. However, my father had his own concerns, and so he sold her. Just like that. I came home from school one day and she was gone. I never saw her again. I never even had a chance to say good-bye. He kept her mother, though. She was a good cook. I never forgave him. He was a very proper gentleman, you see."

"And that is why you try so hard to be unlike him," I said, feeling sorrow for his loss, which he still felt so very keenly, and for his bitterness as well.

"My father," Drew continued, "is an unmitigated bastard and I have not seen or spoken to him in years. But he would disapprove most heartily of what I'm doing."

"What about your mother?" I asked.

"She died of consumption when I was twelve."

I told him I was sorry, and that I understood, for my mother had died when I was very young as well. He asked me then what I was going to do. I told him I could not betray him or any of the others. He replied that he was not concerned about that. He wanted to know if I would help them.

How could I refuse? How could I not help them after all that I had seen and heard that night? I still recall that day in New York City when I saw those awful men clubbing that Negro to the ground and my brothers stopped them before they could abduct him. Even then, deep down, I knew I could never accept slavery, and that I had made a terrible mistake by marrying Travis, though I had been unable to admit that to myself because I loved him. Yet even in that, I had deceived myself.

How differently things have turned out from the way I had expected them to be! If only there was some way the clock could be turned back so that I could not make the same mistake again, but it is foolish even to think about such things, for I have done what I have done. I married Travis, for better or for worse, and if it has turned out for the worse, then I have no choice but to accept it. But there are some things I cannot accept and continue to live with a clean conscience.

Dear God, I can see those awful scars on Solomon's back still! And Eliza, with her children torn away from her, so that she clings to the only one that she has left like a frightened little girl clings to a favorite doll; and Matthew, who has lost his wife; and little Joshua, who wants to be a Union drummer boy so that he can go back to South Carolina with the army and find his mother and his father; and all the others, who represent a litany of sorrows and sins against humanity. How can such things be accepted? They cannot. And if it means that I must be a traitor to my husband's cause, so be it, for I cannot be the quiet Southern wife, knitting quilts and stockings for the troops and supporting the glorious cause of Southern independence if this is what it means.

If I must choose between my husband's cause and that of my own family, then I will choose, in my own small way, to join that of my father and my brothers, for the sake of my own conscience, and I shall take whatever comes.

I told Drew that I would help them in whatever way I could and he nodded, satisfied with my response, though he did not seem at all surprised. Perhaps nothing surprises him. Perhaps knowing the story of the Gallios, which he said he had learned at his mother's knee, he realized that we Gallios, who came from slaves, could never give support to slavery ourselves. Or perhaps, even after such a short acquaintance, he somehow understood me better than I understood myself.

He told me that it would be best for me to leave the home of Carson Slater. I would need a place of my own somewhere, best if it were near the hospital, and I could use for my excuse that it would be much more convenient. Then I would not have to concern myself with accounting to the Slaters for my comings and goings. He said he would see to it.

Needless to say, Abigail had ideas of her own about why I chose to leave their house. She said nothing to me, but the expression on her face spoke clearly for her. She must have thought I was moving out so that I could pursue an adulterous affair with Geoffrey Cord, but she was too much of a lady to bring the subject up. Perhaps she felt guilty for having encouraged me at first, and blamed herself for whatever she imagined I was doing. If she only knew!

Drew found a room for me that was much closer to the hospital, and while it was small and simple, it suited me entirely. The moment I set foot within it, I suddenly felt free. Here, I can keep my journal safely, I think, though I still take pains to hide it carefully. I have devised a secret hidey-hole for it, behind a board that I have pried loose in the floor beneath my bed, and even though I am alone here, I never take it out during the day and always make certain that the door is locked at night when I remove it. I still write in Latin, which few people can read, and I take great precautions. How like a spy I have become! I must admit, there is a certain guilty thrill to all of this.

Each night, when I come home from the hospital, I lay down to rest for a few hours until either Drew or Geoffrey comes for me. Nobody knows me here, and so no one remarks upon my comings and my goings. Indeed, there are several female tenants here who come and go much more frequently than I do, and at odder hours, and rarely alone. Abigail Slater would be positively scandalized.

When Drew comes for me, or Geoffrey, we go to what they call "the sanctuary," which is where they hide the runaway slaves they are assisting. I am always blindfolded when I am taken there. It is in a new location now, for they have grown more cautious, and I am told it is for my own protection that I am kept from knowing where it is, although I think that is not the only reason. I feel that both Drew and Geoffrey trust me, but perhaps Van Owen and the others do not yet have complete confidence in me. No matter. I am not offended. In their place, I would probably have done the same.

The faces change from time to time as some leave to be smuggled North and others arrive, and always there are more arrivals. Those who help the Negroes on their journey are called "conductors" on the Underground Railroad, but for those they conduct to us, there are many who venture to reach the Union lines on their own; I have no idea with what degree of success. But so many of their stories are so heartbreakingly similar. They want freedom. They do not even know, entirely, what freedom means, they know only that they want it, that they want to go where they cannot be bought and sold like goods upon the marketplace. My heart goes out to each and every one of them.

After a day of working at the hospital, nursing wounded soldiers, I try to catch a few brief hours of sleep and then leave again to minister to runaways, some of whom are wounded, some of whom are sick, some of whom are simply tired and dispirited and only need a warm touch of compassion. And I never grow tired, the way I used to. My spirit sustains me, and I stay almost till dawn, when I return to my small room and sleep for perhaps an hour or two before I go back to the hospital once more.

I have become a thief as well. Most times Dr. Van Owen and the others can provide needed supplies, but sometimes medicine is needed that they do not have on hand, and if there is an abundant supply at the hospital, I make off with some, but only if I feel certain there is enough on hand that no wounded soldier will suffer for being deprived of it. Thankfully, this does not happen very often, as supplies are growing scarce everywhere, and the abolitionists in the North send down supplies and medicines through clandestine channels as often as they can. Sometimes if there is enough, I try to replenish what I have taken from the hospital with what the Abolitionists up north have sent us. This once brought about a quarrel with Dr. Van Owen, but I insisted that I would not help one man at the expense of another, no matter what uniform he wore or what color his skin. Dr. Van Owen merely looked at me for a moment, then nodded and said, "Yes, of course, you're absolutely right." So, at least in a small way, I salve my conscience by replacing what I take from the hospital when the opportunity arises.

Still, I have become, if not a spy, at least a criminal, for what I am doing is certainly a crime in Richmond. And while there is no question in my mind as to how Travis would react if he were to know of this, I think my father and my brothers would approve. Or perhaps not. Perhaps they would think I was taking too great a risk. It matters not. Carl Van Owen was right. There comes a time when one simply has to take a stand and I have taken mine. In doing so, for the first time since this terrible war began, I feel a clarity of mind and a strength of purpose that enable me to get through each passing day.

This morning as I was leaving for the hospital I passed a group of children playing soldier. They had little hats with feathers in them, to emulate Jeb Stuart's plumes, and little wooden swords, and wooden broomsticks that they held between their legs for pretend horses. And as they hopped along they sang "Join the Cavalry."

"If you want to have fun,
If you want to see Hell,
If you want to catch the Devil,
Join the cavalry!"

As I listened to them singing I thought how innocent and sad it was that children would sing of going to war and wanting to see hell, when I was just that moment on my way to minister to soldiers who had really seen it and did not think it was fun at all. And I thought that in making the choice to join Geoffrey, Drew, Carl, and all the others, I had indeed caught the devil, caught him by the tail, and now there was no letting go. Perhaps there would be hell to pay for it, but if that should be the price, then I would gladly pay it, for I feel alive and free.

And so, yet another Gallio has chosen to become a soldier.

NOTES

BOOK ONE

Prologue

Colonel Anthony Mark Gallio is a completely fictitious character, and the delivery of Stinger missiles to the Afghan freedom fighters before such shipments were officially authorized is dramatic license on the part of the author. Likewise, Galinov is also entirely fictitious, though Spetsnaz commandos were active in Afghanistan during the Soviet invasion. The Soviet atrocities against the Afghan people are all well documented, however, and in view of recent developments in the Soviet bloc, perhaps Afghanistan will prove to be the last gasp of Stalinist repression.

Chapter One

The Gallio family is fictitious, as are most of the characters and incidents in this chapter, with the exceptions of George Custer and Superintendent Richard Delafield. The incident of Custer stealing his professor's exam notes is true, however, and in his memoirs, he confesses to not having taken his academic studies very seriously. Out of a graduating class of thirty-four, he writes, "thirty-three graduated above me." His many disciplinary offenses included talking in ranks, playing cards, throwing snowballs at marching columns, keeping a stew pot up his chimney, and not getting his hair cut. He once asked his Spanish instructor how to say "class dismissed" in Spanish, and when told the answer, he led a charge out the door. At the time he attended West Point, the course at the Academy was five years, but it was shortened to four in 1861 because of the demand for officers, so that in the year when Custer graduated, there were actually two graduating classes.

Chapter Two

Uncle Tom's Cabin, or Life Among the Lowly, by Harriet Beecher Stowe, was first published in the spring of 1852 and enjoyed phenomenal sales after initially being serialized in an abolitionist newspaper, the *National Era*. The book sold over a million copies in its first year of publication, comparable to a number-one best-seller today, and was also sold in Britain and translated into several foreign languages. Stowe, the daughter of an abolitionist clergyman, claimed that she was influenced by God in writing the book. It is true, as Travis claims, that she had no firsthand knowledge of life on a Southern plantation, and used secondary sources as research for her book. Dr. Van Owen is a fictional character, as is Isaac Jefferson. However, the climate of popular opinion in the North as regards the Fugitive Slave Law is accurately portrayed and there were many real-life incidents of people interfering with slave hunters.

Chapter Three

The Coulter family is fictional; however, the attitudes of Samuel Coulter are not unrealistic. Although the families of slaves were frequently sold either together or apart, there were many Southerners who considered this practice cruel and would not sell the children of their slaves. There were also Southerners who were against slavery, as evidenced by the diary of Mary Boykin Chesnut, although the majority of Southerners at the time regarded slavery as an economic necessity.

Chapter Four

With the exception of Colonel May, the characters in this chapter are fictional, though the routine of cavalry school is accurately described. It is also true that at this time, many soldiers believed that war was inevitable. Tremayne's analysis of the upcoming presidential election may seem unusually astute, but it is not beyond the realm of probability that a well-informed individual of this time could have made such a prediction based upon then-current political developments. The remarks about the coming war made by Lieutenant Sharp are actually a close paraphrase of remarks made by cadet P.M.B. Young of Georgia to fellow cadet George Armstrong Custer, as quoted in Custer's memoirs, at West Point during the winter of 1860–61. Benny Havens was a man who operated a tavern close to West Point. The tavern, which was officially off limits to cadets, was known by his name and immortalized in song by the corps. The verses quoted are only three of many verses that were added to the song by cadets over the years.

Chapter Five

Jeb Stuart was actually present at the War Department when news of John Brown's raid on Harpers Ferry came, and he was sent to Arlington to ask Robert E. Lee to take command of the marines under Lieutenant Green. With the exception of Robert Gallio's involvement, of course, the events at Harpers Ferry occurred as described and the exchange between Brown and his interrogators is accurate, although abbreviated considerably.

The use of the rifled musket in the Civil War is very significant. What is even more significant is that the tactics had not kept pace with the weaponry. The Civil War was unique in that it marked a transition of warfare into the modern era. Smoothbore muskets gave way to rifled muskets (though both were in use throughout the war) and cap-and-ball loads gave way to metallic cartridges, all in the space of one war. Tactics, unfortunately, had not kept pace with the development of the ordnance. The commanders were slow to realize that the massed, Napoleonic-style infantry assault, wherein troops would advance to within relatively close distances of one another and open fire, was rendered obsolete by the rifled musket. Smoothbore muskets were vastly less accurate than rifled guns, and as a result, the tactics up to that point had stressed putting out a "wall of fire," getting as many projectiles into the air against the enemy as possible. With the advent of the rifled musket, from which we get our modern term "rifle," the guns were far more accurate, which accounts for the staggering body counts of the battles of the Civil War. As the war progressed, the commanders eventually realized the folly of using outmoded tactics with new weapons and started to adapt accordingly, resorting to trench warfare and greater firing from concealment. It is ironic that General Winfield Scott had ramrodded, if you'll excuse the pun, the adoption of the rifled musket precisely because he had realized that it would revolutionize infantry warfare. Eventually, it did just that, but it was a brutal lesson that was learned the hard way, with painful slowness, and at a staggering cost.

BOOK TWO

Chapter One

The incident at West Point with Cadets Ball and Kelley leaving the Academy to go South, borne up on the shoulders of their fellow cadets, actually happened and is taken straight from the memoirs of George Armstrong Custer. Mark Gallio, being a fictional character, was obviously not with him, but otherwise, the incident is genuine. It is also true that Major Anderson had been Beauregard's gunnery instructor at West Point.

The journal entry of Valerius Marcus Gallio is fictional, but the description of a Roman camp is accurate, as is the description of Julius Caesar and the political climate that led to the crossing of the Rubicon and the civil war in Rome.

Chapter Two

Many of the remarks attributed here to Winfield Scott and George McClellan are either direct quotes or close paraphrases. It is fascinating to speculate what the difference would have been had Scott's Anaconda Plan been adopted, although in a sense it came to that, as control of the Mississippi and the blockade of the Southern coast became important objectives in the war. Ironically, many of the lessons learned during the Civil War were soon forgotten and had to be relearned, the hard way, in the First World War.

Chapter Three

The meaning of the term "brevet" has often not been properly understood. Custer is a case in a point. He was made a brigadier general during the Civil War, and afterward, in the Indian Wars, he was a colonel, which has led many people to believe he was demoted. In fact, such was not the case. At least, not technically. At the time, the army had no policy concerning retirement and it was not uncommon for officers to continue serving well into a fairly advanced age. Scott, for example, was in his seventies when he retired as general-in-chief, a position basically similar to that to the chairman of the Joint Chiefs of Staff today. Officers in the regular army were promoted as vacancies occurred, but they could be "brevetted," which was like a provisional promotion and entered into consideration of seniority. During the Civil War, many officers, such as Custer, actually held two separate ranks. At the close of the Civil War, Custer was a brevet brigadier of volunteers, but in the regular army he held a commission as a colonel. So when the war ended and the volunteer regiments disbanded, he was not, in fact, demoted, but reverted back to his regular-army rank.

It seems almost impossible to do justice to the description of a Civil War battle in a novel. Robert's anxieties in setting down his impressions were also felt acutely by the author. For example, despite a hands-on familiarity with a wide variety of firearms, including black powder muskets and revolvers, and a reasonable textbook familiarity with many of the weapons used in the Civil War, it was not until I saw some canister shot in a museum exhibit that the horror of it truly struck home. Imagine a shell loaded with round metal projectiles, in the same manner as buckshot, only canister shot ranged from something the size of an egg to projectiles about the size of a baseball. The thought of getting hit by even one of these, much less a spread, is unsettling in the extreme. And even the smallest projectiles used, such as the lead Minié balls, were about the size of a sewing thimble. A wound from one of these could be devastating, shattering and pulverizing bone, usually resulting in amputation, assuming one survived. Cinematic depictions of battles in the Civil War have often been inaccurate in that it was in reality probably a great deal like fighting in a fog. So much powder smoke was released into the air that it rained after almost every battle.

The duel that resulted in Mark's arrest is actually based rather loosely on a real-life incident, except it was a fistfight and not a duel and the one actually arrested in the incident was Custer, who was not participating, but who, as officer of the guard, should have stopped it. Instead, he chose to act as referee, and was arrested and court-martialed as a result. However, friends in Washington interceded for him and the verdict was set aside, as happens with Mark in the story.

The characters and incidents of Cyrene's story are fictional.

The slave auction witnessed by Maria is a bit of dramatic license. In Richmond, slave auctions were generally conducted indoors, in an auction house, though in many places throughout the South, they were frequently conducted on the streets, in front of a courthouse or in a square.

Introduce a friend and save £25

What to do

Ask your friend to complete the application form opposite. Then send us the whole of this leaflet, together with their payment. For each valid subscription we will then send you vouchers worth £25 which can be used as a credit against the cost of your own subscriptions or book purchases. (Please allow 14 days for despatch).

PLEASE WRITE YOUR OWN NAME AND ADDRESS HERE SO THAT WE CAN SEND YOU THE VOUCHERS.

NAME

COMPANY

ADDRESS

POSTCODE/ZIP

COUNTRY   TELEPHONE

POST TO:
**Aerospace Publishing Ltd, FREEPOST, PO Box 2822,
London W6 0BR, UK**
NO STAMP NEEDED IF POSTED WITHIN THE UK

New Subscriber

please complete

SAVE MONEY

☐ **YES,** please enrol me as a Subscriber to **WORLD AIR POWER JOURNAL**

☐ **YES,** please enrol me as a Subscriber to **WINGS OF FAME**

I enclose my payment of £48.00 (UK) / £56.00 (Europe) / £72.00 (Rest of World) for the first four volumes (these prices include postage). I will receive a FREE issue as an introductory gift plus a £10 book voucher.

If I am subscribing to <u>both</u> journals I will double this amount and receive a FREE issue of each journal as an introductory gift, plus a FREE copy of your giant 448 - page Encyclopedia of World Military Aircraft (single Volumn edition) worth £40. As a subscriber I will also qualify for special rates for all your other publications.

NAME

COMPANY

ADDRESS

POSTCODE/ZIP

COUNTRY   TELEPHONE

☐ I enclose a cheque payable to Midsummer Subscription Services

☐ Please charge my credit card

☐ Visa   ☐ Access/Mastercard

CARD NUMBER ☐☐☐☐ ☐☐☐☐ ☐☐☐☐ ☐☐☐☐ ☐☐☐☐

SIGNED   VALID UNTIL
IAFD99

N.B. *If you subscribe to <u>both</u> World Air Power Journal and Wings of Fame you will receive a **FREE** copy of our giant 448-page Encyclopedia of World Military Aircraft (single volumn edition) worth £40.*

Dear Subscriber,

WORLD AIR POWER JOURNAL and WINGS OF FAME have become tremendous successes, with thousands of subscribers all around the world.

But we know from experience that, even after lots of publicity, there are enthusiasts who are still unaware of these wonderful publications. Some of them may be friends or colleagues of yours.

If you introduce them as subscribers using this order form, we will give you vouchers to the value of £25 for each new subscription. You can use these to buy books from our catalogue or as a credit against the cost of your own subscriptions. So please tell your friends all about these great journals, and you can benefit from these vouchers!

Yours sincerely,

Stan Morse, *Publisher*

P.S. If you would like more forms for more friends, just let us know. We'll send you as many as you need.

Guarantee

Aerospace Publishing Ltd will – without question – refund in full the price paid for any volume returned to us within 14 days of our despatch. Subscriptions can be cancelled at any time with full refund for unmailed copies.

Chapter Four

Hiram Ulysses Grant is, of course, better known to history as Ulysses Simpson Grant. Simpson was his mother's maiden name and the error was an incorrect assumption on the part of Thomas Hamer, the congressman who gave him the appointment to West Point as Ulysses S. Grant. Grant's skill with horses was truly legendary and he was said to be the most daring horseman at the Academy. He set an academy jump record that stood for twenty-five years, tamed a horse named York, whom no one else could handle, and could hang off the side of a horse like an Indian. "A more unpromising boy never entered the Military Academy," said Sherman. Grant had a hard time with hazing, couldn't stay in step, was bad on the parade ground, and sloppy in his dress. He read romantic novels, and only went to Benny Havens's once. It is interesting to note that the two most successful Union generals, Grant and Custer, had considerably less than exemplary records at West Point.

The army punishments described are accurate, though the author knows of no instance of soldiers square dancing during drill. Captain John Kinchloe is a fictional character, but the incidents he describes involving Grant really happened as depicted. Stories of Grant's drinking have been much exaggerated. It is true he was forced to resign for drunkenness at Fort Humboldt, but there are few documented instances of his drinking while in command, during the war. His adjutant, John Rawlins, was very opposed to drinking and had rigorously defended Grant against such charges, which, it should be remembered, were frequently leveled against officers by people wanting to find fault with them. McDowell, for example, was accused of being drunk at Bull Run, and McDowell did not drink at all. It is true, however, that when Grant did drink, he was apparently a binge drinker. He was probably an alcoholic, at a time when alcoholism was not recognized as a disease, but regarded as a moral weakness. It was probably a source of great pain and humiliation to him. The famous story of Lincoln offering to send a case of whatever brand of whiskey Grant drank to his other generals is apocryphal, probably stemming from an incident in which, when pressured to get rid of Grant, he replied, "I cannot spare this man. He fights."

Chapter Five

Winfield Scott started off liking McClellan, but in the end was undermined by him and wound up feeling understandable resentment. When McClellan first arrived in Washington, he came like a conquering hero and was greeted with much fanfare. When Winfield Scott left, only his staff officers came to see him off at the station, in the rain. It was an ignoble exit for one of the nation's finest soldiers. That McClellan was egocentric and extremely full of himself cannot be argued with. It comes across clearly even in his own writings. Yet when he came to Washington, he was widely perceived as a winner, whereas Lincoln was perceived as being weak and indecisive. There was even some talk of offering McClellan a dictatorship, though there seems to have been little serious possibility of that. Just the same, the treatment accorded to McClellan when he arrived in Washington clearly went to his head, though he seems to have required little encouragement to think well of himself, and his subsequent treatment of General Scott was disgraceful.

The Battle of Belmont occurred pretty much as described, though Grant's troops seem to have opened fire from the woods before they advanced across the open ground. Grant's daring feat of horsemanship in urging his mount in a slide down the steep riverbank actually happened, but he was not quite the last man to leave the field. He was the last to board the transport, and he believed at the time that he was the last man to leave the field, but some of the troops were evidently left behind and later rendezvoused safely with the transports.

Chapter Six

Chimborazo Hospital was opened on October 11, 1861, and headed by Dr. James Brown McCaw, a thirty-seven-year-old Virginian who had been serving in the cavalry. It was built on the east end of Church Hill, on the Chimborazo Heights plateau, on a high bluff overlooking the river. McCaw developed the hospital much like a small town and was unique in his time in understanding the relation of mental health to physical health. He paid special attention to the diet of his patients and saw to it that there was plenty of fresh air and space and sunlight. Chimborazo was a state-of-the-art medical facility, with eight thousand numbered beds and a ratio of about one doctor to every seventy or so patients. Seventy-six thousand men were treated there during the war, and McCaw trained over four hundred students. Unlike most other hospitals of the era, throughout the war, Chimborazo Hospital maintained a mortality rate of only about 9 percent, an amazing record unequaled until modern times.

Chief Matron Phoebe Yates Pember was a widow from Charleston, South Carolina, who came to Richmond to help the wounded and later wrote a book about her experiences.

BOOK THREE

Chapter One

It seems to have become fashionable nowadays for historians to indulge in "McClellan bashing," but the fact is that McClellan was a good general in many ways. He took the rabble that was left after Bull Run and organized them into an army that had fine discipline and esprit de corps. While his personality seems to have left much to be desired, in that he unquestionably possessed an enormous ego and there is much to support Robert's opinion of him as "a pompous ass," his soldiers loved him and Custer defended him ardently in his memoirs, making a good case for Lincoln sharing at least as much responsibility for the failure of the Peninsula Campaign as McClellan.

In many ways, parallels can be found between McClellan and General Lord Howe, who commanded the British forces during the American Revolution. Both were capable officers, both had sound strategies, yet both seemed very hesitant to commit their troops. Unlike Grant, McClellan was the most conservative of field commanders and did not believe in hurling his troops against entrenchments and fixed defenses. He believed in winning a war by maneuvering his forces into superior positions rather than by all-out assaults, which was more Grant's style. He was the type of general who cared very much about his troops; he loved them, and they loved him, and he was very careful of their lives. He was also greatly hindered by Alan Pinkerton, who supplied him with extremely faulty intelligence about the numbers of the Confederate forces. McClellan always believed he was outnumbered, when quite the opposite was true.

Robert's fight with Custer is, of course, entirely fictional and I know of no such comparable incident in Custer's history. The poet Walt Whitman was actually present in Washington at the time, working as a volunteer nurse.

Chapter Two

John A. Rawlins, Grant's chief of staff, was not a military man, but a lawyer who came to Cairo from Galena, Illinois. He was extremely dedicated to Grant and saw it as his responsibility to dispel the rumors about Grant's drinking. He would not allow any liquor at Grant's headquarters and the exchange between him and Congressman Washburne regarding the rumors of Grant's drinking actually took place. According to historian Bruce Catton, Rawlins wrote to Washburne that "much as he loved Grant, he loved his country more and if for any reason he ever felt Grant was unfit for his position, he would let the Congressman know. He showed Grant the letter before he mailed it and Grant told him: 'Right; exactly right. Send it by all means.' "

The incident referred to with the lawyer Leonard Swett actually happened as well. Swett did, in fact, complain to Lincoln, who replied by warning him that if Grant said he would shoot him, he was likely as not to do it.

Flag-Officer Andrew Hull Foote was passionate in the cause against slavery and had served with a navy ship that patrolled for slavers off the African coast. He was also passionately opposed to the use of alcohol, and convinced his officers to sign the temperance pledge. A devoted Christian, he held regular services aboard his vessels and even held Bible classes for his men. The incident on board his gunboat with the torpedo actually happened, except for Mark's presence, of course. It should be remembered that during this time, "torpedo" was the word for "mine."

The story of the toast to George Washington, the father of his country, "And the first rebel," is true. It happened after the Battle of Belmont, and the toast was proposed by Colonel Buford. Polk made the witty addendum, which was accepted with grace and amusement by the Union officers and the toast was drunk.

Chapter Three

The primary period of activity for the Underground Railroad was not, in fact, during the Civil War, but in the decades prior to it, with evidence of activity as early as 1820. The author has used a certain amount of dramatic license in depicting Van Owen's group, and while there were undoubtedly people assisting slaves to escape to the North during the war, large numbers of them escaped unassisted. A popular image of the members of the Underground Railroad has had them as being mostly white

Northern abolitionists, and while there were many such people involved, it seems the majority of the organizers and supporters were free blacks, notable among them Harriet Tubman, Frederick Douglass, and Sojourner Truth. Harriet Beecher Stowe, whose novel *Uncle Tom's Cabin* was widely attacked in the South as being full of falsehoods and exaggerations, in fact based her book on the actual stories of runaway slaves assisted by the Underground Railroad.

Chapter Four

The incidents of the capture of Fort Donelson occurred pretty much as described, and many of the remarks made by Grant and General C. F. Smith are either direct quotes or paraphrases. The incident with the Union soldier trying to offer the Confederate soldier a drink from his canteen and Grant giving them both a drink, then seeing to it they were both attended to, is true. The words of Simon Buckner, in asking for terms and in surrendering to Grant, are given verbatim.

Walt Whitman's conversation with Robert is entirely fictional.

The surrender of Nashville occurred as described in Colonel Gallio's letter to his son.

Chapter Five

The events of the war described at the beginning of the chapter, as well as the climate in Richmond, are factual. The remainder of the chapter is entirely fictional.

BIBLIOGRAPHY

A Battlefield Atlas of the Civil War, by Craig L. Symonds, The Nautical and Aviation Publishing Company of America, Baltimore, 1983

A Community in Search of Itself: A Case History of Cairo, Illinois, by Herman R. Lantz, Carbondale, South Illinois Press, 1972

All for the Union, The Civil War Diary and Letters of Elisha Hunt Rhodes, ed. by Robert Hunt Rhodes, Orion Books, New York, 1985

Arms and Equipment of the Civil War, by Jack Coggins, Broadfoot Publishing Company, Wilmington, North Carolina, 1989

Battle Cry of Freedom, The Civil War Era, by James M. McPherson, Ballantine Books, New York, 1989

Battles and Leaders of the Civil War, four volumes, Castle Books, Secaucus, New Jersey, 1989

Black Powder Guide, The Complete Guide to Muzzle-loading Rifles, Pistols and Shotguns—Flintlock and Percussion, 2d. ed., by George C. Nonte, Jr., Stoeger Publishing Company, South Hackensack, New Jersey, 1988

Campaigns of the Army of the Potomac, by William Swinton, The Blue and Grey Press, Secaucus, New Jersey, 1988

Carbines of the Civil War, 1861–1865, by John D. McAulay, Pioneer Press, Union City, Tennessee, 1981

Cavalier In Buckskin, George Armstrong Custer and the Western Military Frontier, by Robert M. Utley, University of Oklahoma Press, Norman, Oklahoma, 1988

Charleston, Come Hell or High Water, photographs collected by Robert N. S. Whitelaw, text by Alice F. Levlsoff, The R. L. Bryan Co., Columbia, South Carolina, 1975

Civil War Ladies Sketchbook, Vol. 3 by K. A. York, The House of York, Elgin, Illinois, 1984

Civil War Men's Sketchbook, by K. A. York, The House of York, Elgin, Illinois, 1988

Civil War on the Western Border, 1854–1865, by Jay Monaghan, University of Nebraska Press, Lincoln, Nebraska, 1984

Civil War Small Arms, American Rifleman magazine reprint, National Rifle

Association, Washington, D.C., 1960

Civil War Soldiers, Their Expectations and Their Experiences, by Reid Mitchell, Touchstone Books, New York, 1988

Colt, An American Legend, by R. L. Wilson, Abbeville Press, New York, 1949

"Co. Aytch," The Classic Memoir of the Civil War by a Confederate Soldier, by Sam R. Watkins, Collier Books, New York, 1962

Cry Commanche, The 2nd U.S. Cavalry In Texas, 1855–1861, by Colonel Harold B. Simpson, Hill Junior College Press, Hillsboro, Texas, 1979

Custer in the Civil War, His Unfinished Memoirs, ed. by John M. Carroll, The Presidio Press, San Rafael, California, 1977

Custer Victorious, by Gregory J. W. Urwin, University of Nebraska Press, 1990

Doctors in Gray, The Confederate Medical Service, by H. H. Cunningham, Louisiana State University Press, Baton Rouge, Louisiana, 1958

Five Years a Dragoon, 1849–1854, and Other Adventures on the Great Plains, by Percival G. Lowe, The Franklin Hudson Publishing Co., Kansas City, Missouri, 1906

Forged in Battle, The Civil War Alliance of Black Soldiers and White Officers, by Joseph T. Glatthaar, The Free Press, Macmillan, Inc., New York, 1990

Freedom, by William Safire, Avon Books, New York, 1988

From Manassas to Appomattox, by Gen. James Longstreet, C.S.A., Mallard Press, New York, 1991

Gardner's Photographic Sketch Book of the Civil War, by Alexander Gardner, Dover Publications, New York, 1959

George B. McClellan, The Young Napoleon, by Stephen W. Sears, Ticknor and Fields, New York, 1988

Grant Moves South, by Bruce Catton, Little, Brown and Company, Boston, Massachusetts, 1960

Grant Takes Command, by Bruce Catton, Little, Brown and Company, Boston, Massachusetts, 1968

Gray Fox, Robert E. Lee and the Civil War, by Burke Davis, The Fairfax Press, New York, 1966

Great Battles of the Civil War, by John Macdonald, Macmillan Publishing Company, New York, 1988

Harper's Pictorial History of the Civil War, The Fairfax Press, New York, 1966

History of the U.S. Cavalry, by Albert G. Brackett, Harper & Brothers, New York, 1865

Hospital Sketches, by Louisa M. Alcott, Hurst & Company, New York, 1863

Jeb Stuart, The Last Cavalier, by Burke Davis, The Fairfax Press, New York, 1988

John Ransom's Andersonville Diary, by John L. Ransom, Berkley Books, New York, 1988

Judah P. Benjamin, The Jewish Confederate, by Eli N. Evans, The Free Press, New York, 1988

Ladies of Richmond, Confederate Capital, by Katherine M. Jones, Bobbs-Merrill Company, 1962

Lee and Grant, by Gene Smith, McGraw-Hill Book Company, New York, 1984

Mary Chesnut's Civil War, ed. by C. Vann Woodward, Yale University Press, New Haven, Connecticut, 1981

Memoirs of Robert E. Lee, by A. L. Long, The Blue and Grey Press, Secaucus, New Jersey, 1983

Military Uniforms in America, Long Endure: The Civil War Period, 1852–1867. The Company of Military Historians, John R. Elting and Michael J. McAfee, ed., Presidio Press, Novato, California, 1982

Mr. Davis's Richmond, by Stanley Kimmel, Coward-McCann, Inc., New York, 1958

Never Call Retreat, by Bruce Catton, Washington Square Press, New York, 1967

None Died in Vain, The Saga of the American Civil War, by Robert Leckie, Harper Collins, New York, 1990

On The Western Frontier with the United States Cavalry . . . Fifty Years Ago, by Herman Werner, (chapbook)

Rank and File, Civil War Essays in Honor of Bill Irvin Wiley, edited by James I. Robertson, Jr., and Richard M. McMurray, Presidio Press, 1976

Richmond Virginia in Old Prints, 1737–1887, by Alexander Wilbourne Weddell, Johnson Publishing Company, Richmond, Virginia, 1932

Sentinel of the Plains, Fort Leavenworth and the American West, by George Walton, Prentice-Hall, Englewood Cliffs, New Jersey, 1973

Sherman's March, by Burke Davis, Vintage Books, New York, 1980

Soldiering, The Civil War Diary of Rice O. Bull, K. Jack Bauer, ed., Presidio Press, 1977

Soldiers Blue and Gray, by James I. Robertson, Jr., University of South Carolina Press, Columbia, South Carolina, 1988

South Carolina, A Bicentennial History, by Louis B. Wright, W. W. Norton & Co., New York, 1976

Stonewall in the Valley, Thomas J. "Stonewall" Jackson's Shenandoah Valley Campaign, Spring 1862, by Robert G. Tanner, Doubleday & Company, Garden City, New York, 1976

Stonewall Jackson and the American Civil War, two volumes, by Lieutenant Colonel G. F. R. Henderson, The Blue and Grey Press, Secaucus, New Jersey, 1989

"Tardy George" and "Extra Billy": Nicknames in the Civil War, by Carl M. Becker, from *Civil War History.* Vol. XXXV, No. 4, Kent State University Press, 1989

Ten Years in the Saddle, The Memoir of William Woods Averell, 1851–1862, Edward K. Eckert and Nicholas J. Amato, ed., Presidio Press, 1978

Terrible Swift Sword, by Bruce Catton, Washington Square Press, New York, 1967

The Americans: The National Experience, by Daniel J. Boorstin, Vintage Books, New York, 1965

The American Heritage Picture History of the Civil War, by the editors of *American Heritage* and Bruce Catton, American Heritage/Bonanza Books, New York, 1960

The Army of Northern Virginia, by Philip R. N. Katcher, Osprey Publishing, London, 1975

The Army of the Potomac, by Philip R. N. Katcher, Osprey Publishing, London, 1975

The Army of the Potomac Trilogy: Mr. Lincoln's Army (Vol. 1), Glory Road (Vol. 2), A Stillness at Appomattox (Vol. 3), by Bruce Catton, Anchor Books, New York, 1990

The Beleaguered City, Richmond, 1861–1865, by Alfred Hoyt Bill, Alfred A. Knopf, New York, 1946

The Blue and the Gray, by Henry Steele Commager, ed., The Fairfax Press, New York, 1982

The Civil War, A Narrative, three volumes, by Shelby Foote, Vintage Books, New York, 1986

The Civil War, A New One-Volume History, by Harry Hansen, Mentor Books, New York, 1961

The Civil War Day by Day, by John S. Bowman, ed., Dorset Press, Greenwich, Connecticut, 1989

The Civil War in Song and Story, collected and organized by Frank Moore, P. F. Collier, 1889

The Code of Honor or Rules for the Government of Principals and Seconds in Duelling, by John Lyde Wilson, Ray Riling Arms Books Company at The Packard Press, Philadelphia, Pennsylvania, 1971

The Coming Fury, by Bruce Catton, Washington Square Press, New York, 1967

The Family Album, Ladies Wear Daily, 1860–65, by Jaunita Leisch, Wearlooms, Berryville, Virginia, 1986

The Horse Soldier, 1776–1943, Vol. 2, The Frontier, the Mexican War, the Civil War, the Indian Wars, 1851–1880, by Randy Steffen, University of Oklahoma Press, Norman, Oklahoma, 1987

The Illustrated Confederate Reader, by Rod Gragg, ed., Harper and Row Publishers, New York, 1989

The Rebel Yell and the Yankee Hurrah, The Civil War Journal of a Maine Volunteer, by Private John W. Hanley, 17th Maine Regiment, by Ruth L. Silliker, ed., Down East Books, Camden, Maine, 1985

The Siege of Charleston, 1861–1865, by E. Milby Burton, University of South Carolina Press, Columbia, South Carolina, 1970

The Story of the U.S. Cavalry, 1775–1942, by John K. Herr and Edward S. Wallace, Bonanza Books, New York, 1984

The Underground Railroad, by Charles L. Blockson, Berkley Books, New York, 1989

The Union Reader, by Richard B. Harwell, ed., The Blue and Grey Press, Secaucus, New Jersey, 1958

They Called Him Stonewall, A Life of Lieutenant General T. J. Jackson, C.S.A., by Burke Davis, The Fairfax Press, New York, 1988

Walt Whitman's Civil War, by Walter Lowenfels, ed., Da Capo Press, New York, 1960

War of the Rebellion. A Compilation of the Official Records of the Union and Confederate Armies, prepared under the direction of the Secretary of War, by (Brvt.) Lieutenant Colonel Robert N. Scott, Third U.S. Artillery, Washington Government Printing Office, 1881

CASCA

THE ETERNAL MERCENARY
by Barry Sadler